Shenkin's
VENGEANCE

Davey Davies

Clink
Street

Published by Clink Street Publishing 2023

Copyright © 2023

First edition.

ISBN: 978-1-915785-03-9 Paperback
ISBN: 978-1-915785-04-6 Ebook

Acknowledgements

Port Arthur Historic Site Management Authority –

for answering many questions.

Experiences of a Convict by J.F. Mortlock, edited by

G.A.Wilkes and A.G. Mitchell.

The History of Bare Knuckle Prize Fighting by Bob Mee.

For the Term of his Natural Life by Marcus Clarke.

Escape from Port Arthur by Ian Brand.

The *Sydney Cove* series of books by John Cobley.

My continued thanks to John William Foster; he knows why.

To family and friends for enduring my continuing talk

about that man Daniel Shenkin.

Also my thanks to everyone at my publishers

AUTHORIGHT for their patience.

NEW SOUTH WALES

SYDNEY

VICTORIA

MELBOURNE

CAPE HOWE

TASMAN SEA.

KING ISLAND

BASS STRAIT

FLINDERS ISLAND

(TASMANIA)
VAN DIEMEN'S LAND

HOBART

MARIA ISLAND

PORT ARTHUR

VOYAGE OF THE SCHOONER TEMPEST
AND OVERLAND TO PORT ARTHUR
1836

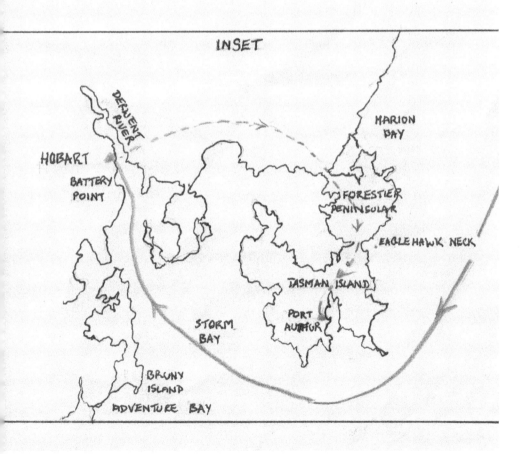

INSET

DERWENT RIVER

HOBART

BATTERY POINT

MARION BAY

FORESTIER PENINSULAR

EAGLE HAWK NECK

TASMAN ISLAND

PORT ARTHUR

STORM BAY

BRUNY ISLAND

ADVENTURE BAY

For Celia, Shirley and Curtis for all their encouragement
and support during my writing of the Shenkin Saga.

Our greatest glory is not in falling,
but in rising every time we fall.

Confucius

PREFACE

Following the response to my first book I received a number of emails asking what happened to Shenkin, Regan O'Hara and Elizabeth Moxey. It was my original intention to write one complete book about Shenkin but my publisher felt the book would be too long and too heavy to handle in this age of ebooks and paperbacks. So the second *SHENKIN book in the series* is really an unbroken storyline; it begins exactly where the first book ended. For those who have read the first book you will remember they are going to search out Abe Goldspick, the former London fence, to sell him the diamond pendant.

For those new to Shenkin it is still a complete story but I hope you will be tempted to read how it all began. There is a third book in the series, but more about that when the time comes.

For me, while writing about him, Shenkin became a close friend, a travelling companion on airlines, ships, climbing mountains or after a day in a recording studio or on stage: in fact any quiet moment that allowed me to write and talk with him. We have spoken about the 19th century and its unfair social injustices, his fight against them which in the end resulted in his dangerous days on the convict ship and the penal colonies of Sydney and Van Diemen's Land. We share in many ways a similar background, for like Shenkin I too grew up in a Welsh mining village. Given the different time period, mine was not as brutal as his in the 19th century, but I knew the history of his period very well, told to me by my own family about their lives in the black collieries of South Wales.

Due to my good fortune to possess a strong bass voice I escaped into the world of music and on to the opera stage. Therefore, the dramatic period that Shenkin lived in, while brutal, also appealed to my sense of theatre. It was a story that for me had to be told, for it is writ large on the canvas of life, the miners' struggle to survive in the harsh world of the 19th century. I only hope I have done them justice.

But come now and join Shenkin and I in the telling of his story and judge for yourselves. I hope you enjoy it and it gives you food for thought, for while in the 19th century men of good faith were trying to level up society – they didn't achieve it. Regrettably, we still haven't managed it even now in the so-called enlightened age of the 21st century – it was ever so.

CHAPTER 1

'Fifty pounds is a bloody insult, with the rest of the necklace this pendant will more than triple its value, and you know it' said Shenkin.

Goldspick moved nervously at the long ale-stained bar of the 'Fortune of War' pub in the Rocks at Sydney Cove. 'I'm taking a big risk handling this stone and you know that too, do you not?' said Goldspick, in a strained voice. He tried to move again, but was pinned between the two powerful figures of Daniel Shenkin and Regan O'Hara. Shenkin was a shade under six foot and broad shouldered. A striking looking man with a mane of jet black hair tied in a ponytail at the nape of his neck. The scar on his cheek was placed there by a splinter of wood during a roof fall in a mining pit in South Wales. It gave him a roguish buccaneering look.

Regan O'Hara was a giant of an Irishman, six foot four inches tall and built to match. They had been together since being sentenced to twenty years hard labour in Australia's penal colony. They had now gained their 'tickets of leave' having spent the first two years in Sydney's convict barracks.

A man the other side of O'Hara pushed his way to the bar, then taking in the size of O'Hara smiled a sickly smile and walked to the other end of the crowded room. Hard-faced men stood around them drinking Bengali rum or ale of questionable strength. The room was smoke filled with burning weed of god knows what assortment of plant leaves. Men coughed and swore into their overflowing tankards of ale and were pushing to the bar or pushed from it. One man turned to look down at a small figure beside him.

'Get your fucking elbow out of my side, or this empty tankard will rip open that ugly face of yours,' shouted a hard-faced man glaring down at an undersized cherub-featured dwarf.

The small man pulled a knife from his wide leather belt. 'Before you lift it I'll rearrange your ale belly from left to right,' he said, in a thin dry whispered voice.

'Well! Want to try it?'

The bigger man grunted and turned his head. 'He's not bloody worth it, let's have some more ale before I dry up.'

'Or bleed to death, Jacko boy,' laughed his friend pouring ale into his tin.

The dwarf pushed his way to Goldspick. 'Having a problem, Abe?'

Seeing the dwarf, Goldspick noticeably relaxed. 'These two gentlemen don't seem to trust me, Mr Teal.'

'Is that so?' said Teal, the knife again in his hand.

Goldspick smiled. 'Let me introduce you, Shenkin, to my associate Mr Thomas Teal, late of the East End of dear old London. A man of few words but very fluent with his well-honed shiv. He's had a lot of practice, so to speak, for he's carved his name across most of London. Where for many years he took care of my business interests, is that not so, Thomas?'

Teal said nothing; his upturned eyes and the knife spoke for him.

'Well!' said Shenkin, turning to Regan. 'It seems we have another Kettlewell, he too was handy with a knife. But Ketch must have told you, Goldspick, what happened to poor Kettlewell, didn't he?' Goldspick visibly paled. Teal, his face a fixed mask, the side of his month turned down unsmiling, the eyes dead and cold, stood back a little to give his knife hand more room to work. Shenkin moved forward at the same time to close the distance; he remembered Kettlewell making the same move. As he did so Shenkin smashed his bottle of rum over the edge of the brass-trimmed bar.

Daniel Shenkin was an impressive figure, tall with broad shoulders that tapered down to a slim waist. The scar that ran down the left side of his face had a strange blue tinge to it, while his eyes were dark brown, steady, alert, dangerous. He looked down at the dwarf then in a quiet deep voice he said. 'If it's a knife fight you're looking for, you little runt, then tonight's your night,' said Shenkin, his voice steady, chilling, all emotion gone. The place had gone very quiet; only the landlord spoke. Shenkin took in the men around them. No one moved to back up the dwarf. Good: one on one, no problem.

'Take it outside,' shouted the landlord. No one moved. Regan O'Hara, the man at Shenkin's side, was a quick-tempered Irishman, always ready to rearrange the furniture, and a few faces.

Both men were former convicts now holding 'tickets of leave', which meant they were permitted to work for themselves and to acquire property on condition that they lived within the district of Sydney and reported regularly to the magistrate court of the penal colony. The tickets could be withdrawn for any misbehaviour and the full sentences would be enforced. That was the risk they were now taking.

'Wait,' said Goldspick, putting up his arms. 'Let's not be in a hurry to see blood, after all we have business to settle, which is far more important, so to speak.' Quickly adding, 'Do you have the goods with you?'

'Do you think I'm a bloody fool?' said Shenkin, not taking his eyes off Teal.

Teal switched hands. Shenkin stepped right to shorten the possible sweeping arc of the knife. The blade picked up the light from a lantern near the door; the flash catching the landlord's eye.

'Sweeny, Blackie, throw the bastards out.' Two men crossed the room both tall, both marked by their past: shaved heads, exposed scars, noses decorating their faces like flattened mud. As they advanced they spread left and right. Men around them hurriedly moved out of the way spilling ale and grog as they did.

'Wait, wait!' shouted Abe Goldspick again. 'We are going to leave peacefully; we'll conclude our business outside. Is that not so, Shenkin?'

Shenkin looked at Regan O'Hara who nodded. 'Yes, but first tell your man to put away his knife,' Said Shenkin.

Goldspick turned to Teal smiling. 'There, there, my dear, no need to get all protective, but stay close to me for old time's sake, so to speak.'

Slowly they moved to the door and the outer darkness, Shenkin making sure both Goldspick and Teal were in front of them.

The night folded around them like a black cape, the rough road was poorly lit by dirty glass-framed lamplights. For heartbeats they stood on the brown ochre-coloured carriage-rutted road of Sydney Cove.

Goldspick turned. 'What you do not want, Shenkin, is to find yourself back in the barracks and on a chain gang, do you? For this time you'll serve your full term, twenty years was it not?'

Shenkin allowed himself a tight smile. 'We seem to be at a stalemate; you're only prepared to offer a measly fifty and I have the pendant stone that will make you a lot of money. Perhaps Lord Feltsham would buy it. I understand he has the money, in coin of the realm, in silver too.'

Governor Bourke had been pressing hard these past months for the British government to supply the colony with silver to counter the mix of assorted currency the colony used, which included rum and cotton as payments for goods or land.

'He may, he may not. In the meantime I'm holding a very expensive piece of merchandise that would be difficult to explain, would it not?'

'I'm sure you have your safe places even in this godforsaken place,' said Shenkin.

Port Jackson itself was certainly a safe harbour for shipping. In 1788 the then governor, Governor Phillip, called it 'being without exception the finest in the world'. But between that date and 1792 they had already landed over three thousand male and some seven hundred female convicts; since then the numbers had steadily climbed until the streets were now full of the unwanted of the mother country, particularly once the sun went down. Convicts, ruffians and the adventurous of the colony pushed and hassled for space on the narrow dusty road, while the blare of music and loud voices competed for the night air.

Goldspick did not respond to Shenkin's safe place statement. Around them the night had turned a little chilly after the long day's heat, while the sound of the drunken voices became louder as they walked to the waterside. Across the road down by the Custom House women's high pitched chatter vied for the oldest profession in the world.

'Bugger off. I'll not pay that price for a raddled pox-ridden piece of shit like you,' said a slurred male voice. 'But what about you, my little gem, young and fresh so you are, a shilling and we'll share half a bottle of rum,' said the man to a girl of sixteen or seventeen standing at the side of the older woman.

'Go to hell. I'll find a toff soon enough who'll pay double,' she shrieked, then screamed as they heard a blow struck.

The men were coming up the small hill from the harbour side. One of them slid back down the hill coming to rest against the wall of the Custom House. 'I just pissed there Billy, so don't stand to close to us.' Said one of the group. They all laughed then began to sing a licentious song as they helped their friend to his unsteady feet.

'Let's get some ale, there'll be more whores in The Union than you can shake a tankard at,.' said the one with the stinking trousers, as they pushed past the silent group on the road.

'Come, we'll go to the peace of my lodgings,' said Goldspick, stepping aside to avoid the drunken group of men. Turning, he stepped up onto the raised wooden walkway that passed the pubs, brothels, gambling places and warehouses that made up the waterfront of Sydney Cove. Goldspick beckoned Shenkin to join him.

Shenkin shook his head. 'We'll stay in the middle of the road. Goldspick, that way we won't be passing any dark alleys.'

'Our friend is very cautious Thomas. It's a wonder he ever got careless enough to be sent to the penal colony of Sydney, so to speak, wouldn't you say?'

Teal added nothing but his silent menace to their slow dark procession. Passing open doors to smoke-dense rooms reeking of cheap ale and vomit, they made their way cautiously to the long row of lodging houses away from the Dock Yard area.

Three years ago in 1831 Shenkin, a miner, ironworker and bare-knuckle fighter, had been one of the leaders of an uprising in the black Welsh valley town of Merthyr Tydfil. They were demanding votes for the working man, better wages and living conditions. But the rising had turned into a riot, many had died, they had clashed with the sovereign state and they had lost. Sentenced to hang, both he and the big Irishman had been first sent to Cardiff Gaol, where the sentences were commuted to transportation to Australia for a term of twenty years' hard labour. First they were sent to the stinking Hulks of London's Woolwich Docks. There they waited for transportation to 'a place beyond the seas'. But the ordeal of the hulks was as nothing compared to the convict ship the *Runnymede* and its voyage of brutality under Captain Moxey and Sergeant Ketch. On board they also had the dubious pleasure of meeting Lord Percival Hugo Feltsham a man who, after Shenkin learned of the stolen goods he had aboard the ship, was determined to cut short Shenkin's future. Shenkin had almost died after a knife fight with one Ebenezer Kettlewell, a London thief who had lost both his life and a valuable diamond during his encounter with Shenkin. Cholera had broken out on board the *Runnymede* decimating the convicts, crew and passengers. The only good thing to come out of it all was Shenkin's meeting with the captain's niece, Elizabeth Jane Moxey. Their love had survived cholera, Feltsham's pursuit of Elizabeth and Shenkin's two year term in the convict barracks of Sydney. Due to his and O'Hara's contribution in assisting the Surgeon-Superintendent Michael Patrick Tarn in containing the fever, they had been given a reduced sentence of two years hard labour on chain gangs and finally their 'tickets of leave'. Lord Feltsham had searched in vain for the lost five carat diamond pendant. It was this diamond that Shenkin now intended to sell to the former London, now Sydney, fence Abe Goldspick. It was now 1834. The money they got for it would secure his, Elizabeth's, and

Regan's future. A lot was at stake this dark ale-fumed filled night in the penal colony of Sydney. As they walked, Shenkin went over all of this in his mind, everything that had brought them to this dangerous night.

Finally, Goldspick stopped and taking a key from his grease-stained waist-coat unlocked an almost derelict house on Argyle Street.

'Come in, my dears. I'll light your way,' said Goldspick, lighting a candle in a brass holder, carefully putting out the flame on the spill to save it for future use. 'Be careful of the floorboards, they're a little fragile, so to speak.' Shenkin looked down and stepped over a wide space that had nothing beneath it but dirty black water.

'There we are. All neat and cosy, so to speak,' said Goldspick, lighting a number of tall wax-caked candles. They lit up the most depressing of rooms, where curtains hung in rotten shreds at fly-blown windows that looked out onto a blank stone wall.

Goldspick smiled a black-toothed smile. 'Sit yourselves down my dears. Thomas, chairs for our guests,' said Goldspick, as he placed bottles of rum on the table. Teal kicked a chair over to Shenkin while Regan pulled one out from under the table that was stacked high with dirty plates and food waste. Disturbed mice scurried from their meal of leftovers into the dark recess of the room.

'Good, good. Now, Shenkin where's the stone?'

'Where's the money at what value and in cash?'

Goldspick sat down placing a bottle of rum between them. 'Cash you say, you'll not settle for barrels of rum or bales of wool?'

'Their value has gone down Goldspick, now that more English silver and Spanish dollars are in the colony,' said Shenkin, sipping some rum from a broken glass. Regan drank from one of the bottles, the rough rawness of the liquor caused even a hard drinker like Regan to cough.

'Good is it not?' said Goldspick, looking up at Regan. Teal didn't drink at all. He just stood there, his baby face belying the ruthlessness of his nature; it spoke of a coiled menace, every fibre of his body wanting to use that sharp knife. Shenkin sat close to Teal's right hand, Regan close to Goldspick; the atmosphere palpable, for heartbeats no one spoke.

Shenkin needed the money from the diamond, because at the moment they were living off Elizabeth's kindness and any odd jobs they could find along the waterfront. Shenkin hated being dependent on a woman, never mind how much she said it did not matter. All the while Lord Feltsham was pressing Captain Moxey for his ward's hand in marriage. He could offer her position, wealth, and a grand house, while Shenkin could offer her only what came out of this night's business and his love. Shenkin guarded himself from being too eager in Goldspick's eyes. So he took a deep breath.

Then in a sudden violent move Shenkin got to his feet. 'To hell with you. I'll take it elsewhere.'

Startled, Goldspick looked up. Teal made a move for his knife but Shenkin held his knife arm tight. 'Don't even think about it my little man,' said Shenkin. Regan smashed the rum bottle over the edge of the table, the jagged broken glass bright and sharp in the candle light.

'Let us all calm down my dears. No need for threats, we'll consider the situation in a friendly manner, so to speak' said Goldspick, anxiously.

'Firstly, I have the rest of Kettlewell's necklace from which the stone hangs, so you will not get a better price. Also, I'll buy it from whoever you sell it to for less then I'll pay you.'

'Perhaps but not if I sell it to Lord Feltsham,' said Shenkin.

'He hates the very smell of your shadow Shenkin, and you know it. Why, he'd have you dead just to clear his way to that pretty niece of Captain Moxey's and shut your voice for ever about Kettlewell's stolen "goods" that he and Moxey have brought into the colony. No, no my dear, it would suit us both to come to an agreement on the stone and its value, here and now, so to speak.'

'I'll not take fifty pounds. I'll see you dead first, so to speak,' mocked Shenkin. Teal moved closer.

'Tell him to back off or you'll never get the stone.'

'Be tolerant Thomas, tolerant. This a delicate situation. Please return your sharp friend to his sheath,' Goldspick said, turning back to Shenkin. So doing, Teal reluctantly pushed the sheathed knife back into his belt.

'It is indeed a stalemate,' said Goldspick, adding, 'I wonder which of us wants the deal the most?'

Goldspick smiled. 'Mind, it would make a beautiful wedding present for Feltsham's bride.'

Before even Teal could move, Shenkin had Goldspick by the throat. Regan smashed the broken rum bottle over Teal's head; he went down as if a trap door had opened under him.

Gasping, Goldspick tried to speak while his face was turning blue, his tongue purple in the candle light.

'Listen, you miserable piece of shit, it's worth more than fifty. I'd say a hundred and fifty at least and you'd still make a handsome profit selling the complete necklace.'

Teal was coming around, he had lifted himself on to his knees. Regan hit him again but much harder this time.

'Well!' said Shenkin, to a gasping Goldspick, as he released his grip.

Rubbing his throat, Goldspick uttered in a breathless voice, 'Such violence my dears, let us reconsider' he said, looking down at the now unconscious Teal.

Even under these circumstances Shenkin had to smile as Goldspick still haggled the price. 'A hundred and fifty! Never my dear, but given the fuller value of the necklace then I'd go as far as sixty, part in rum, part in wool and the balance in dollars, Spanish dollars.'

'Hundred and ten all in silver,' said Shenkin, flatly.

'Hundred all in Spanish silver?' said Goldspick, grimacing.

'English,' said Shenkin.

'Mixed,' said Goldspick.

'Half and half,' said Shenkin.

'Sixty: forty in favour of Spanish,' said Goldspick.

'Done,' said Shenkin, putting out his hand. Goldspick met Shenkin's hand across the table. Teal groaned.

'Regan will go for the stone while you and I have another drop of this gut rot rum and watch over our dreaming friend here,' said Shenkin.

'I think our little friend would be better cooling off, rather than you watching both,' said Regan, with a wink at Shenkin.

'Right,' said Shenkin, turning back to Goldspick.

Goldspick gave a shrug as he poured the rum into the broken glasses. 'But of course, I don't keep that kind of money here, Shenkin, no. I'll pay you at an arranged place.'

'Yes you do, you'd not trust your money anywhere else except close at hand, Goldspick, so let's not play dangerous games.'

Goldspick smiled while again shrugging his narrow shoulders. 'One cannot be too careful in this unpredictable world, so to speak.'

Shenkin nodded to Regan, who had removed Teal's knife, then threw Teal's still unconscious body over his shoulder and made for the door.

'Do be careful with Thomas,' said Goldspick adding, 'so to speak'.

'I'll treat him as if he was a baby, so I will,' said Regan, tapping Teal's bottom.

The bottles of rum between them, Shenkin and Goldspick settled down to wait. After a moment Shenkin said, 'Let's not waste time Goldspick. I'll take a drink while you get the coin ready.' Reluctantly, Goldspick went into a back room. Shenkin heard furniture being moved then the clink of coins.

Outside Regan walked straight into the path of two special constables. 'Evening, officers. I always seem to be the one that has to carry the other home. He's small but drinks twice his size. Drunk to the world, so he is.'

They both laughed, then one turned. 'Well, he certainly couldn't have carried you, Paddy. Home with you for you're not in our beloved Ireland now,' he said, in a broad Irish brogue.

'Right I'll be on my way, so I will,' said Regan, moving down the road quickly. 'Good bless Ireland,' he added, under his breath as he quickened his pace. The splash they heard a few minutes later was the sound of Teal going over the harbour wall.

At Moxey's King's Wharf warehouse, Regan threw a few small stones up at the window of Elizabeth's bedroom. The window opened almost immediately. 'I've been so worried Regan. Is Shenkin alright?' For a moment Regan said nothing. The sight of this girl was breathtaking. She was indeed a beauty. Her round heart-shaped face spoke of all that a man would want: love, warmth, desire.

'Well Regan! Is he safe?'

Regan shook himself out of his reverie. 'Yes! All is well. He's with Goldspick now and they have agreed a price. So I need the stone, my darling girl.'

Elizabeth nodded and disappeared inside. In a moment she was back, a small box in her hand. 'Here it is, be careful.'

'I will indeed, as if it was your very self that jumped,' said Regan.

Catching it Regan smiled up. 'That's my darling girl, I'll be off now while you get some beauty sleep. We'll see you in the morning up at Millers Point at ten o'clock.'

'Right,' said Elizabeth, out of breath with excitement adding, 'what did he get for it, Regan?'

'Now, now, don't go worrying your pretty head about it. Just go to sleep and dream of the most you can think of and then double it,' said Regan, already disappearing into the light sea mist.

Even though it was now almost midnight the waterfront public houses and brothels were doing a roaring business. Regan pushed his way through the mobs of drunken men, while prostitutes of all colours and creeds sold their wares. One man lashed out at Regan as he walked back into a crowed bar. Regan ducked, catching the drunk before he fell into the road. 'There now, unsteady on our feet are we? Time for home man, before you're tumbled in an alley for whatever money you still have left,' said Regan, holding the man up.

'Leave me go. I can hold my liquor better than any man,' said the drunk, pulling away from Regan and falling flat on his face in the road.

'My mistake,' said Regan. 'So you can.'

At Goldspick's lodgings, Regan eased the door open, where he found Shenkin and Goldspick still seated at the table. In front of Goldspick was a large leather pouch of money.

Abe Goldspick looked up. 'You have it?' he said, unable to keep the excitement out of his voice.

O'Hara handed the box with the diamond inside to Shenkin. Carefully untying the twine around the box, Shenkin rolled out the pendant on to the table. The stone hungrily sought out the light of the dying candles; the facets of its surface shone in a kaleidoscope of colours. For moments all three of them just took in the wonder of the diamond. At last Abe Goldspick spoke, his voice dry. 'As fine a piece as my eyes have ever seen,' he said, his face alight with a mixture of admiration and greed as he pushed the money over to Shenkin.

Tearing his eyes away from the stone he allowed himself a smile. 'Be careful on your journey home my dears, that's a lot of money to have on your person, so to speak.' Then looking at the giant Irishman, added, 'still you do have formidable insurance, speaking of which may I inquire after dear Thomas I notice he is not present, so to speak?'

Regan O'Hara lifted his arms in resignation. 'He wanted to go for a swim.'

'To my knowledge Teal cannot swim.'

'Then this was a very poor night to begin to learn, for he was not in the best of health, and that's the truth,' said Regan.

'I see, but I do hope he may recover since I regard him as a valuable part of my little business ventures.'

'He may,' said Shenkin. 'After all it's a deep water harbour so the cold water may revive him, on the other hand,' said Shenkin, shrugging his broad shoulders.

Standing Shenkin looked down at Goldspick. 'We've enjoyed your hospitality Abe, but we really must be going. I trust you realise a good profit on the complete necklace.'

'Oh! I will my dears, I will.'

Once outside Regan turned to Shenkin. 'Damn me we did it Shenkin, we did it. But he's right; that's a hell of a lot of money. What do we do with it?'

Shenkin felt the weight of the coins in the leather bag that Goldspick had lent him, for he gave nothing away. Meanwhile they had to find a safe place for it. But Regan was right; what did they do with it? 'I don't know Regan, and that's the honest truth, but I'll come up with something. We'll sleep on it.'

'Whatever it is it'll have to be soon for we can't spend it or eat it, can we?'

Shenkin nodded. 'Let's get to our lodgings. It'll go under my pillow for tonight.'

They had found, with Elizabeth's help, a small room above one of the warehouses on Campbell's Wharf. The landlord, James Harris did business with Moxey's Chandlers. His wife, Phoebe, was a friend of Elizabeth who promised she would keep the place a secret from her uncle, and so would her husband if he wanted a quiet life. It was small alright; just a few pieces of furniture, two beds, a table and three chairs. Elizabeth had bought candle holders and curtains for the high windows that looked out on to Sydney Cove. As Regan said, 'It's better then the dormitory in the Barracks.' Where they had had to sleep to the sound of chains and guards.

Climbing the shaky wooden stairs at the side of the warehouse, Shenkin turned around to Regan whose weight strained the sea-weathered timbers, setting them creaking at each heavy footfall. 'I think I know where we can safely keep the silver,' he said adding, 'yes, I believe I have the answer.' Continuing their swaying climb upwards. At the top of the stairs Shenkin turned the rusty iron key in the lock. The door opened with a creak on to a dark sea-dank room that seemed held together by no more than flaking paint and willpower. Seagulls had once called it home and their white stain marks were the only decoration left on the paper peeling patterned walls.

After a long moment, one that had taken them inside their room and in which Shenkin had lit the candles, Regan sighed in disbelief, his big shoulders dropping in dismay.

'Is it so secret that even I'm not going to be told?'

'I'm still thinking it through Regan. I'll tell you in the morning, you and Elizabeth together, so let's sleep.'

'Sleep you say, sleep and me all of an um and ah about the coin, so I am. Sleep says the man, I'll not sleep this night!' said Regan O'Hara, his temper a spit away from exploding.'

But Shenkin only smiled then teased him further. 'You'll like it Regan. It will meet all our needs but I need to work out how best to arrange it, so to speak, as our new friend Abe would say. So let's get some sleep for it'll be morning soon and our meeting with Elizabeth at Millers Point.'

Regan grunted and shook his great head in disgust. But for all that, he was soon fast asleep and snoring as Shenkin thought out his plans. Tomorrow they'd begin to put them in place. Sliding the heavy bag of coins into the bed beside him, he too was soon asleep.

CHAPTER 2

The wind on Millers Point blew off the sea in gusts so strong that morning that Shenkin was sure a storm must be brewing on the Pacific Ocean. White horses raced across the waves, while gulls dived and swerved across the blue sky. It was their screaming that had awakened him from a restless night of thinking about the money and where to keep it. As they made their way up to the Point, the silver clicked in Goldspick's bag, every sound an alarm bell to Shenkin's ears. He must be rid of it into a safe place as soon as possible; he was sure he was right in his decision as to where.

Elizabeth Jane Moxey waved from on top of the Point it reminded Shenkin of Cathy O'Hara doing the same on the mountain above the Ironworks and Coal Pits of his black town in Wales, four summers and a thousand years ago. Would he ever see it again or his mother, or sister Rachel, or small brother Owain or indeed Cathy? His father had died that fateful day of the rising that had turned into a riot. He looked over to Regan, whose brother Sean had also died along with all the others that had fallen under the shot and sword of the soldiers from Brecon barracks. What had they achieved but death, transportation to a penal colony, convicts clothes and a lifetime marked as criminals?

The morning had come with light rain and a blustery wind. Sheltering under the balcony of the old mill, they both watched Elizabeth.

'Still thinking are we?' said Regan, waving to Elizabeth.

'No I've made my decision, that's if you and Elizabeth agree,' said Shenkin, as he too waved to Elizabeth.

Elizabeth stood atop the high ground near one of the windmills facing Cockle Bay. It was owned by a former convict John Leighton, known locally as Jack the Miller, hence Millers Point. Her fair hair was blowing wild in the wind that pressed hard against her full figure that took Shenkin's breath away. She began to run to them, and at last they all stood together. Elizabeth threw her arms around Shenkin's neck and kissed him full on the lips. Shenkin hurriedly broke from the embrace. 'Steady cariad, you'll be embarrassing Regan with your wayward ways.'

Regan smiled. 'It's not embarrassed I am, but jealous,' he said, a beaming grin on his broad Irish face.

Elizabeth affected a demure pose. 'Sir I am ashamed of my behaviour; it will not happen again,' she said, giving a small curtsy to Regan.

'Away with you for now I am embarrassed,' said Regan, causing them all to laugh.

After a while, when they had found a place to sit out of the wind near the wall of the big windmill, Elizabeth turned to Shenkin excitedly. 'Well, what did Goldspick give for the pendant stone? Where is the money? Where do we keep it?' said Elizabeth, in a rush of words.

'Sure and wouldn't I like to know some of those answers, for he's been keeping it to his self since last night,' said Regan.

Shenkin looked across to the Argyle Cut where convicts were working in chain gangs. The main construction had been stopped for the moment, due to difficulties with the ground, but the breaking up and the taking away of the already dug out rocks continued. The spot was marked by plumes of sandstone dust rising in the windy morning air, the faint sounds of the rattle of the convicts chains, shouted orders from the guards and metal striking stone; a symphony of suffering. Regan followed his gaze, a knowing look appeared on his broad Irish face. 'Let's get it right Shenkin, for I'll not go back there,' said Regan, all the joy of a moment ago gone in the remembrance of their time on the chain gangs, the marks of the fetters still visible on their ankles in the morning light

Shenkin nodded. 'Not if I can help it.' Elizabeth placed her hands on their shoulders, tears springing to her eyes. Wiping away a tear she opened a basket that she had been carrying. Taking out a bright-coloured cloth from the basket, she began with difficulty to spread it on the ground. Quickly she placed bread, cheese, some pie and a bottle of ale and water on top to hold it down.

Then with a smile she said, 'I'm guessing you've not had breakfast, am I not right?'

The sight brought back smiles to all their faces. 'You are indeed right for we cannot eat silver,' said Shenkin.

'Silver! How much, Shenkin?'

'We'll eat first shall we?'

Elizabeth punched him. 'This man is insufferable is he not, Regan?'

'Sure I've been suffering ever since I've met him, and that's so.'

'Alright, alright we got a hundred and ten pounds in English and Spanish silver,' said Shenkin.

Elizabeth threw up her arms. 'One hundred and ten in hard coin, why it's a fortune Shenkin,' she said, her voice trembling with excitement. Then added, 'but where do we keep it?'

'A very good question,' said Regan adding, 'perhaps Shenkin will tell us?'

Shenkin, a piece of pie in his hand, smiled. 'Doctor Tarn.'

Regan smiled. 'Of course the doctor, where safer a place, but will he be willing to hold it?'

'I have an appointment to see the doctor tomorrow,' said Elizabeth.

Shenkin turned to her in some alarm. 'Are you ill, cariad?'

Elizabeth took his hand. 'It's nothing, an upset stomach. We are still not used to this rich array of fruit we are eating and I have been sick a few times. Please let us not speak of such indelicate matters. He'll make up a powder that will settle my stomach and that will be the end to it. But this will give me the opportunity to discuss the silver and arrange a meeting will it not? In the meantime, where is it kept?'

Shenkin lifted up the leather bag at his side and shook it. 'Safe.'

Elizabeth's eyes opened wide. 'You are carrying it about with you?'

Regan O'Hara, holding a large piece of bread that looked small in the grip of his big hand, lifted his head. 'It's in our sight all the time, in plain view. Who would think two convicts recently granted their tickets of leave would have so much coin about them?'

'But the sound it makes, or while you are working at your odd jobs, it's too suspicious and too perilous. We must leave it with Doctor Tarn as soon as we can,' said Elizabeth, her tone anxious.

'We were not intending to carry it about for the rest of our lives Elizabeth, so do not fret,' said Shenkin, smiling his most beguiling of smiles. 'So we are agreed, the doctor is the best plan.'

Both nodded. 'I'll see you here tomorrow at noon,' said Elizabeth.

'I'll see you tonight if you can get away from your uncle,' said Shenkin. 'I'll be outside the warehouse at seven o'clock. I'll leave the silver with Regan. It would be a very stupid man who would chance his arm or neck at trying to get it away from this big ox.'

O'Hara beamed. 'That's true so it is,' he said, and straightened his back to his full six foot four inches, while flexing his muscles.

'Alright but it can only be for a short while, for my uncle is watching closely since you had your freedom. I have but a few months to go Shenkin, to my twenty-first birthday then I too am free. My uncle's tenure as my ward will be over legally, and my father's will can be executed in my favour. Then I can offer you myself and a dowry,' said Elizabeth, in a proud tone.

Shenkin looked down at her with a serious look upon his face. 'I'll consider the offer carefully.' It collected him another punch on the arm.

That evening they spent an hour locked in each other's arms. The back room of her uncle's warehouse was where he stored bales of wool that made an excellent downy bed. They lit no candles for the dark was bright enough for their love making. Falling back, Shenkin gave a sigh of pleasure as he sank into the warm dry wool. 'So, now that you have had your way with me you are out of my arms. Well! I will not have it so Daniel Shenkin; you will continue to hold me close,' said Elizabeth, in a mocked angry tone.

Shenkin a look of satisfaction on his rugged face, turned to her. 'Anything for a large dowry my Lady.' Which brought a howl from Elizabeth as she tumbled him over onto her bale.

'Still not paid in full my Lady very well, but I demand a bonus.'

Laughing, they held each other close. 'Seriously Shenkin, I love you as savagely and tenderly as my own heartbeat. Never stop loving me for if you did that heartbeat would surely stop.'

'For ever and for ever until our hearts beat their final beat,' said Shenkin.

With a sigh, Elizabeth held him close. 'Now you must leave and I must to my room. We'll meet as agreed on Millers Point at noon tomorrow.' Reluctantly they disengaged from their warm embrace.

Later at their lodging Regan said he had stayed in all evening just in case the silver was put in danger. 'Thank you my wild Irish man, it'll soon be off our hands, I promise you Regan. But that is not the end of things for we will have to give account of our new found wealth. I have been thinking to go back to prize fighting, here in the colony, where it's a big gambling sport attracting large purses. I'll need to get back to fighting weight and fitness mind. What do you think?'

'Its been three years Shenkin. You're a bit older and your body has taken some hard blows what with the floggings, the treadmill, not to mention the knife wound.'

Shenkin studied Regan's face and read his friend's concern. 'Damn it man! I'm still only in my twenties; hell, I'm in my prime. But I grant you I'll need to get some training in. Up and down Millers Point would do it and some road running.'

'As long as Elizabeth is not at the top of the Millers Point Shenkin, remember that. There won't be another tonight for at least two months,' said Regan firmly.

'No! Do you think she'll understand?'

'You're the expert on women Shenkin, not me, what do you think?'

'She will not be pleased to hear I intend to bare-knuckle fight, but it'd be the answer to the money we'll be spending, would it not?'

'It would so,' said Regan. 'When do we begin?'

'Tomorrow morning, ending with a run up to the Point to meet Elizabeth to tell her,' said Shenkin

'Right but you'll run I'll walk,' said Regan. Smiling, they settled down to sleep. Soon the snoring of Regan shook the frail surroundings of their room but kept the gulls away, while Shenkin's mind still planned their future. First they'd need to find out about the prize fighters already in the colony, then who was the current champion and who arranged the bouts and where. He'd get some vinegar and brine to pickle and harden his fists again, then start the training. He wished he had his father here. Idris Shenkin had been a bare-knuckle champion, beating Tommy Morris the Neath middle-weight over eighteen blood-soaked rounds. In his mind's eye he could see again his father looking at his timepiece with the inscription inside.

Idris Shenkin
Bare Knuckle Champion 1810
A fighter of courage, and valour

How his father loved that description; he was a proud man who had given his life for his fellow workers on that fateful day of the Merthyr Tydfil Rising. And Willy Stitch, his flowing white hair turned to red in the riot that followed. He could do with Willy now, the best cut man in any prize fight. Shenkin's hand went up to the scars on his eyebrow and the side of his face. But they were not here for him. So he, with Regan in his corner, would fight alone, thought Shenkin. Slowly, he too drifted off to sleep.

'Sweet Mary in heaven what time is it?' asked Regan, waking with a start at Shenkin's loud call.

'It's about five o'clock, the sun is beginning to rise,' said Shenkin, pulling back their newly hung curtains. The view was slightly misty but the shipping on Sydney Cove was already at work. The whaling vessels sent their odorous smell up to Shenkin's nose causing him to move back from the window with its cracked panes of glass. The window had a latticework of seagull-striped marks with a few new ones being added as he spoke.

'Come it's the first day of training. You'll want an early start will you not for you'll have to pace me.'

'It's the middle of the bloody night Shenkin, why don't you begin without me and I'll catch you up in about an hour or so.'

In answer Shenkin pulled the threadbare blankets off of Regan, with such force that it rolled Regan on to the floor; the crash brought dust and pieces of timber from the ceiling.

'Alright, alright and me dreaming of Ireland and colleens as sweet as the morning dew.'

'Well I can promise you the dew or sea mist at least, so let's go.'

Shenkin had stripped down to just his old Parramatta trousers that were held up by a piece of rope, into which he had tucked a shirt with no sleeves. On his feet were a pair of leather boots which Shenkin had acquired in return for half of his food rations for one week while in the convict barracks. It had been worth it for they had, these past two years, protected his feet well, unlike Regan whose rattan shoes were continually having to be repaired. Finally, tying the shoes with twine laces, he announced himself ready for the road. They would fold the silver into a bundle then strap it to Shenkin's back. It would make for a good training weight. Regan still grumbled his way into his shoes. Neither wore socks for they rotted quickly in the heat, causing sweat rashes. At last they were on the road, or what passed for a road, rutted by subtropical rain and the iron rims of carts. A chain gang clanked their way past them. A few nodded to Shenkin or raised an arm in greeting. The gang were making their way to the Argyle Cut, where they were clearing away the big sandstone rocks, that one day would join Sydney Cove with Millers Point. It was hard punishing work. It would take a long time yet but that was something these convicts had in plenty.

'Poor bastards,' said Regan.

'Amen,' said Shenkin, stretching his legs and breaking into a run.

By midmorning Shenkin had left Regan a long way behind. Sweat was running freely down his body, his shirt soaked through. The weight on his back felt like a ton. It reminded him of the coal he used to carry as a child in the pits of the black valley back home. His father had told him to go through the barrier of pain then it became easier. He did, but finally he stopped. He needed water or his muscles would go into spasms. At the corner of the Old Burial Ground and Bathurst Street, Shenkin walked across the foundations of St Andrews Church where Regan caught up with him by the watch house. 'Sweet Mary in heaven I'll have a heart attack if we keep this up, so I will.'

'You're supposed to be pacing me Regan, not bloody strolling behind me.'

They walked into Kent Street. 'Right let's get some water,' said Shenkin, taking the bundle of silver off of his back.

'Sure, no one would believe what's in there, and that's a fact,' said Regan, still out of breath.

'A tree in a forest is a good place to hide a tree. Look around us, carts full of vegetables or fruit, women with loads of washing on their heads. Convicts carrying timber, they'll not think it strange to see another bundle. We'll get some water and be on our way,' said Shenkin.

After drinking the water fresh from Busby's Bore that now supplied Sydney with fresh water. The Tank Stream, the first water supply that Sydney had, was now little more then an open sewer causing the colony to be reliant on wells or water carted from the Lachlan Swamps until the Bore had finally been opened in 1830. The water was fresh, sweet to the lips and cleared the throat of the dust from the road. Soon they were revived enough to start again, this time the length of Kent Street and up to Millers Point, it would be a good beginning to Shenkin's training. 'I'll give you a start Regan, say two hundred yards then try to keep ahead of me,' said Shenkin, waiting for Regan to move.

After a moment Shenkin turned to Regan. 'We are going to it today aren't we?'

Regan got to his feet in a rush of temper. 'Right you bastard, catch me if you can.'

Shenkin smiled as the big Irishman stretched his long legs up Kent Street. With that temper of his he'll give me a run now, thought Shenkin. At the top of Millers Point they collapsed in a heap at the feet of Elizabeth. 'Well what's all this about? Racing each other are we? And what's the prize to be, a bag of silver? For I can hear it clinking,' she said, laughing out loud. 'Let's hope no one else can hear it, or if they can, can guess what it is. And before you ask yes I have some ale, bread and cheese with me.'

Shenkin still gasping said, 'Thank you cariad, but no ale for me. I'll have some water.'

'It becomes stranger and stranger,' said Elizabeth handing the ale to Regan who drank it down in one gulp.

'It will become stranger yet, and we hope you are in good humour to receive it,' said Shenkin.

Elizabeth threw up her arms. 'I am in very good humour, for I too have news,' she said, a pleased-with-herself look upon her face.

Shenkin moved to her side. 'So what is your news? Are you well and did the doctor agree to see us about the silver?'

'Tell me your news first,' said Elizabeth, firmly.

Regan looked at Shenkin. 'Well, tell the darling girl or are you faint of heart, is that it?'

'You know better,' said Shenkin, bridling at the remark. Taking a deep breath, Shenkin began to explain his plan. 'There must be an explanation for the money, where it comes from, agreed?' Elizabeth nodded.

'So once the silver is safe with the doctor, I intend to prizefight for the purse money and any side bets, this will cover our show of increased spending. A few fights and everyone will assume any buying of lands or houses has come from the bouts.'

Elizabeth's face had turned to alarm. Before Shenkin could go on she cried out, 'No, no I'll not let you get hurt or worse. Listen Shenkin, my dowry can be explanation enough can it not?'

'How will I look living off your money? Anyway it will not be sufficient for what I have in mind.'

'And what is that pray?' said Elizabeth, her temper only just in control.

'Land stocked with sheep,' said Shenkin flatly. 'The wool industry is booming Elizabeth, the demand in England and the rest of the world is growing fast. We can also sell meat from the sheep to feed the colony and maybe elsewhere. The work to be done by hiring convict labour most of which will be free. It would mean a fine house for us, servants, fine clothes, a carriage to drive around in, a life we can build together.' Shenkin paused then added, 'for the three of us.'

Elizabeth looked at Regan. 'Do you share this dream of two ex-convicts in a fine house?' Then she stopped. 'I'm sorry for that remark, but I'm concerned that you're over stretching what is possible. You only have conditional tickets of leave, not an absolute pardon. Prize fighting is dangerous and takes place in the most notorious of areas where drinking and rowdiness is commonplace. Any misbehaviour on your parts will see your tickets withdrawn with you both having to serve your full term. Maybe not even here in Sydney but possibly Port Arthur. I could not stand that, now more then ever, because we have much more to consider,' said Elizabeth sobbing, the tears running down her beautiful face.

'Well, are you satisfied now?' said Regan.

Shenkin held Elizabeth by the shoulders, as a sudden terrifying thought sprang to his mind. 'The doctor, what did he say? Are you very ill? Is it more then an upset stomach cariad?'

'Yes it is more a great deal more, my wild wonderful Welshman,' said Elizabeth, falling into Shenkin's arms.

Over her head Shenkin indicated to Regan to give them some time alone. Regan nodded and began walking away towards the Argyle Cut. Once alone Shenkin said. 'What is it cariad, are you very ill?' Not waiting for an answer Shenkin went on, 'I could not bear the thought of losing you. You are my day, my night, my very breath of life.'

They held each other close, the world reduced to only their heartbeats. After a while Shenkin turned her face up to his. 'Well, what did Doctor Tarn say about your bouts of sickness?'

Elizabeth looked up at Shenkin and smiled. 'He said I was in excellent health, in fact I was blooming with good health, as all expectant mothers are.'

A gasp left Shenkin's lips like a blow to his belly. His skin drained of colour as he took the moment in, then slowly a big smile spread across his rugged face, lighting up his eyes into a look of wonder and joy.

'Cariad, Cariad!' shouted Shenkin, so loud that Regan turned around with a start to look in their direction. What he saw was the two people he loved most in the world. They were wrapped around each other while jumping up and down, the wind blowing around them in a turbulence that seemed to match their excitement.

'What is it?' called Regan, running back to them.

Shenkin grabbed the man he had once fought on a mountain top for arguing about how best to challenge the owners for better working conditions and wages. They had been through a great deal since then, their friendship growing to an unbreakable bond of trust, even love. Not that they would admit it to each other in words: it would remain unsaid, yet stronger because of it.

'I am going to be a father. And you are going to be a godfather,' said Shenkin, breathlessly.

The big Irishman stood looking at them in astonishment. Then slowly he took in a deep breath. 'As if one child to take care of was not enough,' he said turning to Elizabeth, adding, 'you're going to give me another version of this Welshman?' Then with a smile he said, 'I pity Australia with two of them to cope with, so I do.' His eyes brimming with tears, adding quickly, 'damn this gritty old wind.'

Then looking at Elizabeth, he said, 'Is it a boy?'

'Of course it is, is that not true Elizabeth?' said Shenkin. Before she could answer Shenkin placed her gentle on the ground. 'You must rest my cariad, no more jumping around or any physical exertions.'

'No more exertions, are you sure about that Shenkin?'

'There you go again, embarrassing this poor innocent Irishman, for he thinks all babies come from under four leaf clovers,' said Shenkin, the joy still in his voice.

Regan clipped his ear in response. Then more seriously he said, 'Elizabeth is right Shenkin, there is much more at stake now. If we're in any trouble again, who will greet this child into the world? Not you or worse still, not me either if we're both in Port Arthur.'

For a long moment there was a silence that only the wind marked. Dust and the rattle of chains underlined the possible risks they would take.

Shenkin jumped to his feet, unable to hold his thoughts a minute longer. He needed to move, to act, lash out at some hidden menace that was holding him back. 'I'll not have my son born into poverty into a convict's home. With no future but to raise his cap to the gentry as I was forced to do. Owing his life to another man's whim and fancy.' Bitterness tempered every word like a barb of wire as Shenkin clenched his fists so tight the skin became red, the knuckles white.

Elizabeth stood up to stand at his side. 'Please Shenkin, do not let anger spoil this moment.'

But Shenkin's jaw was clenched. 'It is more important now than ever for me to carve out a future for us Elizabeth, you must see that.'

Elizabeth knew instinctively that this was not the moment to pursue the point, instead she held his arm. 'Doctor Tarn said for us to meet with him tomorrow and to bring the silver with you.'

Shenkin relaxed. 'And you my cariad, how will you spend your night? Do not spend it worrying on my account, we will find a way through this one that will ensure our child's future.'

'Of course Shenkin, of course,' she said, kissing Shenkin gently on the cheek before turning to walk down Millers Point back to King's Wharf.

They watched her go, both of them deep in thought as her figure dropped below the rise of the hill. Then Regan broke the silence. 'I know you know how fortunate you are to have a woman like that love you, but are you just as sure of the future you wish her to travel with you?'

'I can't see my son, for I am sure it will be a boy, burdened with my past. If that means taking risks then so be it.'

'It will be interesting to hear what Doctor Tarn has to say, so it will,' said Regan, starting down the other side of the hill as the chain gang too made their way down. It was a further reminder of an uncertain tomorrow.

CHAPTER 3

'Think, Shenkin, think damn it,' said Tarn.

'I am thinking. I'm thinking about my son. What future will he have here in a penal colony, the son of a convict?' said Shenkin.

Tarn rested his hand on Shenkin's shoulder. 'He'll have a loving family, ones who will care for him and an uncle,' said Tarn looking up at Regan O'Hara.

The rattle of carriages filtered through the windows of the doctor's rooms in Elizabeth Street. Michael Patrick Tarn had been the Surgeon-Superintendent aboard the convict ship the Runnymede. He had treated Shenkin for a knife wound after his fight with Kettlewell on the first few days of their voyage out of England. Shenkin had almost died but Tarn and Elizabeth Moxey had saved his life. They had all worked together to contain the cholera that had broken out. Tarn had even acted cupid between Shenkin and Elizabeth by passing messages between them when Shenkin was in the prison barracks. Now he again offered his help by agreeing to hide the silver at his rooms.

'Well! Regan what do you think?'

'I've argued all night with him Doctor, but his mind is set, so it is, and there's no changing it,' said Regan.

Tarn shrugged his shoulders. 'Well what about Elizabeth? She with child and when her time comes to give birth you may well not be here. I assume you have given that the thought it merits. Well?' said Tarn, almost savagely.

Shenkin, his face set. 'Of course I have. Also, before you say it, I know her uncle will not help her; she'll be a social outcast. I know, I know, but I must roll this dice for it's the only chance my son will have.'

'If it's a son, but what if you have a daughter? A penal colony is not the place for two women alone for she'll be a grown woman by the time you're out of prison. That's if you both survive for you'll be double convicts, it will mean hard labour from day one,' said Tarn, searching Shenkin's face for any sign of uncertainty. He found none.

A sob from Elizabeth broke the silence but none of the men looked at her. It was as if each felt they had failed this beautiful creature.

At last, as a vendor outside called out his wares, Elizabeth spoke, 'Men, you are all driven by pride, by class, by a determination to better yourselves whatever the cost to others. You Shenkin, and your rising that in the end became a riot back in your dark mining valley, many of your loved ones died. And you too Regan, your brother dead, both of you now in a penal colony. Was it worth it?' The sobs coming quicker, her body trembling. But she would not stop. 'Regan, what price did you pay? Brothers died for the cause in Ireland and another in the cause for a vote for the working man in a black mining valley far from your beloved emerald island. Well, was it worth it?'

She finally turned her anger to Michael Patrick Tarn. 'Well, Doctor, are your countrymen free from toiling for a fair wage in the vegetable fields of your father's estate in Ireland? While you sit here practising medicine on convicts. Was it worth it?'

For heartbeats no one spoke. 'Buy your ribbons and cloth all at low prices,' shouted the vendor, his cart rattling up the street. 'Yes, madam, red or blue, all one price.' In response to a shrill female voice. The clock ticked away in the doctor's rooms. The clanking of chains from a gang of convicts making their tortured progress up the road brought home the facts of Elizabeth's words. Finally, Shenkin spoke, 'Yes it was worth it, for if just one man speaks out then a small justice is done.' Both the Irishmen looked up: one educated, the other with no education at all, but both with a deep regard for the sorrows of his fellow man. Deep in their hearts they both knew it was worth it.

Tarn put his hand on Elizabeth's slim shoulder. 'I understand your anger and concern, my dear but man has endured through the ages by his struggle against his own suffering and the suffering of others. Shenkin feels he must not give up that fight for if he does then what will you measure him by?'

By now Elizabeth was in a state of uncontrollable tears. Tarn poured her some sherry and bade her sit. Turning to Shenkin he said, 'I'll hide the silver here behind the wall panels of this room. Let me show you in case anything happens to me.' The doctor prised open one of the panels that had the decoration of a red rose upon it. Slowly it came away; behind it was a small tin box. 'In this are expensive medicines and what money I have saved. Now pass me the silver coins,' he said.

The bag untied, it became obvious that they needed a larger box. The doctor emptied a wooden box full of instruments, placing the silver inside, he put it below the first box then, closing the panel, he handed the leather bag back to Shenkin.

Shenkin sighed. 'Thank you, Doctor. I know it will be safe with you for it represents all our futures.'

'I know,' said Tarn, adding, 'now tell me what is the first part of your plan?'

Gazing across at Elizabeth who sat acquiescent in her chair, the sobbing slower, deeper resigned to the future that was to unfold, Shenkin turned back to the doctor and in a firm voice spoke, 'We will find out first where the fights are held and who arranges or promotes them, who the current prize fighters are and who is the champion among them. Then we need to bring me to the attention of the sporting fraternity here in the colony. I need to find someone to put up a purse for me, someone already in the gambling circle of the colony. I will be training each day and we will find work where we can at night. Regan will be in my corner to insure the purse money and bets are safe. I'll also need a doctor to examine me before and after each contest,' said Shenkin, pausing.

The doctor smiled. 'Alright, I'll do it,' said Tarn.

'Thank you, Doctor, we'll also look around for a good cut man for between each round,' said Shenkin. Then looking at Elizabeth, he quickly added, 'just in case he's needed mind, which I doubt.'

Elizabeth looked up. 'Dear god is no one on my side?'

'My dear, if Shenkin is determined to do it then we must give it the best chance of success, for all your sakes. But especially for you now that you are with child.'

Shenkin was moved by this man's steadfast friendship for if ever there was a friend in need it was the good doctor.

'It seems I am continually in your debt, Doctor Tarn. First you saved my life on board the Runnymede, now you preserve it as best you can, thank you.'

Elizabeth looked up. 'We all thank you, Doctor.'

Regan O'Hara nodded his great head, a smile spreading across his broad open face. 'If I'm to watch the fight money you'll need another in your corner to help, so you will.'

'Yes I will,' said Shenkin, thoughtfully.

Elizabeth stood up. 'Why can't I? For I've worked with thick-headed patients before.' At last the mood changed as they all laughed out.

'You would too my cariad, if I let you for you are the best of us.'

'Both of us,' responded Elizabeth, proudly holding her tummy. For she was fully resigned now to Shenkin's plans and god help them all.

***

Ketch had placed a tankard of ale in front of the dwarf. 'So tell me again what Abe did.'

'He says he can't use me any more, that I'm useless to him now that both my arms are busted up,' said Teal.

'I don't give a shit about you, what about Shenkin, Abe and that pendant stone? I always knew Shenkin may have had that for he was in the same cell as Kettlewell on the Woolwich Hulk and again on the Runnymede. The bastard had hidden it somewhere, god knows where for we looked everywhere.' Ketch brooded on the problem for a moment or two before looking at Teal. 'So now we have a complete necklace do we? Worth a bloody fortune that piece of merchandise, mark my words if it ain't,' said Ketch. He had been the sergeant in change of the soldiers on the Runnymede, a brutal man, that the war with the French had mapped his face with a patch over his right eye after the battle at Badajoz. He was a sworn enemy of Shenkin for they had clashed a number of times. It was Ketch who had tried to arrange Shenkin's death while he was in the prison Barracks. His patron was Lord Feltsham whose bidding he still did since giving up the army and buying a public house in the Rocks, all from the proceeds of Kettlewell's loot that they had hidden in the hold of the convict ship. His lordship would be interested to know this information: he'd need to search out Abe Goldspick for a meeting.

Teal had finished his ale. 'I want my revenge on that bastard Irishman that tipped me over the wall, leaving me with these useless arms,' said Teal. Both arms were still in wooden splints, so that Teal could only drink by holding the tankard with his teeth and tipping it up into his mouth, not a pretty sight but effective if you didn't mind the spillage.

'I'll play you in when the time comes Teal, and that's a promise,' said Ketch. 'In the meantime you can do a few odd jobs around the pub here for ale money and some grub, what do you say.'

Teal jumped awkwardly off of the stool and began, with difficulty, to sweep the floor.

'That's the spirit,' said Ketch, a smile, or what passed for a smile, upon his face. Teal, when the time came, could take the blame for any little problem that might befall Shenkin, thought Ketch. A sort of pocket-size alibi, so to speak, as Abe would say.

With a sneer Ketch headed for the door and Lord Feltsham's estate towards Woolloomooloo Hill or Darlinghurst as Ketch preferred to call it for the aboriginal name defeated him.

It only took a short while to get to his lordship's place that stood up on Potts Point a few miles east of Sydney. Feltsham had extended an imposing house on land that was termed 'town allotments'. These land allotments were granted for purchase to a circle of select citizens, who Lord Feltsham had by now ingratiated himself into. His lordship was slowly buying up much of the surrounding land and now had over four hundred acres on which to build and extend his property. This together with the sheep farm he already had was fast making him one of the colony's largest landowners.

Ketch's approach took in the extensive gardens of the house. The gardens and grounds were tended by free convict labour. He swept up to the front wrought-iron gates, the letter 'F' was woven into the iron frame, below which was the crest of the house of Feltsham. Ketch made his way along the wide avenue of red cedar trees, rose myrtle flowers that cascaded down in front of him as his head caught the overhanging foliage, their white flowers forming a carpet on the drive, while at the sides were tree ferns, their long delicate fronds waving like fans in the wind. All of this was lost on Ketch who knew only the law of brutal survival, he was impatient to get to the house, conduct his business and return to his harbourside pub. More trees were still being planted along the half-mile drive that led up to the big house. Once there he had to wait while Feltsham's private militia sent a runner to advise his lordship of his visitor and to enquire if his lordship was at home to receive a caller. Ketch had passed a sealed letter for his lordship, advising him that he had news of a certain necklace. Soon Ketch was on his way to the main house. Through the cedar trees he saw the big house, it was built in the Colonial Regency style by John Verge, the most prominent architect in the colony. Not for Feltsham but for one of the influential citizens of the previous few years. The money he had offered for its purchase was too good to ignore. Having acquired the property, Feltsham had built a further wing, larger stables, a gaming room and cellar. Finally, at the main wide circular drive, a groom took Ketch's horse from him. At the top of the sandstone stairs with its statues of lions heads stood Lord Percy Hugo Feltsham, late of his ancestral estates in Norfolk England, that's if his creditors had not by now acquired them. He was a man in his late forties, his hair greying at the sides and with a petulant shaped mouth. His eyes were slightly rheumy, they conveyed a look of boredom. He was an addicted gambler and rake who, with consummate ease, had lost most of the family fortune at the gaming tables of London. Leaving his mother, the only surviving family member, to face the creditors. She was by now at Southwark's Marshalsea Prison for debtors in London. If he thought of her at all, which was rarely, it was only to reflect that time was not on her side, that at seventy-five years of age she would soon meet their noble ancestors and in so doing his creditors may well give up the chase. He was a thin tall aristocratic-looking man with a hatchet face divided by an aquiline nose willed to him by his Norman lineage. He did have bearing, some say an overbearing presence, that now stood him out from the stone statues and placed him perfectly in his grand setting. The curled lip upon his face gave expression to the lesser mortals of the human race that, with difficulty, he struggled to tolerate.

'This had better be for a good reason Ketch, for I do not wish to see you here at my estate. I have convicts with more grace than you bring to it, so get on with it man, and be gone, for I have guests.' Ketch saw a black carriage at rest at the furthest part of the sweeping drive. Ketch had little doubt these were his lordship's gambling cronies; indeed the place was becoming known for gambling, drinking and scandalous behaviour throughout the colony.

Ketch forced a smile to his lips, adjusted the patch over his eye, removed his straw hat then took a deep breath. 'Never a kind word your lordship, never a warm manner, or a concern for my well being. For have we not gone through a great deal together?'

A look of surprised amusement came across Feltsham's face. 'You are nothing more then a means to an end, you ignorant cretin,' snapped his lordship. Exasperated, Feltsham flicked a piece of lint from his sleeve. 'I can do without your lamentable attempt at sarcasm Ketch. What is it you have about the necklace that is so urgent?'

'It would be better if we went into your drawing room sir,' said Ketch, twisting the straw hat.

'The drawing room! Good god no, we can talk here in the gardens.'

'Just as your lordship likes.' Said Ketch deciding to get to the point. 'Abe Goldspick has acquired the pendant stone my lord. The necklace is complete.'

'Are you sure, have you seen it?' said Feltsham excitedly.

'No but his former carer Thomas Teal by name, came to see me this very morning. He was present when, and this will convince you sir, Shenkin offered it for sale. Both he and that big Irishman had sought out Goldspick as the best means of selling it, him being a fence and all. But I ask myself how did he know about Goldspick? And I answers, Miss Elizabeth Moxey by name. She has seen Goldspick many times at her uncle's warehouse on King's Wharf. Where we transferred Kettlewell's "goods" over to him, and always for a tidy sum' said Ketch, pulling down his waistcoat over his ale belly, it crept back up his chest, Ketch put his hat in its place. His lordship said nothing then slowly began to walk down to a large round pond where disinterested ducks querulously quacked at each other. A convict tugged his forelock, as another waded into the pond to retrieve plant leaves that had been blown into the water. Although Feltsham was looking in the man's direction, his mind was thinking hard about what Ketch had said. After a long moment that had Ketch becoming more and more edgy, Feltsham turned away from the pond and began walking towards the stables. Ketch hurried to catch up.

'Who is this man Teal and why is he so eager to speak to you?'

'He wants revenge sir. O'Hara rearranged his arms in an altercation they had in Goldspick's lodgings; he rendered Teal unconscious then threw him over the harbour wall, where he struck the rocks hard like. It's put him out of business, for his arms were very necessary to his trade as a knife-man, by which he kept Goldspick safe from unwanted attention. Now Goldspick says he's no use to him any more,' said Ketch.

'We have concluded our business with Goldspick,' said Feltsham, thoughtfully. 'All the goods have now been converted into cash or the like by Goldspick.' Feltsham added, 'can this man Teal get us back close to Goldspick, or rather you close to Goldspick, and by association the necklace? He can let Goldspick know that I'm interested in acquiring the necklace,' said Feltsham.

Ketch gave a smile. 'He works for me now my lord, sweeping floors collecting, with some difficulty, the used tankards and any other odd jobs.'

Feltsham nodded. 'Tell him you have a job for him and that if it works out right, he'll have his revenge both on Goldspick and the Irishman. Once arranged let me know, by which time I will have a plan in place,' said Feltsham turning back for the house.

Ketch did not move but stood smiling shiftily, his one eye in a stare, he knew this was a difficult moment. 'Well! What is it?' Feltsham asked, turning.

Hesitantly Ketch spoke, 'Do I take it my lord, that our usual agreement is in place, that is to say, a share of what ever the necklace is worth?'

Again brushing some invisible lint from his lapel, Feltsham sighed. 'Yes man, have we not all shared Kettlewell's ill-gotten loot from the beginning of this distasteful but most profitable business?'

Ketch relaxed. 'Thank you sir, I'll be back to you here tomorrow.'

'No Ketch, you will not come here again. Send a message as to where we can meet, somewhere more in keeping with your class and surroundings and at night. I will let Captain Moxey know,' said Feltsham turning back again towards the house. He was impatient to get back to the green baize of his gaming tables. Ketch snatched the reins of his horse from the convict groom. Then mounting, he pulled viciously at the horse's neck glad to be able, at last to vent his anger. He'd have his share and one day he'd put paid to his bloody lordship, the snivelling lint-picking bastard, thought Ketch, digging his spurs into the horse's flanks. At a gallop both rider and ridden hated the day, the country and each other.

CHAPTER 4

The bar of the Woolwagon Inn at the corner of George Street and Campbell Street was notorious, a colourful spirit and beer house. The room had no tables or chairs, the space it did afford was for drinking and betting only. It was the watering hole for much of the gambling activities in Sydney, which included horse racing, dog fighting, cock fighting, rat killing and prize fighting. Shenkin was ordering tankards of ale while Regan mixed with the men around the tavern, most of who were former convicts or assigned convicts working close by. Shenkin had had to shout his order to be heard above the general noise of the room.

'Twwo als, wight,' said the bar man, a huge man over six foot tall and around fifteen or sixteen stone. His flattened nose caused him to be barely able to make clear-sounding words. While the big man poured the ales, Shenkin asked him who was the landlord. 'Vellgate at end of ar,' said the man, his fist almost covering the side of the two tankards.

'Who?' said Shenkin.

The stare the big man gave left no room for further discussion except for a curt. 'Vuck off.'

Regan took his ale from Shenkin as he pushed to the bar. 'Publican here is a Mr Fellgate, the fat man at the end of the bar by the door. There's a bout on tonight up towards Cooks River, some open ground in the forest that they have cleared where they hold regular fights. The purse tonight is twenty pounds between a prize fighter from the Hunter Valley and a prize fighter owned by Fellgate who arranges a lot of the contests. They are always well attended by one and all including the sporting gentry of the colony, one of which owns the Hunter man,' said Regan, stopping to down his dubious drink. The man at his side had manacle marks around his wrists and smelt as bad as the grog he was drinking.

'What the hell are you drinking man, it smells foul?' said Regan, looking down at him.

'God knows! But I'd not inquire my friend, for the barman is very sensitive.'

Regan gazed over at the barman, who was standing right opposite him at the other side of the bar.

'Vot's your vucking problem hen?' Shenkin quickly held Regan's shoulder as the Irishman moved to vault the bar.

'No problem mate, we just wanted a word with Mr Fellgate, then we'll finish our drinks and be on our way,' said Shenkin, with a smile.

'Did I hear my name spoken?' said a fat man who had moved along the bar. He said putting out his hand. 'Tommy Fellgate at your service. So who may you be?'

Shenkin took his hand; it was damp with sweat or grog. 'Daniel Shenkin and this is Mr Regan O'Hara late of Wales and Ireland respectively. We are interested in the noble art of bare-knuckle fighting and are hoping to see the bout tonight, thereby speculating in a small bet or two,' said Shenkin, taking a swallow of his ale.

'It's my boy against a gentleman's fancy from the Hunter Valley. I'm giving goods odds on my fighter to win.'

'Who's your man?'

Fellgate gave a proud shrug. 'Why Jacko "Giant" Timms, you've met him,' he said, turning to the barman. 'Twenty fights, nineteen straight wins by knock outs, isn't that right Jacko?'

'Vucking truf it is,' he replied.

'Impressive, but it's a good thing he doesn't have to outspeak his opponent,' said Shenkin, making a face as he drank more of his brew.

The prize fighter was quick on his feet for a big man as he sprang over the bar. The man at Regan's side was knocked out of the way, his clay pipe and tin of grog going up into the air. As Timms hit the ground the big barman raised his fists, his body balanced, he was ready.

'Hold it Jacko, let's not cause damage to the pub or your delicate-shaped fists, not with the fights coming up tonight,' said Fellgate, firmly.

Shenkin just stood there, the room around them already cleared. 'Come on Jacko think, Mr Fellgate is not paying you to brawl. He's paying you to fight. And why fight when you're not getting paid for it?' said Shenkin.

'That's right,' said Fellgate adding, 'you fight tonight, then I'm sure he'll request your forgiveness. For you speak your most eloquent when in the ring. So let us settle down.' Fellgate had called up two more of his men who were now holding on to Timms, with some difficulty, as Timms swung the men from side to side.

Shenkin smiled. 'Sensitive soul aren't you? But yes I'd like to see you fight Jacko, and we'll speak after,' adding, 'well, speaking may be stretching it a bit far, don't you think Regan?'

'I'd say so, so I would,' said Regan trying to keep himself from laughing.

'Batltard,' said Jacko, struggling again to break free.

'Right, we'll see you at the bout. That's if you're able to place good size bets, or are you all talk?' said Fellgate, with a sneer.

Shenkin nodded. 'Two Spanish silver dollars, the gents "fancy" to win. It's all we have.'

'Excellent, so it's a sporting man you are,' said Fellgate, unimpressed by the size of the bet. Nevertheless, Tommy Fellgate poured them both a glass of the new Tooth Brew. 'They're on the house and no hard feelings, for I'll get the money back at the field.' Everyone in the room laughed, except Giant Timms.

Stepping out on to the unpaved road, they drank their Tooth beers, which to their surprise were good, hardly watered down at all. Afterwards, standing for a moment on the dirt road of George Street, Regan turned to Shenkin who was dodging a cart of hay being pulled by a huge bullock.

'Move yourself unless you want big Fred to stamp all over you,' shouted the man holding the reins with difficulty.

Shenkin looked up at the driver. 'My friend, you need a bigger driver or a smaller bullock,' said Shenkin, with a smile.

'And that's a fact,' said the small man, struggling to hold onto the cart.

Downing the last of the beer, Regan turned to Shenkin.

'Well I'd say we were off to a good start. It will be an interesting evening, so it will.'

'Let's get back to some training. Twice around Campbell's Wharf and Kent Street sound good to you?' said Shenkin.

Regan winced.

'Unless we can push for a fight tonight,' said Shenkin, with a wink.

Regan brightened.

***

The field at Cooks River was packed with crowds of people: men, women, children, pickpockets and vendors of all the usual vices. The clamour of the crowds, even at the distance they had had to walk, which was about four miles south-west of Sydney Town, became louder and louder by the time they came towards the Botany Bay area. Once at the mouth of Cooks River valley, the noise at the cleared area for the bout was deafening. Convicts who had been working on the new dam across the river stood around looking at the motley groups on the field. Their guards from the nearby stockades began shouting out orders to return to the compound of the stockade. The ones that tried to get lost in the big crowds were soon brought to heel by whip and bayonet, their leg irons preventing them from running far. At the turn in the road Shenkin was stopped by a toll-gate. The keeper stepped out from a small bark hut and demanded payment of two coppers or the equivalent in any coinage.

Shenkin waited for Regan to catch up with him. 'Needs a toll charge Regan, what do you think?'

'Well we could go across the mud flats like many others have or take him and the hut apart, for it's probably illegal,' said Regan.

Taking in Regan and Shenkin's sizes, the man stepped aside. 'Be my guests gents. I see from your arm marks you're not long off the chain gangs, a fellow traveller so to speak. So I'll not detain you,' he said, in a broad Irish accent, standing to one side.

'Most kind of you,' said Shenkin, turning to Regan. 'Your countrymen Regan, I despair of them.'

'Sure he's only hoping to earn a copper or two while the bout is on, taking advantage of the moment.'

Shenkin laughed. 'Is that so?'

At the field they had to push their way to the front. Shenkin needed to see how the two fighters matched up. A call went out from Tommy Fellgate, 'So you did come, good, where's your bets?'

'Let's see the other man first,' said Shenkin, looking over to the opposite corner. He was much younger than Timms, slight of build. His patron was dressed in well cut clothes. He too was young with a pleasant open face that spoke of good living, if a rather rakish one. Shenkin pushed over to his side. 'So is your man up to this contest sir? For he looks a little under size to me,' said Shenkin.

The young gentleman turned his face alight with the excitement of the sport. 'We'll soon see, but I regret to say this is the third "fancy" I've put up against Fellgate's man. Also the purse at twenty guineas is, I don't mind confessing, almost the last throw of the dice for me,' he said with a grimace.

'If he's light on his feet and keeps moving, he may outlast Timms, and be able to land a telling punch,' said Shenkin.

This caused him to look more closely at Shenkin. 'You sound knowledgeable of the sport and have the looks of a possible prize fighter yourself, for you certainly have the build for it, is it so?'

'I'm here to hopefully make some money my lord.'

'Not a lord I regret, for I left England in a hurry, creditors don't you know, a very unsympathetic lot. But let me introduce myself, Sir Edward Standish, late of the Standishes of Mayfair and the gaming tables at Crockford's.

'Well, will you be sporting enough to place a bet on my man, for the odds against him are high, you'll make a fine bundle if he wins, what say you?'

Shenkin looked again at the two fighters. 'Yes I'll give it a spin.'

At that moment Fellgate pushed his way over to them. 'Right the purse Sir Edward, if you please. It'll be held by W.C. Wentworth esq. Is that to your liking Sir Edward?'

'Indeed it is sir. Wentworth is a most worthy sporting gentleman sir,' said Sir Edward, nodding over to who Shenkin assumed was Wentworth.

Shenkin placed their bets and returned to stand with Regan. 'The bets are on but I have little faith in the "fancy"; he's too slight in build but he's all the gentleman can afford. Still, the point is to get us in with the sporting crowd,' said Shenkin.

The fighters came up to the scratch and, after the usual inspection of their hands, and feet and to see if any salt or sand was in the sashes holding up their knee-length breaches, to the roar of the crowd, the fight was underway. Shouts from vendors and the delighted screams of the loose women of the colony added to the general hum.

Both men circled each other for a few moments, then Timms let loose a swinging right that caught the younger man on the side of his head sending him to the ground. To his credit he struggled to his feet only to be met by Timms' knee to his face while he was still bent over. Late bets changed hands and shouts rang out all over the field. Some bluebottles had now arrived after receiving a tip off about the bout. The authorities had already driven the bouts out of Sydney, declaring they were disorderly. They could prosecute the contestants under the Vagrant Act. Regan nodded his head over to the police who were made up of watchmen and constables from nearby Surry Hills barracks but so far they were just watching.

'We are alright here Regan, it's just scrubland and swamps, also it's well outside of the town,' said Shenkin

By now Jacko 'Giant' Timms was hitting the younger man all over the ring. Sir Edward's man was indeed in a bad way but had courage as time and again he came up to the scratch. Shenkin saw Timms look over to Fellgate who nodded. With that nod, so ended Sir Edward's "fancy" a mighty blow almost lifted the younger man off his feet, but Jacko wanted more satisfaction. To boos from the crowd, he smashed blow after blow into the other fighter's body and face until Fellgate called a stop. They dragged the beaten man back to his corner, his nose broken, lips split, one eye closed. Fellgate, the purses in his hand, walked over to Standish. 'Too bad Sir Edward, better luck next time,' he said, a smile on his face as he rattled the purses. Turning to Shenkin he offered similar condolences. 'Going to give your apologies to Jacko for this morning's rude remarks about his small speech problem?' Jacko, a robe over his shoulders, stood at his side waiting for the apology.

Shenkin sighed. 'Well he's good against a small but gutsy youngster. I wonder how he'd fair against someone a little more his own weight and size?' said Shenkin.

'Do you have someone in mind?'

'I do,' said Shenkin. 'Sir Edward was telling me about the very man.' At this, Standish turned away from his man who he had been trying to revive.

Fellgate turned to Standish. 'Well Sir Edward, still determined to beat my man. Your addiction to gambling is going to ruin you sir.'

Standish gave an inquiring stare at Shenkin. 'Perhaps you'll be good enough to tell me who this man is?'

'Can we discuss it somewhere privately Sir Edward? Regan and I will help you with your man then we can talk,' said Shenkin. Without another word Regan lifted the unconscious fighter over his shoulder and moved through the crowd closely followed by Shenkin and Standish.

'Let me know Sir Edward, when you're ready to lose another bout and some more money,' shouted Fellgate after them.

Turning back to Timms he said, 'Another fight Jacko my boy, then back to the pub.' But Jacko was looking over at the constables. 'Don't worry about the bluebottles, I've already paid them off, anyway we're well away from the town.'

'Wrte,' said Timms, climbing back into the ring.

They found a place by the river's edge. Regan began to bathe the fighter's brow with the cool water. Standish placed a rolled jacket under the man's head. 'Who is he sir, what's his name?' said Shenkin.

'Works on a small place I have up in the Hunter, goes by the name of Bill Thomson, son of a convict worker I employ. I saw him fight a few local lads and thought I'd take a chance on him. I'd give anything to get even with Fellgate for I have lost a great deal of money to him. Also to Wentworth and a fellow called John Piper: both sporting gentlemen of the noble art of prize fighting but so far,' said Standish, throwing up his arms.

Shenkin slapped Thomson on the face. 'Come on lad, it's all over.'

Slowly Thomson began to regain consciousness, then with a start he lifted himself up. 'There, there, you're alright now. It's all over,' said Standish, placing a few coins in his hands and opening a bottle of rum. They all had a swig from the bottle while Sir Edward put a silver flask to his lips.

'Now tell me who you have in mind?'

'Me,' said Shenkin, bluntly.

'You? But have you ever done bare-knuckle fighting? I admit you are strong enough looking, but Timms is a hard man to beat with an impressive record. You want me to put up a purse of, what? Another twenty or perhaps thirty guineas on the chance that you may beat him? And what is it you will risk?'

'I have some Spanish silver dollars that I will bet on myself. Can you find the purse?'

Standish was quiet for a long moment. 'I could, but what makes you think you can beat him?'

'That's something you'll have to gamble on; you do like a gamble don't you?'

'We would certainly get high odds against you. So as I understand it I need to put up the purse and be able to place a substantial but risky bet. While you only get the winnings on the silver dollars that you bet, is that correct?'

'Yes,' said Shenkin. Standish again became very thoughtful. Finally he took a deep breath and a long look at Shenkin. 'Thomson, are you fully recovered enough to find your way home if you take my horse?'

'Yes sir,' said Bill Thomson still shaking his head.

'Right, let's find Fellgate,' said Standish, turning to Shenkin.

'Well here we go,' said Regan to Shenkin. 'Let's see if you're fit enough.'

They found Fellgate surrounded by well wishers, some clapping Timms on the back with a 'Well done Jacko.' While another fighter was being carried out of the ring. Fellgate, a fistful of money in his hand, looked up as Standish approached. 'It's getting late Sir Edward, another time maybe.'

Standish got straight to the point. 'I'm putting up my land in the Hunter Valley against a hundred guineas' purse from you. It's worth a great deal more than that but I can't raise the coin so I'll put it up as the purse.'

For heartbeats no one spoke. The crowds, thinking the fights were over, were already moving away.

'That's a hell of a risk on someone you have never seen fight Sir Edward,' said Shenkin.

Fellgate didn't hesitate. 'Where's the paper on the land?' he said.

'The deeds are back at my place. I'll have to give you an IOU paper on it. It will be witnessed by Wentworth if you would be good enough to do the honours sir.'

'I will,' said Wentworth.

Fellgate, his greed slowly getting the better of him, began to be tempted.

'Tke the vucking bet Towwy,' said Timms in his almost intelligible words. 'I'll qill the bathstard who wver he is.'

'Who's your "fancy", Sir Edward?' said Fellgate.

Standish turned around to Shenkin. 'He is.'

Fellgate laughed out loud as did many of his supporters. 'If you had said the big Irishman I may have believed you, but Shenkin!'

'Et me ave him Towwy,' said Timms, excitedly.

'Well?' said Standish.

'Let's have the note for the land dated signed and witnessed,' said Fellgate. 'I'll give you eight to one if you include any livestock you have on the land. Are you game?'

'Agreed,' said Standish looking over at Shenkin. Shenkin just nodded.

While the purses were being arranged, Regan placed their bet then got into Shenkin's corner. Shenkin slowly stripped down to his waist. The late sun caught the muscles of his back and forearms as he danced on the balls of his feet.

'Well he can dance,' said Fellgate. 'Let's see how long he lasts fighting.'

In their corner Shenkin turned to Regan. 'Did you notice Regan, how Timms drops his left when he breaks from a body hold?'

Regan nodded. 'He's a big bastard mind,' said Regan, glancing over at Timms. They had dispensed with any preliminaries because just about everybody had left including the referee and bell ringer. Even the constables had begun their walk back across the scrubland towards Surry Hills.

At the mark, Timms spat into Shenkin's face. 'I'm ging to vucking merdar you,' said Timms, throwing a swinging right which Shenkin ducked under leaving Timms to hit empty air. Spinning around, Timms trapped Shenkin in a bear hug. Shenkin chopped down with the edge of his palms into Timms' sides causing Timms to break and move back. As he did he dropped his left, that was his first mistake. Shenkin stepped inside Timms' defence, blocking first Timms' right then his left. It left Timms' chin exposed, that was his second mistake. Shenkin's right cross must have barely moved six inches but it was brutal. Timms' head snapped back so hard that it sounded like a musket shot. Jack 'Giant' Timms' mouth dropped open, that was his last mistake. Shenkin chopped down with a vicious blow to his open jaw. Timms crashed to the floor, his body lay spread eagled, his arms were flayed out over his head. He was out for the count, any count.

All was silent as Shenkin slowly returned to his corner and put on his rough Parramatta shirt. Regan held out a towel but Shenkin had hardly broken a sweat. 'Unfit so you are' said Regan, adding, 'we'll need to do some work on that right cross too, so we will.'

Standish rushed to his side. 'Shenkin, Shenkin, I've never seen anything like it. I've made a small fortune and you have increased your silver considerably,' said Standish, breathlessly.

Fellgate joined them, a dark look on his face. He handed over the purse and Standish's paper together with the side bet winnings. He turned to Shenkin. 'I'll give you twenty-five percent of any contests I arrange if you fight for me, plus board and lodge at the Woolwagon free for you and Regan as your corner man.'

'No' said Shenkin, walking away.

Fellgate stood legs apart, anger in his voice. 'I'll get that money back, Sir Edward, mark my fucking words if I don't. He's a ringer if ever I saw one. You won't get away with this, you fancy-dressed bastard.'

'Temper, temper, Fellgate, you're a poor loser sir,' said Standish. But Fellgate had turned his back. He didn't even bother to see how badly Timms was hurt.

'Then you'll fight for me Shenkin, yes?'

'No, Sir Edward. Thank you for risking all on me but I or rather we, have other plans.'

Sir Edward Standish shook his well-groomed head. 'Well Shenkin, anytime you're in the Hunter you will always be a welcome guest. If I can return the favour in some other way please let me know.'

'I'll remember that Sir Edward, thank you. Now if you'll excuse us we must be returning to Sydney.

'Your servant sir,' said Standish, in a light-hearted tone.

'Now that will be the day sir, for it's our aim in life to bring it about.'

'Ah! A reformer Shenkin, well I wish you luck,' said Standish, with a bow. 'It's been a pleasure to watch you prize fight, until another time then.'

'Another time Sir Edward.'

On their walk back to town they discussed their plans. 'Well! We have established ourselves into the prize fighting business, now we need some good bouts, ones that will offer the largest purses,' said Shenkin.

'We need a patron: someone in the colony for we can't leave the district of Sydney, the tickets of leave will not allow it,' said Regan, shrugging his broad shoulders.

'That's why Sir Edward was not the man Regan; we need a sporting gentleman in town.'

Elizabeth was waiting at their usual meeting place on Millers Point. 'You're not hurt are you Shenkin?'

'No cariad, I'm fine,' said Shenkin holding her to him. 'And you my cariad, are you well?'

'Sick twice this morning for this baby is as troublesome as his father, but I am glad you won and no marks to show for it.'

'Bit slow mind, it took all of ten minutes to win the bout and that included getting into the ring and taking his top off, so it did,' said Regan, with pride in his voice.

'So you are still going ahead with your plans to prize fight Shenkin?'

Shenkin gently touched her arm. 'It is the only way cariad, to justify the money we spend, to which I can now add more silver,' said Shenkin, adding, 'we'll soon be able to buy land, a large area that we can stock sheep with.'

Elizabeth looked up at Shenkin. 'If you say so, Shenkin, so it will be.'

CHAPTER 5

The message was written in the poorest of hand and spelling.

Der Lord Feltsham,
Meeting arranged tonigt at Captain Moxey's warhouse on King's Wharf
Ketch

Feltsham turned the paper over, it was a label off a box of Spanish figs. He wiped his fingers in a monogrammed silk handkerchief to remove the sticky remains of a fig. 'The sooner I am free of these uncouth layabouts the better,' he said to himself, ringing the silk cord at the side of the grand fireplace.

A man entered the drawing room, his clothes made up of an array of colours and fashions, he clutched a straw hat in his hand. 'You rang sir?'

'Saddle my horse ready for me to go into Sydney tonight, make sure the leather is polished and given a good buffing,' said his lordship, ruffling up the sleeves of his Savile Row cut shirt. As he did he thought of Cork Street and the many times he had walked into Savile Row, and the superb tailoring to be had there. Blessing, as he had many times, his forethought to bring so much of his wardrobe with him from England for the clothes in the colony were of poor quality. He dismissed the servant with a lift of his hand.

'Very good sir.'

Feltsham raised the sherry he had been drinking to his curled lipped mouth, while pondering on the evening ahead of him. He'd finally get the complete necklace then deal with Goldspick and Shenkin; it would mean a number of loose ends would be tied up and be behind him. After all he was now a wealthy respected landowner with business interests in a number of lucrative areas: sheep, wool mills, property. Yes it was time to distance himself from his rather murky but profitable past. Shenkin had been a thorn in his side long enough. After a number of failed attempts to rid himself of Shenkin, this could be the time. In so doing it would clear the way to Elizabeth Moxey and her hand in marriage; she'd make a fine adornment for him together with his imposing house, handsome carriages and sleek horses. The house was furnished in the best London could supply. At the side of the Robert Adam fireplace stood a Japanned escritoire flanked by two Dutch Colonial chairs, while behind his well shaped aristocratic head hung an Irish Border glass mirror. While in front of him stood a fine satin birch sofa. A Burgermeister chair had found its place in front of a stylish Japanese knee-hole desk. The walls were covered in fine art and his lordship was also covered in the latest London fashion from his cravat to his Henry Poole frock-tailed coat while his waistcoat was decorated by a superb gold fob that led to a 1786 Josiah Emery 18ct cased pocket timepiece. With a deep sigh of well being, Lord Percival lit a cigar, the smoke encircled him while he sipped some sherry, smiling smugly as he did so. One way or another tonight he would set in motion the plans to add the necklace to his trophies together with the head of Shenkin.

***

Josiah Moxey was not pleased to be told that Feltsham wanted a meeting at his warehouse that night, he had long pondered on the wisdom of his continued association with his lordship, and Ketch in particular for both were dangerous men, one powerful and wealthy, the other a man capable of the most heinous of crimes. However, Moxey was tied to the one by a business partnership that had proved to be very profitable and if he could persuade his ward Elizabeth to marry Feltsham his business and social future would be secure. They already had a number of ships plying their trade between England and Sydney in the transportation of convicts to the colony and also to Van Diemen's Land with cargoes of all kinds of goods that they sold at a handsome profit in the colony. As he waited for the arrival of the Feltsham carriage he looked around at his warehouse. It was full to the ceiling with all manner of products: wool bales, rum barrels, timber, dressed stone for buildings that the new class of gentry wanted for their grand houses. Fortunes were being made in a range of fast growing enterprises from sheep to convict slavery. He just could not give it up; why in a few short years he could return to England a very rich man. With this thought in mind he turned to welcome Lord Feltsham.

'A fine sight Moxey,' Feltsham said, looking around the packed warehouse. 'We will make a fortune, Captain, but first let us tidy up the loose ends.'

'I want that necklace now that it is returned to its former completeness, it would make a fine wedding gift for Elizabeth, what say you?'

'It would indeed, if I can get her to alter her mind, and if Goldspick will sell it.'

'Damn, if he won't I'll have the bastard in front of the Supreme Court for dealing in stolen goods, don't you know,' said Feltsham in a rush of words. 'I'll not have a bloody Jew stand in my way sir, no indeed.' A knock at the side door announced the arrival of Ketch.

'Good evening your lordship, Captain Moxey,' said Ketch, with a nod of his head.

'Right, lets get down to it. Have you arranged a meeting with Goldspick?'

'Yes sir, for this time next week, to be held here.'

'Here!' said Moxey, in alarm. 'Can we not make it somewhere less conspicuous?'

Feltsham ignored him. 'Will he have the necklace with him?'

'He has a friend resetting the stones over this period so that the necklace looks at its original best, but not the same if you take my meaning,' said Ketch.

'Good then we can lay our plans; to begin with, Goldspick knows too much, agreed?'

'Yes,' said Ketch quickly. Moxey said nothing.

'So it's time we removed Goldspick from the colony, a short sea voyage perhaps, or something more permanent. Whatever it is we desire to remove Goldspick from us and the necklace.' Not waiting for any responses Feltsham continued. 'I intend to mention Goldspick's activities to a few well-placed friends of mine who just happen to be magistrates. One in particular owes me a large sum of money that he lost at my table during cards. This sum will be considered paid should he arrange for Goldspick's incarceration.' At the use of the word his lordship looked at Ketch. 'Imprisonment man.'

'Thank you sir, yes sir, very good sir,' said Ketch, flustered by his own ignorance.

Moxey moved uncomfortably in his chair. 'But he may implicate us, to save his own skin.'

'Have you not been listening Moxey? I have the magistrate in my pocket sir. Goldspick will not be allowed to defend himself. The verdict will be swift; the court limited to a general sentencing of a number of felons on the day, among them Goldspick. He will find himself on the very next ship, one of our ships in fact, to Van Diemen's Land and hence to Port Arthur. I felt you would find this far more palatable than the more permanent solution I was considering, would you not sir?'

Moxey nodded, his greed and future more dear to him then Goldspick, and indeed it would neatly tie any loose ends that might in the future prove embarrassing, in fact it would only leave Shenkin, O'Hara, and Ketch able to connect them with the stolen property that they had brought with them on the Runnymede.

Feltsham poured himself a tot of rum, while offering none to the others. 'Excellent, I'll offer him a sum of money for the necklace that he will be unable to decline, the money to be paid in coin within seven days. He will of course, not pass over the item until then. On his arrest Ketch, with the assistance of Goldspick's former carer Teal, will search Goldspick's lodgings very destructively. I require the necklace only, the rest to be shared out between Ketch, and as a reward for his aid and loss of employment, Teal. Teal when in possession of a goodly amount of funds, can purchase the assistance of some of Ketch's more violent persons to visit Shenkin at his lodgings.' Feltsham paused, he looked at each man in turn. 'You do see how our possible problems begin to disappear gentleman, do you not?'

'It still leaves the Irishman O'Hara,' said Moxey, adding, 'and he too has proved to be very difficult to remove.'

'On Ketch's visit to Shenkin will not O'Hara also be present?' said Feltsham. 'Two for one, so to speak, as our soon to be departed Goldspick would say.'

'As neat a plan as ever there was your lordship,' said Ketch. 'I've been wanting to get even with Shenkin for a long time, and that Irishman.'

'Right, we are in agreement. Ketch make the necessary arrangements.'

'Yes, sir. I'll need some coin to oil the wheels, if you follow me.'

Feltsham gave a knowing smile; he had come prepared. 'This should more than cover it.' Handing Ketch a small leather bag. 'Use it well Ketch, now leave us for the captain and I have other business to attend to.'

'Thank you sir,' said Ketch, dropping the pouch of money into the right hand pocket of his rather soiled jacket, the other pocket hung torn and frayed.

Closing the door firmly behind him, Ketch began to slowly walk towards George Street. At the corner he noticed Elizabeth Moxey hurrying along the unpaved road in the direction of Campbell's Wharf. He would not mind betting that Shenkin had his lodgings there. She was at play while her guardian was busy with Feltsham. Following her at a distance he saw her go up a flight of stairs to rooms at the top of a warehouse. He was gratified to see Shenkin come to the door. 'That's saved me time in tracking you down Shenkin, for

I'm sure I'll find O'Hara there too,' he mumbled under his breath. As if on cue Regan O'Hara also appeared at the doorway. With a smile Ketch stood watching for a moment then said, 'Next time I'm here Shenkin, I'll have a few of my colourful friends with me, the kind who'd cut their own mother's throat for the price of a glass of grog.' So saying, he turned on his heel and headed back to his pub, the Royal Crown on George Street, which was the second of two public houses that Ketch now owned. He had first bought The Iron Duke in Sussex Lane. Both were doing well but the Crown placed him on the main road through the colony where his activities both legal and illegal could flourish.

The first person he saw on entering was Thomas Teal trying with difficulty to climb onto a stool at the bar. The men around him were laughing at his efforts, it's something they would not have done if his arms were still able to function.

'Shut up you bastards,' shouted Teal, his mouth pulled back to show his uneven teeth, most of them a dark shade of rotten black.

'Come along now my friends, is that anyway to treat a fellow convict?' said Ketch, adding, 'are there no gentlemen among you, no men of good manners?'

'No!' came a chorus of replies.

'Then the next man to laugh will answer to me,' said Ketch, his army musket in his hands and cocked. He kept it under the bar top for just such moments. The room went very quiet.

'You Charlie, help Thomas up onto the stool, for I see no one thought to offer him a chair.' Charlie was a human misfit if ever there was one, his right ear had left the side of his face while separating two fighting dogs in Wapping. One of which was his that he'd placed a large bet on. The dog, the ear, and the bet were all lost at the same time.

'There you go my little man,' said Charlie, placing Teal on top of the stool.

Walking back to his place at the bar Charlie whispered, 'Ketch is up to something. I've never known him care two shits for anyone.'

The man nearest to him nodded. 'That's the honest fucking truth mate. I was with him on the Runnymede; he treated us like animals.'

Ketch reached up for a bottle of rum. Then turning to the barman he said, 'Well keep serving them, don't just stand there. Where's that other bloody layabout of a barman?'

'Gone for a piss Ketch.'

'What!' said Ketch

'Gone for a piss, Mr Ketch.'

'That's better. When he comes back tell him I pay him to serve, not piss. I'll tell him when he can piss.'

'Yes, Mr Ketch.'

'Now, Teal let's you and I have a quiet drink together,' said Ketch, pouring them both a very liberal amount of Bengali rum, the rings on the tables bore witness to how well it removed paint. Ketch gave a knowing smile. 'It's all arranged my son; this lot of fucking riff-raff will soon be working for you. Yes! That's right for you Thomas,' said Ketch in response to Teal's look of surprise. 'But first I need to know the places that Goldspick is most likely to hide his ill-gotten gains, for we are going to pay his lodgings a visit.

**

Shenkin held Elizabeth in his arms as they stood alone at the top of the stairs. 'What is it my cariad, you're shaking?'

'Feltsham is with my uncle and Ketch at the King's Wharf warehouse. They are planning to report Goldspick to the authorities then take the necklace from his lodgings, together with everything else he may have.'

'It's a risky business being a fence Elizabeth; did you hear anything else?'

'I heard Regan's name and someone called Teal, but bells on a passing ship were ringing and I could not hear what was said. I'm sure they're intending to rid themselves once and for all of anyone who knows of their past doings. And that will mean you too Shenkin, which is why I came straight to you, for you must be on your guard still.' It had been a few months and already Elizabeth's condition was beginning to show. To hide it she now wore loose-fitting dresses.

Shenkin placed a hand upon her belly. 'How is my son this evening?' At that very moment the baby stirred, causing Shenkin to quickly remove his hand.

Elizabeth gave a laugh. 'There is your answer sir, he is eager to join us. But what with Lord Feltsham and your prize fighting let us hope you are here to welcome him,' said Elizabeth, tearfully.

'I will be my cariad, I promise,' said Shenkin, pulling her close. She would be even more worried had she known that Shenkin was fighting tonight for a purse of five pounds and any side bets he could place. He needed money as soon as possible and the temptation to use the silver he had got for the pendant stone was strong, but to use it would draw attention to him.

'We will soon have enough coin to purchase property, by which time you will be free of your guardian. Then my cariad, we will wed and start life together on our own land,' said Shenkin.

'I hope so my love, for I fret that time and plots will prevent us.'

'Come now let me see that smile before you leave, for your uncle will be wondering where you are at this time of evening.' In answer she went up on her toes and kissed him ardently on the lips. Shenkin felt his manhood stir, but this was not the time or the place.

'Off with you my girl, for you could tempt a saint,' said Shenkin.

Elizabeth sighed. 'Very well but you'll get no better offer sir, this side of your black Welsh valley.' They both laughed as Regan came to the door.

'What's this, are we celebrating the liberation of Ireland?'

'Not yet Regan, but a few small steps in the right direction,' said Elizabeth smiling.

Regan nodded then turned to Shenkin. 'We must go. I said we'd be there at eight o'clock.'

Shenkin gave Regan a look of betrayal as Elizabeth gave him an accusing stare. 'So you are prize fighting tonight and not a word to me,' she said.

'I saw no need to worry you cariad; if this big oaf could only keep his mouth shut you'd not have known till it was over,' said Shenkin, throwing Regan an angry look.

'Sure I'm sorry my darling, but I can tell you it'll be over in no time at all, so it will.'

Elizabeth turned to go then looked over her shoulder. 'If you win, remember Feltsham is in the other corner, just waiting for his chance.' With that she began to carefully descend the rickety wooden stairs. Once she had gone Shenkin turned to Regan. 'Big man and an even bigger mouth.'

'Sorry Shenkin, but what's this about Feltsham?'

Shenkin told him what Elizabeth had said.

'He'll not stop trying to silence us and that's a fact.' Said Regan. 'Still, one thing at a time for I can hear the bell for the first round already.'

By the time they arrived at the Winged Dove on George Street, Shenkin's opponent was already in the makeshift ring in a large room at the rear of the pub. Stale beer and eye-stinging smoke filled the room, the ceiling was stained a dark yellow. The publican met them with a snarl.

'Where the hell have you been? I've had to keep this mob from starting a fight of their own.'

Shenkin began to remove his top; done, he then tightened the scarf around his ponytail. A man near him called out, 'He looks like a bloody girl.'

Regan whispered into Shenkin's ear, 'Now where have I heard that before?' Shenkin smiled. It was the words his father used to use before every fight Shenkin ever had back in his black mining valley of South Wales.

Shenkin turned to the man. 'Regan here will take any size bet you'd like to place, unless your mouth is larger then your pockets.'

'The name's Galby and it's my man you're fighting. Why, Jesse Clark will tear that scarf off and ram it down your throat.' Galby had been a prizefighter himself, a very good one too.

On hearing the name, Shenkin turned to him. 'I've heard of you, it's a privilege to meet you. That fight against Chalker is still being spoken of.'

Galby smiled. 'It's good to be remembered but it does not change my support. Here's another five in Spanish holey dollars to prove it,' said Galby. Regan took the bet and all the others that were being placed. At the back of the room, which was in shadow, a man placed a purse of money in the publican's hand.

Having counted it he said, 'That's a lot of money sir. I'm not sure if it can be covered. I'll speak with the backers.' Galby and the group around him conferred with each other, then Galby lifted his head and nodded.

The crowd was by now shouting for the bout to begin. At last the publican got into the ring for he would also act as referee. After explaining the very rudimentary rules that allowed everything short of murder, the two men returned to their corners. Above the deafening noise Shenkin leaned out of the ring. 'Isn't Jesse a girl's name?' he called over to Galby.

'Your about to find out Shenkin, the hard way,' said Galby.

Someone hit a round metal bar and the fight was on. They sparred around each other for a few minutes. Clark was powerfully built, a little shorter than Shenkin, but he moved well on his feet; his bare fists, broad across his knuckles, flicked in and out towards Shenkin, but just testing which way Shenkin would move. Then he threw a much stronger punch to the side of Shenkin's face aimed at the scar. Shenkin feinted then counter punched as he danced backwards. Coming back in, Shenkin crouched down to come in line with the shorter man. The crowd roared, some booed, while others jeered at the slowness of the fight. Ale and grog splashed around the floor, a man was hit over the head with a rum bottle for trying to pickpocket the man next to him. Egged on by his backers, Clark drove a straight right into Shenkin's face; the force of the blow stopped Shenkin momentarily. In reply Shenkin hit Clark in the kidneys causing Clark to wheeze. As Clark took in breath Shenkin hit him once, then again in a barrage of telling blows, the last of which sent Clark to the ground. Round one was over.

'Strong boy this Jesse; he's no girl,' said Regan.

'Good weight to his punches too and he's light on his feet. Galby's picked a good fighter,' said Shenkin.

The iron bar struck and they were up to the scratch again. 'I'll have that scarf now,' said Clark, grabbing Shenkin's head. Shenkin danced away, hitting the other man as did so. Shenkin kept moving backwards, Clark followed him around the ring.

'Stand and fight, you big bloody boozer,' shouted someone as another fight broke out at the door of the room. Two bouncers threw them out onto the street. Clark caught the top of Shenkin's right eye, splitting the eyebrow. Shenkin dropped to his knee and the end of round two was called.

'Bloody hell Shenkin we didn't think we'd need Doctor Tarn tonight, keep your left up for Christ's sake,' said Regan trying to stop the bleeding, as Galby shouted.

'Next round Shenkin, and I'm in the money. A black hand put something into Regan's hand. 'Put this on the cut fellow.' Regan turned to find an aboriginal standing at his side.

'Do it,' shouted Shenkin.

'Get that black bastard out of here,' screamed the publican. Regan placed the wad of god knows what onto Shenkin's eye; the bleeding stopped while Shenkin winced at the sting it caused.

Up at the line Clark snarled, 'This fucking round Shenkin.'

Shenkin went into a crouch swaying from side to side as he brought his left up to protect his eye. Clark came forward for the kill. Shenkin danced backwards then stopped suddenly, all of Clark's weight was still coming forward. The blow to his stomach made him fold over, the right uppercut that followed straightened him out with a jarring crack. Clark's legs seemed to turn to jelly as he crashed to the ground. For moments a hush spread around the room. Clark didn't move; he lay still, crumbled up like a rag doll.

'Jesus,' said Galby in wonder, tinged with admiration.

It was all over.

Regan first collected the purses then the bets, both of which were held by the publican.

'Well done Shenkin,' said a cultured voice behind him. Turning he found Sir Edward Standish counting his winnings.

'Sir Edward, still on a winning streak I see,' said Shenkin.

'Thanks to you Shenkin. That was a remarkable blow; the poor fellow did not expect it.'

'He wasn't meant to Sir Edward,' said Shenkin.

'Quite so. I'm told you have been doing a lot of prize fighting over the last few months Shenkin, but for very small purses: five and ten pounds, I understand. Why so?'

'You need wealthy backers for large purses. I'm afraid I do not mix in their circle.'

'But I do Shenkin, both here and further afield.'

'While on a conditional ticket of leave, I regret Sydney district is the limit of my territory, and therefore my bouts,' said Shenkin.

'Then be my "fancy" in the colony. I'll put up the purses and arrange for bouts with other sporting gentlemen of the noble art of prize fighting. We'll make a fortune together. I'll split the purses down the middle with you, for I owe you that after saving my property. What say you?'

'Its tempting Sir Edward, but first I'll need to allow this eyebrow to heal.' So saying, Shenkin looked around for the aboriginal.

'He was thrown out,' said Regan, adding 'they're not allowed in here.'

'We need to find him Regan, that wad, of whatever it was, stopped the bleeding even if it stung like hell,' said Shenkin, his hand to his eyebrow. 'Damn he's as good as old Willy Stitch; remember him Regan?'

'I certainly do, he put my jaw back in place after our fight on that bloody coal tip of a mountain back in Wales.'

Shenkin nodded then turned back to Standish, putting out his hand as he did. 'Very well, we have an agreement: fifty-fifty of any purses and bets go to the placer.'

'Agreed,' said Standish, with great enthusiasm.

'I'll have a few stitches put in and be ready to fight again in about a week,' said Shenkin.

'We'll meet here in one week, during which time I'll arrange a contest with a more deserving opponent and for a larger purse,' said Standish.

'Till then Sir Edward, and thank you for your patronage,' said Shenkin, putting out his hand.

'The pleasure will be all mine, Shenkin. The privilege to watch you fight and the joy of the sporting gambles that will ensue.' Standish beamed, leaving the room.

'I feel we are at last on our way Regan, property and fortune awaits. As for Sir Edward, better the man we can trust for we failed to find anyone else.'

'Amen to that,' said Regan.

CHAPTER 6

In the cool night air they began to make their way back to Campbell's Wharf. A call made Shenkin turn. Sitting on the makeshift wooden walkway was the aboriginal, his face so black neither of them had noticed him.

Shenkin rushed to greet him. 'We intended to search you out, that salve you put on my cut stopped the bleeding immediately, but it still stings. What was it and who are you?' said Shenkin, pressing some money into the man's hand.

His rich voice rang out into the night. 'My name is Tallara Warron-Wurrah but I'm known as Tinker.' His white teeth lighting up his smile.

'I'm glad it's Tinker for I think we'd struggle with your real name, so we would,' said Regan.

Standing, he was a nerve tingling sight. Black as the night, his broad forehead was topped by tight black curls, his broad nose flat against his face, while in his left ear was what looked like a gold earring. He wore poor fitting clothes, his feet shoeless, over his shoulder he carried a large swag-bag. Not as tall as Shenkin but just as sturdily built, he moved with the powerful slow grace of an animal.

'What was it you used Tinker?'

'An old remedy of my people. I mixed a dried plant from the rose family with some water then made it into a poultice wad. I have herbs and fluids to make medicines that can cure all kinds of ailments sir.'

Shenkin smiled. 'Well it worked, but there's no need to call me sir, my name is Daniel Shenkin and this towering lumbering man is Regan O'Hara. We are pleased to meet you Tinker; we'd like to offer you a job.' It took a while, but in the end he agreed to become Shenkin's cut man.

'There are many places I am not allowed to go into,' he told them.

Shenkin assured him they would take care of that little matter.

'Where are you sleeping, Tinker?'

'Wherever I can, in the bush, under a bridge, or on the sand of the beach,' he said, shrugging his wide shoulders in an acceptance of his place in the world.

'Not any more, you'll move in with us, is that not so Regan?'

'It is so, but I must tell you that I snore,' said Regan.

'Not after tonight, Regan for I have the very thing for it,' said Tinker.

'Thank god for that,' said Shenkin. 'You've already earned your keep Tinker.'

Laughing, they made their way home.

After the first peaceful night's sleep that Shenkin could remember, they made their way up to Millers Point.

'Who have we here?' said Elizabeth.

'This is Tinker Elizabeth, a new member of our team. He is to take care of any cuts I may collect in the ring.'

'I see you collected one last night,' said Elizabeth. 'It is why I will not see you prizefight Shenkin. But I am thankful you have someone that can heal the wound. I am pleased to meet you Tinker; thank you for taking care of this blockhead.'

Tinker smiled his bright gleaming smile. 'You are most welcome my lady. I also see you are with child. I will make up something to ease the morning sickness.'

Elizabeth looked horrified. 'Does it show that much already?' she said.

'No, but I know these things just by looking at your eyes and the way you walk and move lady.'

'Please Tinker, my name is Elizabeth. I know Shenkin would prefer you to call me that.'

'Thank you cariad, I would, how well you know me.'

'I'd say very well,' said Tinker.

This caused them all to break into roars of laughter. Then Shenkin told Elizabeth about Sir Edward and their plans.

'Good, hopefully this will reduce the bouts you feel you need before you can stop. Then we can buy the land we need to stock with sheep.'

At this Tinker spoke up. 'You have been very kind to me, first a place to sleep, food to eat, then welcoming me to your side. Let me offer more than herbs for wounds and births. If you need grazing land I can help both with the land and the rearing of sheep, for my people are very knowledgeable in both. We work on large sheep farm stations around Sydney and also in the wool mills,' said Tinker excitedly.

'Better and better Tinker, for we have very little experience in either, but are determined to learn, and soon we'll have the money to begin,' said Shenkin.

'After your morning's training, I'll look at the cut and make up more herbs to speed up the healing. Then I shall speak to my people about where the best places for sheep runs are,' said Tinker.

'Thank you Tinker,' said Shenkin. Turning to Elizabeth he added, 'we will meet again here tomorrow at the same time. In the meanwhile, please be careful: do not stand too long, or work too hard. Has your uncle noticed anything yet or questioned your absence from the warehouse?'

'No nothing, he is so busy with Feltsham and their business plans that he notices very little else. I also stay out of his way a much as possible.'

'Till tomorrow then,' said Shenkin, kissing her on the cheek as Regan and Tinker made their way down the point. In the distance, convicts hammered their way through sandstone rock, causing a plume of dust to rise into the late evening darkening sky. The rattle of their chains made Regan look down to his scar-marked ankles. 'It's a hard harsh world Tinker my lad, so it is.'

Tinker nodded knowingly.

At Campbell's Wharf Shenkin and Regan had set up a training area with some old iron bars for weights, and a small ring for sparring with Regan. They busied themselves making skipping ropes while Tinker prepared his ointments and linctus that filled the old warehouse with the most stinking of odours. Tinker just smiled his bright smile.

All the while outside, the small figure of Teal stood at the corner of the building, watching, waiting, his right hand now out of its splint. He flexed and unflexed his stubby fingers. Time and again he had to pick up the new knife he had acquired, it just didn't fit into his hand. 'I'll soon get my friend back,' he whispered to himself. 'I'll take it from your dead hand O'Hara, see if I don't,' he said dropping the knife onto the ground yet again.

Tinker leaned over Shenkin as he examined the cut. 'It's healing well, another few days and it will begin to close up. It will leave a small scar to join the big one on your face Shenkin.'

'My father would always tell me, it takes ten scars to make a man,' said Shenkin.

'And mine would say the sharp strokes of life shape a man,' said Tinker, adding, 'they would have got on well with each other, but I am black and you are white.'

'All were black where my father worked Tinker, no colour separated us in the dark black coal mines of Wales.'

'Amen to that,' said Regan.

The next morning they were eager to continue with the training, even Regan was up and about early.

'Right, another run to Millers Point,' said Shenkin, heading for the door.

The bright sunshine was blinding as they began to descend the shaky wooden staircase. Thomas Teal, who had spent the night in his hiding place, moved quickly behind the building. As he did so the knife clattered to the ground. Shenkin turned in the direction of the noise but saw nothing.

'You're jumpy Shenkin, what is it?'

'I've been feeling we're being watched Regan. Don't you sense it?'

'No it's the bloody heat; it's putting you on edge, so it is.'

As they began their run, Teal too began to leave the place and head back to Ketch's pub. On George Street men were already drinking their first of the day. Ketch looked up as Teal sat down at his side. 'Well, what are they doing my faithful little friend?' said Ketch, pouring some beer into an empty tankard. It was lukewarm but Teal drank it down fast, some spilling over his chin and onto his waistcoat.

'Thirsty work is it?' said Ketch.

'Bloody hot out there, it's no place for a Londoner, and that's a fact. As to what they are doing, well they now have another in their camp: a black bastard abo. This morning they all went up to Millers Point to meet the girl you spoke of, Moxey's niece. Good looker, nice arse, do we get to share her too?'

Ketch sneered, 'It's possible, if she happens to be there at the time it would be a shame to waste the opportunity. Mind, I think his lordship would cut your balls off if you tried,' said Ketch.

Startled, Teal said, 'What's it to him, he only wants the necklace?'

Ketch leaned closer. 'You know what these gentry are like, they want it all. You see Teal my old son, the daft bastard wants to marry her. And him with the pick of the colony to choose from. There's no understanding it but the silver you'll have will see you with any of the colony's dollymops that you fancy,' said Ketch adding, 'that's if you can get on top of them.'

'Very funny Ketch, I've heard it all before, but I can manage; they're all the same size lying down, are they not?'

'So they are,' said Ketch, laughing as he poured some more grog.

That night Shenkin went into the Soldier of Fortune pub. Regan was already sitting at the far end of the bar, a beer in his hand. 'Hot isn't it? But you can forget having a beer Shenkin, for you're in training, so you are.'

'Right enough Regan, I'll have a tot of rum instead, it's good for the circulation,' said Shenkin.

In through the door came Goldspick seeing Regan, he joined him at the table. 'This is the sixth pub I've been into looking for you and Shenkin, where is he?'

'Getting a small, I hope, tot of rum.'

'What is it Goldspick, have you come to tell us how much you got for the necklace?' said Shenkin, joining them.

Goldspick did not respond. 'It's Feltsham and that bloody excrement Ketch who tells me Feltsham wants to buy the necklace. They want to meet with me, but I don't like it Shenkin, Feltsham is too willing, too eager, so to speak.'

'What is this to do with us? You want to be rid of it don't you? And Feltsham can pay a good price in English silver too,' said Shenkin.

'I have no one to protect me Shenkin, since Regan put Teal out of his trade, so to speak. Will you both come to the meeting? A show of support an insurance for me, so to speak. I'll make it worth your while, say ten pounds in coin.'

Shenkin looked at Regan. 'Do we want to hold his hand Regan, while the eye cut heals? It's better than collecting empty tankards or cleaning out the bars for some living money, or worse still spending our hard earned coin from the bouts. What do think?'

Regan pondered the problem while Goldspick shifted awkwardly in his chair. 'Well not for twenty anyway, what do you think your hide is really worth Goldspick?'

Sour faced, Goldspick grunted. 'Fifteen then,' he said in a rush.

'Eighteen, Goldspick, or take your chances with Ketch's boys,' said Shenkin.

'Bastards, but agreed,' said Goldspick, grudgingly.

Shenkin nodded. 'Right! where's the coin?'

'But you may not turn up. I'll give it to you when the deal is sealed and I'm in one piece, so to speak.'

'Half now, half on the night, for I assume it will be in the night. Feltsham prefers the dark; he won't want to be seen down here in the sunlight, is that not so Regan?

'It is so, he's a slimy piece of shit, as we know from close experience on the Runnymede; watched his own wife die of cholera, he did.'

Goldspick gave a slight shudder. 'The people I have to do business with, it destroys my faith in mankind.'

Shenkin gave a laugh. 'They're the only ones who'll do business with you Goldspick, and you know it. So where and when is it to be?'

Goldspick sighed. 'My lodgings on Argyle Street at nine tomorrow night.'

'Right,' said Shenkin. 'You can buy us both a rum to seal it.'

Later at their rooms, Regan asked Tinker if a fresh poultice was ready for Shenkin's eyebrow. 'It is, and so is the mixture for Miss Elizabeth to drink when we meet in the morning.'

'I hope that's safe,' said Shenkin.

The aboriginal gazed at Shenkin. 'If it's not I wonder how come we've been surviving for thousands of years before you Europeans arrived to show us how.'

'I apologise Tinker,' said Shenkin.

'Bring the tin down Regan, let's put this money of Goldspick's into it.'

Regan brought down an old biscuit tin from the roof rafters above them. 'How much does that make Shenkin?'

After a moment, Shenkin announced they now had about fifty pounds in mixed coins.

'I've been thinking Regan, what we need is a big purse that Standish can arrange and put the lot up as a purse, the gentry would have that kind of silver. What do you think?'

Regan looked both alarmed and excited by the idea. 'You'd be up against the best in the colony with that kind of money at stake.'

'But just one fight Regan, and we'd be set. We could buy property, or even better, buy a yearly licence. We could claim as much land as we liked then use the silver to buy sheep.'

'Tinker, how big a sheep run will we need to supply our own wool mill?'

While Tinker thought about this, Regan looked at Shenkin. 'You're thinking big, perhaps too big, and it's all based on you winning.'

'Don't you have faith in me Regan?'

'You know better than to ask, but it's a hell of a gamble.'

'I've been taking on all comers, sometimes three a night for small purses. This way one fight Regan, and we are really free. Standish will find a sporting gentleman to put up an equal purse I'm sure.'

'Well Tinker, what would we need?'

'The land is better for grazing than farming, so sheep or cattle is the best stock. You need at least two thousand acres to start with, access to fresh water, free convict labour to help run it, horses to cross it, dogs and men to round up the sheep, building material for the mill and skilled labour to build and work it. Then all you need is a great deal of luck with the weather and a lot of guts,' said Tinker with a smile. 'My people had a place over in Blackfellas' Point, we got hold of some stray sheep and began grazing, but some whites took it over because they wanted the water from the Towamba River. That's when I left and came to the colony to get work, but it all went poor for me. If I had not met you at that pub I was going to go walkabout in the bush towards the mountains.'

For a while no one spoke, the gulls called to each other as if in mockery of their flying. 'Right, we need a licence for the land-taking rights, then we search out some land and move onto it,' said Shenkin firmly.

'First we need to convince Elizabeth, then arrange the fight and above all win it,' said Regan.

'Alright, alright,' said Shenkin. 'I'm seeing Elizabeth tonight.' Seeing Regan's face he added, 'To talk Regan, nothing more.' In response to Regan's grunt. 'We are seeing Sir Edward tomorrow night at six, hopefully he'll have a contest arranged. I'm sure he'll be confident that I can win,' he said, looking accusingly at Regan.

'Praise be to that,' said Regan, crossing himself.

'Then we have to hold Goldspick's hand during his meeting with Feltsham.'

'We have our presence and Teal's knife and nothing more, but I think that will be more then enough,' said Regan.

Tinker beckoned Shenkin to a chair, the fresh poultice in his hand. After a moment Shenkin called out. 'Bloody stings, my eyebrow's on fire.'

'That is what stops the bleeding; tomorrow I'll put on a healing salve, by next week it'll be fine,' said Tinker, the smile never leaving his lips.

Outside the evening was more pleasant after the heat of the day, causing Shenkin to take a deep breath. The waterfront was its usual busy self, carts full of ships, cargo moving to and fro across the length of Sydney Cove. At King's Wharf Shenkin stood in the shadow of an overhanging jury block and tackle that had been used to unload a whaling boat moored at the jetty.

A light shone out as Elizabeth stealthily came out of a side door of the warehouse. They fell into each other's arms in a passionate embrace. Shenkin could feel his manhood stir again. Apparently so could Elizabeth; she moved away quickly. 'I understand you are in training, Shenkin. I have no wish to be the cause of your downfall sir, so unhand me this instant,' she said mockingly.

Shenkin broke away quickly, a sad miserable look on his face.

'Well, well, Shenkin, you are serious about your strength and that I may weaken it.'

'I'm concerned what Regan may say tomorrow as we climb Millers Point, cariad.'

'Ah! I see, very well, goodnight to you Shenkin, and sweet dreams,' she said beginning to turn away. She got as far as turning around before Shenkin spun her back into his arms. They made love there on the side of the whaling boat. Given her condition, Shenkin was gentle and considerate; lust and love were in perfect balance. Each sighed as their moment of release arrived. 'I love you Shenkin, with every breath I take, I love you.'

'And I you cariad, no moment of the day passes without me feeling empty at the loss of your nearness, the scent of your body, the warmth of your arms,' said Shenkin. Elizabeth gave a small sob at this man's tenderness that was hidden so well in the power of his masculinity.

Later, in a rush of words, he told her of their plans. 'Wait, wait, Shenkin, I am with child. How can I go out into the bush to breed sheep when I need to breed myself? I must be near to Doctor Tarn when the time comes for the birth, do I not?'

'We can travel back to town when you are ready,' said Shenkin adding, 'there's another five months yet, cariad.'

'But we could be a hundred miles away, the journey back would be over difficult roads or no roads at all,' said Elizabeth, becoming more anxious.

For some time Shenkin became very quiet, then in a soft tone he said, 'What if you stayed with Doctor Tarn for the last month?'

This seemed to settle Elizabeth down. 'Yes, I am sure he would be agreeable, also he has an old servant woman in the house so the proprieties would be served.'

'Good,' said Shenkin, relieved they had found an answer. 'I must go now Elizabeth, I have training early on the morrow and you must get back to your room for the night is now getting late.'

'I see sir! You have had your wicked way so now you would leave me, to cry upon my lonely pillow.'

'If you can take me to that pillow then I'll stay,' said Shenkin, with a roguish look.

'That is for the future my love, soon may it be so, now go and we'll meet tomorrow at Millers Point,' she said going up on her toes to kiss Shenkin's cheek.

'What time do you call this then? I just heard six bells for the first watch just rung out from the barque, the Numa, moored off the cove. Is this what you call training? With all our futures at stake, so they are, and I hope you behaved yourself.'

'You sound like my mother Regan, go to sleep.'

'Sleep? I have not had a peaceful sleep since I first came to your black valley and met you, and that's the truth.'

But soon, knowing that Shenkin was back, Regan fell into a deep sleep and a quiet one too since Tinker had been giving him drafts of god knows what in his tea.

Sir Edward Standish, his courteous presence commanding the corner bar of the Fortune of War pub, greeted Shenkin with a firm handshake.

'Landlord, three glasses of your best grog. Well Shenkin, I have our first contest arranged for four days' time, but how is the eye?'

'Healing well Sir Edward,' said Shenkin passing a glass to Regan.

Regan took two glasses off Shenkin. 'You're in training, either water or a tot of rum,' he said firmly. With a sigh of resignation Shenkin sat down. When they were finally settled Shenkin told Standish of his thinking.

'That's a great deal of purse money Shenkin. This bout is for one hundred, I am not sure the backer would go to three hundred, but I'll ask. Also an aboriginal in your corner is a difficult one,' said Standish.

'If we held the bout in a field not a room would that be acceptable?'

'Possibly, again, I now need to go back over the arrangements and they may not be pleased about that.'

Shenkin could see this was placing Standish in a difficult position. 'If it can't be done then I'll fight this bout for the agreed purse. Who's the "fancy"?'

'A London bare-knuckle exponent, Charlie Benson by name, brutal by inclination, with some thirty fights behind him, that has made his backers a tidy sum of coin,' said Sir Edward, adding, 'all knock outs by the way'

'We are increasing the risks Shenkin, so we are,' said Regan.

'Let me see what they say. Back here in one hour, is that alright?'

Shenkin nodded, sipping his rum slowly.

'Good evening again Sir Edward,' said Thomson. He was a well-dressed man, a grazier of merino sheep, a heavy drinker, and one of the top sporting gentleman of the colony. 'Why back so soon?'

Standish pulled up a table in the crowded noisy bar of the Wool Pack pub. 'I have a new offer on the table. Having spoken to my man we would like, if the odds are good, to go to a three-hundred-pound purse. If necessary all in mixed coin to that value.'

Thomson smiled. 'You sound confident. What odds are you looking for?'

Standish sipped his rum then placed it carefully on the table. 'Five to one.'

'Too strong, too certain, I'll give three to one but increase the purse to four hundred.'

'Really. Without seeing my fancy? Now that is what I call very sporting,' said Standish. 'Also we have an aboriginal in our corner, a cut man. If we hold the bout in one of the Brickfield Hill fields, say well to the west of Surry Hills, would you have any objections?'

'I'm a former convict Sir Edward, I've spent the better part of my life with criminals and I have found the aboriginals to be far more acceptable company,' he said smiling.

'Then we have terms sir,' said Standish. 'It will draw big crowds, the vendors will have a field day in every sense.'

'As you know, I own this pub and I'll have my beer and grog sellers at all the entrances, hot pies too if the night is cool, blocks of ice if it's not,' said Thomson with a smile.

'Your business sir, mine is purely a sporting one.'

'Money makes money Sir Edward, so whatever happens it'll be a good profitable night. So you see it's not entirely sporting for me but I'll enjoy it, if your man's as good as you seem to think he is.'

Standish grinned. 'Your good health sir.' He raised his glass. 'Now if you'll excuse me I must advise my man that we have terms.'

'Strange to have your man call the tune Sir Edward, if you don't mind me saying.'

'Not at all, we have a history and I have a great respect for him.'

'You have yet to tell me his name.'

'Daniel Shenkin a "ticket-leave-man" transported for causing a riot leading to damage to property and the death of soldiers; it took a detachment of a Highland regiment to stop him.'

'Ah! Irish is he?'

'No, a Welshman but a shared cause, the suppression of another people don't you think?'

'Don't look now Sir Edward, but your Whig politics are showing.'

'It is why I find myself in the colony sir,' said Standish, with a smile, as he headed for the door.

Back at the Fortune of War, Shenkin was becoming concerned. 'If he's not back soon we'll have to leave or Goldspick will be having a fit of nerves.'

'So he will,' said Regan. At that moment Standish came through the door, his very dress and manner opened a path in front of him.

'We have an agreement, but the purse is now four hundred at three to one against you,' said Standish.

'We have only three hundred Sir Edward. Can you meet that purse?'

'Did I not tell you that was my side of our joint venture?' said Standish putting out his hand.

'You did indeed. I hope I will meet my side of the bargain Sir Edward.'

'Amen to that,' said Regan closing his eyes and saying a small prayer.

'Do not take any notice Sir Edward, he's just a suspicious Irishman who only believes in shamrocks and leprechauns.'

'And the power of prayer,' said Regan, crossing himself. Then turning to Standish, he added, 'also the fists of your man here, for I've felt the weight of them and seen them in action. Why, I'm sure he's really an Irishman in disguise or a Welshman that could not swim across the Irish sea.'

Laughing they downed their drinks.

CHAPTER 7

'Well, well, Shenkin and your Irish lap dog.'

Shenkin held on to Regan as he pushed his way to Feltsham. 'Leave him Regan, evil is that evil does,' said Shenkin. 'We are here at Goldspick's invitation to see that fair play is done your lordship, for I see you have Ketch and Teal behind you in the darkness of the room, most appropriate places for them.'

'Dear me Goldspick, did you not trust me?'

'A small insurance, so to speak,' said Goldspick.

'So what do you want for the necklace, which really belongs to me anyway?'

'To Kettlewell in fact, or whoever that London thief stole it from in the first place,' said Shenkin.

Feltsham turned in anger to Shenkin. 'Your words and accusations are going to get you killed one of these days Shenkin.'

'You've tried a few times already Feltsham, but with little success,' said Shenkin. Ketch began to move forward into the light of the dripping candle sticks. A flash caught Shenkin's eye, as Teal too began to move forward. 'I see you have acquired another knife Teal, together with another master.'

'I'll see you and O'Hara dead from my loss of it and that's a fucking promise Shenkin, or I'll die in the attempt.'

'Then begin planning your funeral you runt of runts.'

Thomas Teal gave a strangled squeal and rushed forward, but Feltsham pulled him back. 'We are here to buy a necklace Teal, not settle your personal grievances. If I am in any danger then you can act, but not before. That goes for you too Ketch. I am eager to do the business and leave this den of filth.'

No one answered.

Feltsham stepped forward. 'Is that understood?' said Feltsham, raising his voice.

Both nodded.

His lordship removed a pouch of money from the red-coloured inner lining of his cloak. 'Well, Goldspick!'

Goldspick took a deep breath and placed the necklace on the crumb decorated table. 'Two thousand in English silver.'

'Bastard,' said Shenkin under his breath.

'Out of the question, I'll give one thousand and no more,' said Feltsham.

Goldspick began to put the necklace back into its box. 'Then goodnight, Lord Feltsham, and be careful of the night with its dark alleys.'

Feltsham placed his hand over Goldspick's. 'I'm pleased to see you have it in full view, Goldspick. I thought Ketch would have to search for it and you can imagine how destructive that would have been.' Then turning, he said, 'Stay out of this Shenkin, I have arranged for some magistrate friends of mine to send some carefully selected constables and watchmen here. They will arrest Goldspick for attempting to sell back to me a necklace that he had stolen from my estate only last week.' So saying, Feltsham pressed the side of his gold pocket watch, causing the dust cover to spring open. 'We have just ten minutes before they arrive, this would have given Goldspick time to have the necklace in his hand. However, he's been most obliging for it's already on the table,' said Feltsham, a satisfied look upon his face and a cocked Henry Nock pocket pistol in his hand. 'This is double barrelled Shenkin, so no sudden moves, for I assure you I know how to use it.'

Ketch placed the necklace in Goldspick's trembling hand. 'Teal, stand behind Goldspick and let him feel the point of the knife,' said Feltsham. 'As for you two,' he said, turning to Shenkin and Regan. 'Well, it could not be better; both present and future plans settled in one night. When they arrive I'll simply advise them that you all were the thieves that stole the necklace from me, here to collect your share. It's even better then my original plan. Exceedingly neat do you not agree?'

Shenkin stood very still. Then, almost in slow motion, Shenkin kicked the table over; the room plunged into darkness. 'Drop to the floor Regan,' Shenkin shouted. The flash of the pistol marked out Feltsham's place. Standing, Shenkin swiftly stepped forward hitting out into space. He was pleased to feel his fist connect with bone. A scream left Feltsham as he sank to his knees.

'Shenkin,' called Goldspick. 'This way quickly,' he said, turning to make for the back door, but Teal drove the knife into him. With a small sound of the air leaving his lungs he fell towards Shenkin, the weight of his body told Shenkin he was dead. They were all adjusting to the darkness. Ketch lunged for the necklace that was now on the floor. Securing it, he placed it under him. Regan hit him hard across the head with the back of a chair. Footsteps sounded on the wooden walkway outside, then knocks at the door.

'Open up in the name of the law.' There was no time to roll Ketch over.

'Quick Regan, down the hole between the floor boards,' said Shenkin. They landed in the filthy waters of the cove. On hands and knees they crawled under the houses; finally they came up at the top end of Argyle Street. To the sound of Goldspick's door being broken down they hurried over to the Spread Eagle pub on Harrington Street. Standing at the bar in a pool of water, Shenkin ordered two rums. The publican looked at the floor and handed them a mop.

Holding Regan back before he hit the landlord, Shenkin took it. 'Right you are sir. We fell out of a whaling boat, landlord, so eager were we to get to our first drink,' said Shenkin, mopping up the floor. The men around them laughed.

One held his nose. 'Fell into the sewer line by the smell of it,' he said.

After mopping up they made their way to a table with their drinks.

'Now that was bloody close, so it was,' said Regan.

Shenkin looked up from his drink. 'Goldspick is dead but strange as it seems he tried to save us.'

'He did so, but there goes our other half of the protection payment and the necklace.'

Shenkin nodded.

'Will Feltsham still try to implicate us in this?'

Shenkin shook his head. 'No, he'll be too concerned about us telling what we know about the stolen goods that he's been involved with, so drink up and we'll get out of these wet clothes.'

Almost in stunned silence they walked down towards the warehouse. 'Wait, listen,' said Shenkin. In the distance they could hear the commotion coming from Argyle Street.

'My carriage is around the corner, Constable, be so good as to tell my driver to come over here,' said Feltsham, holding a handkerchief to the swelling under his eye.

Turning to the officer in charge, Feltsham went back over the facts. 'This man, what was his name again: Goldspick?'

'Goldspick, my lord.'

'Quite so, he and the small man began to argue most violently over the sum of money they were demanding for the return of my property. Damn me sir, if the little man didn't go ahead and stab him. Right in front of me, most upsetting, most upsetting,' said Feltsham, the silk handkerchief marked with blood.

'Indeed sir, we'll have him safely under lock and key in no time, he'll hang for the killing of the other man this Goldspick; he's been known to us for some time. But at least you have your property back. I'll let the magistrate know of the outcome. Will you be alright to make your way back home sir, what with you being hurt and all?'

'Yes Constable, thank you, you've been most helpful and understanding. I shall so report it to your superiors. But my good friend Mr Ketch, we were on the Runnymede out of England together, don't you know. He had kindly offered to escort me down here tonight, it's not an area I frequent. Both he and the driver will see me safe, but thank you again.'

'Then I'll say goodnight sir.'

'Goodnight,' said Feltsham, his other hand firmly holding the necklace in his pocket. Teal had been screaming all kinds of accusations until a constable rendered him unconscious and carted him into a waiting carriage.

'A good outcome, don't you think?' said Feltsham when they had left. 'I have the necklace, you have whatever you can find back in there, we are free of Goldspick and this fellow Teal. As for Shenkin, engage the services of some friends to pay him and O'Hara a visit as we originally intended, but say in two weeks' time; we need to let this fracas die down first. There is a bonus in it for you, Ketch, if I hear that they are both no longer a threat to me or to my future wedding plans. What say you?'

'Considerate it done my lord,' said Ketch, adding, 'and Captain Moxey?'

'He's too deep into our business arrangements to cause any problems. Let me worry about the captain.'

'Now where can I find me a willing whore to ease my way home?'

'Back to my place my lord, for I have some of the choicest there,' said Ketch with a licentious grin.

'Lay on, Macduff,' said Feltsham, in good spirits, feeling again the cool diamond necklace in his pocket. 'A necklace worth a great deal of money, two loose ends tied tight, indeed all in all it's been a fine night's profit. Damn me, I'll have two of the sluts as a reward to myself,' he said under his breath, as Ketch went to the other side of the carriage and got in.

Ketch had a bewildered look on his face. 'Who's Macduff, sir?'

'It does not matter Ketch, get in the carriage and let's be off. I will not come into your place, you'll send the slatterns out to me two at a time for me to choose.'

'Of course my lord, it's not a place for you to be seen in.'

'Quite so,' said Feltsham, settling back into the comfort of his carriage. His face still stung but the two whores would ease the pain, so to speak, he said to himself with a laugh.

Tinker held his nose as they came through the door. 'Phew! Where you two been?'

'Disturbing the waters under the Argyle lodging houses,' said Shenkin.

'And a lot else by the smell of it,' said Tinker moving away from them. 'I have your healing salve ready, we'll put some on tonight.'

'Good I hope to hear from Sir Edward tomorrow about the date of the bout, so let's hope it's healed by then. Still make up that ointment you used to stop bleeding Tinker, just in case we need it. Now, let's get a wash, clean clothes and some sleep.'

'Its been an interesting day, so it has,' said Regan, the bed creaking under his weight.

On Millers Point the next morning, after Shenkin had already run a good five miles, he told Elizabeth about the night before also his decision to place all the money from the previous fights on one big bout.

'But you are risking everything Shenkin, what if you lose? I know there's the silver from the pendant, but you don't want to spend that yet do you?'

'Have you and Regan no faith in me cariad?' said Shenkin, looking at them both.

'Its not that Shenkin, it's just if you lose and your badly hurt what if…'

Shenkin stopped her. 'Stop it cariad, I'll win and we'll start putting our new lives together.'

'May all the saints preserve us,' said Regan, closing his eyes and genuflecting.

In some annoyance Shenkin said, 'These fists will preserve us. I'll trust in them, while you trust in god.' Then with a smile he placed his hands on their shoulders. 'But it would not hurt to have as much help as possible. I only hope god knows how to fight.'

'Sure, he was good at keeping his fists up back home, so he was,' said Regan.

'Then let's go and see Sir Edward since we are all ready,' said Shenkin.

'Elizabeth, have you taken Tinker's medicine?'

'I have and it tastes foul and your son does not like it either, but I have not been sick this morning.'

'Good till tomorrow then,' said Shenkin, starting down the hill with Regan.

They both instinctively looked over to the sound of the working chain gangs, to the rattle of chains, the shouts of the guards, the rise and fall of picks tolling out their music of misery.

Shenkin turned to Regan. 'I know much is at stake Regan, but all of life is a balance between feeling alive and being dead.'

'Well we've certainly felt alive these past few years, even if pain and pleasure have been out of balance from time to time.'

'That's life my friend, that's being alive. Now let's go and place our bet. What do you say?'

'You know the answer to that, so you do.'

The Fortune of War was packed. Men pushing their way to the bar spilled some of the ale of those leaving it, causing a few fights to break out. They swore at each other, laughed at jokes, smoked foul-smelling tobacco in chipped clay pipes and spat into spittoons that they mostly missed.

'Charming place, so it is,' said Regan lifting one man out of his way and dropping him into a corner.

The man looked up at the towering figure above him and just nodded. 'Sorry mate,' he said, 'didn't notice you were wanting to pass.'

Sir Edward Standish, his clothes cut to the latest London fashion, at least it was when the clothes left London three months ago, walked into the room. His black silver-topped cane made a path before him as he went to the bar. 'Landlord.'

'Yes, sir.'

'I need a private room for my friends and I.'

'Best I can offer is the back room sir: it's where we hold the cockfighting and like so it's not that clean.'

'That will have to do; and bring in three rums, no make it two bottles.'

'Right away, sir.'

They found some stools and a three-legged table. Standish poured three liberal amounts of rum. 'Well, Shenkin, it's all arranged, it will be held at Brickfield this coming Saturday at eight o'clock, we'll meet at the Wool Pack for the purses to be placed, both fighters to be examined and the rules to be agreed. Then into carriages for the short journey to the field. The backers have roped off the area, set up stalls, placed some seats at the front and generally prepared the place for the bout. You will fight under Broughton Rules except, because it's in a field, the chalked square yard mark will be replaced by a scratch mark.' Standish paused. 'Is this acceptable to you, Shenkin?'

'Yes, I fought under Broughton Rules back in Wales, also coming up to the scratch after a knock down within thirty seconds or being declared beaten.'

Standish began to pour another round of drinks. Shenkin covered his glass with his hand.

'Of course Shenkin, please forgive me.'

'Till Saturday then Sir Edward, if you'll excuse us, we have a lot to do,' said Shenkin.

Regan drank his rum fast. 'I'll take the other bottle, Sir Edward, for rubbing your man down and medicinal purposes,' said Regan smiling.

Outside, Shenkin turned towards Elizabeth Street. 'We need to see Doctor Tarn, have him look me over and see how well this eye is healing.'

'Right you are, can't be to careful. As good as Tinker is, we don't want it opening up.'

'Come in, both,' said Tarn, pleased to see them. Shenkin explained their visit. 'Who treated it?'

'Aboriginal named Tinker, he's joined us as my cut man.'

'These natives have some strange but effective herbal remedies, we could have done with him on the Runnymede during the cholera outbreak,' said Tarn, looking with admiration at the condition of the wound. 'It's almost healed, you've found a good man.'

Shenkin nodded. 'So it'll hold during the fight, Doctor?'

'You are not a bleeder Shenkin, and the skin around your eyes is thick, so I'd say yes, it will hold, but protect it at all times. Remember if the crowd turns nasty and the constables are called, you could be charged under the Vagrants Act and find yourselves back in prison. At least this time you will have sporting gentlemen present but it's still a risk. Governor Bourke has appointed magistrates who are empowered to select a non-military police force to deal with any public disorder.'

'And isn't General Sir Richard Bourke an Irishman too?' said Regan, with pride.

'He is Regan, and a credit to our country he is.'

'But they'll have lookouts posted as usual, Doctor, who'll be well paid by the backers,' said Shenkin.

'Then I wish you luck, now tell me how Elizabeth is.'

Shenkin did but left out the part about Tinker's morning sickness remedy.'

'Good, tell her to come and see me within the next week.'

'I will Doctor, thank you. If I win the fight then I'll be able to take the silver off your hands for I intend to commence buying property and stock.'

'I am pleased to hear it for it weighs heavy on my mind to have it here,' said Tarn.

'I know Doctor as soon as we can, we'll come for it.'

Walking back to their lodgings, Shenkin was deep in thought, he began playing with the scarf around his long hair.

'Now that's a bad sign, so it is,' said Regan.

'I was just thinking, these are the only shoes I have,' said Shenkin looking down. 'I need better grip if I'm fighting on grass. I need boots.'

'Is it something like military boots you had in mind Shenkin?'

'Yes! They'd be fine,' said Shenkin, adding, 'light weight, strong underneath and good leather.'

'You go away home now, I'll just go up to the Duke of Wellington on George Street. It's where the military officers pass the evening telling each other of the battles they've been in. I'm sure I can separate one from his nice shiny boots,' said Regan, smiling.

'I need you as my second Regan, so be bloody careful.'

'Sure, it'll be just like a quiet night's fight back in a pub in Ireland. A little light entertainment to while away the evening, so it will.'

Eagerly, Regan cut into East King Street, leaving Shenkin to make his way back to Campbell's Wharf.

In the early hours of the morning the door of their room flew open. Regan shouted at the top of his voice that the cobbler had arrived. He was as drunk as a lord, slamming the door so hard behind him it came off its hinges. Gulls on the roof screamed at being awakened in such a violent manner. Knocking over the table, Regan broke into the Irish rebel song 'Bold Robert Emmet' swinging two pairs of officers' boots in time to the tune.

'Shut up,' said Shenkin. 'You'll have every bloody watchman from miles around here.'

'I met one on my way from George Street. Tried to take the boots from me, so he did. He's resting peacefully now propped up against the side of the Custom House wall.'

'Tinker, get that door back on its hinges quick. I'll put Regan to bed.'

It proved easier said than done, but in the end the big man was sleeping like a baby. Before he fell asleep, Shenkin asked him, 'Why two pairs?'

'I wasn't sure of your size,' he said.

In the morning, Regan slowly lifted himself onto the edge of his bed. 'Sweet Mary, why is the room spinning and I'll kill those bloody gulls, so I will.'

'We're going training, and Tinker has made you a drink of god knows what that he says will make you feel better, isn't that so, Tinker?' said Shenkin.

'My people make a brew from the trunk water of the cork wood, damn strong stuff. The following day we place the leaves of this plant in hot water, which I have done for you, Regan.'

'It looks like tea,' said Regan.

'It's not, but you whites are confused by it so you calls it the "ti tree plant", anyway it'll help. It starts you sweating which is good to get the alcohol out of the body,' said Tinker.

'I have the very thing to help you sweat, Regan. Two runs up to Millers Point and back, so sip away then we'll go,' said Shenkin.

Regan made a face of despair, but began drinking. Four hours later Elizabeth was commiserating with Regan who, while ashen white, swore he felt better.

Shenkin had used the best-fitting boots on the morning's training to break them in, the other pair were far to small. Regan said he intended to take them back to the Duke of Wellington pub, he'd tell the publican that he found them in the street and ask if there was a reward for their return.

'He will too,' said Shenkin, standing in front of her with a shrug of his broad shoulders. Elizabeth noticed how good he looked, how wonderful was his sheer masculine presence. She blushed at the thought.

'Are you alright cariad? Remember you need to go to see Doctor Tarn in the next few days.'

Recovering her composure, she turned to Shenkin. 'Stop fretting Shenkin. I feel wonderful and Tinker's remedy worked fine. I am more concerned about this forthcoming fight, will the eye be healed by then?'

'So Tinker says and Doctor Tarn is satisfied that it will.'

'Is he fit Regan?'

'If he isn't then I am with all this running. Away with you, he's fine, so he is.'

Elizabeth left first so that they were not seen together, then they slowly began to walk down. 'She's a lovely girl, so she is and if you lose this bloody fight I'll beat the living day lights out of you.'

'Say a small prayer for me Regan, for I've heard this one is the best one yet. The boots will help and I'm grateful for your efforts in getting them.'

'Now don't go getting all mushy on me, and me a good Catholic and all.'

Shenkin smiled, but he knew this man's worth. He'd fight with all his strength not to fail him.

The Wool Pack was crowded, men spilling into the road, the noise deafening. Shenkin had to push his way into the long bar area then into the back room. Sitting at a long makeshift table sat the backers and Charlie Benson. The sporting gentlemen dressed as if on their way to a ball. They drank from silver flasks or pewter tankards. All the patrons and backers were in deep conversation with each other. Looking up, Standish quickly stood up. 'Gentlemen, I'd like you to meet my "fancy" Mr Daniel Shenkin and his second, Mr Regan O'Hara. We have the purses of four hundred to be held by the landlord of this establishment, he will sit between two gentlemen. Any private bets can now be placed at three to one against Shenkin. Do I have takers? First here then open to any member of the public at the field.'

Shenkin stepped forward with a pouch in his hand. 'Fifty pounds on me as the winner just to start it off,' he said.

Bets were placed around the room. From the back of the room a voice Shenkin knew only too well spoke up. 'I envy you Shenkin, it must be quite a gambling thrill to bet more money than you can afford to lose,' said Lord Feltsham, the curl of his lip perfectly in place.

Shenkin just smiled.

Sir John Piper, a leading landowner and sporting gentleman of Sydney also one of Benson's main backers, stood up. His bearing proclaimed his military background; he had been at Waterloo and had shared the moment of victory by Wellington's side. Clearing his throat and with a brush of his waxed moustache he said, 'Shall we first go over the rules gentlemen, then the independent examination of both prize fighters, also the seconds and corner men. We will then select the umpires, one by each opponent from the gentlemen present. The rules to be Broughton except that the square yard mark to be replaced by a scratch mark for the set-to. Once the two fighters are squared up, the area shall be cleared except for the seconds, cut men are to stand at the side and are not to lend aid or interfere at any time until the round is over. The round ends when a man is knocked down, if his second fails to bring his man back to the line in thirty seconds, he shall be deemed a beaten man.' Sir John took a breath.

'There is no limit to the rounds or length of the bout. Failing to come to the line signifies the end. Kicking, gouging, head butting and wrestling are allowed to win the bout. But no man shall be hit while he is down; a man on his knees is reckoned to be down.' Piper paused. 'Are we agreed gentlemen?' The gathered sporting gentlemen, backers and opponents nodded.

'Mr Benson, Mr Shenkin?'

Both nodded again.

'Right, gentlemen, to Brickfield Hill and hence to the field of play.'

During this time Shenkin had been studying Charlie Benson: they were the same height, same build and there was hardly a mark on Benson's face. He had muscular arms, his hands were pickled almost yellow, the knuckles hard lumps of skin. He moved light on his feet for a big man, a springing movement which spelled agility. He would not be easy to beat.

In the carriage ride to the field they found the road full of people walking or riding to see the bout. Shenkin turned to Standish, who he had picked as his umpire. 'Have you seen Benson fight Sir Edward, how good is he?'

'Well they have not brought him here to lose, Shenkin. As I told you he does have a reputation for knock outs, in fact he has changed his name a few times because of it.'

Shenkin turned to Standish. 'Because?'

'He could not get any bouts so he fought in outlying places of Australia and Van Diemen's Land. They say he's tipped to be the Bare-Knuckle Champion of New South Wales.'

'Well, the first round will tell me how high he carries his fists and if he stands upright or crouches,' said Shenkin.

Tinker was running at the side of the carriage in an effortless lope, as they made their way up Brickfield Hill. Sir Edward told him to jump on the step down at the door. Soon Tinker's smiling face appeared at the window.

'Thank you Sir Edward, he's a good man and my friend,' said Shenkin.

'You really are a reformer Shenkin. Earl Grey would be proud of you.'

'It has cost me many loved ones Sir Edward, but one day we will see the wisdom of it.'

'Well, one fight at a time Shenkin,' said Standish, as the rattler pulled up at the entrance to the field.

A roar came up from the crowd as the two prize fighters made their way to the roped-off area in the centre of the field. Ale and grog sellers lined the approach while others were selling tobacco to smoke or chew. The noise was a roar of heart-thumping sounds. The whole place had a fairground feel to it as Shenkin began to strip to his waist. The boots felt comfortable and firm underneath his feet. His scarf was holding his long black hair tightly back in a ponytail. Regan had tried to get him to shave his head, but as always he refused. The discussion had reminded him of the arguments he had had with his father over his long hair. 'The other man will pull your head down, Daniel,' he would say. Shenkin wondered, if his father had lived, what he would make of all this. So far away from their black coal covered valley of Wales. It would be winter there now, the Brecon Beacons would be mantled with snow in stark contrast to the black coal fields. Shenkin brought himself back to the roar of the crowd as Regan pulled on his ponytail. 'He'll bloody hang you with this, let me cut it off.'

'Don't start again, it's staying on and that's that,' said Shenkin.

'Alright, alright,' said Regan turning to Tinker. 'Do you have everything?'

'For the tenth time, yes,' said Tinker.

Benson on the other hand, had no such needs, for he was shaved completely bald, one ear was crumbled flat to his head, which Shenkin had not noticed at the Wool Pack, it would be a target.

Feltsham sat at the edge of the roped-off area surrounded by his cronies. He had placed a large bet on Benson and had covered other bets from his sporting friends. Silver flasks flashed in the last of the evening light while cigar smoke spiralled into the darkening sky. Tar-filled torches stood at the ready, while pickpockets waited for the dark to shroud their night's work. Constables and watchmen stood among the crowd hoping to keep control, mindful of the gentry that were present; it would need to be a killing for them to stop the bout, besides they too were busy placing bets.

CHAPTER 8

Their seconds brought them up to the scratch. While so doing, each fighter turned the palms of his hands upwards to show they were not hiding anything. 'Seconds leave the centre, only the principals to remain. Umpires stand at the sides, do not call out advice to your man,' called the publican, the purses tied tight to the wide leather belt around his ample belly.

'Seconds, are they squared up?'

Both nodded.

'Commence.'

Shenkin broke from the set-up first, dancing lightly, he moved around Benson. They sparred for a while testing the length of each other's arms, their speed of movement forward and backwards. Then Benson threw the first blow, it landed at the side of Shenkin's head. A roar went up from the crowd as they pushed forward for a better view. Lord Feltsham smiled, this was going to give him great pleasure, seeing Shenkin being beaten. This man who had humiliated him on the convict ship and thwarted his efforts to take Elizabeth to wife, he'd now watch his downfall. Even as he thought it, Shenkin hit Benson with a brutal right cross that stopped Benson short in the middle of the of the ropes. Another shout went up as Shenkin drove the other man backwards with a barrage of blows, finally hitting Benson in the chest with a vicious kick that sent him to the floor. Seconds rushed across to their men as the seconds ticked off the timepieces the umpires were holding. Nineteen, twenty, twenty-two. Benson was at the scratch, a slight lump just under his right eye. He nodded to Shenkin as they came at one another again. 'You're good,' said Benson, wiping a trickle of blood from the side of his mouth. There was no expression on Shenkin's face. In a low crouch Benson rushed at Shenkin, putting him into a bear hug, his powerful arms squeezing the breath from Shenkin's lungs. Shenkin got his left arm under Benson's chin and pushed upwards until he had enough room to chop down at it with his right fist. They broke, Benson counter punched as he moved backwards. One of the blows caught Shenkin solidly on the brow and Benson moved in quickly, hitting Shenkin with a swinging head butt to the face then swinging his head left and right across Shenkin's head. Shenkin went to his knees. Standish screamed out for Benson to stand back. He did, dancing nimbly on his feet, his fists raised in an open stance waiting, ready to pounce.

Regan came to Shenkin's side. 'Take a breather Shenkin.' Seventeen, eighteen, nineteen, Shenkin was up and squaring off. Benson went in straight away but was met with a right fist then Shenkin's elbow. Stunned, Benson dropped to his knees, his mouth open, blood streaming from broken teeth and split lips. At the set-up both men were breathing hard. Shenkin dropped his arms and danced backwards. Benson did the same. 'Fight,' came a call from the gentlemen around the ropes.

Benson lifted his fists and came forward landing a flurry of blows on Shenkin, then grabbed him and threw him to the floor. Shenkin came to his feet quickly. The umpires called for a set-to but were ignored. Both held each other in an attempt to throw the other. Benson got Shenkin in a head lock and began punching him about the face. Shenkin chopped into Benson's side then hit him hard in the kidneys. They broke again, each moving back into the centre. A wild swing came from Benson, Shenkin ducked then drove blows into Benson's stomach then up under his heart. Benson was almost lifted off his feet by the power of the blows. Shenkin moved back just enough to place a right cross to Benson's jaw. He went down as if a trap door had been opened under him. Benson's second ran over to him and threw water in his face. Shaking his head, he got unsteadily to his feet. At the scratch mark, Shenkin could see a glazed look in Benson's eyes. They had been fighting for over an hour, both carried marks about the body and head, but Shenkin was looking the stronger. Benson grabbed on to Shenkin and head butted him in the face. The scar on Shenkin's eyebrow split open, blood streamed down. He could not see as Benson began hitting with lefts and rights, then to the stomach, then back to the head. Shenkin was being driven back across the open ground. Feltsham was shouting his delight. 'Hit him, hit him.'

The gentleman at his side was Piper. 'Do you mind, sir, please desist from such poor sportsmanship.'

Feltsham sneered. 'You enjoy your sport your way and I'll enjoy it may way,' he said.

Piper turned away from him in disgust. But Shenkin was back up to the scratch, a wad of Tinker's herbs around his cut. It flew off at the first blow but the bleeding did appear to have slowed.

Regan had shouted into Shenkin's ear, 'You'd better finish this fast or that cut's going to start bleeding again.'

'Have a word with Benson, he seems to have other plans,' said Shenkin. After three hours they were beginning to hold each other more than throw punches. Both had been down a number of times, but both refused to stay down. The torches were burning low, the night turning chilly except in the circle of the bout where both men hit each other around the open lonely area of their own personal torments.

Around Shenkin, all was happening in slow motion, blow after blow found or missed its mark. Benson dropped to his knees, not from a blow but from fatigue. 'Foul, the man has not been hit,' called Standish. 'If he can't make the mark quickly I declare my man the winner.'

Benson's umpire looked at Benson still on his knees. 'Well, man, what's it to be?'

Benson spat blood onto the ground and got to his feet. In spite of himself, Shenkin nodded his admiration. He moved back to give Benson a moment longer to recover. Benson acknowledged the act of sportsmanship, then threw a brutal left that sent Shenkin staggering backwards.

'Sweet Mary in heaven we're not in a bloody charity Shenkin, don't give him any time man,' called Regan.

'Seconds will not give their man advice,' shouted Benson's umpire.

Both men locked each other in an arm wrestle. Shenkin brought his knee up into Benson's groin. Gasping he broke away as he did, Shenkin hit him with a right upper cut, causing Benson's head to snap back like a pistol shot. As Benson's head came back down, Shenkin's elbow struck him across the jaw. He was down, this time a hush spread across the field as they waited to see if he could get up. Eleven, twelve, thirteen, fourteen, fifteen, Benson stirred, pressing his hands to the ground, he slowly began the painful effort of coming to his feet. Twenty-seven, twenty-eight, Benson's second took him back to the scratch. They squared up again, it was now almost four hours and neither man giving way. Tinker had treated the cut time after time but the cut was getting longer and wider. He told Regan it was not good, the wound was becoming too wide to fill; it needed a stitch that he already had needle and thread ready for.

'Right, next time he's down,' said Regan.

Benson kicked out with his right foot. Shenkin caught it and swung

Benson around, hitting him full on the side of his jaw as he did so. The combined weight of their bodies sent Benson down onto his back with a thump that the first few rows heard clearly. Was this it, could he get to his feet again? He did, but staggered. The umpires looked at Benson's second, as he brought his man yet again up to the scratch. Shenkin, a look of disbelief at this man's endurance braced himself again, his right fist high protecting the cut. Parrying to his left then right, Shenkin moved inside his man. In his mind he heard his father's voice. *'Kill the body Daniel, and the head will die.* Right Da,' he said under his breath.

Punch after punch went into Benson's stomach. A tattoo of non-stop blows like the beating of a drum started at Benson's waist and ended under his heart. Benson's fists and then his head, began to fall until his arms were hanging at his side. Shenkin breathed in deeply then stepped up close to Benson. Shenkin's right fist moved maybe four to six inches, but in that short space his fist delivered a brutal, vicious blow. Benson was down, he was unconscious before he hit the ground, it was over.

A deafening roar went up as bets were called in and fights broke out to settle any differences. Broken bottles were thrown, constables restrained who they could but soon gave up.

Standish, his arm around Shenkin, guided him to the side. Purses were passed over, private agreements met, which Feltsham did with little grace. But watched by Piper with great satisfaction and, although he was one of the backers of Benson, he shook Shenkin's hand. 'One of the finest bouts I have ever seen, it was a pleasure to watch you work Shenkin.' But Shenkin was helping Benson to his feet; still groggy, he looked at Shenkin. 'I never thought anyone could do that to me, but now I know what the other man feels like after a beating. You are a natural gentleman sir, it was an honour to fight you,' he said, shaking Shenkin's hand.

Shenkin with some difficulty, raised a smile. 'Well, it was a close-run thing, for a moment there I thought I was about to lose the fight together with every penny I had, or rather we had,' said Shenkin turning to Regan and Tinker.

'Generous of you to say once we are cleaned up, or rather stitched up, can I buy you a tankard of beer?'

'You can Charlie, and it will be my privilege to sip with you.'

Back at the Wool Pack, Tinker began to place stitches in the cut, it took five to pull it together. 'Bloody stupid way to behave if you ask me, and us black fellows are supposed to be the savages,' said Tinker.

At this, Standish stood and raised his glass. 'To Shenkin, Regan, Charlie Benson and the only civilised man amongst us, Tinker.'

Laughing, they raised their drinks as Charlie Benson joined them. They all stood up. 'Sit down please. Regan, if you would.' Handing Regan some silver. 'A beer for the best damn prize fighter I have ever fought.'

'Amen to that and long live Ireland,' said Regan, making his way to the bar to refill their tankards and glasses.

Doctor Tarn came into the room. 'That was a hell of a fight; can I take a look at the eye?' he said, adding, turning to Tinker, 'with your permission of course.'

'You honour me sir,' said Tinker, with great dignity.

'Damn me but that's fine work though it'll take a time to heal. You'll not be fighting for some time, Shenkin.'

'I don't intend to, Doctor, we have what we wanted and I promised Elizabeth if I won I'd not fight again.'

'I'm pleased to hear it. So you will be coming to see me soon to regain your property,' he said, lowering his voice.

'I will Doctor,' said Shenkin.

Everyone was talking and drinking, but he'd promised Elizabeth he'd let her know how the bout went, so he began to excuse himself when Benson put a hand on his arm. 'Can I have a word with you before you leave?'

Shenkin stared for a moment at Charlie Benson, both of them were looking battle scarred. Benson's lip was split, his left eye cut above and below, a swelling under his right cheek. While Shenkin had a swollen eyebrow with stitches, both were tired. 'What is it Charlie, you need some coin?'

'Thank you, but no that's not it. You were very fair to me tonight Shenkin, and I may be able to return the favour.'

'In what way?' said Shenkin.

'This Lord Feltsham is no friend of yours is he?'

'No we go back to the convict ship, the Runnymede, that we were on from England. He was one of the passengers, a business partner of the captain, a man named Josiah Moxey.'

'Was there a man called Ketch on board?'

'Yes there was, why?'

'Lord Feltsham was a poor loser tonight. You cost him a great deal of silver, Shenkin. After he'd paid up to the other gentlemen, he called this man over this Ketch. They stood talking for a while, but then they came up close to where I was dressing behind one of the tented stalls selling ale. They could not see me, but I could hear all that they said. Feltsham said he wanted Ketch to pay you a visit tonight while you were recovering from the fight. That this would be a good time, that he was to take a few of his more violent friends with him, it could be blamed on some men who had lost coin tonight on the fight. He expected to hear the grave news of your and Regan's sad killing in the morning.' Benson paused, for heartbeats neither spoke. 'If I can help, Shenkin, you have only to ask. You've busted me up quite a bit, but I can still throw a punch.'

Shenkin nodded. 'Thank you, Charlie, but it's best if you're not involved in this; it's something between us and Feltsham. But I appreciate your warning he's a well educated, high-born out and out bastard and Ketch is his guard dog; he was the sergeant in charge of the military escort on the Runnymede. We suspect he murdered his corporal and the ship's first mate. Feltsham has set him up here in the colony. Ketch now owns two pubs and is ready to do Feltsham's dirty work whenever needed.'

'Deadly partnership Shenkin, you need to be careful, at least you know what's coming your way, so there's time to duck and get that right cross of yours in before they do.'

'Thanks again Charlie, and I wish you well, hope the cuts heal soon.'

'Same to you Shenkin,' he said, heading for the door. The crowd parted in front of him. A few men slapped him on the shoulder, but Shenkin had put paid to him ever becoming the New South Wales champion and he knew it.

Returning to their table, Shenkin excused himself saying he and Regan needed to leave. 'But the night's young Shenkin, stay a while longer,' said Standish.

'What's this and me only on my fourth beer, is it eager you are to get home to that lovely girl of yours? If that's the case I'll stay here, for you'll not be needing or wanting me, and that's so,' said Regan.

'But I do need you Regan, soon you'll be too drunk to keep the coin safe, whereas the two of us and Tinker outside will be able to make sure all of us and the coin get back to our lodgings safely.'

'He has a point Regan, the night time is not the time to be walking the streets of Sydney Cove alone with a lot of money on you,' said Standish.

'It's everything we have, Regan, once back you can go up to the Fortune of War if you want.'

Regan brightened immediately. 'Let's be on our way then, for you're wasting time away from your colleen and I'm losing a few ales.'

They said their farewells. Outside, Shenkin told Regan what Charlie Benson had told him. 'The bastards, they're going to make damn sure this time, Shenkin. What are you like in a fight, Tinker?'

'I have a boomerang back at Campbell's Wharf with an edge as sharp as a bloody knife,' said Tinker.

'I'm concerned because I told Elizabeth that if she could get away from her uncle then to meet us there after the fight,' said Shenkin.

'Hell it's getting late, if Ketch got some men together they could already be on their way,' said Regan, hurriedly following Shenkin to the door. Men wanted to shake his hand but finally they were crossing Bathurst Street then running down into George Street passing St Andrews Church and the old burial ground, which took them all the way down to the Custom House and down the steps to Campbell's Wharf. Passing the Naval Office they slowed up, all of them out of breath, blood beginning to seep from Shenkin's eyebrow again. The lamplights were lit and the noise of the pubs and brothels was ringing in their ears. Damn it to hell thought Shenkin, I should have left earlier.

At the turn off to Campbell's Wharf Shenkin stopped to see if he could see a light from their lodgings or any sign of Elizabeth. There was none. Out of the darkness, Shenkin could make out a lantern swinging in a man's hand. The watchman turned as they approached.

'Evening to you all.' Then looking at Shenkin he said, 'Don't you look a mess, been in a fight?'

'Something like that,' said Shenkin quickly. 'Tell me have you seen a number of men coming up from Campbell's Wharf?'

'I did about an hour back, right looking lot they were too, even pushed me to the side when I enquired who they were,' said the watchman. 'Still, didn't seem to be causing any trouble so I let them pass, too bloody many of them to argue the point.'

'Sweet mother in heaven,' said Regan.

'Is everything alright?' said the watchman seeing the alarm in Regan's face.

'I want you to come with us to our lodgings at Campbell's Wharf,' said Shenkin, breaking into a run.

'Right, or perhaps I should go for more help,' he said, turning up towards the Custom House where he'd last seen some armed constables.

'Damn,' said Shenkin, watching him go, but he didn't stop running.

Tinker was already far ahead of them, having not stopped as they spoke to the watchman. At Campbell's Wharf he took the wooden steps up to their rooms two at a time. There was a dim light inside as he swung the door open.

The scene that greeted Tinker took his breath away.

Elizabeth was on one of the beds, her dress was above her waist, her legs open, blood running down the inside of her thigh. Tinker turned back to the door as Shenkin took the last few steps.

'Stop Shenkin, it's not good. Quick Regan, hold him for a moment.' Regan's large arms locked Shenkin in a bear hug. Shenkin struggled, but after the fight his strength was no match for Regan. Tinker went back inside. He felt for a pulse and by all that was sacred he was pleased to find one. She had fought hard, scratch marks covered her face and bare shoulders, but her breathing was slow and laboured. He covered her up and placed a blanket over her, before he came back to the door. 'She's alive but only just. I can heal the body and facial wounds, but she needs a medical doctor. She's been raped a number of times, I'd say.'

'Dear god let me go, Regan,' said Shenkin, the tears running freely down his face, the salt of them burning the cuts from the fight. Tinker nodded to Regan who let him go. Going to her he knelt by her side. 'Cariad, cariad what have they done? I should have been here to protect you. He buried his head in her hands and kissed them gently, they were bleeding and cold.

'Regan, get Doctor Tarn quick.'

'Tinker's already left, and I've given him the money from the fight to give to Doctor Tarn to keep safe, is there anything else I can do?'

'Pray to that god of yours,' said Shenkin, adding, 'if he is there then let him bear witness, that I swear Ketch and Feltsham will pay dearly for this.'

'Amen, with all my heart and soul, amen,' said Regan.

Regan handed Shenkin some warm water and cloth. Gently, Shenkin began to bathe Elizabeth's face, his tears mixing with the tepid water.

Regan turned away, his vision too was blurred at the sight of Shenkin's sorrow and sure didn't he love them both? The wife of the owner of Campbell's Wharf, Phoebe Harris, stood in the doorway, at her side was Captain Moxey.

'Stand aside, woman,' said Moxey.

'I didn't know what to do Shenkin; we heard Elizabeth screaming. My husband tried to stop them, but was knocked to the ground. A gash to the head rendered him unable to do anything.'

Moxey went to pull Shenkin away from Elizabeth. It was a mistake; with one blow Moxey was on the ground. 'Touch me again and I'll kill you,' said Shenkin.

Moxey got slowly to his feet. Regan held him firmly. 'Captain, if you value your life don't go near them. We've already sent for Doctor Tarn,' said Regan.

Moxey was no match for the big Irishman, but it did not stop him from talking. 'You have been nothing but trouble ever since you came aboard the Runnymede in chains and I'll see you in them again Shenkin. I too have sent for someone. Lord Feltsham will be here soon, together with some constables.'

Phoebe Harris protested. 'It was not Shenkin Captain Moxey, he was not even here,' she said.

'If you know what's good for you you'll keep out of this. Your husband is in debt to me for a considerable amount of money madam,' said Moxey with a snarl.

The sound of a carriage came up from the road. Soon the place was full of men. 'Unhand the captain, you papist bastard,' said Feltsham. Regan O'Hara's reply was to backhand Feltsham across the face then drop the nearest man with a clubbing blow to the side of his head. Shenkin went to get up from beside Elizabeth, but a strike from a truncheon sent him unconscious to the floor. Soon Regan was overpowered by a number of men who placed manacles on his wrists and legs.

They dragged both of them outside and bundled them into a cart. Once alone Moxey turned to Feltsham. 'This sir, is your doing. My niece has been raped and not by Shenkin, but by Ketch and his fellows. The woman Harris told me as much.'

But Feltsham silenced him. 'I've brought my own doctor to care for her sir, and you would best be advised to be silent,' said Feltsham in a whispered tone.

While the doctor tended Elizabeth, Feltsham took Moxey outside. 'I did send Ketch here tonight but not to do this. After the bout I thought Shenkin would be here alone with his Irishman, we could have blamed it all on some bad losers.'

'I will see to it that Ketch is brought to justice for this my lord, for she was of my blood.'

'Ketch will implicate us in all we have done, stolen goods, Goldspick, Teal, who has not been hung yet remember. Would you lose everything in one rash move?'

Both were silent for a moment as the doctor came out from the room. 'She is very ill my lord, badly torn internally, still barely able to talk. Also the baby may not survive without a great deal of care.'

'Baby sir, baby you must be mistaken,' said Moxey, his voice shaking.

'Sir, I have been practising for many years. I know a pregnant woman when I see one,' said the doctor indignantly.

'Its Shenkin's, of course, the bloody man. I see it now. It all began on the long voyage aboard the Runnymede,' said Feltsham.

Moxey was struck dumb, for heartbeats no one spoke. Then a light came to Lord Feltsham's eyes that brought a smile to his lips. Given the circumstances it was not a pleasant sight.

'You find something amusing, sir?' said Moxey, angrily.

'It's a social scandal, is it not? It places your niece outside of decent society, unmarried and with child. The father serving a long term of imprisonment, and if sent to Port Arthur he may never return to Sydney. Your business prospects, by association with the affair, now look very poor. I suggest sir that you reconsider involving Ketch and the risks that that may entail. To stir the pot more will only add to your problems. When Shenkin and O'Hara are safely incarcerated for a very long time, only Ketch will remain who knows about our past actives. I assure you he will be dealt with quietly and effectively,' said Feltsham.

'But my niece?'

'I have been pressing for her hand in marriage, have I not?' Not waiting for a reply, Feltsham continued, 'A wife cannot speak against her husband in a court of law. After a year recovering I will reintroduce her back into society as my wife. She will pass her dowry over to me, in her state of health it should be quite easy to get her to sign the necessary papers,' said Feltsham, in a rush of words.

Then brushing down his tailored coat he turned to Moxey. 'We have carriages outside the doctor will take her to my estate, where he will give her the best attention possible. The whole affair will be hushed up. You will pay the Harrises off, but keep them in your debt for no one must know what really happened here tonight.'

Captain Josiah Moxey looked a beaten man. He was getting old; this was his last chance to secure his future and into the bargain, that of his niece. Out of sight at Feltsham Mansion, away from prying eyes, she could recover from this and become Lady Feltsham. If the child survived then they would both be well taken care of financially and socially.

'But she is now damaged goods, Lord Feltsham. You cannot want her, surely not?'

'Damn it, man! She is insurance, she brings a dowry, she will be on my arm in society as my wife. As to damaged goods, I will get my pleasures elsewhere, the majority of which are certainly damaged goods. If she dies at my estate, as my wife, I will play the heartbroken husband, who society will be eager to open their hearts and social events to. In fact, the more I think about it the better it fits both our futures,' said Feltsham, adding, 'get the marriage plans arranged Moxey, within the next few days before she either dies or regains her faculties.'

Moxey was both stunned and appalled by the plan.

'Well,' said Feltsham, irritably tapping his fingers on his silver-topped cane.

After a moment Moxey glared back at his lordship. *As rotten as any piece of worm-eaten wood he had ever seen in the ribs of a ship.* Then with a sigh he said, 'Agreed.'

'Doctor,' called Feltsham.

'My lord,' said the doctor, coming to the door.

'Can she be moved?'

'Only with great care, but yes she can.'

'Good I want you to put her into your carriage. My driver and Captain Moxey will assist,' said Feltsham, after all he saw no point in getting his fine carriage stained with blood.

Slowly they made her as comfortable as possible in the carriage. 'Shenkin, Shenkin, please I want Shenkin. Where is he?' said Elizabeth, her voice hardly audible.

'Right, driver, if you go into or over a rut in the road I'll have your hide, you'll be back on a chain gang come morning is that understood?' said Feltsham.

'Yes, sir.'

Moxey watched as the carriage disappeared into the dark gloom of Sydney Cove.

Turning, Moxey began to go into the rooms of James Harris but the lantern lights of another coach stopped him. Feltsham backed into the overhead timber cover of the warehouse.

Tarn stepped down from the rattler, Tinker at his side. 'Well, Captain how bad is she?'

'Who?' said Moxey.

'Elizabeth of course, this man told me she had been molested. I would have been here sooner were it not for a case I was on some ten miles outside of town towards Parramatta,' said Tarn.

'Why would she be here, Tarn? I'm here to collect rent from James Harris who rents this part of the stockroom from me. If she would be anywhere it would be at our place on King's Wharf would she not?'

'Then I wish to see her sir.'

'She is not there sir. She's away at the moment visiting friends. She's been looking rather pale of late; the rest will do her good.'

'This fellow is untruthful, sir,' said Tinker. 'I saw her, touched her with my very own hands in the rooms above, Doctor.'

'Touched her! touched her, you?'

'Doctor he is lying sir.'

'You dare to question a white man, you black abo bastard?' said Lord Feltsham stepping out of the shadows. 'Who are you and what have you stolen from around here? The owner here Captain Moxey, has been missing a number of barrels of rum of late, he tells me. I'll see you're punished severely for it,' said Feltsham. Tinker turned to run but was stopped and then hand-cuffed by the constables at his lordship's side, his struggling was to no avail.

Tarn turned to face Feltsham. 'The plot thickens, if you are here at this time of night and in this area, my lord.'

'Come now, Doctor, surely you'll not take this man's word against ours?'

'Then why did he come to fetch me?'

'To lure you into the night and rob you most likely.'

Tarn was shaking his head. 'Shenkin and Regan, for this is their lodgings, where are they?'

'Not the company I keep, Doctor, as you well know.'

Tarn was not satisfied with Feltsham or Moxey's explanation. 'This bears further investigation, my lord and I'll see to it that it is done thoroughly. You have my word on it.'

Feltsham smiled. 'But of course Doctor, do that my all means. Now if you'll excuse me I must be getting along, time of night don't you know. The constables will do their duties and I will bear witness in court tomorrow, as will Captain Moxey.'

'Indeed I will,' said Moxey, his words somewhat strained.

'Till the morning then, for I too will be there,' said Tarn, looking once more up at the broken door at the top of the stairs before turning back towards his abode.

Moxey moved close to Feltsham and began to say something. 'Shut up man, we have made our story now we stick to it,' said Feltsham sharply.

'But they will all be there, all giving evidence to the contrary.'

Lord Feltsham straightened his back, his hand loosely holding the silver-topped cane. He tapped Moxey on the shoulder with it. 'Come, come, my dear man, two former convicts and an aborigine, have you no faith in British justice and my very good friend Judge Hendry?' Not waiting for an answer, his lordship turned on his well-shod heel. Walking forward, he avoided a questionable pool of water. Stepped into his carriage, removed his hat and leaned out of the window.

'Till tomorrow then.'

Then looking up at the coachman, he spoke in a voice quite unruffled by the night's events. 'Thomas, take me home by way of Ketch's pub.'

'Sir.'

Ketch backed away from the bar as his lordship came through the doors. A whore came to greet him, her breasts barely covered. Lord Feltsham struck her across the face with his cane. 'Out of my way, you pox-ridden gutter whore.'

Letting out a scream, the woman fell backwards onto one of the tables, scattering tankards of ale over the men at the table. One of the men pushed her off the table. 'Polly you useless ugly slut, you'll pay for those drinks in cash or in tricks for all of us.' Lord Feltsham didn't falter. He sidestepped the pools of ale on the floor, the sawdust slowly turning it into a mush. A look of disdain on his face, he pointed to the back of the room.

'Ketch, in the private room now.'

'Wait your lordship, I can explain,' said Ketch, as Feltsham raised his cane while Ketch moved into one of the corners of the private room.

Very slowly Feltsham lowered the cane. 'I should strike you, you bundling miscreant. It was Shenkin you were supposed to deal with not the girl.'

'It got out of hand sir, they were on her before I could stop them. I was guarding the door waiting for Shenkin when it happened. Then what with Captain Moxey's niece screaming and men fighting to get to her, well the noise was disturbing the area. Lights were going on all around; I thought it would be better if I left, like.'

'I want you to leave, Ketch. Leave Sydney until this blows over. I'll send for you when I need you. Tell your dregs here that if asked, you left two days ago, do you understand?'

'Yes sir, two days ago, but what about the running of the pub?'

'Arrange for someone to take care of it. Tell them I will be sending someone down to collect the week's takings.'

'But...' began Ketch. Feltsham cut him short.

'No buts she knows you were involved man, it will help them bear witness to the act.'

'Very well my lord, I'll go first thing tomorrow.'

'You will go tonight, Ketch. I will be in my carriage watching you go. Do not fail me Ketch, for if you prefer the chain gang then that too can be arranged.'

'Tonight it is sir, and I appreciate you watching out for me, your lordship, yes indeed I do, thank you, sir.'

'Think nothing of it, Ketch. You have been useful to me so far; let us hope that continues,' said Feltsham, pressing a small pouch of silver into Ketch's hand.

'It will sir, you can depend upon it, and thank you again, sir.'

Feltsham gave a lip-curling smile. 'Good then get on with it. I'll give you thirty minutes past midnight,' he said, looking at his engraved full gold Hunter fob watch, his cigar-cutter tapping gently against the gold chain. The inscription read: *To my devoted son from his loving mother, may his time upon this earth be long and bountiful.* It always gave him a sense of the rightfulness of life, he did hope Marshalsea Debtors' Prison was agreeing with her, for he was certainly pursuing a bountiful rich life.

Placing the Hunter back in the bottom pocket of his waistcoat, he walked back through the ale-swilling pub, the air thick with smoke, Polly leading another man out into the side alley. 'You'll be the last, and my debt is paid in full,' she said.

The Right Honourable Lord Percival Hugo Feltsham, an English aristocrat to his manicured finger nails, his fingers tapped the Hunter into its rightful place. Not quite a devoted son and very far from honourable when it came to paying his debts. *I must say, he thought, you do find the payments of debts in the strangest of places* as Polly disappeared through the side door.

Having regained consciousness for the hundredth time, Shenkin twisted his hands in the iron cuffs.

'They'll not come off, remember?' said Regan, his heart heavy with the sadness of the last hours.

'Dear god Regan, did Tinker get the doctor, did he get there in time?'

'God knows but I hope he's watching over her,' said Regan, with a deep sigh.

'I swear, Regan, I'll kill Feltsham and Ketch for this, so help me god.'

'I don't think that's what god helps with Daniel.'

'Then to hell with him. I'll damn my soul if I must.' A tear ran over Shenkin's fight-scarred face.

The rattler bumped over the rutted road towards the prison barracks.

CHAPTER 9

'What bloody time of night do you call this?' said a man coming through the heavy wood doors of the barracks in answer to the hammering on the door. 'It's almost bloody morning and you bring me prisoners,' said Isaac Blake, with a snarl. He was the Night Overseer at the convict barracks at the top of Macquarie Street and not the sort of man you would wish to disturb from his sleep. Still grumbling about the lateness, he looked into the cart. 'Well, well if it isn't my old friends Shenkin and O'Hara. So glad to see you back, and so soon.'

Turning to the constable he said, 'These two cost me a good hut overseer position and a good friend to boot by the name of Fleet. I'll see they get a really warm welcome back, Sergeant. They'll look even worse come morning.'

The sergeant constable slowly stepped down from the cart. 'Whatever you have in mind Blake, forget it. They're to go into solitary for tonight only. Tomorrow they go up in front of Judge Henry; it's all been arranged. They're bound for Port Arthur for rape, their tickets of leave revoked. They'll serve their full sentence there so you'll not see them again.'

'Still it's a few hours yet till morning Sergeant; you never know, they may have an accident,' said Blake.

'Now listen Blake, I don't give an abo's ass about them, but I'm responsible for them until sentence is passed see, and I don't want to be explaining no accident. If I have to explain I'll be back here to have a few words with you. You got that?' The sergeant was banging his heavy stick into the palm of his hand.

'Alright, alright,' said Blake leading the two constables into the barracks. Chained together, Shenkin and O'Hara stumbled after them.

'Well now I never thought I'd have the pleasure of seeing this place again, and your smiling face too, Blake,' said O'Hara.

'Shut your mouth, you Irish bastard,' said Blake, lifting his cosh.

'Weren't you bloody listening, Blake?' said the sergeant behind them.

Blake kicked a cell door open. 'Get them in there before I risk what the sergeant is threatening.'

The constables pushed them in and slammed the door. Blake stepped forward and turned the key in the lock. Looking through the grill in the door, Blake whispered. 'Let's see if you can make it till morning.' Then turning back to the sergeant, he raised his voice. 'They'll be safe and sound in there, Sarg.'

Standing in the middle of the cell they looked at each other. O'Hara was the first to speak. 'Sure I can't believe we're back here.'

Shenkin was still silent as he had been for the last hour or so. The sadness in his face was terrible for Regan to see. Then after a moment he turned to O'Hara. 'Regan I must get out, somehow I must she's all alone, she's hurt and scared. Dear god why didn't we leave earlier, why?'

'Its no good going over it Shenkin, and as to getting out how?'

Shenkin thought for a while. 'If the guards come in the morning to feed us we could overpower them then make a run for the front door.'

'We'd never make it and you know it. It would also give Blake the excuse he's looking for to beat all kinds of hell out of us.'

Shenkin knew it, but he had to do something. Everyone he had loved or cared about seem to have been either killed or hurt. The miners who had died in the bowels of the black earth back in South Wales, the siren sending out its mournful sound at their passing. His father, Sean O'Hara, Willy Stitch, Dic Penderyn and Billy One-Leg when the rising turned into a riot. The list went on and on. The family he had left behind, the wild Irish beauty Cathy O'Hara, Mary Jones, the prostitute who gave her life for him, and now Elizabeth. The world seemed to be crushing in on him as tight and pressing as the walls of their cell, the darkness engulfing his mind, his very soul, as tears clouded his vision. He wanted to scream. The big Irishman stepped closer to his friend then he rested his hand on Shenkin's shoulder. 'Sit down, Daniel.'

Only at very difficult moments did he ever call him Daniel. Shenkin was grateful.

Embarrassed, the big man removed his hand and sat down beside him. 'Well now, if not a run for the locked door in these chains, what about as we come out of the court still in chains but no locked door? Why we are halfway there so we are.'

'What if I faked a fit?' said Shenkin. 'They'd send for Doctor Tarn, who is now the barracks doctor, wouldn't they?'

O'Hara shook his head. 'We can't expect him to risk everything, Shenkin, he's helped us so many times.'

'But who else can we turn to who has any authority?'

They talked on through to the first light but were still no further in a plan of action. It was beginning to look very doubtful if they'd get away or worse, ever see Elizabeth again.

'Did you see what happen to Tinker, Shenkin? For I lost sight of him what with all that was going on, and truncheons tend to blur the sight.'

Shenkin bent his head. 'No, let's hope he at least got away.'

They were quiet for a while, lost in their own thoughts. That they were back in the barracks was hard to come to terms with after all that had happened since they had left. The light rattle of chains from the sleeping huts as men turned in their sleep, the sweep of lanterns as guards made their rounds.

Shenkin's mind went over and over the last hours, the hurt look and pain in Elizabeth's face, the blood, the violence, their child, the shattering of dreams. The sheer hatred that coursed through his veins at the men who had visited this upon them. They would pay for it if it was the last thing on this god's earth that he would do, he would have his vengeance.

He didn't even know if she was alive or dead; the hate was eating him alive. He let out an anguished shout, 'Dear god, why didn't we leave earlier?'

Regan moved to his side. 'It must be almost morning Daniel, let's see what the day brings,' he said, resting his hand on Shenkin's shoulder.

Down near King's Wharf, two constables were frog-marching Tinker to a jail set aside for aborigines only. Out of the dark came two figures. Silently they came up by the side of each of the constables. With hardly a sound the guards crumbled, their legs seem to have turned to jelly beneath them.

'It seems you need a little help, Tallara,' said the taller of the two. As he spoke he rubbed an oil into Tinker's wrists. Closing his hands as small as possible, Tinker slid the handcuffs off.

Three sets of pure white teeth lit up the dark. 'Thank you my brothers, but I do not want you to get into trouble, you came about the sheep grazing land and now I have brought you into this trouble of my friends.'

'Friends who befriended you are our friends too,' said the smaller man. 'We must make plans to see how we can save them and their woman.' With that they moved, as if they were nothing more then floating black smoke, and were gone.

CHAPTER 10

'All rise for Judge William Hendry in the hearing of the crown versus convicts Daniel Shenkin and Regan O'Hara,' called the clerk of the court, a small man with a squint who appeared to be looking in the general direction of the court. Each side of the Judge sat officers of Sydney's military garrison, many of who were card-playing drinking partners of Lord Feltsham. With some noise, scraping of chairs and clouds of dust, the people present got to their feet. However, most were still talking to someone or other.

'Silence in court!' shouted the clerk, his glasses sliding down his long nose.

Finally, silence did rule. Breathing, coughing and settling dust were the only sounds that confirmed that the room was just under half full. Waiting to be called, Shenkin saw Doctor Tarn. Nudging O'Hara, he nodded his head in Tarn's direction.

'Good for the doctor a friend indeed,' said O'Hara.

But sitting beside him were Lord Feltsham and Captain Moxey.

Judge Hendry blew his nose to clear the dust then looked up. 'Witnesses for and against the accused.'

The three men stood. Feltsham was immaculate in his riding coat of rich red brown, his waistcoat was a buff colour richly braided with white and complete with silver buttons. The trousers a checked single-milled cashmere, completed his morning suit, which had come direct from Geo. D. Doudney of Fleet Street, London. Very few knew this and even less cared.

Moxey was in his captain's uniform. Just to look at him caused Shenkin to stiffen as he remembered his brutality on the convict ship the Runnymede.

Doctor Tarn wore a sober dark suit.

'I call Lord Feltsham to the stand to bear witness.'

Standing with his hand placed lightly on his silver-handled cane stick, he began to slowly walk to the witness stand. The clerk stood. 'Do you swear to tell the truth and nothing but the truth?'

'Of course,' said Feltsham, indignantly.

'Yes or no please, your lordship,' said the clerk.

'Yes!'

'Please commence Lord Feltsham,' said the judge.

Feltsham proceeded to condemn them out of hand for rape, stealing and general misconduct further stating that the lady was one who he had had the honour of meeting on his journey out to Australia. He stressed the word lady. Then fixing his gaze over the assembled platform where the judge sat, he said, 'She is, sirs, one of us, an exclusive in this colony of Sydney. A niece of Captain Moxey in whose ship we travelled, but even so this man Shenkin showed disregard for the lady's station and had to be reprimanded a number of times for speaking to her or calling to her from the forecastle. Having with Captain Moxey's permission, taken the lady into my home for care, I am advised by my physicians that after her dreadful ordeal, Elizabeth Moxey may die unless she receives a great deal of care and treatment. I have undertaken, with her uncle's permission, to take it upon myself to ensure she does receive the very best care possible.'

Shenkin let out a gasp. 'If she does die Feltsham, I'll kill you and that bastard Ketch.'

'Restrain the prisoner,' called the judge.

With this Feltsham sat down, his cane still in the upright position his hand resting on the top while fluff needed to be brushed from his coat sleeve.

'The court thanks his lordship for taking the time to come here today. I now call upon Captain Moxey.' Moxey followed suit almost word for word.

Tarn raised the question of doubt about the night in question: that there had been a running feud between Lord Feltsham and Daniel Shenkin ever since the voyage from England; that that night an aborigine named Tinker came to his establishment urging him come quickly to Shenkin's lodgings in the docks area where a lady had been attacked by a gang of men.

At this the judge interrupted the doctor.

'Can you produce this man, sir?'

'No my lord, he slipped his chains not far from the scene and ran into the warehouses of the docks. It's a warren of back streets and alleys. After a long search, the constables failed to find him.'

'So much for his evidence then,' said Judge Henry, lifting his nose wipe up to his nose and blowing hard. Then added, 'please continue, Doctor.' Tarn holding himself in check, continued to praise both men, together with his firm belief in their good characters. This he stated, was shown in their stalwart assistance on the Runnymede during an outbreak of cholera.

The judge ruffled papers blew his nose again, cleared his throat, then raised his eyes first to Lord Feltsham then to the court in general.

'We find Daniel Shenkin and Regan O'Hara guilty as charged.' Tarn got to his feet to protest.

'Sit down sir, unless you wish to be charged with contempt.' He then turned to the men before him. 'You will both serve out your full original sentences,' he said, looking down at a sheet in front of him. 'Twenty years at Port Arthur convict settlement with hard labour, in chains and working on the roads. Sergeant, take them down,' he said. Then without hardly taking breath, he called, 'Next case.'

Lord Feltsham gave a satisfied smile. The hearing had taken scarcely thirty minutes. Minutes that sealed both Shenkin and Regan's futures and most likely their lives.

Outside stood a cart, the horse stamping his hoofs into the ochre-coloured earth. The rising dust was making small red stockings around his front legs.

'They're not wasting any time are they?' said Shenkin, shuffling down the court steps. At that moment Feltsham also came down the steps. Shenkin called after him. 'Feltsham, I demand to know how Elizabeth is.'

Lord Percival Hugo Feltsham, as was his want, removed once again some invisible lint from the sleeve of his Doudney coat and walked on.

Again Shenkin called after him, 'If she dies I'll kill you, Feltsham. I swear it by all the gods and saints that this unequal world has come up with.'

The guard struck him across the head and he went down on his knees. Shenkin mustered all his energy to get to his feet. O'Hara hit the man, first with his fist then followed through with his elbow. The man's nose split open and blood ran down his face at the same speed as his body hit the ground. More guards and military men rushed forward, beating O'Hara and Shenkin to the ground.

Doctor Tarn closed his eyes and buried his head in his hands at the horror of it all. When he looked up, their bodies were being thrown into the back of the cart as it turned in the direction of the docks where the prison ship for Port Arthur awaited them.

'God help them,' said Tarn to himself. One thing was certain, god would not be in Port Arthur's penal settlement to welcome them.

CHAPTER 11

Although Shenkin had regained consciousness, by the time they were sailing out of the harbour, he remained silent. Regan was rubbing the side of his jaw and a large swelling was coming up on his right temple. Their legs were fettered. The chains ran through two metal brackets fixed to the deck of their makeshift cell below decks.

Above them the noises of the crew came down in burst of orders and responses. Running feet pounded the deck, causing a fine wood dust to fall on them. Chains and ropes falling or coiling onto the deck added to the fine shower of dust. Soon their heads, hair, eyes and noses were covered with it. Breathing became difficult as they coughed their way out of Port Jackson into the Tasman Sea named after Abel Janszoon Tasman, a Dutch explorer, by Lieutenant James Cook in the 1770s as part of his first voyage of exploration in the area. Neither Shenkin nor Regan cared who discovered what or when, they only knew they were heading for Hobart and Van Diemen's Land for the journey down to the notorious Port Arthur penal colony.

Around them were stored crates, sacks and timber but no other prisoners. They were the only convicts aboard.

'This voyage was put together in haste Shenkin, not for the need of cargo at Hobart Town but to get rid of us,' said Regan coughing out his words then adding, 'the bastards have it in for us this time and by the way we look, and fettered as we are, they may just do it.' O'Hara hoped this challenge may gain a defiant response from Shenkin.

Still Shenkin remained silent, his sorrow covered him as thoroughly as the dust from the deck above them.

The hatch opened. A small-faced man called down. 'Which one of you is Shenkin?'

There was no reply from Shenkin. 'Come on, I haven't got all bleeding day. The captain wants to speak to you.'

Shenkin raised his arm with a sigh. He spoke his first words in many hours. 'I am Shenkin,' he said, adding nothing more.

'Isaac, give me a hand here.' The two men came down the companionway in a rush. Keys found the locks to their chains and Shenkin was pulled to his feet. O'Hara was secured again and Shenkin was led up to the top deck.

He welcomed the fresh air but wondered if this may be his moment of going overboard.

Captain Stephen Saxon was on the bridge giving orders to his first mate, but turned as he saw Shenkin emerge from below decks.

'Carry on and remember none of this.'

'Very good, sir.'

'Bring the convict up to my cabin.'

'Sir,' called the small man at Shenkin's side.

The first thing about the captain that Shenkin noticed was his broken nose, it caused the captain to snuffle slightly as he spoke. He was a big burly man broad shouldered, tall and in good shape. No fat hung from his face, arms or body, it all looked like muscle and bone.

There was also something else about the man that Shenkin could not place, not that it mattered, he was sure this man was to be his executioner.

'So what does Feltsham have in mind, a big splash and that's the end of me? Will it be the same for Regan O'Hara too?'

The captain smiled a slow long smile.

'My orders are to ensure the safe delivery of the cargo at Hobart Town. There I have to present your papers to the authorities for registration before you can be taken down to Port Arthur. While doing so the ship's cargo will be unloaded. I will then sign over the cargo against a receipt from Moxey's clerk at his chandlers in Hobart Town. This will take a day or so depending upon the amount of shipping at the docks. Then together with one of my crew, I'll escort you both overland to the penal settlement at Port Arthur. We will actually sail past Port Arthur on our way to Hobart but no shipping is allowed in the waters around the penal settlement for security reasons, so we cannot dock there.' Taking a deep breath he continued, 'All the paper work for your crimes and sentences are duly sealed and signed, here in this leather wallet,' he said, tapping the wallet on the desk in front of him with his fingers.

His face became grim. 'It contains your destinies. Make no mistake Shenkin, Port Arthur is regarded as a place of no return, and with good reason. The Commissariat Officer is a strict disciplinarian; any breech of the rules is met with severe punishment. The solitary confinement block has a rule of silence where convicts can spend up to five years. The asylum building is immediately outside of this cell block, which speaks for itself. The road gangs work from sunrise to sunset. They are made up of double convicts, that is to say men like yourselves, who have committed further crimes since arriving at Sydney Penal colony.' Again the captain paused for a moment then went on, 'To my knowledge no convict has ever escaped from there. The only leaving is out to sea in a rough-made wooden coffin where they are buried on a small island just off Port Arthur. Those who are serving sentences of ten years to life are doomed. Both your futures are very bleak,' he said, looking up at Shenkin.

Then to Shenkin's amazement the captain said, 'First let me pour you a glass of brandy.' Shenkin looked at the captain dumbfounded. Everything was happening too fast; he could not take it all in. Elizabeth being attacked, the barracks, the short trial, now aboard this ship Port Arthur bound. It was just too much to take in.

Offering Shenkin the glass, the captain smiled. 'You are surprised my friend, are you not. Let me explain.'

CHAPTER 12

Before the captain could say anything, Shenkin in a rush of words said:

'Why, Captain, have you brought me before you? Why trouble yourself in explaining anything. For your orders, and it seems our fates are sealed, are they not?'

'It would appear so.'

'Then…' started Shenkin.

The captain stood up. 'Simple, I wanted to met the man who beat my brother in what he tells was the hardest fight he had ever had the misfortune to find himself in,' he said, a smile breaking out on his face. He held out his hand to Shenkin. 'Please sit Shenkin, and drink your brandy for you look as if you need it.'

'Charlie Benson of course, I see it now in your face. Well I'm damned. I'll tell you this Captain, it was a close-run thing. Your brother was the best I've ever fought. Tell me is he on board?' For a brief moment all the sadness of the last few days left him, he even felt guilty at his joy at the chance of meeting this man again.

The captain shook his head. 'No, but he sent word for me to watch out for you and that big Irishman. It must have been a hell of a fight for Charlie was the best this land had ever seen.'

'Was,' said Shenkin, stopping to raise his glass.

'He's retired; says its all over for him. He can't hope to be champion now not after the beating you gave him. Nobody will back him so he's to settle down to farming in a place called Blacktown just outside Parramatta.'

'Then I wish him well,' said Shenkin, raising his glass in a toast.

'Thank you Shenkin, I'll tell him. Now as to your spot of trouble, what is the sentence? For I cannot open this wallet.'

'Twenty years hard labour, on the roads and in chains.'

'God in heaven you'll never make it man.'

'I think that was Lord Feltsham's intent.'

'Charlie told me about the conversation he overheard. The problem is, the crew are all Moxey's men or in Feltsham's pay, for they own this ship.'

'I see,' said Shenkin.

'You are in front of me for me to read the rules and penalty if you try to escape. No one knows of any connection between us. At least not on board, but Feltsham may know. Which is why I think I was given command of this voyage. He probably feels I would be hard on you in revenge for the beating you gave my brother. He of course, knows nothing of the respect you have for each other, it would be outside his thinking, for he is a small-minded vindictive man.'

Shenkin nodded his head. 'He is indeed Captain, we have been enemies these past years. He has made a few attempts on both mine and Regan's life; this time he may well achieve it,' Shenkin said, with a sigh.

'But his last attempt, resulted in harm to the woman I love. Come what may I have vowed to avenge her,' said Shenkin, with a snarl.

Captain Saxon poured another glass of brandy for them both as a knock came to the door. 'One moment,' said Saxon placing the glasses under his table and indicating Shenkin to stand.

'Come.'

The man who had brought Shenkin to the captain's cabin entered.

'Yes, what is it, Dobson?'

'Shall I return the convict to below decks, sir?'

'Return to your other duties. I'll call when I am ready.'

'Sir.'

After the cabin door closed, the captain turned to Shenkin, glass in hand. 'He suspects something, but is not sure. Finish your drink; we'll talk again before Van Diemen's. We can do five knots in this schooner, so given a fair to moderate crossing say two weeks to Hobart Town. If the weather changes then maybe longer,' said Saxon in a low voice. Saxon then filled a hip flask with whisky. 'Dobson may search you so put this down the front of your trousers, he'll not search there,' he said, with a grin. adding, ' it's damn cold down in that hold, this will keep you both warm.'

'Thank you, Captain,' said Shenkin, placing the flask securely.

'Ready?'

'Yes, ready.'

Standing at the cabin door Saxon called out, 'Dobson.'

Shenkin heard a distant 'Sir', followed by hurried footsteps across the deck.

'Take this man back to the hold.'

'Sir.'

Shuffling across the deck then down the companionway with some difficulty, Shenkin took in the layout of the ship. She was neat well ordered, and bustling with activity. A few of the crew turned their heads to look at Shenkin before returning to their work. Shenkin took in deep breaths as the ship made her way down the coast of Australia towards Van Diemen's Land. When telling Shenkin how long the voyage would take, the captain had told him about the ship. The *Tempest* was a schooner, rigged with fore and aft sails on her two masts and weighed a hundred and forty-four tonnes. Built on the river Tweed in England by the Berwick Boat Yard, a sturdy ship that had done good service since her build in 1781. She first plied her trade as a London coaster before Moxey bought her in 1830 when he sailed her to Sydney. She was ideal for light cargo at a reasonable rate of knots between Sydney Cove and Hobart Town. Feltsham and Moxey owned two others all of which returned a handsome profit. This time part of her cargo would also see the burying of their dubious past.

As Shenkin was pushed into their makeshift cell in the hold, Regan rushed to his side. 'I thought I'd never see you again.'

Shenkin struggled to his feet. 'So did I. But believe it not we have a friend on board,' he said. He told him all that the captain had said.

O'Hara could hardly believe their good luck. 'Good for Charlie Benson but can his brother help us to escape?'

'Its some of the crew members who have been put on board, to make sure we get to the penal settlement, that's the problem. One in particular by the name of Dobson, a small shifty man eager to earn his grog from his masters. 'We seem to be dogged by these little men who while small, are deadly in their purpose,' said Shenkin.

'Another bloody Teal by the sound of it,' said the big man.

'A few of the crew look to be the muscle for Dobson, if he needs it.'

Both were quiet for a while, each deep in thought. 'Can we make a jump for it at Hobart harbour?' said Regan.

'And fight the sharks in these chains?' replied Shenkin, with a lift of his arms causing the chains to make their point.

'So what can Charlie's brother do?'

Shenkin shrugged his shoulders. 'He says he'll speak to me again before we land. Hopefully with some kind of plan, but he is taking a risk.' Then with a sigh, 'as everyone does who helps us.'

'That's so,' said Regan.

Finally they made themselves as comfortable as possible for the long night ahead. They had had no food or water when suddenly the door swung open.

'The captain gave orders to bring this to you,' said Dobson, placing a tin plate holding some bread and a little cheese together with a tankard filled with water. 'If it was me I'd see you starve. The captain must be getting soft, and I worry about weak captains, I does.' So saying he slammed the door. The key scraped the bolt lock into position. Then he called out, 'Watch out for the rats.' and laughed.

'Rats are the least of our worries, but let's eat up before they get to it,' said Shenkin, struggling to reach the flask.

'You're not going to piss here are you?' said Regan, then he saw the flask.

'Compliments of the captain,' said Shenkin, with a smile.

'And isn't he a wonderful man, so he his,' said Regan.

Shenkin raised the flask to his mouth. 'To Charlie Benson and his brother,' said Shenkin, passing the whisky to Regan.

'Amen,' said O'Hara.

While they drank and ate, O'Hara asked how long before Hobart.

'Could be well over a week or say ten days if the weather holds,' said Shenkin.

'Plenty of time to think then.'

Shenkin swallowed his last piece of cheese. 'I wonder how she is Regan, and the child too.'

'May sweet Mary in heaven watch over them,' said O'Hara, crossing himself.

'He didn't do much of a job at Campbell's Wharf did he?'

'Now don't go speaking against him, we're alive aren't we?'

'Yes, for what its worth.'

'One thing at a time. Let's get off this water bucket first.' Drinking down some water, a look of disgust on his broad Irish face. 'Water! God in heaven what have we come down to? Still the whisky was a treat and no mistake.'

For Shenkin there was a deep sick feeling in the pit of his stomach, for thoughts of Elizabeth were back with him as he sailed further and further away from her.

It is all happening too fast and I can't control any of it, he thought with a feeling of grief that kept rising up into his mouth like bile.

CHAPTER 13

They spent their coming hours then days, in planning. But came up with nothing definite. 'We have little detail of this ship, the land we are heading for, or the people we will met. It's down to the captain I fear,' said Shenkin at last.

'Tomorrow will be our fourth day but at least we are being given food and water; it will keep our strength up for whatever he has in mind Shenkin,' said Regan.

'Yes, but this waiting, this not knowing, this lack of action. All the while Elizabeth is in pain, alone and at the mercy of Feltsham. If only I could get my hands around his soft-skinned neck.' As he said it his hands tightened around the thick tin cup of water, the metal slowly began to buckle then the seams split.

'Well he'll not survive that, if you ever get your hands on him.'

'I will Regan, somehow and however long it takes, I will have my revenge.'

The lock in the door grated then opened. In the doorway stood Captain Saxon.

'It may well be over another week before we reach Hobart Town Shenkin, for the weather is turning poor. The wind is failing and I have to tack our way forward. It'll add time to the voyage I fear. Two crew will be down here in a moment when I shall have you both taken up on deck for some fresh air.'

'Thank you Captain, we are in need of it.'

Two crew members appeared; one was Dobson, a disgusted but resigned look upon his face.

'Take them up Dobson, but check their chains first.'

'Sir,' said Dobson, running his hands over the chains. 'Come on you lazy bastards move.' he said, pushing them through the cabin door of the storeroom.

On deck the wind hit them hard but both breathed in the cool fresh air gratefully. The crew's eyes were on them as they made their way unsteadily to the ship's portside rail. Shenkin felt one of the belaying pins under his hand and looked at Regan. 'Brings back memories Regan, of our time on the Runnymede.'

'It does so.'

'No talking or you'll go back before your hour's up,' said Dobson.

'Bastard,' mouthed O'Hara

The captain stood on the quarterdeck and catching Shenkin's eye, he shook his head.

The hour was up only too soon. Dobson shouted for another of the crew and they were manhandled back below deck. Sliding and stumbling down the companionway ladder, they found themselves back in the makeshift cell.

The repeated tacking caused the ship to roll first one way and then the other. O'Hara planted his big feet between the bulkhead deck timbers. 'What ever the captain has in mind I reckon it's on land,' said Shenkin.

It was another six sea-rolling days before a call went out above them, 'Hobart Town harbour off the port bow.' But it was still a full day before they finally dropped anchor.

'Thank god,' said Shenkin, with a sigh of relief.

'Amen to that,' said O'Hara.

Opening the cabin door, Dobson beckoned them out. 'The captain wants a word with you both.'

Now inside the harbour, the sea was calmer, the deck full of activity as the crew began the task of unloading their cargo.

Dobson closed the door to the captain's cabin. As it closed the captain waited a few minutes to make sure Dobson was going back to his duties.

'I do not have long as I must oversee the docking and unloading. The only way of escape is by sea from Port Arthur,' said Saxon.

Shenkin looked surprised. 'I thought it would be back over land for sure.'

Saxon shook his head. 'Out of the question Shenkin, you would never make it, first the sea then over land.'

'But we don't know how to sail a boat,' said Shenkin.

'No. That's where I come in. I'll bring a boat around the heads into Port Arthur pick you up and head out to sea for a few miles, then steer a course back to the land the other side of Eaglehawk Neck. I cannot explain now there is no time, so I have written it all down on this paper.' The captain placed the paper into Shenkin's loose top shirt. 'Make it secure when you go back below.'

Shenkin lifted his arms causing the chains to play their rattling tune. 'We can't expect you to take such risks,' Shenkin protested.

The captain smiled. 'Charlie is expecting me to help, if not he'll more than likely break my nose again as he did when we were kids.'

'But…' The captain cut him short. 'It's all there on that piece of paper, the whole plan,' he said, then added, 'You can read can't you?'

Indignantly Shenkin replied, 'Yes I can.'

'Good thing Shenkin can for I can't,' said O'Hara.

'Good go over the plan and keep a record of the days, for I'll be there in one month from today. You will find the date on the paper together with a small rough calendar; it will also have the time. Now do not get into any trouble either of you for you'll be put in solitary ending this plan in a waste of time, making any risks taken for nothing' he said, getting to his feet. 'Understood?'

'Yes and thank you for this. I hope someday we'll be able to repay you,' said Shenkin, offering his hand.

At this there was a knock on the cabin door.

'Yes.'

'Long boats coming alongside, sir.'

'Very well.'

Turning back to them he whispered, 'Good luck and May your god go with you.' Not waiting for a reply the captain called, 'Dobson.'

'Sir,' said Dobson, obviously he had been very close outside.

'Take these men below. I have advised them against trying to escape in these shark-infested waters, even this close to the land.'

'Indeed, sir,' said Dobson, carefully looking around the cabin.

'Get on with it, man,' said Saxon.

Back in their cell, Shenkin carefully took out the paper the captain had given him. In a low voice Shenkin slowly read it out.

The top of the page read:

PORT ARTHUR

The area surrounding Port Arthur makes it an ideal place for a penal settlement. It is on a peninsula, giving only one land access along a very narrow strip called Eaglehawk Neck. This is guarded by an armed military party, together with a pack of large guard dogs. At night this area is lit up by a line of lamps. If they got past this, a convict would have to find his way along the Forestier Peninsula where he would again face a well-guarded area called East Bay Neck before reaching the main land of Van Diemen's Land. Therefore, I propose an escape by way of the sea, sailing around these two necks and landing on the coastline above them. A month from now, I will bring a whaleboat around the Heads of Hobart Town to Port Arthur.

Once there I will lay off from the settlement for one whole day in the pretence of fishing. Then in cover of darkness I will sail in as close as possible to the shore. Today is Tuesday the 13th of November. On the 13th of December, at 5:00 am that morning, I will be anchored opposite the small settlement church which is almost on the water's edge. How you get there is for you to work out, but you must give me a sign that all is well. A thumbs up will do it. If you are not there, I will try again on the 13th of January at the same time. I will have three other trusted men with me. Together with you both, it gives us a crew of six and all the oars we will need for a quick row out to sea. Frankly, Shenkin it is not the best of plans but the only one I can think of that might, just might, work.

God be with us.

It was unsigned.

Below was a small handwritten calendar, the dates circled in red ink.

'He's taking a hell of a chance,' said Shenkin.

'He is so,' said O'Hara, adding, 'we must be there ready for him.'

'It'll take some working out. The cells, the chains, the guards and god knows what else we'll find there. The journey will give us the lay of the land but that's a long way off yet.' A plump rat scurried between two sacks of oats as they both fell silent.

CHAPTER 14

In chains and also chained together, they stood in front of the officials of the government offices in Hobart in the early hours of the following morning. Within a very short time their papers were presented by Captain Saxon. They were recorded, processed, and given numbers. In less then thirty minutes they were ready for their transfer to the penal settlement at Port Arthur. A coach was waiting for them outside. A bar had been fixed to the bottom floor of the carriage to which Dobson secured their chains then sat opposite them. Papers in hand, the captain joined them. Two outriders on mounted horses escorted them out of the town one each side of the coach, which was pulled by two black mares. The coachman shouted a command, the whip cracked and they were off.

Slowly they made their way through the town of Hobart, small in comparison to Sydney. It was concentrated around Sullivans Cove. Like in Sydney, convicts were a common sight to the people of Hobart, no one gave them a moments glance. As the coach left the town limits, their escort left them. The driver shouted further commands to the horses, causing them to break into a quicker pace. Soon they were out into the dense scrub of the countryside, this gave way to forests of high trees and tangles of fauna and vegetation. It was a world that went back to the beginning of time. The roads became narrower, the plants spilling onto the makeshift roads causing the carriage to rock over the uneven ground. Shenkin glimpsed a kangaroo, a male of the species, it looked cautiously at the intruders into his domain while behind him the rest of the herd grazed peacefully under his protection.

'Kangaroo, big bastards aren't they?' said Dobson adding, 'the male grows up to 6ft 7in and can weigh as much as 200lbs.'

Shenkin looked at Regan with despair, as if saying, *this will be a difficult land to cross.*

O'Hara nodded. The waters too seemed full of fish or larger forms of life, a head broke the surface, brown in colour with scale-like skin. Its mouth opened wide, a row of teeth flashed in the bright sunlight. The sight was over in a moment as the carriage bumped its way along. The captain caught Shenkin's eye. 'It's a freshwater crocodile, they can be 9ft long and weigh around 220lbs. Nobody swims or walks across shallow rivers out here if they can avoid it. So be warned. Now settle down for we have a long journey ahead of us if we are to get there by night fall, for we have to travel first by ferry across the Derwent River then around other rivers. It's a difficult journey over rough terrain before our arrival at the penal settlement.'

Dobson smiled a slow long lingering smile. 'A natural prison it is; forget the rivers, they are all full of those crocodiles and poisonous snakes too. But there is the sea if you survive the sharks that is. There is only one way off and that's by way of a coffin.' At this last remark Dobson started to laugh.

'Shut your mouth Dobson, that's enough,' said the captain.

'They are just riff-raff sir. No good to man or beast. Convicts they are and will always be.'

'As you were Dobson, only two years ago, is that not so?'

'I was innocent I was,' responded Dobson, indignantly.

'As is every convict that was ever transported to the penal colonies. All as blameless as the day they were born. And you, Shenkin, are you innocent?' asked the captain.

'Me! No not me or O'Hara here. We did it alright and would do it again if we only had the chance.'

'What about your recent crimes, just to satisfy Dobson's curiosity.'

'Of that sir, we are indeed innocent, so help me god, if he exists at all.'

'See Captain, blasphemous and all. They deserve to die they do.'

So went the long, tiring, coach jarring journey to the settlement. Apart from one stop at a Coaching Inn to change horses they kept going through the humid day. The clip clopping rhythm of the horse's hoofs soon made them drowsy, making the inside of the coach free of any further talk.

It was late and dark when they finally arrived. Stiffly, Dobson climbed out of the coach, tipping it sideways as he did so. The motion pulled on the chains, making Shenkin and O'Hara's ankles even redder from the jerking movements of the drive.

When Dobson had gone, the captain leaned forward. 'Keep that paper safe and keep out of trouble. God willing, I'll see you next month.'

'Thank you again, Captain,' said Shenkin, adding, 'give our thanks to Charlie too.'

'I will. Now I must hand your papers over to the Acting Commandant, a Major Harris. He is a strict disciplinarian, ambitious and ruthless. He is awaiting the return of Commandant Booth from London, so is determined to make his mark and hopes to become Assistant Commandant on Booth's return. He will want a clean sheet when he hands the running of the settlement back to the commandant Shenkin, and will impose his will upon any who break the rules.'

'I understand. We will toe the line. And thank you again.'

In the commandant's office they met Major William Walter Harris, a tall man in stature, but very short in temper. 'Close the bloody door can't you?' he screamed at Dobson.

He was a mean-faced thin-lipped man. On his desk lay a riding crop. They were to get to know that riding crop very well. In the first month that Commandant Booth was away, Harris had a convict punished with a hundred and fifty lashes. The man died a day later. Harris had covered the matter up by entering into the records that the convict was killed while trying to escape. Hobart accepted the explanation. Such was the commandant's total authority, the body was buried on the Isle of the Dead and by now eaten by all manner of wildlife.

Turning to Captain Saxon he took in the captain's sea attire. 'What's this? No military army or constables in Sydney any more? No wonder I've been kept up so late awaiting your arrival.'

'My orders came from my ship's owners sir, and theirs by way of the court in Sydney. It was felt necessary to have these men into your safe keeping without delay, hence the overland journey,' said the captain, placing the papers on the commandant's desk. 'I think you will find everything in order even coming as they do, from a sea captain,' said Saxon, barely able to hold his tongue.

Harris sneered at the captain's discomfort. 'Come, come, Captain we all have our cross to bear in life. It is late I have not had my supper and you must be on your long journey back sir, is that not a fact?' said Harris, looking hard at Saxon. Making the point that he had no intention of inviting the captain to sup with him or stay overnight. The captain gave a forced smile. He resolved to find lodgings somewhere else rather then suffer Harris's company any longer then he could help.

Bristling then in a low voice, he said, 'For the first time sir, I see the benefit of ex-convict Dobson's company. I bid you goodnight sir.' The slammed door lifted the dust off the floor.

'Well so much for the seaman. Now to your papers,' he said, spreading them before him.

After a while he put the papers down. 'I now see the urgency in your arrival at our penal colony; you will go into solitary for three days after which you will be placed in chain gangs.' He paused, then added, 'in different gangs, there to be put to work on the roads,' said the commandant, pausing again. He looked up from the papers then with a curled lip he said. 'This excessive energy you appear to have will be put to good use for we are still building this settlement as a secure prison. By the end of one month I guarantee you will be pleased to settle down to a long and active life at Port Arthur.

'Guards.' Two armed men came through the door.

'Sir.'

'Take these men to the solitary block for three days detention.'

'Sir.'

'Timms my bloody supper, if you please,' shouted Harris, as they were frogmarched through the double office doors.

At the same time, a tray came through the now open doors followed by a pimply faced young man. The tray trembled, the china rattled, as the youth attempted to keep everything steady. The chains on his legs did not help his unsteady gait, as he tried not to get tangled up in Shenkin and Regan's chains going the other way.

'For god sake man, get on with it. Must I go to my bed hungry because of your ineptitude?' The word was lost on the frail youngster but he nodded.

'Sorry sir.'

'Put down the tray you misbegotten scum, and get out...'

The door slammed shut as Shenkin shuffled behind the two guards. He gave a look of dismay to Regan who just inclined his head as if to say, *that's bastards for you.* Shenkin nodded.

'Come on keep moving, we want to get back to bed,' said the leading guard. Adding, 'you are going to like it in solitary, won't they Smithy.'

'They will that.'

Both began to laugh as their prisoners stumbled forward out into the cool night.

CHAPTER 15

The barracks, or penitentiary as Shenkin was later told it was called, appeared to form a square. Cells were placed both sides of the corridor of the structure where some were still being built. Chippings and dust covered the floor. The floor was cleaned daily by the inmates, the walls white washed regularly. It was a never-ending job while further cells were being added. Walking under a large muster bell they were led along the solitary cells. Stout heavy timber doors lay open to unoccupied cells. The doors fitted so well that once inside, the prisoner could hear very little from outside or in the next cell. Finding himself inside as the door slammed shut behind him, Shenkin took in his surroundings. The guards had said nothing, nor was he given any food or water.

One guard stood at his doorway, the other at Regan's. 'Right, Billy they're all locked up for the next three days. I've put the keys back; also they are on bread and water only. We are off to bed. It'll be bloody morning soon enough,' said the lead guard

'What about their broad arrow clothes?' said Billy.

'Get them ready for when they get out,' shouted the main guard.

'Right you are, it suits me,' said Billy, then laughed. 'Suits me, get it? Suits me, now that's good, that be.'

Doors closed, chains rattled, lights went out, all now familiar sounds to Shenkin. Finally, all became silent.

Standing quite still in the centre of the dark cell, Shenkin waited for his eyes to adjust to the darkness as he had so many times back in the mines of Wales. Then he took another look at his surroundings. One that would be his home for the next three days. Former inmates had cut marks into the part-timber walls of the cell. It seemed to have been done with what looked like the tips of sharp metal nails or the like. There was a record of time in days or god forbid, years. There was the crude shape of a naked woman laying full length on one of the stone blocks, while another had the words *God save us all* scratched on it. Yet another had *Lord forgive them for they know not what they do*, each letter carved deep into the rough stone.

Shenkin gave a grim laugh. They seemed to have had plenty of time on their hands, he thought, with a shudder.

Then he got to wondering if O'Hara was in the next cell. Shenkin called out then he banged on the wall. Nothing, not the smallest of sounds came back to him. In the end he made himself as comfortable as possible on a straw-filled mattress in one corner and tried to sleep.

The night drew out like a long cold knife; he was disturbed only by the scratching and squealing of rats. They must be feeding the prisoners or these bastards would not be here thought Shenkin, that's something.

The morning brought little relief to Shenkin; indeed he did not know it was morning until a guard opened the door. Another armed guard stood behind him.

'Some bread and water, which is all you'll get during the time you'll spend here. It's a softening up process, see? You'll be more ready to adjust to your life here,' said the guard. The outside light seemed harsh on his eyes causing him to stumble forward and almost miss the tin mug and plate offered him.

Shenkin said nothing.

'Strong silent type are you? Well we'll soon free your tongue from its slumber, if only by your protests of pain.'

Shenkin said nothing.

'Stand up let's see your size, for we are getting some tailored bright-coloured clothes for you.'

Shenkin said nothing but stood up.

'Jesus you are a big bugger, broad chest, and good shoulders for pushing trams with the chain gang; overseer is going to be pleased to have you, he will.' Then after a moment longer he turned to the armed guard.

'Right, I've got it, or near enough. Let's see the other one.'

Shenkin said nothing.

Through the part-open cell door Shenkin heard, 'Good god, we haven't a thing to fit him.'

Then Regan's deep voice. 'Now don't you worry your small selves, I'll just go on wearing what I have and be on my way back to Ireland, so I will.'

At this Shenkin heard a new voice in a broad Irish accent, which must have been the armed guard.

'So he would too, the big bastard. Sure now we're going to have a fine time with this one, and the both of them together, why it'll be like Dublin on a Saturday night.' A laugh followed that brought the head overseer down the corridor of cells.

'What the hell's going on? Why is that cell door open? You're supposed to be fitting them up for yellow jackets, not playing silly buggers. Now get on with it before the major is on his rounds.'

He looked into both the cells. 'Bloody hell,' he said.

'I want three guards in here whenever we have to deal with them. Got it?'

'Good thinking, Overseer Hogan. We'll do that, so we will.'

The doors slammed shut. The silence wrapped itself around Shenkin like a shroud.

The next days went slowly, very slowly. Shenkin put his mind to the escape plan. How to get down to the water's edge, how to get out to the boat and how to stay out of the commandant's way in the meantime. He decided he would need to see the general layout of the place before any firm decisions could be made. At last, after three days, they were led out to a large yard. Shenkin, his eyes blinking in the bright light, saw a pile of clothes on a table in the centre of the square of buildings.

'Get a move on, we haven't got all day,' said a big burly man. 'When you strip off, the guards will give you a wash down with buckets of cold water. Dry as best you can then put on your new clothes. Nice colours they are too all yellow and bright, so's we can see you good. While that's being done I'll read you out the rules and regulations of Port Arthur penal settlement on Vandermonia as we likes to call the island. It's where you're going to spend the rest of your useless lives, got it?'

Shenkin said nothing. Regan just nodded.

'Good, a peaceful quiet start to the proceedings; that's what I likes, got it?'

Shenkin said nothing. Regan nodded again.

Prompted by musket prods from the guards, they began to strip off. The leg irons were still around their ankles, but this proved to be no problem as one of the guards produced a knife and cut their trousers away from their legs. This was done none to carefully, the guard cut into Shenkin's hip while cutting through his belt. Finally, they stood naked apart from the leg irons.

'Right, my name is Hogan. I am the overseer of this here solitary cells block. Over in the corner there you will see punishment apparatus.' He pronounced the word with an 'h' and paused while they took in the whipping post, neck irons, branding irons and racks. Sets of cat o' nine tails hung from nails on the walls. 'Got it?'

Shenkin said nothing. Regan nodded.

Then humiliated and naked, they stood ready for the cold water. The sting of it took their breath away. In the chill of the early morning they began to shiver. Shenkin gritted his teeth to stop them from chattering. Using their old clothes they dried themselves as best they could. A guard kicked the yellow striped clothes to them. They were part black, part dark brown and yellow uniforms reserved for the lowest class of convict assigned to chain gangs and hard labour. The trousers had a row of buttons at the side legs and a front waistband detachment to enable the removal of the trousers without having to remove the leg irons.

'Come on, get them on. I'll flog the man who starts to drag his feet. Got it?'

Shenkin said nothing. Regan tore his top while trying to get into it. It was just too small for his broad back; the trousers too began to come apart at the seams, the side buttons stretched to breaking point.

Hogan looked up at the sound of the tearing. 'That's damaging government property that is; the punishment is ten lashes. Smithy, take this man over to the flogging post. Smartly now, I want them on chain gangs this morning,' said Hogan.

Shenkin turned fast and stepped towards Hogan, who took a step backwards. The guards swung their muskets upwards. 'Can't you see the bloody clothes are to small for him?' said Shenkin, his fists balled at his side.

'Right, ten lashes for him too,' said Hogan.

Shenkin shouted, 'Bastard.'

'Add five more for both,' said Hogan.

So saying, the guards dragged them over to the flogging posts. Their tops were pulled off, their hands tied above their heads and their legs spread eagled and tied to the bottom triangles of the frame.

'Settle the cat hard and well, my lads. I'll not have these bastards answering back or destroying good clothes. Lay it on while I read out the rules.'

The first cut dug deep into the skin.

'One,' called the guard.

After a deep breath, Hogan began, 'I want the lashes in time with the reading of the rules. Got it?'

'Sir.'

'Punishment will be dealt to prisoners for—'

'Two,' called the guards to the sound of the snap of the cat.

'Communicating with each other.'

'Three,' cracked the cat.

'Reading aloud.'

'Four.'

'Not rising when the first bell rings.'

'Five.' The flails spluttering blood over the floor.

'Not keeping their persons, cells or provided articles clean.'

'Six.' The flesh on their backs splitting open

'Damage to utensils.'

'Seven.'

'Not treating officers with respect.'

'Eight.'

'Allowing their lights to burn above a moderate height.'

'Nine.'

O'Hara turned his head. 'Bastards.'

'Right,' said Hogan. 'Add five more.'

'Sir.'

'Unrolling bedding before bell has been rang.'

'Ten.' Both backs were now in shreds

'Having unauthorised articles in their possession.'

'Eleven.'

Hogan looked up from the sheets. 'I can't read them all, they will be posted on the wall of your cells. Read them well for your lives will depend upon it.'

Looking down he continued, 'Rule 262. A prisoner wishing to see the governor, Chaplain or medical officer will ask the officer on duty.'

'Twelve.'

'Rule 263. Any complaint about food must be made before it is taken into the cell.'

'Thirteen.'

'Rule 264. Any other complaint must be made to the commandant or Officer in Charge.'

'Fourteen.'

'Rule 265. These rules will be posted on the walls in each cell and remain there undamaged.'

'Fifteen.'

'Right, cut them down; then let's have them on a road gang.'

'One has passed out sir.'

'Bucket of cold water it is then, until he is fully back with us, leave their clothes torn. We will replace them tonight. Damage to clothes is no food for two days. Got it?'

'Sir.'

Grabbing a hand full of hair he twisted Shenkin's head towards him. 'Welcome to Port Arthur,' he said.

CHAPTER 16

The doctor turned to Lord Feltsham. 'She is dying my lord. I have done all that I can.'

Feltsham walked slowly across the wide stable area. 'Indeed you have Doctor, over these last months you have hardly left her side. I am most grateful for your efforts in trying to save my dear, dear wife, but there you have it.'

The doctor bridled slightly. He had been expected to treat the poor girl, for that is all she was, here in a stable. When questioned, Lord Feltsham refused to have her in the main house.

'Dear me no, she is damaged goods don't you know?'

'But you married her sir, the very night she was brought to your house. Why?'

Feltsham a smile or curl upon his face. 'This is my business, Doctor, yours is to redeem your gambling debt and hold your tongue. At least the child if premature, has survived. And a baby girl no less, if she has her mother's looks she'll be an adornment to my social engagements. I am having an upstairs room in the main house decorated into a nursery. Once the mother is dead the child will be moved into it and become my ward.'

The doctor who had been holding Elizabeth's hand, gently put it down. A piece of straw was caught between two of her fingers. The doctor covered her beautiful face with a horse blanket. She had found peace at last. Sighing, the doctor stood up to face Lord Feltsham.

'Sir, my debt is for gambling but yours sir, is a debt against all that is decent, may god forgive you, for I can't. You are sir, the coldest of men. It chills my heart and offends me to breathe the same air as you. The death certificate is here on the bed.' So saying, the doctor closed his bag and, with his head hung low, left the stables.

Lord Percival Hugo Feltsham said nothing, flicked a piece of invisible lint off his cuff, picked up the certificate, turned towards his grand mansion and walked into the night.

Later, standing in front of his Adam fireplace, the fire in it ablaze for the nights were growing chilly after the hot day, Feltsham poured himself a brandy, lit a cigar and rang the bell cord.

'You rang sir.'

Placing his cigar carefully on the edge of the mantelpiece, Lord Feltsham sighed as if bored. 'You will find the body of the woman the doctor has been attending in the stables; see to it she is buried, away from the main building. A simple wooden box and cross will suffice. The baby is to be brought into the main house. Tell the housekeeper to find a wet nurse by tomorrow. I have no wish to hear the bleating of a child during the night or any other time,' said Feltsham, reaching for his cigar.

The butler, a man with a dubious past, who had been brought out from England at some expense, inclined his head. 'Very well sir.'

Settling into a comfortable armchair, Lord Feltsham went over in his mind the events of the last months.

In case Elizabeth had lived, he had hurriedly married her, for a wife cannot bear witness against her husband. But regardless, alive or dead, her dowry would now come to him. Captain Moxey was in too deep to cause a problem. Ketch was now out of the way in Van Diemen's Land. An accident one night would resolve that loose end. Goldspick was dead, as was Teal, while Shenkin and the Irishman were in chains in Port Arthur for the next twenty years, that's if they survived, which was very doubtful. There was Doctor Tarn but what proof did he have? None.

Puffing deeply on his cigar he felt a sense of satisfaction. *Yes, very neat indeed, very neat. Now that everything is precisely in its place I will continue to build myself an empire in this 'land beyond the sea', one of great wealth and power. Give me just ten years and it will see me the richest most powerful man in New South Wales. So thinking, he settled more deeply into the expensive silk material of his armchair.*

Sir Edward Standish sat opposite Doctor Tarn in his surgery rooms and shrugged his shoulders. 'Is there nothing we can do?'

Tarn poured some sherry and handed it to Standish. 'We need proof, damn it, proof. It's all happened so quickly Sir Edward. Feltsham has seen to that. He has so many of his gambling cronies in high places, both in the courts and the prison services. We could appeal to the governor but Bourke, while a fair man, also needs proof. Let us be frank, Shenkin will hardly be seen as an upright citizen. We would be asking him to release Shenkin, a double convict, from Port Arthur on what grounds? Our say so alone.'

Standish slowly sipped his sherry. 'Then what do you suggest?'

'Firstly, I want you to meet a friend of Shenkin's. Tinker, would you come in please?'

Tinker stepped swiftly into the room, big white smile and all. 'Good evening sirs.'

Sir Edward too gave a smile. 'We have met Doctor; it was my pleasure to meet Tinker at Shenkin's last fight.'

Tarn nodded. 'Tinker ran away from the constables on the night of the attack on Elizabeth, having first tried to bring me to the lodgings, but Feltsham was already there with his own doctor and the law. He believes he can help Shenkin and Regan escape from Port Arthur. Please explain Tinker,' said Tarn, offering Tinker a glass of sherry.

'No thank you Doctor. I never touch the European devil water.'

'Very wise.'

'I found Charlie Benson, who is now retired in Parramatta, and explained everything to him. His brother is a sea captain and by good fortune works on Moxey's ships, although both Lord Feltsham and Moxey now own so many of the ships in Port Jackson that most of the sea captains work for them. Charlie would make it known to Feltsham that he wanted to get even with Shenkin and that his brother could make things very unpleasant for Shenkin, even an accident maybe. Feltsham was eager to accept the idea and Benson's brother was made captain of the schooner to take Shenkin to Van Diemen's Land. On board, Charlie's brother told them of an escape plan he had in mind.'

'Which is?' said Standish.

Tinker explained. For heartbeats they sat still while weighing the probabilities.

Standish was the first to speak. 'It's very risky; so many things could, and probably will go wrong. How do they find their way across the land? Let us say they do get back to Sydney; where do they hide?'

Tinker's smile grew broader. 'Well sir, it so happens that we abos were here a long time before you came. The Palawa tribe of Van Diemen's Land speak Kani which I have a good knowledge of sirs, they will help me to guide Shenkin across the land up to the Derwent River for a ship to Sydney,' said Tinker adding, 'it will be a hard walkabout, maybe two months or longer.'

'But you have to get to Van Diemen's Land Tinker, how?' said Sir Edward.

If it was possible Tinker's smile widened even more. 'As your servant sir.'

'Ah! Now I understand the call from Doctor Tarn to meet.'

'It is our only hope Sir Edward, a very risky plan I agree, but the only one we have,' said Tarn. refilling their glasses.

Standish was quiet for some time, while the other two hardly moved.

At last Standish stood up, took a long sip of sherry, smiled and said, 'I am a gambling man as you know, and I owe much to Shenkin. Indeed he, or rather his fists, restored my fortune and therefore my public standing here in Sydney. I can think of a number of reasons that I would wish to go to Van Diemen's Land both business and sporting,' he said. Then looking at Tinker adding, 'the need for a servant would certainly be required.' A liberal Whig to his finger tips, he stretched out his hand and well-manicured fingers to Tinker, giving him a firm handshake. 'Your lord and master, my good servant, he welcomes you.'

Laughter rang out around the earlier sombre room, as they settled down to make their plans.

CHAPTER 17

'Bend your backs you bastards, or you'll feel the cat again,' shouted the road gang overseer.

The open wounds from the lashings they had had that morning burned like hell, every movement was sheer torture. The cuts on their skins cracked open wider as the sun dried the wounds. Having to carry the large blocks of rock on their shoulders did nothing to ease the pain.

Regan caught Shenkin's eye. 'Dear god, how do we survive this?'

'We think of another place: you of Ireland and me of Wales,' said Shenkin. A light smile spread over his face. 'I am walking at the moment through my black valley of South Wales. My father is at my side; he is telling me that ten scars make a man.'

'Well you've got them and more,' said Regan with a grunt, the rock cutting into his left shoulder as he spoke. Shenkin noticed Regan was beginning to limp.

'Shut up talking,' screamed the overseer. Adding, 'the next man I hear carries twice the weight of stone.'

So went the day until finally it thankfully came to an end and they were marched back to the penal settlement. The road was uneven, causing the sharp stones to cut into their lightly shod feet. Regan's limp became more noticeable. Some sixteen convicts made up the road gang, as far as Shenkin could make out most were Irish. Marching at the side of Regan he said. 'You should feel at home here Regan, for most of Ireland seems to be here.'

The big man nodded. 'That's so, for the English want rid of us. And what are we doing but building them bloody roads to make sure we know our way here? Is there no justice in the world?'

'No,' said Shenkin, trying to straighten his back but the pain was too severe.

Regan pulled himself up to his full six foot four inches and felt the skin split further across his back. 'The bastards, the lilywhite loathsome bastards, may every mother's son meet his end in pain.'

'Feel better?'

'No.'

The prisoners' barracks was a series of timber huts set in a square. The outer perimeter were the dormitories. Other smaller huts that Shenkin saw were single cells all built of rough-cut timber, some of which were in the middle area of the ground. Apparently the settlement had started as a timber station surrounded by tall trees so access to building material was plentiful. Shenkin saw some chained convicts coming down from this area of the forest. They had been felling the large trees which lay scattered around the apron of wood.

Finally, all were gathered outside the huts, the dust lifting in a cloud around them, their leg chains settling with a clang into the dust.

The overseer looked up and down the ranks of dirt-covered sweat-bathed men. 'The new men step forward two steps,' he screamed.

Shenkin and Regan moved out of the line together with three others.

'Right guards, get these miserable bastards into their cells.'

'Sir,' came a chorus of voices, their dark blue uniforms also covered in dust from the day's work areas. But they would soon be going home to the military compound, to their wives, to hot food and comfort.

Shuffling forward towards the group of timber huts, Shenkin noted the arrangement of the timber structures. There were four long huts and a row of what looked like single huts at the top end of the quadrangle. A guard at his side pushed him towards one of the smaller huts in the middle of the square. Inside were two cells; the guard opened the door to one. Shenkin was manhandled inside. Adjusting his eyes to the dark, Shenkin was pleased to see the floor was earth, the walls rough-cut timber with one single window at the top. Shenkin smiled in spite of his aching tired body. *Better than the stone cells we were in at the guard house on the first three days of solitary confinement. Yes, the possibilities to get out of here are a great deal improved*, he thought.

The door opened again. No one entered, then a guard threw clothes into the cell. 'Damage these and the lashings will be doubled. Your food rations are listed on the wall, any wastage will result in punishment. Spoons and a tin mug will be issued with your first meal. They will be kept clean. Any loss or damage will result in punishment,' he said.

The door slammed shut; the key turned. It was an all too familiar sound to Shenkin, only the construction of the cell made any difference. He shuffled over to the wall where a dirty notice board was nailed.

Breakfast
½ pound bread
1 ½ pints of Gruel
Dinner
½ pound bread
12 ounces salt beef or pork
1 ½ pints soup, small amount beef, vegetables and flour
Supper
Same as breakfast.
One keg of water will be supplied daily
Any wastage of food or damage to utensils will result in punishment
Could be worse, thought Shenkin.

The clothes consisted of one jacket – grey in colour, one waistcoat, one shirt, one pair of trousers, one pair of boots and one cap. There was a bucket in one corner but no washing services. *Must be outside.* One small stool, the bed was low, the mattress straw or wool filled, no blanket.

He took off the torn clothes, the top shirt first. Most of the material was stuck to the wounds. Very slowly and painfully, he finally managed to get it off. He undid the trouser buttons and stepped out of the torn dirty leggings. A noise from outside of metal clanging and wood door flaps opening or closing, a small flap in the door frame gave way to the appearance of a tin tray with food and an empty tin mug on it. 'Come on, move yourself. I haven't got all bloody day. If you're slow tomorrow, you'll go without.'

Shenkin snatched the tin tray from the long box-like opening.

Pouring a little water from the keg over his hand, he wiped his lips, which were caked with dried dust and blood. Wetting his old top shirt, he cleaned himself the best he could. Looking down at the tray he saw a tin bowl of thin gruel, a small amount of flour unsweetened. *So it could be worse.* In the days to come Shenkin would find it would be much worse.

While he ate what little there was, he thought of Elizabeth and their picnics on Millers Point back in Sydney. Was she safe? Was the baby alright? Was Feltsham treating her well? Dear god, was she alive? 'If only I had not stayed so long after the fight I may have been in time to save her,' said Shenkin, out loud. At the thought of it even the thin gruel was hard to swallow. 'I will have my revenge in this life or the next,' he said, throwing the gruel across the dirt-covered floor.

Stupid, stupid. I must eat it, dirt and all. Which, slowly picking out as much of the dirt that he could, he began to do.

It was still dark. How long had he slept out of sheer exhaustion? He didn't know. All time had become one long painful nightmare.

'Wake up, you lazy swines, breakfast is being served now, not later, but now. Any man not at his flap goes without.'

Shenkin stood waiting, lessons learned. The tray appeared: a piece of bread, green in parts, but no gruel. He tore the bread into small pieces and ate.

Doors swung open. Armed guards swinging short thick sticks stood waiting.

The overseer looked down at Shenkin's trousers. 'Make sure these men are dressed correctly. Come on, come on, be smart about.' One leg iron was quickly unlocked. Shenkin adjusted his crumpled out of line clothes.

Outside, the sun was slowly beginning to rise over the mountain behind the peninsula. Guards pushed them towards the other convicts lined up outside. Regan nodded. 'A good night's sleep makes all the difference, don't you think?'

The nearest guard brought down his stick across Regan's back. A line of blood appeared where it had opened up the lash wounds. 'One more sound and all four convicts will be on the punishment list,' screamed the guard. Outside the red ball burned its white heat into the settlement of living horror.

Walking down the line, the overseer inspected the convicts one by one. 'Right, my name is Overseer Flint. I want strong men for ploughing the farm fields.' So saying he began to travel back along the line. As he did, he put his hand on the ones he wanted. It included both Shenkin and Regan. In the end he had a team that added up to twelve convicts.

The overseer took one final look at them then turned to the four nearest guards. 'Take them up to the unbroken ground above the Guard Tower construction. By the end of the day I want to see the ground ready for the officers' wives to plant vegetables and herb seeds. Got it?'

'Sir,' came the unison call.

The overseer turned to walk away then looked back. 'I'm away for my breakfast; don't let me be disturbed or I'll have that man on double duties. Got it?'

Those two words would become very familiar to Shenkin in the coming days. Indeed the guards had 'got it', for they marched the ploughing team briskly on their way up the slope. In front of Shenkin, Regan limped forward, the leg chains thumping on his badly swollen foot.

Shenkin moved forward to catch up with him. 'What's the problem with your foot?'

Regan didn't turn but said, 'Something's cut or bitten me; I don't know which but it's bloody painful.'

'Tell one of the guards, man. They'll get it looked at. You can't work with that.'

'I mentioned it last night while being placed in the cell, do you know what he said?' Not waiting for a reply Regan went on, 'Let me know when it falls off; we'll give it to you as a little Port Arthur gift.'

Shenkin considered asking the guard near him. Sensing that is what Shenkin would do, Regan said, 'Leave it I'll see how it is tonight. Got it?'

Shenkin gave a laugh. 'Yes, I've got it.'

By the time they arrived, many convicts were already at work on the building site of the Guard Tower. It was needed to be finished as soon as possible for it was to form a central part of the penal colony's security. Even young boys were busy at work, some not more, thought Shenkin, than perhaps nine or ten. He was to learn these came from the small island across the bay called Point Puer. They were employed in cutting the stone for the buildings on the settlement. It reminded Shenkin of the cheap child labour of the mining villages in South Wales. Had he not been one of them? Had he not fought to free young lives from this harsh exploration?

His reminiscences were brought back to the moment. 'Get these men chained up into twos: six long.'

Once done, a timber pole was passed through chain rings on the poles leaving just enough room for each man to grip the pole. A leather strap went around each man's neck and was tied to the pole. A long chain went from the last two convicts to another chain that was fastened to the plough, the knife blade buried into the ground that would till the earth. The plough went up to two handles which were guided by one convict. Guards were placed at the two sides and the top and bottom of what was to be the field.

Shenkin was in the third group, Regan in front of him. Their light shoes were not going to stand up to this, nor Regan's foot, thought Shenkin.

'Pull, you bastards. I want to see half done by midday. Got it?' the overseer was back.

The effort to pull the plough dug in to their necks as their arms and legs took the strain. Rocks impeded the ploughshare from cutting through the soil. When this happened, the jarring increased the strain on their bodies. So went the long, long morning. At midday they stopped for water and a little food; this was placed in a trough at the side of the field.

'We are being treated like animals,' said Shenkin. Regan was silent.

'How's the foot?'

Grudgingly, the Irishman stood up straight. 'I am sorry Shenkin, but I can't go on,' he said. The saying of it hurt his pride, his manhood.

Shenkin looked at the foot. It was twice its normal size; how he had kept going this long was incredulous.

Shenkin called the armed guard behind him.

'Who the hell are you talking to, you piece of shit?'

'This man is injured. He cannot go on,' said Shenkin, adding, 'the field will not be finished by this evening.'

The guard looked at the foot, turned and walked away towards the overseer.

'Well, what is it man, out with it?'

'It's one of the convicts sir. His foot it's swollen and turning black it is.'

Sergeant George Flint strode purposefully towards Regan. 'Let's see it then; lift your leg up man, for I am not bending down to look at it.'

Regan winced.

'Bloody, bloody. You careless bastard, you've stepped on a copperhead snake. Venomous they are, you'll be lucky to save your miserable leg you will. Get him to the medical officer then get a replacement for the ploughing team, and be quick about it. Got it?'

'Sir,' said the private. 'Shall I take his leg irons off sir?'

Exasperated, Flint screamed, 'Jesus, at the bloody double man, move it, if he loses the leg what bloody difference does it make? Just get him out of here and get me another convict. Got it?'

The reply of 'sir' was lost in the clanging of chains and rising dust.

Flint called down the line, 'Get them back to work damn it. We're losing time. Don't let me see the earth turned over less because we're a man short. Got it?'

'Sir.'

The red ball in the sky burned a white heat into their straining backs, the dust choked their throats, the stony ground dug and cut into their feet. Their bodies life force seemed to drain from them. Shenkin gritted his teeth. *I'll get through this come hell or high water. I'll see Feltsham again. My hate alone will see me through this.* The leather strap cut into his neck, but he smiled a slow seething smile.

CHAPTER 18

Given the abundance of timber, most of the buildings at Port Arthur were built of wood. The hospital was no exception. It was constructed of rough-cut timber logs with a roof of slit-timber tiles. Built in 1830, it stood slightly apart from the other structures. The medical officer hated it, as he hated the convicts and the whole bloody penal colony of Port Arthur. His wife was unhappy, his children irritable and mostly ill with one damn thing or another.

At the knock at his office door, which caused flakes of wood and dust to lift into the stifling air, the medical officer, Captain Charles Bickle, gave a sigh. Raising his head from his weekly report to the governor's Office in Hobart on the state of the convicts' health, he put down his pen and in a weary voice called, 'Come in.'

The guard and Regan stood on the threshold. 'Well, what is it?' said Bickle.

'Convict bitten by a snake. Sergeant Flint thinks it's a copperhead sir.'

'Does he really? Let's take a look then. Send in one of my orderlies.'

'Sir.'

Regan shuffled and limped his way in. 'Get up on that bunk bed.' Regan was glad to lay down; he did so with a deep sigh.

Bickle examined the site of the bite. 'When were you bitten?'

Regan eased his leg. 'Yesterday morning I think, or maybe the night before.'

'Make your mind up, you dolt. I haven't got all day.'

The orderly, an old stooped convict, nodded. 'Can't be a brown or copperhead sir, he'd be in a state within a few hours. Could be a white-lipped though.'

The medical officer continued his examination. 'Foot is swollen, no fang marks, but a deep red inflamed mark.' Standing up, Medical Officer Bickle made his diagnosis. 'It's a spider bite: red-back, funnel web or mouse, who knows?' he said, adding, 'do you have a headache, some dizziness, severe pain?'

'Yes.'

'Right! Pass me the ointment, Owens.' Turning back to Regan, he said, 'We can only hold about thirty patients at a time here. We have very little medicine due to slow delivery of supplies. This is painful but you'll live. If any serious cases come in you go back to your cell, understood?'

Regan nodded.

'How long will it take to heal?' asked Regan.

The doctor sighed. 'Doctor, Officer or Sir would be more respectful, you bloody ungrateful miscreant, you're all the same. Get him out of here Owens, then get me some tea or wine or anything that will make this duty easier to endure.'

Owens looked confused. 'En-what, sir? Is it a medicine?'

'Just get out.'

'Sir.'

Regan got off the bed and limped out of the office.

Once through the door, Owens put Regan's arm over his shoulder. 'Haughty bastard thinks we're all fools. I was studying medicine before he was born.'

Regan O'Hara looked down at the thin stooped man, whose voice had changed into a more cultured tone.

But you're a convict too aren't you?' said Regan.

Owens glanced up at the big man. 'A small matter of too many drugs for a very small clinic to need. But I had a number of wealthy patients to supply until one talked while under the influence, at a gambling table where he had just taken a lot of money from a judge. So here I am, an orderly to that obtuse fool.'

Regan stopped. 'Ob-what?'

Owen smiled. 'It doesn't matter. It's Regan O'Hara, right? I looked up your record, twenty years right? Well, I can tell you very few manage to endure it. I'm on my fifth year of ten and it's only working here at the hospital that's saved me so far.'

O'Hara stopped walking, or rather limping. *A useful man to have on an escape and knows the penal settlement well*, thought Regan. He resolved to speak to Shenkin about him as soon as he could. 'There you go O'Hara, rest on this bunk for an hour or so. I'll get some water and food.'

'Thanks my little friend, so tell me, what's your full name?'

'Robert Owens, the late well-known quack with rooms in Camden Town,

London, supplier of drugs, opium a speciality, together with a wide choice of Ladybirds at your service.'

Regan looked puzzled. 'Ladybirds! You had a garden too?'

Owens gave a dry cracked chuckle, his near-bald head bobbed up and down.

'Prostitutes, ladies of the night, dollymops. Where have you been living all your life then?' Not waiting for a reply, Owens went on, 'I've given many a toff a dose of syphilis I have. Then charged them a great deal of money to cure it. Painful cure it is; brings tears to their eyes,' Owens said while continuing to laugh. 'From a comfortable living to this godforsaken place, five years of hell it's been,' he said his voice had now become gravely serious.

Regan ventured, 'Ever considered escape?' He immediately felt he may be saying to much.

But Owens nodded his head, his few straggly grey hairs floated in the dust-laden air. 'Yes, in the beginning I did but how to do it and to where? The land is a natural prison, just a narrow isthmus guarded by men and dogs. The only possible way is by sea. But how? The water is full of sharks and anyway, I can't swim and I have no boat, nor can I sail. So, after three years, when I landed this job I gave up. Now I'm too old.' The words had come at a rush leaving Owens slightly out of breath.

'I understand. Don't worry yourself,' said Regan.

Robert Owens gave a grim smile. 'But a big strong man like you, with the right kind of help might just do it,' he said with a wink.

'It would be a pleasure to get my own back on the medical officer for I can't give him, more's the pity, a good dose of ladybirds can I?' At this both Regan and he fell into laughter. 'I'll get you something to eat and don't worry about having to go back to the barracks. Anyone ill will have to pass me.' Turning, he made for the door. Then out he went, cackling laugh and all.

We have another ally, thought Regan. 'Shenkin will know how to take advantage of it, I'm sure he will,' said Regan out loud to himself.

Shenkin, when he wasn't thinking of Elizabeth, had Regan on his mind for the rest of the day. The extra man failed to turn up, causing Flint to become more and more annoyed. The field was not going to be done by the day's end; two thirds of it stood mocking Flint as the convicts were marched back down to the barracks.

Dirty and sweaty, their mouths dry with dust, the eleven men just managed to hold a steady line outside of the barracks.

Flint, a savage look upon his face, stood in front of them. 'So you didn't finish it, which means I have to explain to the officers why their wives can't plant their bloody stupid seeds tomorrow. Every second man will go without food tonight. Got it?'

Starting from the right of Shenkin, the guard went down the line marking out the men who would go straight to their dormitory or cells. As luck would have it, Shenkin was saved. He whispered a small prayer, then felt guilty for so doing. He was beginning to understand that Port Arthur could change men and not necessarily for the good. Uppermost in all of their minds was to survive. But he still felt that his hate for Feltsham would get him through. In the meantime what of Elizabeth without him…? He could not complete the thought. *Dear god, I must survive. How many times a day did he echo these words in his mind? Around and around they went.*

The bowl of gruel and green tainted bread lay on his tin plate daring him to eat. Well, he would and did. Water never tasted so good, like liquid nectar. A smile came to his cracked lips, who would have thought it? *And you Regan, what water, if any, is passing your lips?*

Regan had just finished a piece of pork meat on his fresh bread, which he washed down with a glass of red wine.

'Thanks, Robert, that was the best I've had in a long time.'

Robert Owens gave his usual dry chuckle. 'Does me good it does to know I've got one over on that bastard I work for. Gone to his quarters he has, the same time every bloody evening. I hope his wife gives him a miserable bloody night.' Adding, 'now tell me your plans to escape.'

Regan looked alarmed. 'I never said I had anything in mind, just a thought is all.'

'Come now, do I look as stupid as the medical officer?'

Regan gave Owens a hard look. 'If you say anything to anyone, I'll kill you.'

Owens said very slowly. 'Don't you think I know that?'

'We'll not take you with us.'

'I know.'

'There's no money to give you.'

'I know.'

'In fact we can't offer you anything to help us.'

'I know.'

Owens sighed. 'It's like this Regan, I think I know how to help you do it. If it's successful, Officer Bickle will get the blame. That's my reward. One of revenge for the three years of petty-minded cruel treatment that I have endured, to use his words, day after bloody day. That's over a thousand days Regan, watching my life slip away at the hands of an arrogant supercilious man.' As he spoke, he seemed to turn into himself, bitterness etched deep into his old lined face. The moment was broken by sounds from outside. It was Flint's voice cutting through the stillness of the hospital ward. The work gang were back.

'Get a fucking move on or you'll all see lights out before you see any food. Got it?'

Regan turned to Owens. 'I can't promise anything. I need to speak to the other convict I came into Port Arthur with, do you understand?'

'Of course, rest here until tomorrow. I'll see you when that stupid bastard makes his round of the ward. He's never early so get a good night's sleep. I'll scrounge hot tea and maybe a few biscuits with your gruel, it'll have flour and sweetener in it,' he said with dry chuckle.

'Thanks again,' said Regan as the door closed.

Strange as it seemed, the foot felt better, thought Regan. *I wonder what Shenkin will make of it.*

Shenkin cut up his bread and dropped the pieces into his bowl of gruel. It tasted bitter with little substance in it. Looking around there was still no sign of Regan.

Shenkin put his bowl down still half full, the convict beside him nudged him.

'You going to leave that then?' he said, reaching out.

'Get your eyes and hands away,' said Shenkin with a snarl. 'Or you'll have no teeth to eat or hands to steal with. Got it?'

'Bloody hell, just asking I was.'

'Well now you know,' said Shenkin in a flat dangerous voice.

Darkness came, the lights went out and the dormitory plunged into shadowy moving forms as men spoke or argued with each other. The night guards took up their duties. Lanterns swung in the steamy balmy night air. Mosquitoes swooped and dived, searching out the body blood they needed to see them through the night. Bush Stone-curlews screeched out their evening chorus and what sounded to Shenkin like an owl hooted his soft notes, a common sound in this land beyond the seas which Shenkin was becoming accustomed to; so went the night.

Morning came with a jolt. 'Up, you lazy bastards. Wash, food and let's have you outside before Sergeant Flint is on his inspection.' There was no need to dress for they never undressed. The soiled clothes were damp from the sweat of the night. The cool water was a relief to the skin and helped to freshen them. Breakfast was not as the ration list promised, most convicts saw no bread, the thin gruel slopped its way over the top of bowls. No one complained for this was life in the penal colony set in a beautiful landscape of lush vegetation and fruit while the sun began to slowly cast its finger of light across the sea. It would be a few hours yet before the red ball danced its way across the heavens while it burned its way into their skin.

Flint stood outside all neat and clean. His boots polished to a shine by some poor convict. 'Right, today we are going to complete our ploughing of the officers' field that will make their wives happy. Any man seen to be shirking will feel the lash, ten for the first offence then doubled for any further offences. We have a full plough team of fourteen men so I feel confident that the midday meal will see the work done. If not it will not be every other man that does not eat tonight, no one will eat and that includes the midday meal. Got it?'

The day became agony as the guards continually urged the team of men to move faster. Then towards midday, the share hit a large boulder that caused a judder to go through the men, tearing into their skins as it did so. Flint screamed for men to be uncoupled to move the stone as quickly as possible. While doing it one convict got his hand crushed under one side of the boulder. 'Get the useless idler out of the way and get me another to replace him, and this time I want the man here in double quick time. Got it?'

A guard was already running down the hill.

The injured convict was pushed up against an outcrop of rock, blood streaming from his arm and hand. 'What about the hurt man, sir?'

'What about him, who cares, you?' said Flint.

'No, sir.'

Flint quickly walked back to where the plough team were being recoupled into their positions. The new man was shackled into the team but was protesting that he should be working in the kitchen today.

Flint stepped forward. 'You talking to me, you sniffling bag of shit? Well, are you?'

'The duty officer gave me the order today, Sergeant Flint.'

'Right, put this man on the end of the day punishment list: ten lashes for talking back to me and another ten for leaving his place of work in the kitchen. Got it?'

'Sir.'

'But—' started the man.

Flint cut him short. 'Double the lashes for arguing. Got it?'

Turning to the now-coupled team, he screamed, 'Come on, come on, you lazy bastards, you're beginning to look at no food today.' The men immediately took up the strain and the ploughing got back under way. By midday they had finished the field. The cost to the team was evident to see. Cut shoulders from the straps, hands bleeding, trousers torn from falling over as some were unable to keep up. Sweat caked on their bodies the backs, legs and arms heavy with fatigue, their breathing in time with the swing of the chains.

'Guard, take the names of all those who have damaged their clothes: that's against regulations that is. It's quite clear in the rules, it is. Ten lashes for each of them. Got it?'

'If the chance comes up before or as we escape, I'll fix you Flint. Two well-placed blows will slow you down for the rest of your life,' whispered Shenkin under his breath, with a grim smile on his face.

'What you bloody smiling at?' said a guard at his side.

'Just glad the officers' wives can plant their seeds, sir.'

'Don't be funny with me lad, or this bayonet will slit your trouser leg open putting you on the punishment list.'

'Do we get any of the vegetables when they come up, sir?'

'Right, you bastard,' said the guard pointing the blade down onto Shenkin's leg.

'What the hell are you playing at, Brittlebank? Get this man out of the harness and into the line for food and don't overfill the plates. I want to see the surplus in a basket by end of day. Got it?'

'Sir,' said the soldier. He turned to Shenkin as Flint walked away. 'I'm watching you, first chance I get I'll have you on the flogging post.'

Shenkin said nothing.

Later, having been fed, which came with less meat than they were supposed to have, the team moved on to another field. So went the day.

The injured convict bled most of his life away before he was taken to the hospital. Shenkin wondered if he'd ever see him again.

After the briefest of examination, Medical Officer Bickle admitted the injured man into the hospital with a shrug. 'He's lost a lot of blood. Put him near the door; he'll probably not see the night out,' he said to a convict orderly.

'Owens, get rid of that convict with the spider bite. Then look sharp with my tea man,' he said, then went on, 'you are nothing but a bloody malingerer, it means a useless layabout, Owens. You think you know a little about medicine, well you don't. You're just an old quack.' After a pause he went on again. 'Don't just stand there, make the tea if you can manage it.'

The old man stiffened. 'Right away, sir.'

'I'll see to you I will,' said Owens to himself. It was a mantra he repeated to himself almost hourly.

The ward smelt of vomit, dry blood and timber while the new patient continued to drain his life blood away.

Standing at Regan's side, Owens shook his head. 'Just a tourniquet to the arm would have saved much of the blood but it's too late now. Still, the flies seem to like it. We'll be taking him over to the Isle of the Dead in the morning.'

'Where's that?' said Regan.

'An island out in the bay. All who die at Port Arthur are buried there, no grave markers for the convicts of course; their graves are on the lowest part of the island. The tide comes in and goes out and the crabs have a feast. It's where I'd like to bury Medical Officer Bickle.'

Stepping back he looked down at Regan. 'Back to the barracks for you. Let me know what your mate says. I know everything there is to know about this blot of misery on the face of the earth so I could be very helpful to you.'

'I will, Robert, and my thanks again for everything,' said Regan. Tenderly he placed his foot on the ground. He was pleased to feel that the foot took his weight with little pain.

'Swelling has gone down, should be fine in a couple of days. Try to stay away from here and the incompetent fumbling of the medical officer.'

'I will, but how do I see you again?'

Quack Owens smiled. 'I'll seek you out, never fear. Now if I call a guard, you'll be back in time for supper. Supper, now there's a word that is misused here.'

Pushed into the food line, Regan looked for Shenkin. He was six convicts further along. Finally he caught his eye and inclined his head towards the barracks building where they could speak later.

Shenkin nodded.

The gruel tasted thicker and sweeter, either that or Shenkin was getting more hungry. The bread was again absent. Shenkin had been told at the midday meal that Flint and the guards sold the bread and meat to local shop owners in Hobart. Which they would then spend in the pubs and brothels of the town.

At last the lights were out and Regan made his way to Shenkin's bunk. A convict stopped him. 'On your way to your poofter are you?'

Regan's fist sent the convict and most of his bedding into the opposite wall, which he slowly slipped down, his face a mass of blood from the split lip.

Regan straightened up to his full six foot four inches. 'Now, before I have a few words with my friend here, does anyone else want to say anything?'

Silence rained supreme. The convict on the floor was unconscious; no one moved to help him.

A voice from lower down the room said, 'The guards will want to know how he came to be in such a state.'

Another voice, also from the back of the room, in a strong Irish accent said, 'Well now, didn't I see the poor man fall over?' Looking around he added, 'and is anyone going to call me a liar?' No one spoke.

'From Cork is it? Sure it's a very peaceful place,' said the Irishman.

Regan O'Hara smiled. 'Rosslare, but close enough so it is, for anywhere on that beautiful land is home. We'll talk later.'

'We will that. Now lads, help me put this poor man back on what's left of his bunk. Do you know, I think he looks better with a split lid.'

Regan sat down heavily on Shenkin's bunk. 'Did you have a good day ploughing?'

How's the foot?' said Shenkin, by way of reply.

'Sure it's fine, but I have something to tell you that will put a smile on that miserable face of yours.'

Regan told him about Robert Owens and what he could offer. At first Shenkin was annoyed that he had said anything about the escape plans. But finally he said, 'I'd like to meet him, if he's genuine he could help in many ways. If not we need to make sure he doesn't speak. I'll not risk this escape failing, Regan.'

'No of course, he told me he'd search us out soon.'

'We need sleep, for god knows what they have in mind for us tomorrow and the coming few weeks. I've been marking off the days to the 13th of December; we have just twenty-two days to go, Regan.' After some moments, Shenkin said, 'We can't wait for Owens to get back to us; we must meet soon, tomorrow if possible. Can you get the foot looked at to make sure it's on the mend?'

'It'll mean convincing Flint,' said Regan.

Someone called out, 'Can't you bleeders stop talking? We need sleep.'

'He's right,' said Shenkin.

Again, Flint was waiting outside of the barracks. 'Well now, all rested are we and ready for a good day's work?' Regan limped forward. 'Can I see the medical officer, Sergeant Flint sir, this foot is still a problem?'

'You are a bloody nuisance like all you Irishmen, you're always on the dodge. Pity it wasn't a snake; we'd have been rid of you in minutes.' For heartbeats the guards and the convicts waited in the coolness of the morning. Then, with Regan giving a silent prayer, Flint spoke, 'We lost a man yesterday and we are in need of a full gang. Thomson, get this man to the hospital and back to us smartly. Got it?'

'Sir.'

Shenkin let his breath out in a sigh, while Regan crossed himself.

'Come on, the rest of you, this isn't a bloody Sunday parade. Get them up the hill, Corporal, sharply now. I don't want to see them. I want a cloud of dust. Got it?'

Owens gave his dry crackle of a laugh. 'So you spoke to him then, your mate. Shenkin by name and also a twenty-year man, I looked up the intake list this morning before his nibs arrives, which will be in about thirty minutes. So what is it to be, can we meet?'

'Yes,' said Regan. 'Tonight if possible in the barracks, can it be arranged?'

Owens nodded. 'I'll be there to look at your foot before lights out.'

'Good enough,' said Regan, then added, 'how does the foot look?'

'It's clearing up fine; a few more days will see it back to normal. But I think I should speak to a friend of mind in the Shoemaking Workshop. If you do make it out you'll need good boots to get you across the land.'

At the Medical Office the doctor looked up. 'Not this bloody man again?' said Bickle, standing in the doorway.

'He's been sick in the night sir, perhaps some poison from the bite. Sergeant Flint sent him to make sure it's healing, sir. Says he needs him for a ploughing team today.'

'I see you have his foot in your hand; what is your medical opinion?' said Bickle sneering.

'Looks to be healing but still a little red. It seems hot too. Also the man's temperature is on the high side. Perhaps it needs to be looked at again after his day in the work gang.'

'I'll be at home by then, Owens, you see to it. I'm not waiting about to examine a bloody spider bite.'

'Of course not sir, it's not important enough for you, sir.'

'Not trying to be sarcastic are you, Owens?'

'Sar… what, sir?'

'Just do it man,' said Bickle in exasperation. 'Now where's my morning tea?'

'Right away, sir,' said Owens, giving Regan a knowing look.

I'm sure Shenkin is going to find this little man very helpful, thought Regan as he limped back outside to the guard and the now blazing sun burning its way over the top of the mountain. It promised to be another hot painful day.

CHAPTER 19

'It's very simple; you're both going to have typhus and die,' said Owens, with a dry chuckle. Shenkin, who had changed bunks with another convict to be close to Regan, looked at Owens in disbelief.

'Typhus,' said Shenkin in a shocked voice.

'Well, it will certainly appear to be typhus, at least enough to fool that idiot of a medical officer.'

'But how?'

'I'll create similar symptoms to typhus; you are both going to be sick, very sick on the 11th of December. And the powder I'll give you on the 12th will turn your skin grey and drawn. Bickle will place you in the isolation room; he'll give the keys to me because he'll be to scared to treat you himself,' said the old convict, pausing for breath.

'But we still have to get to the sea and on to the boat,' said Shenkin.

Owens dropped his voice as the guard walked down the line. When he had passed he turned to Shenkin. 'Leave the rest to me. I'll have you at the shore line by 5am on the 13th, ready to board your whaleboat together with the new boots. But I promise you, you're not going to feel like a sea voyage. In two to three days with plenty of water you will clear the effects of the powders in your bodies.'

'But what about you after we're gone? You'll be accused of helping an escape,' said Shenkin.

'Not if you're buried in a snug grave on the Isle,' said Owens.

'The Isle?' said Shenkin.

Owens went on, 'Regan will explain.'

'But…' said Shenkin, getting no further.

Owens raised his hand. 'You're going to have to trust me, Shenkin. I will have what I want and you will have what you want.'

'At least it's not cholera like the outbreak we had on the Runnymede coming from London,' said Regan.

'If this is a trick Owens, it'll be the last you ever play.'

'Think, Shenkin, what do I have to gain? Nothing. I'm not asking for anything. If I reported a plan for an escape, what would they give me? Nothing. But with Officer Bickle taking the blame I'll probably see the back of him and have an easier life over the next five years. That's all I want out of it, Shenkin, I promise. For what it's worth you have my word, not the most reliable I grant you given its source, but so help me it's the truth,' said Owens. For heartbeats no one spoke. The lights in the middle of the lines of bunks, for it was never completely dark in the barracks, swung back and forth creaking the night away.

'Any plan of escape from here is a high risk venture. Few have made it out of here and the ones that did were soon recaptured or died. One convict by the name of Billy Hunt, a former strolling player in England, even put on the skin of a kangaroo, and hopped his way across Eaglehawk Neck. The guards, thinking he was a big old kangaroo heading for Forestier's Peninsula, decided this was an opportunity for fresh meat for them and bones for the dogs so began to fire their muskets at him. Billy quickly stopped hopping and struggled out of the skin and in a perfectly projected voice called out, 'Don't shoot! It's only me, Billy Hunt.'

Both Shenkin and Regan laughed at the grim comedy of it. 'But surely someone successfully escaped,' said Shenkin.

'Many attempts have been made, my friend, by very desperate men. Most died in the sea or at Eaglehawk Neck by musket fire or the dogs who are kept half starved deliberately. Those that did get across Eaglehawk Neck, either by swimming through the surf or hiding in the sandhills, died in the jungle forest of the mountains,' said Owens. 'I am offering you a better chance of succeeding by giving you inside help for I am sure my plan will work.'

'Can we think it over for the next few days?' said Shenkin, adding, ' we expect news about the boat in a day or two. The man arranging it has friends up the coast who will get word to us.'

Owens shrugged his thin shoulders. 'Time is critical; there are boots to be made, the preparation of the powders and the medical officer to be convinced. Think Shenkin, help from the inside and outside, now that's very rare. You'd stand a very good chance, Shenkin, and you know it.'

Regan turned to Shenkin. 'We've taken higher risks along the way have we not?'

The guard near the door called out, 'What's keeping you, Owens? Either the bleeding foot's going to fall off or not. Get on with it.'

'Almost done, just bandaging it up, seems to be healing.'

Continuing in a whisper he said, 'It'll be more difficult to get in here again. As you can see security is strict; you are always being watched. Damn it, you need to decide now,' said Owens, flatly.

'Well, Regan?' said Shenkin.

'I say we've had to take many risks in the past, and I've seen how much Owens hates the medical officer, it's his only reason for living. You above all know how hate drives you.'

'Right, you're in. But if this is a trap, I swear I'll kill you,' said Shenkin, grasping Owens bony shoulder.

'Then there's nothing to worry about for only you, Regan, me and god, if he bothers about this evil place of Satan, know about it,' said Owens, getting up and making for the door.

At the door the guard looked up. 'At last,' he said.

'He's got a big foot and a long leg; it takes time,' said Owens.

The night guard and Owens passed each other in the doorway. 'About bloody time, you are always late, Williams,' said the day guard to his replacement.

'Alright, I'm here now ain't I? What's the quack doing here then?'

'Read the record, if you can read that is.'

'Touchy tonight aren't we?' said Williams. But the day guard was already out of the door slamming it shut behind him.

The guard slowly walked down the lines of bunks towards his fellow night guard at the other end. 'Here we go for another bloody long night, do you know I feel as if I'm doing a term here as well,' he said.

A voice from a dark corner called out, 'You can have mine Williams, if you want it.'

'Another back talk and I'll put six months on that man's sentence,' said Williams.

Silence finally fell on the Prisoners' barracks at Port Arthur, only the guard dogs up at Eagle Hawk Neck could be faintly heard as they howled at the moon. As he fell asleep, Shenkin thought, *So many barriers to stop a convict from escaping, so many.*

The next days went as if in a living nightmare, land-clearing gangs, road gangs, tree felling. One convict who had absconded five times in the last month had now received a total of four hundred lashes, his back and buttocks were virtually in shreds, but he was still put to work. He died on the first day of tree felling. Some said he walked under a falling gum tree that had just been cut, its weight caused a deep furrow in the ground. It was decided to leave the convict there until they cut the tree into lengths, by the third day the stench was unbearable. Three days later, two died in the ploughing harnesses, no one knew they were dead until they had finished the clearing. Flint drove them relentlessly from early morning to the return to the barracks in the evening. His daily punishment lists grew longer by the day. Those that were on it more than twice had their sentences increased by six to eighteen months, depending on the offence. Somehow both Shenkin and Regan managed to keep out of trouble, despite Flint waiting his chance to get them on the punishment detail. Until the 9th of December that is, then all hell broke lose.

They had been working all day on the edge of the clearing where the stumps of trees were being dug up and dragged away. The work gang, some of them in leg chains for punishment for some offence or other, only Flint knew what or why, young and old convicts, strained and heaved at the heavy big gum tree stumps, their roots as big as a man's leg. One convict caught his trousers in a piece of root; it tore the trouser leg off.

'Put that man on the punishment list for twenty lashes for damaging government property,' shouted Flint.

'Sir.'

One convict had already collapsed twice that morning. He was old, bent and tired. With a long gasp, he went down again over the stump he was pulling. The convicts around him stopped because one of his feet was pinned under one of the large roots.

'Get that bloody piece of shit up on his feet,' screamed Flint to the nearest soldier. The old scarecrow of a man, his skinny legs a mass of ulcer scars, had a crumbled tattoo on his forearm that seemed to say Mum in a heart. He had excrement running down one leg.

'He stinks sir. I think he's passed out again; that's the third time today. Shall I get him down to the medical officer, Sergeant?'

'Medical officer, fucking medical officer, what do you think this is lad? A day out with the bloody family. Get him on his feet.' Then he added, 'never mind, let me see to him.'

'Up, you lazy bastard,' said Flint, raising a corded rope above his head to strike the unconscious man. He never brought his arm down; Shenkin had stepped away from the working gang. Blocking the arm he pressed it back with an inward push; the snapping bone resounded around them. Flint screamed, which Shenkin silenced with a chop to Flint's throat. It was over in seconds. Flint lay twisted up on the ground. Everyone had frozen in the moment of violence: the guards, the overseers, the convicts. The guard who had vowed to get Shenkin rushed forward. He got as far as Regan whose fist dropped the guard as if he stood over a trapdoor. The guards from both sides of the line of convicts, together with the overseers, ran forward. In a very short time everyone was involved in the brawl. Convicts were using their chains as weapons. Overseers were swinging whips and truncheons. The soldiers had their muskets at the ready but no officer was present to issue orders.

The big Irishman from Cork stood by the side of Regan. 'It's just like being at home, so it is. Now don't you go worrying about these two guards coming towards us,' he said, bringing both their heads together in a sickening thud. Shenkin went on his knee to help the old convict get to a safer place only to find he was dead. At that moment three officers arrived, swords in hand. One cut down a convict who was strangling a guard, the sword sliced through the convict's neck, blood spurted like a fountain around them. A captain stood on the high section of a fallen tree.

'On my command, prepare to fire.' Muskets went up to shoulders, clicks sounded as hammers were pulled back. Brown Bess, as the musket was affectionately called, drilled her barrelled one eye into the mass of convicts.

'Armed detachment over to one side, then hold your fire until my command,' screamed the captain.

Walking up the hill from the settlement was the acting commandant with Medical Officer Hunt. Major William Walter Harris's long legs finally brought him in front of the captain. 'What in the name of hell is going on, Captain? Report, damn it, report.'

Captain Watts came to attention. 'Small rebellion sir, all under control now.'

'Small rebellion, you say, it looks like a bloody battle field man.' Harris was not right very often, but in this instance he was. Blood covered the ground, six guards were down, two were without their caps, their uniforms torn, the two overseers were standing, but only just. The convict that was cut down was dead. *That's a long bloody report right there, thought Harris.*

Seeing some convicts were in chains, making it a punishment detail as well as a tree clearing gang, the major said, 'Was there an officer attached to this chain gang?'

The captain turned to Flint who was being held up by two soldiers, while Medical Officer Bickle was examining him. 'Well, Sergeant, was an officer present?' After a moment he said, 'Well man, speak up.'

Bickle turned around to address the commandant. 'He has more then likely said his last word and given his last order, the sergeant's larynx is, I believe, crushed, his right arm is broken and he has passed out again.'

The bloody paperwork is getting longer, thought Harris, and on Booth's return it reduces my chances of becoming Assistant Commandant. 'Good god, give me the name of the convict responsible,' he said.

No one spoke, then one convict stepped forward, until the Irishman from Cork dragged his boot down the inside of the man's shin. The man screamed.

'Well what is it do you know the name?' said Harris, red in the face now.

'No sir, sorry, sir, caught my foot in one of the roots sir.'

'If I don't get a name within the next two minutes, every one of you will receive twenty lashes and your sentences will be increased by three years for this riot.'

For heartbeats only the cockatoos and the buzz of flies could be heard, a wedge-tailed eagle flew low overhead. It cast a shadow over the group. Harris watched it glide across the clearing where it no doubt was hoping to see some prey that had been uncovered on the now open ground. In these few moments the two Irishmen caught the eye of every convict near them.

No one spoke, a screech came from the eagle as it gently swerved to the right of the gang. The chorus of cockatoos sang out their farewell. Turning to the captain, Harris said, 'Take their names and numbers; have it on my desk by end of day.' Stopping for a moment, he looked again over the scene of convicts, dust, hot sun and the bloody cockatoos. He sighed deeply. *This posting is a low point in my career*, he thought. Shaking his head he turned to Bickle. 'Do what you can, Doctor. I'll have your report on my desk too, by end of day.'

Harris turned to captain Watts. 'Get an officer assigned to this chain gang and a sergeant. Flogging posts to be erected on the site for all other chain gangs to see. Lashes to be administered promptly, lay it on. I want to hear the screams, understand?'

'Sir,' said the captain.

Shenkin went to step forward. Regan held his arm. 'This is no time for confessions, we have other plans to consider, not least of all Elizabeth, isn't that so?'

Shenkin hesitated, then the moment was lost. Harris was already down the hill back to his office. A detail of soldiers moved fast to bring up flogging posts. Bickle called for stretchers for the dead convicts and the injured. Flint was still unconscious, his arm at an unnatural angle.

Within two hours the screams from the convicts, as the cat cut into flesh, competed with the cockatoos. Shenkin felt guilty but Regan was right, too much was at stake. As the cat bit, he felt he was paying at least some kind of reckoning for his betrayal of the others.

That evening the hostility against Shenkin was thick in the air. One convict came over to Shenkin after they had had their meal, that few felt like eating. 'Only three bleeding months I had to go, that's all. Now it's another three years on top thanks to you, you bastard.'

At any other time the man would have regretted his remark, but Shenkin said, 'I'm sorry.'

But the convict had walked away.

Regan leaned forward. 'Don't let it fret you, in two days we'll be starting our escape plan and hopefully see the back of this place. How many times have you said to me, it's survival first.'

'I know but...' said Shenkin, with a grim look on his face.

'Sweet Mary, leave it man, we need to concentrate on the days to come.'

So they settled to sleep, which for Shenkin was full of remorseful guilt. An owl shrieked in the darkness outside, probably marking the end of a field mouse or rat; it's all a question of survival.

CHAPTER 20

On the 10th a note appeared in Shenkin's bread. The scribble, unsigned, simply said, *It's on see you in three days.* Shenkin ate the note with his stale bread and washed it down with water.

The morning of the 11th, Shenkin was handed a small white packet by Owens as the quack passed him in the main doorway to the barracks. He whispered to Shenkin, 'Put it into your water at breakfast today, trust me. I'll being seeing you later, tell Regan.'

The gruel was its usual tasteless meal, the bread somewhat better now that Flint had been sent to the hospital at Hobart. However, the medical officer was right: Flint's larynx was crushed to a pulp. He'd never talk again. The new sergeant was marginally better but not by a great deal. Sergeant Watkins was a career army man full of hustle and bustle. He had been in the army for over twenty years. He'd seen it all and was not impressed. This posting he felt, was below him, but another year would see him back in England and thank god for it. In the meantime he'd make the most of it. 'Right, you godless undisciplined bastards, orders and rules that's what it's all about; without rules where were we? no-bloody-where that's where. Do not make the mistake of causing another riot, for it will be your last. If rules are obeyed then we will get along but, as god is my judge, if for any reason you do not, then the devil will prevail and his name is Sergeant Watkins.' At this moment an officer joined them. The sergeant came smartly to attention, shoulders back, chest out. His Waterloo medal glittered in the early morning light.

'All accounted for and ready for the day's work, sir.'

'Very good Sergeant, carry on; I have road work on the schedule, four to be in chains is that right?'

'Correct sir,' said the sergeant.

'Right, move them out.'

'Sir.'

Shenkin had drunk the water with the powder mixed in. It gave the water a bitter taste. By the time he was breaking up rocks on the road his stomach was turning over, vomit slowly came into his throat, he began to sweat. Looking over at Regan he saw that the Irishman was very pale with a slight green-blue tinge around his mouth and slightly bent over. At that moment his stomach went into painful cramps so intense it bent him double.

Both collapsed. 'Corporal, get those two men on their feet and be quick about it.' Seeing the size of Shenkin and Regan the corporal took two privates with him.

After a few moments, the corporal returned to the sergeant. 'They're very sick Sergeant: can't stand. Look like death they do; their bodies shaking fit to bust, Sarge so help me if they don't.'

'Bloody useless loafers, that's what they are.' The sergeant made his way to the officer who was sitting in the shade of a tree.

'Two convicts ill sir. Got the runs they have sir. Not much use to us like that, sir.'

'Get the medical officer or an orderly here, Sergeant,' said the officer with a sigh of resignation.

'Sir.'

At the hospital the orderlies, for it took four of them, half-carried and dragged Shenkin and Regan in front of the doctor.

'Good god, not this man again,' said Bickle, in annoyance at seeing Regan.

Most of their breakfast, what little there was, had long left their stomachs, only fluid now passed their lips.

'Owens, come in here.'

'Sir,' said Owens rushing through the door.

'Get this bloody mess cleaned up then get them onto bunks. Why am I expected to do everything myself?'

'Sorry sir, seeing to the burial party for the convict that died last night, they need to catch the tide,' said Owens.

'This first. The man's dead; he can wait. Just get on with it.'

'Right away, sir.'

Bickle began to examine Shenkin first. 'What have you been eating?' he asked.

'Very little as you well know.'

'Don't be insolent with me man, or I'll recommend a spell in solitary,' said Bickle, adding, 'bloody convicts.'

Owens stood looking over the doctor's shoulder. 'He could have eaten some berries I suppose, but his colour is…..' He got no further as Bickle cut him short.

'Still think you can diagnose do you? Well, Quack Doctor, what's your diagnosis? Come on, let's have it,' said Bickle, smirking.

'I was just wondering if he had a backache and general muscle pains, sir.'

Before Bickle could say anything Shenkin, with great difficulty, straightened up. 'Yes all over, Doctor.'

'He's not a bloody doctor; he's nothing but an old worn-out quack,' said Bickle, irritably. For a moment no one spoke or moved. Medical Officer Bickle considered the possibilities. The man was certainly feverish, was sick, did have stomach and muscle pains. He also seemed confused.

Shenkin had began to mumble as his temperature went higher. Regan, too, mirrored the same symptoms.

Finally, Bickle came to a decision. 'Get them into a side cell, let's see how they are this evening.'

'Straight away sir,' said Owens in a voice full of urgency.

'Then come and see me.'

'Sir.'

In the side room, Owens closed the door quickly when the orderly that had helped him get both men on to narrow bunks left. 'Right I know how you feel but you now need to take this second powder. I'll be in later with something to go around your back and stomachs.'

'Dear god, I never felt so ill,' said Shenkin, in a shaky voice.

'You are going to feel a lot worse, I can assure you,' said Owens with a smile. 'But I'm sure you feel it's worth it for the freedom to come, that's if the rest of it goes well.'

Officer William Bickle sat at his desk, a medical book opened in front of him. 'I know what you are thinking Owens, but there is no rash on their bodies, is there?'

Owens shook his head. 'No, but the rest of the symptoms do seem to point in a certain direction. I'm no doctor sir, it's what you think that matters. However, I did notice as we took them to their room that their eyes seemed very sensitive to the sunlight. As you know, the word that we are not saying comes from the Greek meaning hazy, they are certainly that.'

Bickle looked at Owens as if he was seeing him for the first time. 'Good god, you can't mean typhus?'

'We have the right conditions for it more fleas then we can count, poor sanitary conditions and overcrowding,' said Owens in a now firm voice, adding, 'but as you say, no sign of a rash, yet that is.'

Medical Officer Bickle had gone pale, his fingers twitched over the papers of his medical book, a light sheen of perspiration had spread across his brow.

'It's not possible you fool, it can't be. No, no it can't.'

'If you say so, sir,' said Owens.

'We'll examine them for any signs of a rash in two hours. No wait, you examine them and let me know,' said Bickle, in a hurried voice.

'Very well sir. I expect you'll be getting home now sir, it's rather late. The work gangs are back and we have no other patients. One convict died on the road gang today so he is beyond help. The body will go over to the Isle tomorrow early, together with the other one. Shall I lay him out ready sir?'

'Yes right Owens do that, if these men do have a rash do not come to my house to let me know. I'll see to them in the morning.'

'Very well Doctor,' said Owens with a strong emphasis on the word doctor.

When Bickle had gone, Owens went in to see Shenkin. Both were grey and drawn in the face, even Shenkin's face scar was now grey. Going to a bag in the corner, Owens removed with gloves, some nettles he had gathered earlier. 'This is going to sting like hell but it'll look every bit like a rash my lads, so grit your teeth.' With that, Owens lifted their shirts and wrapped the stinging nettles around their middles.

Both Shenkin and Regan let out a gasp of breath. 'Sweet Mary in heaven, what in the name of god was that?' said Regan.

'The plant urtica my Irish friend, or stingy nettles to you, vigorous out here they are, can raise the skin into red inflamed lumps in no time. Dock leaves are the cure but not yet, for you'll have to endure the pain till morning so the doctor can start the day in good spirits,' said Owens, giving a dry crackling laugh.

Through gritted teeth Regan said, 'Let's hope the escape works after this, for I'll not go through it again.'

'Yes you will if need be, for I am sure our friend can come up with some maladies just as painful and colourful.'

'Indeed I can, why there's one that…' Shenkin cut him short.

'Don't tell us, Owens. We'd rather it be a surprise,' said Shenkin, vomiting and coughing between each word.

'Admirable you are, keeping a sense of wit about you. That's good, for you are going to need it during the night. Indeed you'll think that typhus itself cannot be as bad, so I'll say goodnight to you both,' said Owens closing the door and locking it for now; he also had the keys.

The night was everything Owens said it would be. They tried to sleep but it was impossible, they vomited up nothing but watery fluid causing their stomachs to ache from the strain of it, while the stings made it impossible to find a resting place. They were hot, sweat ran down their bodies, the salt in their perspiration caused the stings to burn even more. It was in every sense, a nightmare when one was fully awake.

Shenkin was grateful when at last he saw light creep through the window of their room. Regan gave a sigh. 'If I live to be a hundred years old I'll not forget every godforsaken moment of that long night, for I've walked with demons and that's the truth.'

'Indeed we did but I fear there is more to come.'

'Now don't go spoiling my morning.'

Their words came with very little energy behind them. Finally, the key scraped its way around the lock letting Owens into the room. 'Well, how do you feel? Just this full day and then in the early hours of the morning we'll see you aboard the whaleboat.'

Shenkin could scarcely lift his head; he was drained of fluid, drenched in sweat and every muscle was as tight as Di the Sound's violin string. He grunted a greeting. 'So what now?'

'First some water and a little soup, you'll not want it, I know. But you need fluid for that long walk down to the sea's edge come morning. You'll vomit most of it so I'll replace it every hour,' said Owens.

'You'll never manage it on your own. Why, Regan alone will take two men to carry him,' said Shenkin.

'I know but the doctor first, then I'll talk to him about your demise from this mortal coil.' Both Shenkin and Regan started to talk at once. Owens raised his hand. 'Believe me I've thought it through, I assure you. Knowing Bickle as I do, my plan will work.' After a long drawn-out moment, Owens spoke again, 'You must trust me, Shenkin.'

'If you are a liar Owens, I'll kill you.'

'And where would you get the strength to do it, may I ask?'

Both Shenkin and Regan looked at each other, they were indeed in the hands of this quack, with only the hope his hatred of Bickle would see them safely onto the boat.

'Now drink this soup, you'll vomit but some fluid will remain in your bodies. I'll bring more after talking to Bickle; he'll more than likely not want to come near you, but he'll have to if he's to report an outbreak of typhus to the Acting Commandant. I'm hoping then that both will avoid coming here,' said Owens, leaving the room and locking the door after him.

Owens knocked lightly on the medical officer's door. 'Come,' called the sleep-stained dry voice.

Owens opened the office door as if not to cause offence. 'Well, how are our malingerers this morning? No signs of a rash, I'll wager,' said Bickle.

'Covered sir, both convicts are also grey of colour, eyes sensitive to light, as last night but now more so, temperature high to burning skin. They must have had it a while for it's now, as I say, in the rash stage. Saw a lot of it in dear old London. It is common in the workhouses and prisons. Indeed you must have seen it in the war with the French sir; the field hospitals were full of it, "jail fever" they called it, as you know,' said Owens, knowing full well that young Officer Bickle had not been in the Napoleonic Wars.

'Yes indeed,' said Bickle, a nervous quiver running through his words.

'You'll be needing to see them then sir, before reporting to the commandant.'

Bickle continued to turn a light shade of white. Then, speaking too quickly, he said, 'Yes, but I'll not examine them again Owens; the symptoms you relate are confirmation enough. However, should the commandant ask, I did see them yesterday, did I not?'

'You did sir.'

Captain Bickle shuffled paperwork around his desk, not wanting to look at Owens he said, 'Strip the convicts to the waist; I'll call in and see them from the doorway.'

'Very well, sir.'

Later at the doorway, Bickle stood with a handkerchief over his nose. He ran his eyes over Shenkin and Regan then let out a gasp. 'Good god, they seem to be dying in front of us, the rash, colour of their skin, the vomit.'

'They are dying, sir,' said Owens.

'Get the vomit cleaned up Owens, use buckets full of water and strong carbolic,' said Bickle, walking hurriedly out of the room.

'So you think it is typhus sir,' said Owens, a shocked look on his thin hatchet face.

'No bloody doubt about it damn it, every symptom matches the clearly described notes in my infectious diseases manual,' he said, slamming the book down.

'I'll see to it sir, don't you worry. I knew you would agree with my diagnosis seen too much of it we have.' A light smile spread across his face as he followed the medical officer out.

'Right,' said Bickle, openly relieved that Owens would deal with it. adding, 'What's to be done? That's the thing.'

'Well sir, you know best of course, but I'd get them off the settlement at the soonest opportunity. Say, over to the Isle in the early hours of tomorrow, for they'll not last the night, I'm thinking. Then into the ground with plenty of earth and stones on top of them, if you don't mind me saying sir.'

For moments, only the rattle of the chain gangs disturbed the still air of the office.

Owens shifted from foot to foot. 'Contagious it is sir, particularly for the old and very young children, like yours sir, if you don't mind me saying, sir,' he said.

It was enough to tip the shaky balance of Bickle's decision. 'Yes, they must be removed from the colony with due haste, yes, most certainly. But how do we get them to the boat Owens, having to handle the bodies, to be in close contact?'

'Well sir, I do know one of the fishermen, an ex-convict in fact. Lives along the coast a bit. He has a whaleboat and for a small amount of coin, he would, I'm sure, take them over. I'd need a few men to get them from the hospital and into the boat of course, say a few of the convict overseers, no need to risk any of the military sir, is there?' adding, 'after all, the convicts are dying of one thing or another all the time aren't they sir.'

'Quite so,' said Bickle, already rehearsing in his mind the best way of putting this to the acting commandant.

'Typhus, you say, are you positive, Captain Bickle?'

Bickle bristled slightly. 'I carried out a very careful examination of the men their symptoms leave no doubt in my mind, sir.'

Major Harris was an ambitious man therefore, an outbreak of typhus on his watch would not be beneficial to his long term plans. 'Spreads like wildfire

Bickle, saw it in the war from Spain to France. We burned the bodies but it just spreads, close contact is to be avoided. What are your recommendations?'

Medical Officer Bickle went over in detail the plan Owens had been considering, except that the idea was all his.

'Excellent, get them off the penal colony without delay; get the men you require tell Owens to enlist the help of this man with the whaleboat, pay him what he wants. I'll reimburse you from the mess funds.' Harris visually relaxed, all was under control.

The medical officer brought himself up to attention. 'Very well sir,' he said making his way out but stopped at the opened door. He turned to the commandant. 'You'll want to see these convicts sir, for your report that is.'

Major William Walter Harris was an officer who knew how to delegate risky tasks, that was the way he survived the war. 'Good god man, you're the doctor: if you say they have typhus so it will be entered in my report, which you will countersign. Is that clear?'

'Quite clear sir. I'll get on with the arrangements immediately,' said Bickle. Within an hour, four convict overseers were on standby for the morning. Owens had been despatched to arrange the whaleboat. He suggested to the medical officer that the earlier the better to take them to the Isle, say perhaps 5am. The tide was right and few inmates or military would be about. Bickle agreed, the sooner this was done the more relieved he would be. He had briefly looked into the room holding the two ill convicts, both were still alive but in a very distressed state. Perhaps come morning they would be dead and the transfer to the Isle of the Dead would be easier.

Owens sat on a rock the other side of the headland. He would give it an hour or so then return to tell the doctor all was arranged. He observed, not for the first time, how spectacular the scenery was that held the convict settlement: lost souls in a paradise of warm colours, a deep blue sea surrounded by a land full of all the colours of the rainbow, topped with the gold of the sun. Breathtaking, and yet men died in its manmade prison of hell. The old quack was lost for a while in his thoughts of the years yet to come. Would he survive? Without Bickle, he just might. He must believe that; he must hope. He had once heard an aboriginal proverb: 'Those who lose dreaming are lost.' One day he would be free again, but first a successful escape would help that dream come true. He stood up with some difficulty then, taking one last look at the bay that echoed with the sounds of brightly coloured birds and the rattling mocking of chains, he made his way back down to the penal colony.

'Well,' said Bickle, looking up from writing his long report to the acting commandant with the main heading *Typhus* at the top of the page.

'All is arranged sir. I asked for them to be at the jetty by 5am: the tide is right at that time and there will be few military and overseers about,' said Owens.

'Excellent, but the bloody men are still alive, damn it.'

'Yes, that's a shame to be sure sir, but we'll soon have them under the ground sir.'

So saying, Owens leaned a little closer to the doctor. The old man's odour swept over Bickle like a rancid wave. In a low voice Owens said,. 'I considered that sir, so I took the liberty of giving them some extra coin for the digging of two deep graves, when they finally have the good grace to die; so no need for our overseers to be troubled.' Owens breathed tobacco-laced breath over Bickle, who visually cringed.

'Yes, very good,' said Bickle moving his chair backwards. 'I'll note it in my report to the commandant.'

Owens knew only too well that the report would be what the medical officer himself had accomplished and no one else. *All the better,* thought Owens. 'Also, sir I have prepared a number of handkerchiefs covered with a light soak of carbolic for yourself, the overseers and the boat crew to cover their mouths and noses with.'

'Your stupidity seems to be taking a turn for the better, Owens.'

Owens touched his forelock. 'That is very good of you to say so sir. You'll want to see them I suppose, sir, before we take them down to the jetty, see them off like?'

'Lamentably I'll have to be here, so have everything ready for a quick removal, Owens.'

'Very well sir, you can rely upon me sir.'

When the doctor had finally finished his report, he left for the commandant's office and then home. He felt sure Major Harris would be pleased with his actions in the matter.

No sooner was the door closed than Owens went in to see Shenkin. 'How do you both feel? For you look bloody awful,' he said with a laugh.

Shenkin lifted himself onto the bunk. 'Bloody awful does not describe it, but a little better than we have been.'

'The powders are working out from your bodies, which is good for all is arranged, but I'll need you to give the nod to your Captain Saxon so he knows we're part of the escape plan.'

'A sign is already agreed but it'll be a rum game, Owens, for Saxon will be suspicious, but again, he knows I had to put a plan together to get to the shore line or the jetty so it may work.'

'It had better,' said Owens, adding, 'if it does not we'll all be here for the rest of our lives, and in solitary too.'

Regan crossed himself. 'Well, and there's me thinking it couldn't get worse.'

Shenkin looked at Owens with a start. 'What about the overseers to take us down to the jetty then across to the Isle?'

'Its been seen to, just trust me,' said Owens.

'It appears we have little choice.'

Owens nodded. 'No, so listen, you will both be weak and ill but still alive when the overseers that I have arranged come to take you to the jetty come morning.'

'But…' said Shenkin.

'Just listen to me damn it,' he said raising his hand. 'They will have masks to their faces and Bickle will watch our departure. We'll signal the boat to come in to the jetty. I'll give the crew handkerchiefs for their faces; you will give your signal to Saxon. Hopefully he'll understand, for it will be our most perilous moment.'

CHAPTER 21

At exactly ten minutes to 5am, Medical Officer Bickle stood, impatient to see them off, while the four overseers placed Shenkin and Regan onto stretchers. Both were groaning in apparent pain, both looked at death's door, while Owens fussed over the proceedings.

Bickle, a cloth mask to his face, gestured to move it along quickly. 'Come on, get them out of here and down to the jetty smartly now,' he said, his voice muffled by the cloth.

'Indeed sir,' said Owens.

The two overseers lifting Regan strained under the weight of his body, but finally the procession was out of the hospital and swayed their way down to the jetty. The morning was crisp and damp with dew as the sun struggled over the mountains behind the penal colony.

Slowly they dropped below Bickle's view. 'Thank god,' he said under his breath, closing the door tight.

Thankfully it was a clear morning, if slightly chilly. At the jetty, Owens scanned the sea for signs of a boat, nothing caught his eye. For a moment his stomach turned over in panic.

Shenkin shared the moment with him, he closed his eyes and almost prayed.

At last the splash of oars came over the water and slowly the shape of a whaleboat came into sight. Saxon stood at the stern, his hands firmly on the long tiller as he guided the boat in. Laying off some distance from the shore, he called out, 'Ahoy there! To the jetty is it?'

Owens waved his arms. 'It is.'

The overseers took up the weight of the stretchers again. Pulling hard to the jetty, the boat drew alongside. It was then that Shenkin lifted his head and gave a thumbs up to Saxon, who hesitated. For long heartbeats no one moved, seconds ticked by, only the lapping of the water marked the passage of time. Shenkin held his breath, then Saxon threw a line to Owens, who quickly secured the boat to its mooring. He then handed the crew handkerchiefs. 'Cover your faces lads, for this is no pleasure trip,' he said.

One of the overseers turned to Owens. 'If you have exposed us to a contagious fever Owens, your life is over,' he said, his voice hard and tight.

Owens smiled. 'No need to worry my dears, in a day or so all will be made clear.' adding, 'it's only a chill from the morning cold that you may catch, but I wager you'll have a good laugh and I'll see a tot of rum finds you,' he said, giving a dry chuckle.

The overseers tipped them into the boat then cast it off from the jetty. Saxon gave an order to his crew and they were away, the oars beating the water into a turbulence of salty spray; they were soon into the darkness.

No one spoke until they were well out and heading for Maingon Bay and the headland off the east coast. Only then did Saxon come forward. 'Well, that was a performance, my sick friends, what do you suffer from, may I ask?'

'Typhus,' said Shenkin. A deep voice from one of the crew split the early morning air, a burly figure stood up from rowing and with care made his way forward. The boat rocked under his weight; it was Charlie Benson.

Shenkin stood unsteadily to his feet. 'Charlie it's you,' he said in delight. 'A poor farmer but the best damn fighter I ever fought,' said Shenkin, putting out his hand.

'Before I shake it, what's this about typhus?' said Charlie.

'There is no need to worry, I assure you,' said Shenkin.

'Well tell us all about it,' said Charlie, eagerly.

After being introduced to the rest of the crew, who Shenkin thanked, he told them all about Owens' plan. At the end all were laughing at the sheer cheek of it. The laughter sounded over the water greeting in the dawn of the morning, as they passed between Cathedral Pillar and Tasman Island. After some hours of hard rowing they rounded the headland. After more hours of rowing they made their way up the coast. Finally, they heard the barking of the dogs at Eaglehawk Neck. Saxon leaned over to Regan 'Would you believe it? This is called O'Hara Bluff; it must be a sign,' he said with a laugh. Regan would have answered but he was being sick over the side. At the peninsula the dogs became fully aroused, causing a necklace of lantern lights to dance in the pale dawn light. They sailed around it to freedom.

After further hours of more hard rowing they were far enough out to sea to put up their dipping lug sail. It soon caught the wind, speeding them along the coast line. After so long in the confines of the penal colony, Shenkin was exhilarated by the feel of the cold sea spray on his face. By late morning they were sailing towards the main land of the Forestier Peninsula. Saxon quickly loosened the sail to spill the wind, then, taking up the oars again, they rowed ashore. 'We spend the rest of the day here,' said Saxon. No one said anything. All were exhausted; sleep came quickly. Come early morning, they again launched the boat into the thankfully calm sea. First the oars to take them out to the deep water, then Saxon put up the sail. The wind caught the sail and they were soon skimming the water at a steady pace. Late afternoon found them in Marion Bay. Saxon let down the sail and steered to the land, bringing them up to Bream Creek. They were free.

The sunlight spread across the water as the day drew to a close. Everyone heaved a sigh. Shenkin and Regan looked better and managed a smile. Charlie Benson turned to Shenkin while his brother stood on the steering platform to navigate the whaleboat towards the shore. 'Good you're better this is the first chance we have had to talk Shenkin. I have a surprise for you: some friends who have been influential in bringing this escape about are waiting for you,' he said, with a smile.

'Who are they, is it Elizabeth?' said Shenkin excited by the thought.

'No,' said Charlie, unseen by Shenkin the smile had turned to sadness.

'Then who?'

'Wait and see.'

Slowly, two figures began to take shape on the shoreline. One was the figure of an elegant man, his hand resting easy on an ebony cane. The other was as black as coal dust but with a smile that lit up his face.

'Regan, it's Sir Edward and Tinker,' shouted Shenkin. 'Well, I'll be damned.'

'It is too,' said Regan, his big Irish face split into a wide smile.

'Ship all oars,' called Saxon.

The sharp bow of the boat cut its way into the shingle of the beach and they were ashore.

Running down to the water's edge, Sir Edward Standish put out his hand in greeting, which quickly turned into him throwing his arms around Shenkin. 'You made it Shenkin, you made it. I'm delighted to see you safe, if a little on the pale side, you too, Regan,' he said. 'Absolutely delighted, and look who is with me.'

Tinker stepped forward. 'Well, you both look whiter then the whitest new convicts from the whitest land of England.'

A roar of laughter cut through the morning air. It was good to be back among friends again, thought Shenkin. Clothes were given to them, rough seaman's clothes but Shenkin was glad to be rid of his convict garb, and with the strong boots that Owens had supplied, he felt they were ready for the journey over land and back to Sydney to settle his score with Lord Feltsham.

Tinker had lit a fire and they all sat around it for a much-needed meal.

When it was over, Tinker took Shenkin aside. 'I have some bad news to tell you.' As he said it the cluster of men near him turned away. Regan sensed the moment and joined Charlie Benson and his brother at the far side of the camp fire.

'What is it, Tinker? You doubt we can travel over this primitive land of yours, is that it?'

'I wish my friend that is what it was.'

'So?'

'It is Elizabeth. I have gone over it in my mind how to say it, but there is no easy way.'

'What? For god's sake what?'

'She is dead Shenkin, there is no other way to say it.'

'No. No. No, please no.' The cry that spoke the words screamed into the air; the alarmed birds filled the air. Shenkin did what no bare-knuckle fighter had ever been able to do to him, he fell to the ground and lay there.

Sir Edward moved forward to Shenkin but Regan put out his hand. 'Leave him; it is his pain. Let him suffer it alone. He knows we care.'

They all turned to the fire. Tinker joined them and began to outline the journey they would need to take, leaving Shenkin to his sorrow and pain.

It was early morning of the next day before Shenkin rejoined them. 'Which way Tinker? For I am anxious to have a meeting with Feltsham.'

Sir Edward looked up. 'You have not asked about the baby Shenkin.'

'I don't care.'

'Yes you do! Tell him, Tinker.'

'She lives. It is a baby girl Shenkin, living in the grand home of his lordship, who they say cares for her well.'

After some moments Shenkin, in a tight voice spoke, 'He's taken my love; he will not take our child too. I'll kill him first.'

'So be it,' said Regan, standing.

Everyone realised it was pointless to discuss the matter further with Shenkin, so they turned to Tinker who was stamping out the fire.

Throwing the last of the hot water on the fire he looked up. 'We go to Sorell first, then across to the town of Hobart where we board a ship for Sydney,' he said, turning to Sir Edward who took up the plan.

'I have, on the advice of Thomas Street, a Sydney merchant who has recently purchased the paddle steamer the James Watt, booked passage for my self, my bare-knuckle fighter and three servants. But the word in Hobart is that she may not sail. This is a great shame, for we could have been in Sydney in eight days, a remarkable speed don't you think?' Not waiting for a response, he went on, 'So we will sail on the first ship out of Hobart bound for Sydney. It will take longer, but six hundred nautical miles of the Tasman Sea, is, as Tinker remarked on our way here, a lot of water to do "walkabout" in. They laughed, which eased the tension of the moment. All but Shenkin whose face remained sad, his jaw set, the scar on his face a deeper shade of blue. He would avenge Elizabeth, of that he was certain. One day soon he would be in front of Feltsham, then god help his lordship for no one else could. He would take their child to himself. He would call her Beth after her mother. In the afternoon's bright light, a silent tear rolled down Shenkin's scarred cheek; he had not shed a tear since as a boy he went down the deep coal pit of his South Wales valley and stood alone in the cold black darkness.

Regan looked at Shenkin, his jaw tightened and he sighed a sigh of pain at the sadness of it all.

Tinker looked at Sir Edward. 'Do we start our journey now? For the sooner we begin the better. The days are short here and darkness is not the ideal time for walkabout in these forests.'

Shenkin stood. 'Yes, let us begin for I am eager to get to Sydney,' he said, in a savage tone.

Charlie Benson placed his hand upon Shenkin's shoulder. 'Careful my friend, if you lose your temper, you lose the fight.'

'Have no fear Charlie, this is one fight I'll not risk losing. Now let us say goodbye to our whaleboat crew with thanks for all they have done. And to you, Captain Saxon, how can we ever repay you?'

'Why you have already Shenkin, by beating the man who broke my nose all those years ago.'

Charlie clipped him across the ear then gave him a farewell hug. 'See you in Sydney after your next voyage.'

'You will and under better circumstances, I am sure.'

Having said their goodbyes, they were soon on their way to Sorell. Tinker with a machete at the ready in his right hand took the lead, together with Shenkin, followed by Sir Edward, Regan and Charlie Benson. They had enough food for two days, after which Tinker told them they would live off the land. Sir Edward had a pistol and assured them that he was indeed a very fair shot; should game present itself they would have meat to eat. Tinker pointed out edible plants, snails and grubs that were favoured by his people. 'No, my friends, we will not go hungry for this land is full of many tasty eats,' he said, the wide smile never leaving his face.

For the first few hours Tinker kept up a fast pace, expertly swinging his machete left to right, cutting his way through the tough vegetation and undergrowth. Soon the growing darkness made it more and more difficult to make any headway. Huge trees towered over them; vines spread across their path causing them to trip or stumble. Shenkin was soon glad of the boots Owens had had made for them but even these after only the first day were cut and frayed. Sir Edward's fine clothes, which had been protected by the coach that had brought him from Hobart, were now stained by fruit juice, torn by barbed creepers and marked by droppings from the forested canopy above.

That evening Tinker, who had set such a punishing pace, quickly made a fire and with much relief, they all sat around it for a meal. The meal consisted of bread, preserved cabbage, some dried meat and tea. The water boiled over the fire in a cut down tin container that had been used to send bully beef to Sydney in British supply ships; they had turned out to make good teapots. As the pot swung to and fro over the fire, it became hypnotic in the fading light. No one spoke.

Tinker smiled his dazzling smile and said, 'Well, my white friends, are you finding the journey hard going?'

No one replied; they did not have the energy.

Tinker burst out laughing, startling multi-coloured birds from the trees around them. 'Come let us sleep, for there is much further to travel yet. We cannot take an easy route or a ride on a coach, for by now the penal colony at Port Arthur will have realised your escape,' said Tinker, trying to smother his laughter.

To complete his report on the death of the two convicts Acting Commandant Major William Walter Harris had gone with Medical Officer Captain Bickle to see the graves of the men on the Isle of the Dead. But they searched in vain for there was no sign of fresh graves to be found on the far side of the island or, for that matter, anywhere else on the island. One after the other of the guards returned to report to the commandant that they had found nothing.

Harris, by this time in a rage, turned his fury on the medical officer. 'You incompetent fool, they duped you. It was an escape, not typhus' he said, red in the face, his blood vessels standing out like the roots of trees.

'But...' Bickle began.

'Shut up, you imbecile. I'll have you removed from this command and reassigned to a company in the West Indies.'

Captain Charles Bickle's face sagged in horror at the commandant's words. 'Sir, I implore you to reconsider. I too was duped by my orderly and the crew of the whaleboat; it was all so feasible. I demand an investigation that will I am sure, vindicate my actions.'

Harris was hardly able to contain himself in front of the guards, who were by now enjoying the spectacle of one their officers being reprimanded. 'Demand, sir, demand? You poor excuse for an officer. You, sir, were the officer in charge and I sir, the senior officer in charge of the penal colony. Therefore, the final responsibility rests with me; do you understand the position you have placed me in? You, you...' But words failed Harris.

Turning to the guards he said, 'We return to the settlement in all haste to report the escape and you, sir,' turning back to Hunt, 'had better hope and pray that we recapture them soon.'

Within hours of their return from the Isle of the Dead, a full scale hunt was underway. Word of the escape spread like wildfire through the settlement. The two convicts who had taken Shenkin and Regan down to the jetty had two large glasses of rum in front of them and a wink from Medical Orderly Owens. Later in the commandant's office, stood Bickle, Owens and the convict overseers that had taken the escapees down to the boat.

Captain Bickle, who had wanted a full investigation, was nevertheless uncomfortable to find himself standing in line with orderlies and common convicts.

Major Harris cleared his throat, he was calmer now that a hunt for the escaped convict was in progress. He felt sure they would soon be recaptured and returned to Port Arthur where he would severely sentence them to punishment and extend their time at the penal colony by another five years.

Looking up from his paperwork he sat back in his chair, placed his hands on the table and began.

'This is a stain upon this administration during my watch, but I assure you that by the time Commandant Booth returns from London it will all be satisfactorily explained and cleared up. Those who are to blame due to their incompetence, will no longer be here.' Acting Commandant Harris turned his head and looked directly at Medical Officer Bickle. 'Your account of the matter, sir, if you please,' he said, sarcastically.

Bickle swallowed hard but his voice still sounded dry and cracked. 'I examined the men when they were brought to the hospital from a work gang, both showed every symptom of typhus. This was confirmed by Orderly Owens who had seen it many time in his medical practice in London,' said Bickle, looking over to Owens.

'Is this correct, Owens? ' said Harris.

'Well not really, sir I'm sorry to say.'

Before he could say more, Bickle screamed at him, 'What do you mean not really? Why, it was you who said everything pointed to typhus, he is nothing more then a lying little jumped-up quack, sir.'

Harris was on his feet. 'Hold your tongue man; if you attempt to disrupt this investigation I'll see to it that you face a court marshal, do I make myself clear, sir?'

'Yes, sir.'

'Continue, Owens.'

'Well sir, with all respect to Medical Officer Bickle, what I said was, if you think it's typhus, Doctor then it must be, for you are the one with medical qualifications not me. I swear, sir, that was all I said.'

Owens looked over at Captain Bickle who had turned a sickly white. 'But...' he stammered.

The Commandant cut him short. 'For the last time, sir, hold your tongue damn it.'

Owens turned to Bickle. 'Sorry sir, we've worked together for some time now and you have always been good to me, but I cannot lie to the commandant can I?'

Harris was writing it all down in a flurry and dip of his pen.

'However, I understand from Captain Bickle that you arranged the boat and crew,' said Harris. 'Is that true?'

Owens made a facial grimace. 'Yes and no, sir, you see I did suggest I may be able to borrow a boat from friends down the coast a little way, honest men, sir, why they are former convicts of this here penal colony, sir.'

'Get to the point man,' said Harris, impatiently.

'Yes, sir. Sorry, sir.'

'Well sir, Captain Bickle asked how long this would take. A couple of days, I said. At this I was told to find any boat near at hand sir.'

'No! This is simply not true,' said Bickle, loosening the collar of his uniform.

The Commandant turned to his medical officer. 'You are I see, determined to face a court marshal, are you not?'

'No sir, but if we could only speak in private…'

Harris cut him short again. 'For the last time remain quiet, or so help me, I will order you be placed under guard.'

Bickle seemed to shrivel up, his whole body sank into itself.

'Go on, Owens,' said the commandant, in exasperation.

'Well sir, it just happens there was a whaleboat near the jetty, fishing they was and not aware of the restriction of sailing so close to the penal colony, sir. So I called out and advised them that if they could do the settlement a favour, we would overlook their trespass. I'm sure we should have sought your permission first sir, but the captain was in a hurry to get rid of these, what he called, transmittable contaminated men. I'm not sure what that means sir, but it sounded really bad.'

Turning to the convict overseers, Harris asked them, 'Did you know this was not the settlement's boat?' Not about to incriminate themselves in a course of action contrary to the commandant's knowledge, to a man they said, 'No, sir.'

One of them spoke up, 'We were acting under Captain Bickle's orders sir.'

Major Harris placed his pen down very slowly. He called for his outside guards. On their entering the office, he told them to escort Owens and the overseers back to their duties.

Turning to Bickle he said, 'You will remain here for immediate orders.'

A beaten man, Bickle simply said, 'Yes sir.'

After what seemed an eternity, the commandant finished writing.

Placing paperwork and pen to one side, he addressed the medical officer in a sober precise manner.

'Captain Charles Bickle, Medical Officer of Port Arthur penal colony, after considering all the facts that led up to the escape of two convicts I find you negligent in every aspect of the matter.'

Bickle began to speak, but the major raised his hand. 'You will hear me out sir,' said Harris, continuing.

'You will return to the officers' quarters where you will commence packing in readiness to leave the Port Arthur settlement. You will remain confined to your quarters until your replacement has arrived from Hobart Town. On leaving, you will have with you a letter stating my recommendation that you be placed in a less responsible post in the West Indies, possibly as an orderly to a doctor on one of the garrisons there.' Raising a sheet of report paper Harris said, 'This also gives my reasons why. You will present it on arrival in England and await your next posting on half pay.'

For heartbeats the only sound was the muffled voices from the outside office the wind, the shout of a guard, and Bickle's whimper.

Placing the report in an envelope, Harris sealed it with wax then imprinted it with the colony's stamp and handed it to a broken man. 'You are dismissed sir.'

CHAPTER 22

'How long now?' said Regan, sweat running down his face, arms, neck and everything that moved in between.

'Not long now,' said Tinker, with a grin. Looking as if this was no more then a gentle stroll.

'You said that hours ago,' said Sir Edward, his fine clothing now torn damp rags, his fine silver-buckled shoes in shreds.

Tinker smiled. 'Your hours ago Sir Edward, not mine. Sorell first, then the Derwent River: lots of whaling ships there so we can get across to Hobart Town.'

'But when?' said Standish.

Tinker spoke but without stopping, 'When we arrive Sir Edward, is when we are there. We stay tonight at the village of a tribe I know, where we will rest and sleep. You will eat what you are given or you will offend my people,' he said, it was not open to discussion.

Regan looked behind to Shenkin who simply shrugged his shoulders. He did not care.

It had been four days now of relentless walking, up to ten hours a day. Days of continual struggle against the dense forest of vegetation, flies, and biting mosquitoes. It was beginning to take its toll on everyone except Tinker.

Shenkin his face a mask of determination, was driven on by his hatred, a hatred so strong he could almost taste it. He spoke to no one, he ate alone and walked alone. Regan kept an eye on him but did not try to intervene for he knew only too well how dangerous Shenkin was in this mood. Nor did any of the others they just followed Tinker in a steady, if exhausting, step after step of growing fatigue and tangled undergrowth. The trail that Tinker took avoided all tracks known to any European. On it, they encountered every form of species except human. At the end of another exhausting day, they reached the aboriginal settlement. It was deep in the forest where a clearing had been made and a number of shelters were erected, all of which looked very fragile to Shenkin. They were nothing more then bent leaning branches covered in what appeared to be bamboo or rattan.

An old man walked towards them and greeted Tinker. 'Ya pulingina Warron-wurrah.' Tinker bowed his head. They spoke together for some time during which more men, women and children came out of their crude dwellings to join them. They walked around the group of pale men. Then what seemed for no reason, they began to dance, dust flew up from the forest floor like a brown carpet, a chant began and grew into a chorus of song. An instrument like a long tube was being blown into. It sounded like the steady thump of a heart, the dance became quicker, the chant louder. It was spellbinding. They watched captivated by the moment, even Shenkin seemed enthralled. The elder raised his hands and, as suddenly as it had begun, it stopped.

Tinker rejoined them. 'The elder says we are welcome, their land is our land, their food is our food and we are welcome as friends of Warrah. Also that a shelter will be erected for us to sleep in tonight. Tomorrow two of his tribe will lead us to the great river,' said Tinker.

'How far?' said Charlie Benson.

Tinker smiled. 'Not far.'

'Will we get there tomorrow, the next day, next week?' asked Regan, trying another way.

'When we arrive, then we will get there Regan,' said Tinker, which ended the conversation. They all followed Tinker into the middle of the settlement. Darkness fell as if someone had dropped a black cape over them. Soon camp fires lighted the night, pots swung over the burning embers, the smell of meat cooking drifted in the air and all of them became hungry. But first colourful berries were produced with side helpings of small white grubs and beetles. Hungry or not, they hesitated. Tinker spoke to them in a steady flow of English, his words edged with annoyance. 'You will eat, do not embarrass me in front of my people,' he said.

Shenkin was the first to try. Starting with the berries, he unhurriedly moved his fingers into the crude wooden bowls of beetles and grubs, many of which were still moving. He gulped down fast, while trying to keep a grimace off of his face. Slowly, the rest followed; each had a small amount and stopped. Tinker raised his voice but with a smile on his face, as if to say, it is good isn't it? Then he spoke, 'You will eat it all.'

'Is there anything to drink, Tinker, just to wash it down like?' said Regan.

Tinker spoke to the elder who had now joined them. The rest of the tribe were tucking into the grubs.

'We are going to be given way-a-linah; it is from the eucalyptus tree. It is like your cider drink, but much stronger for it is fermented gum,' said Tinker, with relish; this was a favourite alcoholic drink of the tribe.

While they struggled with the food, the aboriginals began to fill coconut half shells with the cider-like drink.

Regan's eyes lit up as he reached for the nearest bowl but Tinker stopped him. 'Sorry Regan, but you must finish your very tasty berries and grubs first, only then can you drink,' he said. Adding, 'it is not done,'

Sir Edward Standish laughed out loud. 'And you thought it was only the upper class gentry that pursued such frivolous forms of good manners. It seems we have much to learn from our black cousins.'

Tinker bathed in pride at these comments. 'Many thousands of years before the white man Sir Edward.'

'I am sure Tinker, for we are slow starters but we know the value of good form,' said Sir Edward, as he inclined his head.

Finally, the first course was eaten by all and the drinks were passed around. Regan sighed.

Large palm leaves were filled with the meat of unknown animals; however, the smell was mouth-watering to the hungry travellers. Sitting around the camp fire, they were all soon eating the food ravenously. No prompting was needed this time from Tinker. The velvet dark night was at peace. Apart from some birds and forest animals moving in the black reaches of the settlement perimeter, the world around them was silent. The fires sent columns of red sparks into the air to join the white jewels of stars. Sir Edward Standish turned to Shenkin. 'What have we lost, us Europeans, in our avariciousness for wealth and power.'

Shenkin guilty in this moment of peace, looked at Sir Edward. 'We have lost the simple joy of life, the wonder of our surroundings. We have paid this price for a so-called sophistication, which we call civilisation,' he said, with sadness.

'Indeed we have my friend, such a high cost this loss of our humanity.'

Shenkin nodded his head. 'We are all guilty, Sir Edward.'

The meal over, Shenkin asked Tinker to thank the elder for such a good meal and asked if he could tell them what the meat was.

Tinker said he would but wondered if Shenkin was sure he wanted to know what the meat was.

'Yes,' said Shenkin. 'We may have the opportunity to hunt for this animal on our continued journey to Hobart.'

'Very well,' said Tinker. Addressing the elder he expressed his friend's appreciation and then the enquiry.

The old man talked in a tone of reverence and excitement; all around the rest of the tribe cheered his words, some pointed to the forest, others to a wooden frame from which hung some dead animals.

They all turned to look at Tinker as he translated, 'It is a mix of meat from two forest animals my friends.' He paused.

'Well what is it?' said Charlie Benson, biting into his last piece of meat.

'Rats and possums,' said Tinker, adding, 'good yes?'

If the silence was profound a moment ago, it was now shattering.

Charlie slowly put down his handful of meat. Regan's hand moved quickly to the cider.

Tinker hooted with delight. 'Well, you wanted to know. Now we must sleep because I am told our quarters are ready and we have a long walk ahead of us, and we may be fortunate enough to catch a few rats along the way for our meal tomorrow night.' He was plainly enjoying himself at their discomfort.

For some time no one spoke. Then Sir Edward remarked that maybe the tables of London would appreciate the delicacy, for there are many rats in London.

'Good food while reducing the pest population at the same time. What say you all?' he said, with as much good grace as he could muster. No one responded. Regan burped, which caused a collective moan to run through them. The old man smiled; he felt sure this was a sign of how much they had enjoyed their feast, and offered Regan another helping. Regan smiled a sickly smile and quickly shook his head. To the aborigines, their guests seemed a little paler if that was possible. Perhaps it was because they were tired, but at least they had enjoyed their meal. The elder raised his hand and out of the darkness came dancers. They had finger paint on their bodies and faces; it was a primitive scene that had been performed countless times over thousands of years.

'We are honoured,' said Tinker. 'This dance is not normally performed for outsiders. It is a sacred dance to thank the animals for their sacrifice in giving us themselves to eat. I have only seen it a few times myself.' There was no smile on Tinker's face now it was as if he was in his church of nature, which was solemn and sacred.

Shenkin turned to Sir Edward. 'We have indeed lost a great deal, even possibly our souls.'

Finally, the dance came to an ear-splitting earth-pounding climax.

In the silence that followed the night closed in on them and, stomach upsets or not, under the stars with the warmth of the fires washing over them, they slept soundly.

Come morning in the early light, they were soon ready to go on. The elder had introduced them to their guides, both powerfully built young men who Shenkin recognised from the dance of the night before, but now all traces of the body paint had been removed. Both carried a small spear, a leather pouch of food and some water. Food and water was also given to each of the Europeans with a great deal of ceremony and good wishes for the walkabout to the great river. Shenkin hoped it was not rat meat but said nothing.

The day began well enough, but by midday heavy rain began to fall; their guides assured them it would not last long. However, in a very short time they were drenched, the track became mud covered and treacherous under-foot. Tinker talked in low tones to his fellow aborigines, then turning to Shenkin, he said, 'We will find cover and wait for the rain to stop. To go on I am concerned about the risk of you tripping on the vegetation and sliding in the mud. We cannot afford an injury now.'

All were in agreement. The guides soon had a shelter built for them, and a fire, with some difficulty, was started. The aborigines ate their food with relish, the escapees with reservations which were washed down quickly with the water. Tinker advised them to refill their water carriers with fresh rainwater that was running off the big leaves of their shelter. After a short while the sun came back out, the warm rays penetrating the canopy of the tall trees above them causing steam to rise from the forest floor like a white blanket. Their guides waited for the fog-like steam to clear so they could see the path ahead of them. Soon they were again on their way. Tinker explained that they were travelling to a place above Sorell which would bring them above the waterfront of the town. Then they would continue to the Derwent River where hopefully they would find a ship's captain who would take them across the river to Hobart. No one asked Tinker how long this would take. They were slowly settling into the dream world of the aboriginal people. 'Today is not ours but that of the land around us; tomorrow will come when it is ready, but not before.' and so it was.

Their journey and time became nothing but a walk forward through the tangled undergrowth, the primitive land around them unchanged since the beginning of time. Shenkin felt, if not at peace, at least reconciled to the moment.

During the day they saw a wallaby and Sir Edward was as good as his word. He shot it at a considerable range, much to the alarm of their guides who nevertheless had it hung between them in less then an hour. Shortly afterwards, they settled down for the night. The guides expertly skinned the wallaby the meat was cut off the beast and was soon roasting on a fire. The aroma caught the night air, bringing flies, possums and wombats to the feast. The following day, the aborigines let loose with their spears, bringing down two possums and a wombat. They would not go hungry, at least is was not rat meat.

Late that same evening Regan walked over to where Shenkin was sitting alone. 'And how are we now?' he said.

'It's eating away at me Regan. I can't stop thinking of Elizabeth, her death caused by that bastard Feltsham. I'll kill him I swear it.'

'And I'll help, so I will, but we have to get there first,' said Regan, his tone firm.

'I know, but it is too slow with the need for revenge moving so fast in my mind.'

Regan remained silent.

Shenkin his face drawn, his voice full of grief at the loss of the one that he had loved. 'Dear god Regan, she's gone.'

Regan looked at Shenkin with pain in his eyes. 'I know, I know it's hard to take but there it is,' he said in a tight strained voice. 'But we must go on; we cannot change it, but bear it as best we can.'

Shenkin said nothing, his mind a turmoil of anger and unused adrenalin. He felt the desperate frustration of not being able to confront Feltsham there and then and with Sydney still so far away.

'And what will you call this fine daughter of yours? And don't tell me you do not care,' said Regan.

Shenkin lifted his head slowly, he mumbled something under his breath.

'What's that you say?' said Regan, leaning forward. 'Speak up damn you, for I'll not believe you have not thought of it.'

'Beth,' said Shenkin, in a still lightly trembling voice.

Regan smiled. 'Beth, is it after her mother? Well her godfather likes it so he does. Beth,' he said in full voice. 'Yes I like it for it warms my heart. Elizabeth would have approved too, so she would. Yes, Beth,' he repeated as he began to walk away.

Shenkin's eyes followed the Irishman whose heart was as big as his body. Shenkin called after him, 'Regan.'

Regan turned. The firelight caught the tears running down his strong powerful face. After a moment, he said, 'This damn smoke gets into your eyes. What is it now then?'

'Thank you.'

'Now don't go soft on me, and me with my stomach full of bloody live grubs.' They both laughed out loud, causing Sir Edward and Tinker to turn around.

'Well now that's an improvement,' said Sir Edward, Tinker smiled, his white teeth shining in the firelight.

The following morning, Tinker announced they had to cross an area of land where an unfriendly tribe lived. Settling down on his haunches by the last embers of the fire and in a solemn tone, he spoke to them. 'Since the late 1820s my people have been involved in what is called the Black War. The fighting became so fierce it prompted Lieutenant Governor George Arthur to declare martial law. This the European settlers believed, gave them the legal right to hunt and kill aboriginal people. Soon the native hunting grounds were becoming less and less, food more difficult to gather. Tribes desperately defended their lands. The fighting by this time, had broken out right across the island. By 1830 with British settlers wanting more and more land, a military offensive was created, made up of solders and civilians who formed a line, known as the Black Line, across the island stretching hundreds of kilometres to push the aboriginal people from the colony's settled districts into the Tasman Peninsula and to keep them there.' Then with sadness, Tinker added, 'It is believed that well over a thousand or more aboriginals have already died. Martial Law against the aboriginals ended in 1832. After a while much of the warring ceased, but in pockets it is still happening. In this place we now find ourselves, a kind of "clean up" operation began. Any aboriginals that are captured are forcibly removed to Hunter Island or a detention camp on Flinders Island,' said Tinker.

No one spoke. Tinker took a deep breath. 'So it means we are in danger of being attacked.' He looked around at the small group. There was a deep silence, for long heartbeats no one spoke.

Finally, Shenkin said, 'But the tribe we stayed with who fed us and made us welcome. Why would they do that when they are at war with Europeans?'

Tinker smiled. 'They took my word that you were my friends; it was enough.'

Shenkin sighed. 'Sir Edward is right we have much to learn from your peoples, Tinker.'

'We do indeed,' said Sir Edward.

'If we are seen, we may be considered a hunting party looking for aboriginals, that's your concern Tinker, isn't it?' said Shenkin.

'Yes,' he said.

But we have two, no three, aboriginals counting you with us, Tinker,' said Sir Edward.

'Hired by settlers as guides,' said Tinker, flatly.

Charlie Benson stood up. 'Then how do we cross this part of the land Tinker? We have no weapons apart from Sir Edward's pistol. Can you go ahead and tell them we are friendly?'

Tinker swept his hand across the dense forest around them. 'Where are they?'

Shenkin stared into the thick vegetated darkness of the way ahead. He could see perhaps a few feet past the big trees and tangle of undergrowth.

'So what do we do?'

Tinker stood up. 'We leave the trail and cut our way though the forest; it will take longer and it will be harder, but safer.'

'How much longer?' asked Charlie Benson.

'We will know that when we arrive,' said Tinker.

Shenkin shrugged his broad shoulders. 'Well then, the sooner we begin the sooner we'll know.'

Collecting their belongings, the water and food they left the trail. The two guides were aware that they would have to do this and had already begun the cutting of a new path.

If the last part of their journey had been difficult, it was a gentle amble compared to what they had to endure in only the first few hours of the day. By nightfall they collapsed exhausted onto the ground while the guides began to light the evening fire. They had lacerations on their legs, arms, hands and faces. Charlie Benson dabbed at a cut on his cheek. 'My god, it's like fighting twenty rounds with an invisible opponent,' he said, to no one in particular. 'Those sharp leaves that spring at you and the roots that trip you up. Please tell us Tinker, how long we must endure this.'

'For as long as it takes,' he said.

No one replied; they were too tired. Shenkin looked around at Sir Edward and Charlie Benson.

'I am sorry my friends to have submitted you to this.'

Sir Edward Standish stood up, his fine clothes almost in rags but still every inch the English aristocrat that he was. 'Think nothing of it my dear fellow, why at my public school at Harrow this was nothing more then a pleasant game of paper-chase across Harrow-on-the-Hill, a mere bagatelle don't you know.' He then collapsed to the ground, a line of the blood running down his left leg staining what was left of the fine silk of his trousers.

Charlie Benson smiled. 'I've known harder opponents, you for instance.'

Shenkin grinned. 'Anyway, Regan and I thank you both, you too, Tinker.'

Tinker nodded. 'We continue, yes?'

'Yes,' came a chorus of voices. Their guides looked on in wonder at this strange group of pale-faced men.

CHAPTER 23

For the next long exhausting days they fought their way through the seemingly impenetrable forest. They walked by trees whose branches reached to the sky and formed a canopy so thick that day became night and whose girth was three times the length of a man, with roots that held the earth like the fingers of a giant. The vegetation was a dense blanket of tangled growth that their aboriginal guides fought a footfall at a time. As night fell on that fifth night, or was it the sixth night for all was becoming one in their walking nightmare that measured its days a footfall at a time. Each evening they fell to the ground exhausted so glad to finally stop to drink some water, eat some food and sleep.

Tinker decided they would only have a few hours sleep at a time, more would tighten up their muscles. A shelter was built each night, fires lit and makeshift beds prepared. While they rested the aboriginals hunted for fresh meat, while Tinker made up balm for their wounds.

Sitting in a circle, they slowly and delicately treated themselves. Some of the cuts had become infected, making them inflamed and painful to the touch.

Regan, his big hands carefully spreading the balm over his arms, groaned as he found a needle of a plant that had driven itself under the skin. The worst of the vegetation they had encountered was the aptly named sword-sedge its needle-sharp leaf cut deep into their flesh.

As usual the temperature was dropping after the heat of the day, causing a chill to fall over their encampment. Having smeared the ointment over his arms and legs, Regan walked over to the fire to warm his hands.

No one knew where they came from the first sounded like the flight of a swift bird, then another sound: this time a twirling air-swishing flurry. They both found their targets, the spear went into Regan with a sickening thud, the other into the back of one of their guides. Sir Edward pulled his pistol and fired into the darkness of the forest. Tinker threw water over the fire.

Shenkin rushed to Regan's side and began to pull at the spear. Tinker let out a scream, 'Don't Shenkin, it's barbed.' The other aboriginal turned his friend over, the axe head was buried deep in his fellow aboriginal's back. He was dead.

Shenkin cradled Regan in his arms, he was conscious but only just. Tinker came to their side. 'Regan, listen I am going turn you on to your good side. Can you hear me?'

'Yes.'

Carefully, Shenkin and Tinker turned him over. The point of the spear-head was just visible below the skin. Tinker drew his knife and swiftly made a criss-cross cut over the point. Regan passed out.

'We are going to have to push the spear through his side,' he said.

Charlie Benson and Shenkin held Regan firm. Sir Edward and the surviving guide kept guard but it had gone quiet, not a sound not a movement of bush or leaf. It was as if they had simply disappeared.

With a forward push from Tinker, the spearhead broke through the skin. Bending forward, he cut the stone-barbed head of the spear off and swiftly drew out the spear's shaft from Regan's back. He had plugs of clay ready to seal off the wounds front and back. 'I need to prepare a herbal compound,' he said, leaving them.

They placed Regan down but blood was seeping through the plugs at a steady rate.

Shenkin shook his head. 'We are paying a heavy price, Charlie.'

'We are and it's not over yet.'

Standish was at their side. 'How is he?' he said.

'Not good,' said Shenkin.

That night Regan became delirious; the fever simply went up and up. Tinker had made up a compound from different plants but it just did not bring the temperature down. Finally, he told Shenkin he was going to lance the wound in an effort to remove the infection. With Shenkin holding a burning torch, Tinker cut into the wound. It was as well that Regan was unconscious, for pus and blood came out like a fountain spray.

Tinker, having redressed the wound, turned to everyone around him. 'Now we wait, he will either survive the night or not.'

Shenkin sat with him through the long night. Come morning, Charlie Benson brought Shenkin some hot tea and a dry biscuit.

'Well, how is he?'

Shenkin sighed. 'Not good, it's been a bad night.'

'I heard his calls and moans during my guard duty Shenkin, it looks bad.'

Sir Edward joined them, followed by Tinker and their remaining guide.

Regan's eyes fluttered open but the pain was clear to see. Tinker moistened Regan's lips then examined the wound. He looked at Shenkin and shook his head. After a moment Regan looked up at them, then in a slow hardly audible voice, he said, 'I cannot go on Shenkin, it will slow you up you'll never get out of this tangled jungle.' The effort was almost too much for him to bear.

'Nonsense, we'll carry you out,' said Shenkin. All of them except Tinker agreed.

'We must face the truth that is before us my friends, it would be impossible to carry him out. He would be dead before we covered less then a half a day's walking,' said Tinker.

Shenkin turned on Tinker in a fury at such an acceptance of failure, but Tinker simply smiled a slow, knowing smile.

'I know how you feel how you all feel, the European thinks he is able to control his life and death but it is not so. Inside himself, Regan knows he is dying, for his body tells him. We have just made his last few hours as comfortable as we can, there is nothing more we can do.' With that, Tinker turned back to the clearing to help his fellow aborigine bury the killed guide and to break camp. Later to their horror, Tinker began to dig a second grave. Having done so he returned to the still silent group.

Shenkin finally spoke. 'But there must be something we can do, Tinker.'

'There is, we go on,' he said. It was a flat statement. 'First we bury our dead, the tribe that did this will not disturb the graves, for we believe the bodies are back to mother earth where we all belong. Then we must leave as soon as we can.'

At that moment Regan gave a deep cough, causing a froth of blood to come flowing to his lips. Shenkin moved quickly to his side. Regan gripped his hand tightly, then in a small voice he said, 'May your god go with you Shenkin, for I no longer can.' With that, the once powerful grip on Shenkin's hand went limp, the massive head lolled to one side but the eyes remained open. The wild light in them had gone out. Regan was dead. Shenkin leaned forward and closed Regan's eyes. He held Regan's head in his arms and in a moment of deep emotion, he kissed his friend gently on the cheek, then more urgently as if this would bring the big man back, but Regan O'Hara had, god willing, finally gone home to his beloved Ireland. It was the end of a friendship that had endured so much. The tragic ending of a political uprising, the horror of a convict ship, the brutal beatings in the prison barracks in Sydney and Port Arthur penal colony and the many loved ones and friends that had died along the way. So much, so much Shenkin's body seemed to shrink; his soul cried out in pain. 'No! No!' he screamed, causing the birds of the forest to cry out in mocking imitation.

Sir Edward and Charlie Benson lifted Shenkin to his feet. In a small low voice, Sir Edward said, 'He is dead Shenkin, but we must go on. We have aboriginals all around us, the guards and officers of Port Arthur behind us. Both determined to catch us or kill us.'

Shenkin took one last look down at Regan; to go on without him seemed impossible but he knew Standish was right.

They cut a cross, placing it deep in the earth at the top of a mound of stones. Tinker had begun to carve Regan's name and date of death on it, but Shenkin insisted on doing it. Then with one final look at both the graves, they continued to make their way to the Derwent River in silence.

Shenkin's sorrow was palpable, the rage in every fibre of his body at the man responsible for all of this. First the death of Elizabeth, and now Regan. He vowed Feltsham would pay the heaviest of tolls. His need for this vengeance would get him through all that now stood between him and Sydney until the final day of reckoning.

CHAPTER 24

Tinker pushed them hard day after day after day until even he had to call a halt, he could see that the Europeans were near the very end of their stamina.

'We rest here for a while,' he said. A sigh of relief went up from the group as one after the other they fell to the ground worn out. They had seen no sign of the tribe of aboriginals. Tinker said this did not mean that they were not being watched. From time to time they heard the sound of dogs in the distance. These dogs were from the Eaglehawk Neck kennels at Port Arthur trained to hunt for runaway convicts, vicious brutal animals deliberately underfed to sharpen their hunger. 'They are no more then a day behind us,' said Tinker. adding, 'they can also use the trodden trail making their speed much faster, perhaps just a few hours rest then we need to move on.'

No one argued; their lives were at stake.

The following hours of walking took its toll until Tinker was forced again to stop.

Behind them, Major Harris was on horseback. He had guards, dog handlers and soldiers with him. He cursed the overhanging branches and dense vegetation that blocked their way, even on what the guides called the normal open trail through the primeval forest.

'Bloody country, bloody convicts and this bloody forest,' he said out loud. He had not stopped bemoaning his lot since leaving his quarters at Port Arthur. He'd see these men hung and those that had helped them put in chains. His report to Hobart had been painful to write for however he had tried to word it, the fact was that it was his responsibility, his fault. 'The bastards,' he uttered again and again.

Major Harris came from a military family who regarded his posting to a penal colony on the other side of the world as offering no advancement to their youngest son's military career. The son of a father whose eldest son had distinguished himself at Waterloo and had been posthumously awarded the KCB medal while leading a courageous charge right at the centre of the French attack. The Knight Commander of the Order of the Bath medal now hung in the main hall of the family's mansion in Surrey above which was the painted portrait in full dress uniform of their beloved son. Harris's father Colonel Wilfred James Harris, had been mentioned in despatches, then decorated during the British Expedition to Ceylon. His grandfather and great-grandfather were both soldiers with outstanding military careers. The walls of the great hall dripped with medals and flags. Their youngest son the now Acting Commandant of Port Arthur Penal Colony, was under achieving, unnoticed and under-represented in the great hall. What this Harris needed was a war or, failing that, a position of respect and authority in this new world. The thought stirred him in his saddle, he would distinguish himself regardless of the cost. So saying, he turned in the saddle and called back.

'Give the dogs their heads man, let's get this done.'

' Yes, sir.' But the man knew better than to just let them go, for he'd never stop them or catch up with them. It took all his strength just to hold onto them.

Harris had sent word to the River Derwent and Port Hobart to watch out for the fugitives. Constables and military personnel had been issued with the description of the convicts. He was confident they would be caught, but he had to lead the pursuit for the sake of appearance and his reputation.

A guide came up to him. 'Fresh graves sir, dug not more then a day ago.' Harris spurred his horse into a canter, or as much as the dense undergrowth allowed. He dismounted near a group of his men. 'Well, where are they?'

'Over here, sir.'

The two graves were close together. One was short but wide with a big flat stone over it; the other was much larger and had a wooden cross at the top of a mound of stones. Harris bent down to read the scratched writing on the cross.

Here lies the body of REGAN O'HARA an IRISHMAN freed at last from his bonds. R.I.P. my friend.

Harris got to his feet. 'And the other grave?' Hope in his voice that it would be Shenkin's.

One of the men stepped forward. 'An aboriginal sir, they bury them in a crouched position with just this flat stone as a marker. Sometimes they are cremated but there would not have been the time to do so, sir.'

'Right, dig the convict up. We'll take him back as an example to others.'

'With respect sir, he'll already be decomposing sir, even after this short time and he'll stink to bloody heaven. Begging your pardon sir,' said the guard, touching his hat.

'Yes, yes, very well, but take the cross as evidence.'

'Yes sir,' said the guard, adding, 'begging your pardon sir. We have a slight problem with one of our aboriginals sir.'

'Well what is it man? I am anxious to get on. Where are the guides?'

'That's just it sir, one is very drunk, on gum tree beer I suspect,' said the corporal.

'Drunk,' screamed Harris. 'Bring him to me I'll teach the bastard.'

The aboriginal stumbled forward. The soldiers each side of him let him go, he promptly fell to the ground.

'The other guide refuses to take us further sir, without his brother,' said the corporal.

'Really,' said Harris dismounting.

He walked slowly up to the prone figure of the man, then turned to the sergeant at his side. 'Hang him and make sure his brother sees every twist and turn of the drunken body.'

'But…' started the sergeant.

Major Harris tapped his riding crop onto his polished boot. 'Unless you wish to join him for disobeying an order.'

'Sir. Williams, and you Johnson, get a rope onto that tree. Phillips, bring his brother forward.'

'Sir.'

Not knowing what was happening, the aboriginal offered no resistance and was soon swinging from the branch of a gum tree, which Harris thought was very appropriate.

'Ask his brother if he is prepared to lead us on or does he wish to hang on the other branch?'

The look on the aboriginal's face said it all; he quickly moved to the front of the trail to lead them forward.

The sergeant asked about the body still swinging on the tree.

'Cut it down, Sergeant and throw it into the bushes. I haven't got the time to waste in digging a grave, damn it.'

'Sir.'

Harris remounted, then turned to the men. 'Well get them moving,

Sergeant. We have found one, even if he is dead. If we find the other also rotting below a cross then this may yet turn out a success.'

The faint sound of the dogs carried over the early morning air, bringing both men, birds and beasts into activity.

Shenkin's mind was still full of sorrow at the loss of Regan, who for so many years had been the first person he saw on any day. The big Irishman's usual snoring would keep him awake, how he had complained about it and how now did he wish for that disturbance.

Sir Edward stood above him. 'Time to move. They seem to be getting closer, Shenkin.'

'Indeed they do; perhaps we'll never get out.'

'You are despondent my friend, because of Regan but you owe it to him to get back to Sydney, to us all for that matter.'

Slowly, Shenkin got to his feet. 'I'm sorry, you're right. It's just this terrible moment of loss.' With that, Shenkin went over by Tinker at the head of their now smaller group. The rhythm of their machetes, which were fifteen inches long, began to sing in the morning air. Hour after hour, the two aboriginals scathed their way ahead. At midday they stopped for water and something light to eat. Dried fruit, nuts and small tree grubs for the aboriginals. Shenkin thought how Regan would have reacted to this, it raised a smile to his dry sun-cracked lips as Regan's voice echoed in his mind. He was brought back to the moment by Tinker.

Sitting on an uprooted tree Tinker talked in a slow low voice. 'We have been making no more than six miles a day because of the difficult route and the tribe that attacked us, but I can now tell you that with one final effort, my fellow aboriginal tells me, we will be on the part of the Derwent River that we need to be within one more moon rise.'

Charlie Benson stood up. 'One day only, why we can do it after all,' he said, slapping Sir Edward on the back. They all began to talk at once.

Tinker raised his hands. When he finally had quiet, he again spoke slowly but very deliberately. 'But first we need to rejoin the trail, which I know you will be pleased to hear. However, we will again become more in danger from both the Port Arthur men and the aboriginals.'

Shenkin looked at Tinker. 'But they could have attacked us at any time, Tinker.'

Tinker shook his head. 'No, the dense forest made it difficult for them to run away, and they know we have a gun.'

Within a few hours, they were again on the open trail. Progress was much faster and with the increasing speed their high spirits increased. By mid-morning, on a large clearing, they could see the river in the distance.

'We've made it,' shouted Charlie Benson. His shout was cut short by a spear thudding into his back. Sir Edward span around and fired into the bush, first left then right, but his shots were no more then random aims for he could see no one. Shenkin was at Charlie Benson's side.

'Charlie speak to me, how bad is it?'

Stirring, he tried to sit up but collapsed immediately onto his side, the spear sticking out of his back obscenely, as if it had taken root in his body. 'I can hardly breath Shenkin, for god's sake remove it.' The words came in short bursts of gulped air.

'Tinker,' called Shenkin, but he was already at his side.

'It's impossible to remove it; it's in the centre of his back, the tip is barbed and it would kill him straight away if we were to try. It has penetrated his lungs; a weaker man would be dead by now,' said Tinker, standing back, his gaze turned to scan the bush around them. A dog barked somewhere in the valley behind them. Their elation of only moments ago dashed. 'I can cut the spear's shaft to make him more comfortable if we support the entry area, but nothing more.' Tinker's ready smile was long gone. Three were lost now because he knew there was only a short time left for Charlie Benson.

'Dear god Charlie, I am so sorry; this is all my fault.'

'I don't remember you twisting my arm Shenkin. We all came with our eyes wide open. Listen to me, on our journey these past days,' he said, but he had to stop for breath, then continued. 'I thought, if anything happened to me what would I want done?'

Shenkin tried to stop him. 'Save your strength Charlie, please.'

'For what? You heard what Tinker said. So listen damn it, this is my last round my friend, and I'm not going to hear the count.' Blood came to his lips as he spoke, it was Regan's death all over again.

Part choking, part trying to breathe, he said, 'In my vest pocket are the deeds to my farm. At the farm in a safe, you will find all my personal documents. An ex-convict named Tommy Bright runs the place while I'm away; he'll know how to open it.' Having to stop again for a moment he went on, 'He's a good man Shenkin, you can trust him. He used to be my cuts man for many years; like you and Regan we've been though a lot together, so you can trust him. I've spoken about you to him so he knows everything.'

Again Shenkin placed his hand on Charlie's shoulder, pleading for him to rest.

'I'll soon have plenty of it my friend, so listen.' Taking a deep painful breath, Charlie Benson summoned up his last remaining strength. 'You must become me.' Shenkin pulled away.

'What?' said Shenkin in astonishment.

He grabbed Shenkin's arm. 'Listen to me, it's the perfect solution to your problems: we're the same height, same build. If you cut off your pigtail, grey your hair, your beard is already grown, then have Tinker make a scar above your left eye to match mine. Hell no one would know the difference, Shenkin, you'd be accepted as me.' Benson quickly went on, 'No sentence hanging over you, land to work and the start of a new life.' Charlie gave a deep sigh; his body went limp.

Shenkin again tried to say something.

'Damn it, do it, Shenkin. Then none of this will be in vain.'

'But it should all go to your brother.'

'I'll dictate a note to Sir Edward giving the location of the farm and explaining everything. My brother will not leave the sea to run a farm, he has told me so many times, so sell the animals and give the proceeds to him. Hurry now, for I feel I have only a short time and I need paper and pen. Sir Edward keeps a diary so he'll have the makings.' All this while blood and gasping for breath racked his body.

In a short time it was done and signed, leaving the property and deeds to Shenkin. 'You'll need this Shenkin, only if you're found out.'

When he was finished, he turned to Shenkin. 'It's been a great fight Shenkin, by proxy I'll stand in your corner. It will be an honour for me that you carry my fighting name. Do it man, and take your revenge for us all. Why, you could even fight for the championship of New South Wales.' He began coughing again; it brought up thick clots of blood. When the attack was over, he added, 'remember the cross on my grave needs to read, "Here lies Daniel Shenkin" An hour later Charlie Benson was dead.

Shenkin again found himself carving a name and date on a soft wood cross, but this time it was his own name that he scratched. It weighed heavy both on his shoulders and mind that he was now replacing Charlie Benson's life with his own.

Sir Edward stood by his side. 'Shenkin, it's the perfect answer for you. Don't let this generous gesture of his friendship go unfulfilled.'

'But I have taken so much from you all, now this.'

'You came into his life Shenkin, indeed all our lives, and it's our way of proving our friendship to you. Don't waste it.'

Shenkin had to swallow hard, for the lump in his throat at that moment threatened to choke him. 'I will try to be worthy of his name, Sir Edward.'

'He knows that; that's why he gave it to you. It's the most generous gift I've ever witnessed.'

Tinker came up to them. 'Put the cross in the ground Shenkin, then I'll place a scar above your left eye. I'll make a herbal packing to press into the wound; it will heal quickly but leave a deep scar. I have done many such markings Shenkin, for rituals of my people. It's a pity it's not on the forehead, for I do a very good one there, also elaborate tattoos,' said Tinker, with a smile.

Then his smile went. 'Seriously Shenkin, we have little time. The aboriginal tribe will not come any closer to the river but the Port Arthur men are still on our track and closing ground as we speak. They are now less than a day away.' As if to underline Tinker's remarks, a dog barked in the distance.

The cut was swift. Shenkin felt the sharp knife scrape across the bone of his eyebrow. He almost passed out. He spat the cord of tree twine, that Tinker had had him bite on, out of his mouth. It was done.

The herbal packing would stop any infection; it would also prevent the skin from rejoining, thus insuring a full scar. Then with some ceremony, Tinker cut off Shenkin's pigtail and presented it to Shenkin as if it was a passage of rite and in many ways, it was for Shenkin had had it a long time.

The long tuft of hair lay in his hands. It conjured up all that had happened in the past causing Shenkin to became silent. Sensing the moment, Sir Edward placed a hand on Shenkin's shoulder. 'For the greater good my friend, in a few years you can grow it back, can you not?' Also when you grow a full beard, which will cover your own facial scar, then the disguise will be complete.

'Yes, of course, it's a very small sacrifice indeed compared to what's been made,' said Shenkin, making to throw the pigtail into the undergrowth but he was stopped by Tinker.

'The dogs will pick up the smell, we need to burn it, Shenkin.'

'Of course. I was not thinking, Tinker. Thank you.'

They were now just two Europeans and two aboriginals. They finished the grave then stood in silence for a moment as Sir Edward said a few words. A small fire soon destroyed the pigtail and within the hour, they were on their way to the river and the masquerade would begin.

CHAPTER 25

They said their goodbyes to their aboriginal guide. Tinker told him if he came in contact with the Port Arthur men if possible, he should misdirect them, with that they were soon on their way. Midday found them on the east bank of the River Derwent at a place called Risdon Cove. They enquired after a ship chandlers or any clothing store; directions led them to a small hut that sold ship repair items and rough and ready clothing. Leaving Shenkin and Tinker in the shadows of some large trees, Sir Edward went into the store.

The man sitting behind a solid counter gave him a sour look. 'What do you want? If it's a job you're after then I can tell you I don't need anyone.' Standing, the man began to walk towards the back of the shop.

Sir Edward Standish stood up straighter. 'Dear me, do my clothes look in such disarray? I've been on a survey and my man got us lost, don't you know? Frightful journey back to some sort of civilisation which I assume this is, before making our way to my lodgings at Hobart for a meeting at Government House tomorrow. But I need the best quality clothing your poor establishment can provide. Can't travel over to Hobart like this can I?'

Hearing the cultured voice of a gentleman, the man quickly turned around. 'Begging your pardon sir,' he said, tipping his hat. 'No indeed sir, sorry to hear of your misadventure sir, indeed I am, most sorry.'

'Right, what can you show me?' said Sir Edward, placing a bag of coins on the counter.

The tinkle of the coins lit up the store owner's face. 'They're not up to Sydney or London standards of course sir but I have a few pieces that I keep for officers of the military and ship owners sir, that might just suit you.'

'Well let's see them then for I have no time to waste. I'll also need a fit of clothes for my two men.'

Better and better, thought the store keeper as he hurried into the back room almost falling over a bail of wool in his hurry to please.

The clothes were indeed of poor quality but would serve to get to Hobart.

Having chosen his own he called in Shenkin and Tinker. Tinker stood at the doorway. The storekeeper turned surly. 'I'll have no abo in here. They're not allowed inside any buildings on the cove.'

Shenkin went to grab the man but Sir Edward restrained him. 'It's of no matter; I'll pick something out for him,' said Standish.

'No offence to you, sir, but since the 1804 troubles we are very ill disposed towards the abos.'

'So before this date they were welcome I take it.'

'Well, no not really, sir, reckoned we had stolen their hunting grounds or some such thing.'

Sir Standish turned to Shenkin. 'It seems we are back in civilisation Benson. It certainly smells like it.'

The shopkeeper shrugged his narrow shoulders. 'I wouldn't let it be known that you're on good terms with the aboriginals sir, not here in Risdon Cove if you don't mind me saying sir.'

Sir Edward allowed a smile to cross his lips. 'We'll soon be leaving this small cove and its small-minded people,' he said, while paying the man for the clothes.

'Just trying to warn you sir, help you like…' But Sir Edward cut him short.

'You can help me, which may make up for your insolence.'

'Any help I can give sir, I'll be eager to offer,' he said tipping his hat.

'I need to cross over to the west side and hence down to Hobart. What facilities are available in what passes to be a town?'

'Why sir, we have a ferry, the James Austin by name up at Old Beach just a short walk upriver from here. James Austin died a few years back but his nephews still run it; why, there's an Inn there too.'

'Right, we'll bid you good day then, my man. I'll be mindful of all you've said and not fail to mention your assistance in Hobart.'

'Thank you sir. I'm much obliged.'

Their reappearance on the dirt road cut a more respectable outward show than earlier. Sir Edward also bought a cane and tall top hat. Their picture of respectability and social standing was complete; they were ready to find this ferry at Old Beach. Walking along the water's edge they scanned the line of moored boats. Out on the water a medley of shipping was criss-crossing the short few miles to the opposite side.

Shenkin felt more hopeful that their progress was at last becoming positive. 'I see us in Hobart by nightfall, Sir Edward.'

'Let us hope so but at what times does this ferry cross? I wonder. Once a day, twice a day or continual? Let us hope for the latter.'

Late afternoon they came to an Inn sign. 'This must be it. There's a jetty too but no sign of a ferry,' said Shenkin.

They made their way into the Inn. 'Good day sir, how can I be of assistance? Is it ale or food you require?' said a youngish man behind a heavy timber bar.

Sir Edward placed his cane at a jaunty angle. 'Neither at present, we're seeking out a ferry across the river to Hobart.'

'We own that too sir, but there won't be another crossing until the morning's ebb tide. We can offer a room to yourselves,' he said, looking at the white men then adding, 'but the abo will have to sleep outside in the stable.'

'Then that is agreed. However, we will all have our meals outside on your veranda.'

'Not the abo sir, he must have his at the stable.'

'Then we will all eat at the stable,' said Shenkin, his temper beginning to boil over. Again, Sir Edward placed a restraining hand on Shenkin's shoulder.

'Make our rooms ready landlord, and we will dine on the bank of ground leading down to the jetty.'

'No offence is meant sir, but here in Risdon we've had difficult times with the aboriginals.'

'Right, we'll have some ale to start with which will temper our mood, I'm sure.'

'Ale it is sir, but the abo drinks from his own canteen, which I see hangs from his shoulder. Sorry, but it's the way of things.'

For heartbeats no one spoke, but the tension in Shenkin was dangerous and for a moment it looked as if he would strike the man.

'Come Benson, let's walk slowly down to the water's edge,' said Sir Edward, holding Shenkin's arm tightly and leading him away while calling back to the still figure of the landlord, 'Soon as you can my man, for we're all hungry.' He reinforced the word 'all' with a biting edge.

'Yes sir. Right away sir,' said the landlord, glad the moment had passed.

With his hand still on Shenkin's shoulder and in a hushed voice, Sir Edward said, 'We're not going to change these people's minds Shenkin, regarding their relationship with the indigenous aboriginals. Is that not true, Tinker?'

Tinker nodded. 'In 1804 a massacre took place here between a group of British settlers and a hunting party of my people who were on a kangaroo hunt. Men, women and children from different tribes took part. They formed a wide arc across the valley to herd the kangaroos towards the cove. They had no spears because it would have been dangerous to use them in such an enclosed space. The British settlers thinking they were under attack, called in the military who soon opened fire on them. Some forty to fifty of my people were killed; the only weapons they had were clubs for killing the trapped kangaroos. This incident soon led to the Black War that I spoke to you of when many, many more of my people died trying to protect their hunting grounds from the increasing settlers' need for land.

They remained silent until the food and drink arrived. Two young women placed chicken, rabbit pieces and cuts of bread in front of them, while the landlord brought them ale in pewter tankards.

'Thank you,' said Sir Edward. 'The rooms are being readied and we have places on the ferry.'

'They are and you do sir. Indeed, three military men will be joining you tonight sir, both at the Inn and on the ferry. It's likely that you know the officer in charge sir, Major Harris of the Port Arthur penal settlement. He has been after some escaped convicts these past days. Your paths may have indeed crossed out in the bush.'

'No we saw no sign of any military unfortunately. More's the pity because we would have welcomed the assistance out of that dense forest of tangled growth and the animals and insects it holds. Is that not so, Benson?'

'It is sir,' said Shenkin

Only a few hours earlier in the bush, a corporal from the Port Arthur garrison stood at the side of Major Harris's horse. 'Compliments of the sergeant sir, we have found another fresh grave sir.'

Harris spurred his horse. 'Lead on man, let us hope for the best.'

The sergeant already had the cross in his hands. 'It's the other convict, sir buried yesterday or the evening of the day before,' he said, handing the cross up to Harris.

He read the inscription with great pleasure. All his problems resolved in a few short words. *Here lies the body of Daniel Shenkin who has finally found peace. God rest his soul.*

'Good we have brought about a satisfactory conclusion and a warning to others who would attempt to escape. Take the cross place it with the other.' Turning in his saddle he called out, 'Lieutenant Clements.'

The fresh-faced young officer rode forward. 'Sir.'

'You will take the men back to Port Arthur, making sure you display the crosses in the main square for all to see, while I go on with the sergeant and two men to Hobart in search of those who helped these convicts escape. I'll see them in Port Arthur for a long term of hard labour.' Harris turned in his saddle. 'Well! Get on with it, man.'

'Very good, sir.'

With a deep sigh of relief, Major Harris proceeded onwards to the river. 'Sergeant, fall in with two men behind me.'

'Sir.'

The sergeant saluted but had hoped he too could have returned to the penal colony and his wife and children instead of following this stupid popinjay who he had hoped would have been replaced on the return of Commandant Booth from London, who was a true officer and gentleman. But such was army life. Unencumbered by further searching, Harris was soon in Risdon Cove. Approaching the tavern sign, he pulled up his horse.

Dismounting, he ordered the sergeant to hold his horse's reigns. Turning he strode into the hostel, leaving his men to stand in the blazing sun.

The sergeant spat dust from his mouth. 'The miserable bastard, he's going to let us stand here while he washes his throat out with some cool ale. I hope he chokes on it,' he said, lifting his canteen of water to his mouth. It was empty. Such was army life.

The soldier at his side pulled at the collar of his uniform. ' Yes! I'd be happy to carry a cross with his name on it back to barracks too, the bastard.'

'Shut your bleeding mouth.'

'But you just said…'

'Shut it, he's an officer he is.' Then added, 'the bastard.'

'Yes, Sergeant I mean, no Sergeant,' replied the soldier, all confused.

Sometime later and none too steady on his feet, Harris returned. 'Right, can't stand around here all day Sergeant. Damn it, we need to find our lodgings at Austin's Inn.'

'Sir,' said the sergeant through gritted teeth.

CHAPTER 26

Leaving Tinker at the stables, Shenkin and Sir Edward went up to their rooms which, while simple in structure and lacking any attempt at fineries had beds with sheets, if well worn, something they had not enjoyed for many days. They agreed to have a short rest before going down to a late supper.

Harris banged the bar counter with his riding crop. The young man appeared seeing the uniform, he said, 'Your rooms will soon be ready Major Harris. Your men will share a room in the servants' quarters. Is there anything further you need?'

'Yes! A meal damn it. My men will eat outside on the veranda. What can you offer? Come on, speak up,' said Harris, giving the man no time to reply.

'Cold meat cuts, sir with some local potatoes and vegetables followed by fruit pie.'

'It'll have to do. Do you have a good Claret?'

'Well, we have a red wine, sir but not much call for Claret here in the cove sir, if you follow my meaning sir.'

'Whisky?'

'I have a bottle of 1812 Indefatigable if that's to your taste, sir.'

'It is indeed. Bring the bottle and I'll try to do it justice,' said Harris, beaming for the first time in days.

At that moment, Sir Edward and Shenkin were making their way down the winding wooden stairway from their rooms. Stopping short of the bottom, Sir Edward put his hand out to stop Shenkin's descent.

'Military Shenkin, do you know him?'

'Jesus! It's the Commandant of Port Arthur, Major Harris. He must have taken charge of the search party looking for us. All is up, I fear,' said Shenkin.

'We can't hide in our rooms, so we'll bluff our way through. If we can fool him that you're Charlie Benson then it's a good beginning. What say you?'

'Agreed, we have come too far and the cost has been too high to cower from this moment.'

'Right, deep breath then, but let me do most of the talking,' said Sir Edward while he descended the last few steps. The dark stairwell curved around into the main room of the Inn.

Shenkin turned to Sir Edward. 'Are you sure we can risk it?' But by then they were at the bottom of the stairs and all eyes were on them.

Being very used to being stared at, Sir Edward said in a loud rather haughty voice, 'Well! Fight him you will Benson, or you'll no longer be my favourite.'

Shenkin picked up the line. 'But it's been a while since I fought sir; that last fight almost finished me, and I have a farm to run now.'

'Dear god, Benson! I have, at great expense, followed you to this miserable place to persuade you to fight in Hobart where you've never fought before. There's money to be made, damn it.'

Not waiting for a response, Sir Edward called out, 'Landlord, some whisky, and what's for supper?'

'Cold cuts of.....'

But Standish cut him short. 'Good god man, the whisky first, don't you know?'

'Sorry sir, this gentleman has the last bottle of 1812, sir. Everything else I have is more grog than blended, if you know what I mean.'

Turning to Harris, Sir Edward walked across to him. 'We'll share the bottle sir, and in recompense I'll pay for the bottle and your supper. What say you?'

'Generous sir, most generous,' said Major Harris, smiling.

'Landlord, another glass.' Harris looked up at Shenkin who was still in the shadow of the stairs.

Sir Edward turned to see where Harris was looking.

'None for Benson. He's in training, a bare-knuckle fighter don't you know?'

'Really, under what name?'

'Sir, let me introduce you to Charlie Benson, soon in my view, to be the heavyweight champion of New South Wales. In fact, Van Diemen's Land is to be his next conquest. Is that not so, Charlie?'

For a moment Shenkin did not respond. 'Come Charlie, no false modesty, I beg you.'

Shenkin took a deep breath and stepped out of the shadows. 'If you say so, Sir Edward.'

Harris stood up immediately. Shenkin held his breath. He was sure it was all over. 'Are you Sir Edward Standish, the Sydney sporting gentleman?'

'At your service sir, with my empty glass in my hand,' said Sir Edward, leaning forward for Harris to fill it.

'Then it promises to be an amusing evening after all,' said Harris, pouring the whisky into the proffered glass.

Topping up his own glass, Harris said, 'I too have a keen sporting interest in horse racing, cockfighting and also the noble art of bare-knuckle fighting. But alas, I have little opportunity to indulge them for I am the Commandant of Port Arthur penal colony. May I introduce myself? Major Harris sir, at your service. You'll join me at my table.'

'Delighted my dear fellow, delighted.'

'And your man Benson, he'll join us?' said Harris, looking up at Shenkin.

'Good of you sir, but as I say he's in training. He'll eat at a separate table, a light supper, no drink and early to his bed. Very disciplined in training is Charlie.'

Standing at the darker corner of the table, Shenkin gave a slow smile. 'Sir Edward protects his investment well sir. But first I think I'll go to the stables to see how Tinker is fairing, if you gentlemen will excuse me,' he said, walking towards the door.

Settling back into their high chairs, they both took a full gulp of their drinks.

Rested and relaxed, Harris looked over the rim of his half-empty glass. 'Your Benson sir. I can usually tell a man's accent.' For a moment Sir Edward froze.

'Indeed, and where do you place him?' said Sir Edward.

'Why! Your Benson man is from Cornwall, is he not?'

'You have a good ear sir, for he is indeed from Cornwall.' Then he thought he'd risk a bit more. 'But can you tell which part he hails from?'

'I'd say Truro, for I can hear the slight lilt in the voice and Cornwall was once West Wales in Anglo-Saxon times.'

'Remarkable, my dear fellow, quite remarkable.'

Major Harris, Acting Commandant, preened himself. 'Well, there you have it, always been able to place a man by birth and social standing.'

'A rare gift sir, strangely enough, he and Tinker are not dissimilar in vocal sound.'

'Tinker?' said Harris.

'Our aboriginal guide and Benson's cut man,' said Sir Edward.

Harris looked astonished. 'You actually allow a savage to treat your man?'

'Indeed I do, for this savage has great knowledge of herbs and the stitching of split skin, Major. In any event, Benson will allow no one else to treat him. They have been together for some time now and, in the heat of a fight, you rely upon the ones you trust. It's like a battle Major. Good officers, like yourself I'm sure, are the best to lead and encourage are they not?'

'Yes, quite so,' Harris said. Then added, 'more whisky sir?'

Adjusting the ruffles at his sleeves, Sir Edward pushed his glass across the table for the refill. The bottle was already beginning to feel lighter. By the early hours both men were talking louder and neither were listening. On the night air, the sound carried out to the stables.

'I hope Sir Edward is not becoming befuddled,' remarked Tinker.

'He's as drunk as he wants to be, Tinker. Have no fear, by the time he is finished Major Harris will regard us as friends,' said Shenkin, smiling.

Back in the Inn, Harris stood unsteadily to his feet. 'To bed I think for it's been a long day but I've got my convicts, dead it's true but a good example to others.' He had told Sir Edward all about the graves he had found and the crosses that were now to be trophies of his success.

Sir Edward nodded, tried to stand but gave up. 'Indeed sir, every inch the perfect British officer, the Empire is proud of you. I assure you I will mention your name at Government House in Sydney, that's if I can get a ship from Hobart.'

Harris moved purposefully but, ungainly, knocked his chair over as he did so. Then with great bravado, said, 'I'll see to it that you get a berth on one of the naval ships out of Hobart bound for Sydney.' It came out like Sidley.

'Damn decent of you sir. I would expect no less from an officer and a gentleman.'

'Then I wish you goodnight Sir Edward, or rather good morning,' he said, looking at his Hunter watch.

Both men laughed. 'A friendship forged in good whisky, good food, but above all, good company,' Sir Edward said in a matching slurred voice.

At the bottom of the stairs Harris, with great concentration, began his ascent. He missed the first step entirely, grabbed the rail with his right hand while steadying himself with his left, which was firmly pressed on the opposite wall. Crablike he continued upwards. Sir Edward and the landlord waited for a door to open; it did, then closed with a bang. Then a loud thud above them announced the collapse of Harris's body hitting either the floor or the bed, then silence.

The landlord asked if there was anything else he could do. Sir Edward grinned. Then, in a remarkably sober voice, said, 'You have been most patient, landlord, more than we deserve, so to bed with you and we will see you in the morning for the ferry across the river.'

'Then goodnight sir, you will be called for breakfast and any luggage will be taken down to the ferry. The punt will be full with the major's horses and sheep so I bid you goodnight.'

Sir Edward walked down to the stables expecting Tinker to be asleep but not so, both he and Shenkin were still talking.

Shenkin stood up quickly. 'How did it go, did he suspect anything?'

'He is a man full of self importance, therefore easily flattered. He is prepared to help us find a naval ship to take us back to Sydney,' said Sir Edward raising his arms in triumph.

'Well done, Sir Edward, well done,' said Shenkin.

CHAPTER 27

A few hours later saw them all, except for Tinker, eating a simple meal of some sort of gruel, burned toast and eggs.

Harris, rather pale of face and fragile in his movements, spoke for the first time. After sitting down slowly at the table, every clink of plate or cut of knife seemed to grate on his nerves. 'Good morning.'

The landlord came up to the table and in a normal voice, said, 'Your horses are loaded sir, so when you are ready we can proceed. For may I remind you sir, that we need to catch the high water line.'

'There is no need to shout man,' said Harris in a very small voice.

'No sir. Beg your pardon sir.'

Composing himself, Harris turned to Sir Edward. 'Do I understand that you have no horses with you?'

'I regret we do not. We'll need to get a rattler from Austin's Ferry for Hobart.'

'Nonsense, you will take my sergeant's and the privates' mounts. They can wait here for my return in three days. Did you hear that, Sergeant?' Who was sitting at another table near the door.

'Yes, sir. Very well, sir.' At least, he thought, they would be free of this bloody officer together with a few days' rest. In the army, eat and rest when you can, for you never know when you can next.

The sergeant looked over to the private. 'A small furlough, Private Bean, we'll search out what this miserable place has to offer in the way of drinking holes and whores.'

'If you say so, Sergeant.'

'I do, Bean, I do.'

Within the hour, fourteen foot poles steered the punt through the water and the ferry began its travel across the river.

Leaning on the rail that ran around the ferry, Harris offered Sir Edward his flask of brandy. 'A hair of the dog, Sir Edward?'

The silver flask felt cold to his lips but in recompense the brandy burned its warming way down his throat.

'How can I repay your hospitality, Major? It's all most generous of you, my dear fellow.'

'Well, there is one way you may be able to balance the books,' said Harris, tapping the side of the flask.

'Speak up sir. I am all ears.'

Harris placed the top slowly on the flask, gave it a turn and replaced it in the tail of his top coat pocket, causing the braid and buttons of his uniform to rustle in the morning wind.

'You are hoping to arrange a fight in Hobart before returning to Sydney are you not?' he said, pressing his hand on the wooden rail, causing a creak to run the length of the rail while his fingers, wet from spray, drummed on the wood.

'I am indeed,' said Sir Edward, wiping spray from his face.

I can help you with both: first an introduction to a sporting gentleman of Hobart and also a berth on one of the naval ships bound for Sydney. I am sir, acquainted with a Royal Naval Officer who is also a keen sporting man.'

'In return for?' said Sir Edward.

Harris smiled and leaned forward conspiratorially. 'A sizeable wager on your man placed through you, for it would not be proper in my position that I was seen to be betting in Hobart on illegal bare-knuckle fighting.'

'I see,' said Sir Edward, thoughtfully.

Not wanting to take any chances at being recognised, Shenkin had remained on the other side of the ferry while going through a series of limbering up exercises. Tinker, the only truly civilised man among them, had to travel on the punt with the animals. The wind and spray mixed their sounds with the bleating of the terrified sheep and the stamping of the horses' hoofs while Tinker stood on the side of the punt holding on to a wet rope, his body rising up and down to the pulse of the low but strong waves.

After a short stomach-bouncing time they were across to the east bank of the River Derwent. On the walk up to Austin's Ferry, Sir Edward held out his hand to Harris.

'Agreed, Major. A light meal at the Inn first and then a toast to both our good fortunes.'

Harris smiled. 'And the laying of our profitable plans, Sir Edward.'

'Indeed,' said Sir Edward, his left leg swinging in time to his exaggerated cane movements.

Austin Ferry Inn was certainly an improvement on the Old Beach. It was set in remarkable gardens which Sir Edward was surprised at, apparently Governor Sir Thomas Brisbane had been a visitor to the Inn.

The wine and food was excellent. The spirits of both men increased, which soon had them both talking about their plans.

Eager to define the scope of his possible winnings, Harris had spoken first.

'What purse will you be putting up sir.'

Sir Edward took a sip of his Claret. 'Would fifty pounds be too steep for Hobart, Major?'

'British silver coin or a mix of coins?'

A smile played on Sir Edward's lips. 'My dear Major, coin of the realm, of course.'

'And the odds, encouraging I trust?'

'I think we can get three to one, Major. Let us not be too greedy, or scare your sporting gentlemen off.'

'Benson is that good?'

'Better, for I once saw Daniel Mendoza, the favourite of King George IV, fight and Benson has all the skill that Mendoza had, plus a hammer in both fists.'

Harris warmed to the words and called for another bottle while he cut into his meat from, what animal it was not easy to say but it tasted well enough.

'I'll wager ten pounds,' said Harris with a flourish.

'Considerate it placed, sir.'

Swallowing hard, Harris looked up. 'I have a man in mind sir, a government official no less. John Turner by name, his favourite is an ex-convict, Will Biggins, a giant of a man who has won a number of fights for Turner,' he said, rubbing the thumb and fingers of his right hand together.

'So he is good for the purse?'

'Indeed,' said Harris. 'He rents a timber barn on the outskirts of the town to stage his bouts and is most discreet.'

'Sounds like our man,' said Sir Edward, raising his glass in a toast. 'To our mutual financial gains, my dear fellow.'

The plan was sealed to the clink of glasses. 'I'll speak to him within the hour,' said Harris.

'Good, I'm sure you'll be inviting the Navy officer to our little get together too.'

'First Turner, then the captain; have no fear.' Harris began to rise from his chair. Smiling, he said, 'Make my wager fifteen pounds. Indeed, I would like to place more but I am just a poor British officer of a penal colony on the wrong side of the world.'

Sir Edward held his arms wide in sympathy. 'So it will be, Major. Fifteen pounds it is, you have it on you?'

'No, but the bank here in Hobart will advance me the coin I assure you.'

'Now that the crown has finally sent out gold and silver to the colony, I would require it in such denominations.'

A slight hesitation followed, then Harris nodded. 'Very well.'

'The show of silver always makes for good sport don't you know?' said Sir Standish.

With the rise of an eyebrow, Harris said, 'I see how you've gained your reputation, Sir Edward.'

Again Sir Edward raised his arms in acknowledgement.

When Harris had left, Sir Edward went over to Shenkin's table. 'Well, it couldn't be going better Shenkin. We have a fight with a reasonable purse and modest side bets so as not to attract too much attention. The fight, if possible, will be tomorrow night; a win would secure you as Benson and we would have a berth on the next available Navy ship to Sydney. How do you feel about that?'

Shenkin sat back in his chair. 'Thank you, Sir Edward.' Then added, 'I can't afford not to win.'

'I agree much is at stake, but I have every faith in you, Shenkin.'

'If you will accuse me, Sir Edward, Tinker and I have a few miles to run.'

CHAPTER 28

The evening saw Harris pouring himself and Sir Edward a liberal glass of whisky. 'All arranged sir. Tomorrow night we'll go by rattler to the barn to meet Turner and his associates one hour before the bell. Captain Bellamy will also be present. I've tipped him the wink to back Benson in return for your berths to Sydney.' As an afterthought, he added, 'let's hope Benson is in good form, or we'll have money and face to lose.'

Sir Edward's face lit up. 'My dear fellow I have seen Benson fight; have no fear.' Behind his back he crossed his fingers.

After a number of long runs and limbering excises, Shenkin felt in better form. Tinker had again packed the newly acquired scar. 'Keep your left up during most of the rounds, the scar must be protected but I'm sure you're aware of this Shenkin,' said Tinker, looking closely at the scar. 'Could have done with a couple of weeks more to heal.'

'Tonight it is Tinker, so let's hope you've packed well.'

Tinker nodded. 'Indeed, but I will have a needle and thread ready my friend.'

They were standing at the bar of the Inn when Sir Edward joined them. He was followed by Harris. 'Good we are all ready,' he said. Taking in Shenkin's appearance, he gasped. 'Well Sir Edward, your favourite certainly looks the part for he cuts a very formidable figure, I must say.'

Shenkin was stripped to the waist with knee-length breeches that had ribbon sashes tied just below the knees. The rest of the legs were in white stockings, a wide sash held the breeches up while on his feet he had black lightweight footwear. Shenkin's broad shoulders tapered to a narrow waist, the muscles rippled in the light from the Inn. All had been brought to Hobart by Sir Edward in preparation for a possible fight. Shenkin had smiled at Sir Edward's anticipation. 'What if I had been unable to fight, what then?' he said.

In response Sir Edward had said, 'They took up very little room Shenkin, and knowing that the chance of a fight and the need of money at this time would have been difficult to refuse.'

Harris continued to appraise Shenkin. Indeed, he felt his winnings were becoming a definite possibility.

'He looks in good shape Sir Edward, not an ounce of fat.'

While he was being assessed like a prize bull, Shenkin thought to himself. *The sign of no fat is down to your meagre rations at the penal colony, you bastard.*

The moment was broken by the arrival of their coach. Climbing aboard, they were soon making their way out of Hobart for the barn that Turner owned. The track became uneven and rutted, causing them to hold on to their seats while outside the dust swirled around them covering them in a fine layer.

'Bloody country,' said Harris.

'Its worse for Tinker,' said Shenkin, who was having to run at the side of the aptly named rattler. Tinker was covered in a cloud of dust, an apparition in human form fading in the light only to reappear in a flash of white teeth.

'These abos are no more then animals, Benson; they're used to dust, heat and dirt,' said Harris.

Shenkin leaned forward and held Harris's arm in a vice-like grip, causing Harris to wince. 'This abo as you call him, is my friend sir. He is a man of great dignity, knowledge and concern for his fellow man, which is more than can be said for many so-called gentlemen that I have met.'

Harris pulled his arm away and sunk back into his bouncing seat. 'You forget yourself and who you are Benson, a kept brawler for profit.'

Shenkin crossed the short space between them in seconds, his right fist drawn back as Sir Edward threw himself in front of Harris.

'Come, come now, the fight is at the barn not in this coach.'

Harris fearing the blow from Shenkin's fist, pressed himself into the back of the coach partition and straightened his clothes. 'Indeed, we should bear that in mind. I am grateful to you, Sir Edward,' said Harris, his face had gone very pale.

The moment was saved by their arrival at the barn. Stepping from the rattler, Harris brushed himself down as he walked unsteadily towards a rather portly man standing outside of a low timber building.

'Turner my dear sir, we seem to have gathered a large crowd. I hope they've brought enough coin with them,' said Harris in a still somewhat nervous voice.

Walking behind him Sir Edward turned to Shenkin. 'Damn it Shenkin, hold on to your temper or all will be lost.'

Pulling away, Shenkin spat on the ground. 'I have met these kind of men on both sides of the world Sir Edward. Indeed, I am here because of their kind.' Then in a calmer voice, Shenkin said, 'But you are right. The moment is important; I'll curb my anger.'

'Good, let us take it out on Turner's man,' said Sir Edward, with a warm smile.

At that moment the burly figure of Will Biggins came out of the barn doors and stood by the side of Turner. To say the man was big was an understatement for he must have been at least six foot six tall and built to match, some fat around his middle Shenkin noted, but the rest pure muscle.

'He looks impressive Shenkin.'

'They all do, but can he fight?'

Sir Edward smiled a slow telling smile. 'We are about to find out, my friend.'

Tinker stood at Shenkin's corner needle and thread at the ready, together with balm for the eyebrows and fine dust for the hands. For the last few hours Shenkin's hands had been soaking in vinegar and rum.

Tinker examined them. 'The skin seems to be tough enough and your spell on the chain gangs has done the rest.'

Shenkin nodded as he looked across the makeshift ring at Biggins who towered over everyone around him.

'Well Tinker, what do you think of Will Biggins?'

'The bigger they are, the harder they fall,' said Tinker with a gleaming smile.

'Agreed, the bread basket looks like the main target. My father would say, kill the stomach and the head falls.'

'A wise man,' said Tinker.

The crowd was now numbering in the hundreds. Bets were being shouted, ale and pies being sold, while wine and brandy was being drunk among the rich of the town. Although bare-knuckle fighting was illegal, many government officials were placing bets in their frock-tailed suits, silver-buckled shoes, and tall hats with money in their hands. For Shenkin the noise was a mere muted background; he was deep in thought. Then finally he said, 'He has a long reach Tinker. I'll have to crouch square and get inside his arms for some short-range fighting.'

'If you say so Shenkin.'

'Fighters to the scratch line,' shouted the referee who was a man of about forty-five or fifty. He was of average height but with a muscular build. Shenkin noticed that one of his ears was missing and both eyebrows carried scar tissue: a former prize fighter without doubt.

To much applause, Will Biggins stepped up first to the scratch. Then pulling himself up to his full height, he raised his arms above his head as if he had already won the match.

The roar from the crowd was deafening, a chant went up, 'Biggins, Biggins, Biggins.'

Shenkin so much shorter at five foot eleven, looked completely outmatched, causing even more bets to be placed on Biggins.

'Now listen, you two bastards,' said the umpire. 'I'll allow a lot but when I say break I mean break or I'll use this heavy stick I carry. Do you both understand?'

Shenkin said, 'Broughton Rules?'

'Yes.'

'Which are?' asked Shenkin.

'You know what they are.' He looked at Shenkin. 'Or are you afraid Benson?'

'Yes, it all sounds very frightening,' said Shenkin.

Biggins flexed his muscles. 'I'm going to cripple you, you little runt.'

Again the so-called referee asked if they both understood the rules.

'Yes!' shouted Biggins.

Shenkin said, 'What rules?' But nodded anyway. *So anything goes then, thought Shenkin. Right, let's do it.*

Then turning to the crowd, the referee shouted, 'In the white leggings with a black sash I give you, Charlie Benson of Sydney.' Boos rose from the crowd.

'In red leggings with the white sash, our very own Van Diemen's Land champion, Will Biggins.'

The sound that went up was like a peel of thunder.

Shenkin whispered to Tinker. 'He's not biased then, so that's a help.'

Tinker smiled. 'Lets change his mind Shenkin.'

A bell sounded, the fighters came up to the mark and the match began, slowly at first, as each man sized up the other. Then Biggins threw a right. Shenkin stepped inside the punch and crouched down, causing Biggins to have to hit downwards which was both difficult and tiring for such a tall man.

Shenkin blocked and weaved, blocked and weaved, then danced backwards then forwards. It was all becoming a bit too scientific for Biggins; he was a brawler both physically and mentally. After half an hour, the crowd was becoming restless and frustration began to set in.

'Come on Will, what's the matter? Hit him,' someone shouted. But try as he would he could not hit Shenkin in any effective way: on his arms, yes, on his shoulders yes, but the blows were parried or side stepped. So he blustered and swung wide energy-sapping punches while Shenkin got inside Biggins' long arms and pummelled his stomach, the skin was slowly turning red. The hour mark came up and neither man had gone down. The crowd were beginning to boo and hiss. Biggins rushed forward, chopping downwards as he did. Shenkin smiled it was a big mistake, all that weight coming down and Shenkin's right fist coming up. Together, the combined weight was devastating. Biggins went down as if a bolt of lighting had hit him. The referee shouted at Biggins to get up as he tried to help him to his feet. Sir Edward shouted foul. Slowly, in a dazed state, Biggins struggled to his feet and managed to get to the mark.

'Broughton Rules,' shouted the ref, helping Biggins to his corner.

Turner applauded. 'Quite right, Broughton Rules.'

Harris was on his feet. 'But the rules, what about the rules?'

Sir Edward standing beside him said, ' Forget it Harris. There are no rules. This is a bare-knuckle fight to the end, anything goes.'

Taking advantage of the lull in the fight Shenkin said, 'How is the scar holding up Tinker?'

'It looks good Shenkin,' he said, smearing more balm over the eyebrow, but keep that left up.'

'He's blowing hard. I'll drop to my knee to end the next round then get up quickly to the line, then drop again at his next punch. All of this will first relax then tension him, it will be very tiring.'

Tinker gave a knowing smile.

Both squared up again. No bell was rung but Biggins head butted Shenkin, who feinted backwards, causing the blow to lose any power. He then counter punched a left, a right, another left that went straight into Biggins' stomach. With satisfaction, Shenkin saw the other man wince for the first time. A swinging right brushed the top of Shenkin's head and he went down on one knee. Biggins snarled, 'Got you now, it's almost over.' But there was a sigh in Biggins' voice as he relaxed at the sight of Shenkin on the ground at last.

Then Shenkin jumped up, moved to the mark and turned to face Biggins. 'Is that the best you have, you big lump of shit?'

Biggins rushed and wrapped his big arms around Shenkin and began to crush his ribs. Shenkin got the heel of his left palm under Biggins' chin and pushed up with all his strength, forcing Biggins' head backwards and upwards until he exposed his chin. Shenkin drove his right fist up hard. Biggins' jaw snapped shut, teeth grinding on teeth; the arms fell away. Shenkin feinted backwards then moved forward, then backwards again. As Biggins came after him, Shenkin's counter punching sent blow after blow into Biggins' stomach. Gasps came from Biggins' throat as he absorbed the blows. He delivered a poor miss hit at Shenkin's head. Shenkin went down again; the big man kicked at Shenkin's groin. Shenkin caught the foot, lifted it above his shoulder and stood up. Biggins went flat on his back, the sound of the thud brought screams from the crowd. Biggins began to get up on his one knee and Shenkin hit him square in the face with his foot. Blood spurted out of his nose as Shenkin drove his right knee under Biggins' chin. That sent him backwards, flat on his back. The ref rushed forward and threw a bucket of water over Biggins. 'Get up Will,' he shouted. This time even the crowd didn't like it and jeered.

Biggins staggered to the line, his front covered in blood from his nose, his jaw hung loose. *Perfect, thought Shenkin.* The roar of the crowd was now intense, as Biggins was beginning to punch the air in desperation. By pure luck, one punch caught Shenkin harmlessly on the side of his face so he went down. The relief on Biggins' face was a sight to behold as he thought it must be all over this time for sure, only to see Shenkin get up again and dance up to the line. 'Oh dear you're not really trying are you?'

The ref grabbed Shenkin's arms, pinning them back. 'Hit him, Will. Hit the bastard.'

'How much are you paying the ref, Turner? I would expect better from a gentleman,' said Sir Edward, in anger.

Turner bristled with indignation. 'I assure you sir, he acts on his own view of the fight. There must be some good reason for his act.'

'Yes! It is to help your man sir.' Standish was angry at this blatant display of poor sportsmanship indeed, of fouling of the highest order. And began to shout, 'Foul, forfeit, surrender the purse.'

'I'll do no such thing sir,' said Turner. 'Continue the fight,' he shouted.

His arms still pinned behind him, Biggins came forward. Shenkin waited until he was in leg distance then he drove his foot up into Biggins' groin. If he had balls before he didn't have them now, they were somewhere up inside his intestines. He screamed, it was a sound of pure agony. The ref let Shenkin's arms go. Standing back, he looked at Turner shrugging his shoulders.

Biggins had dropped to his knees clutching his manhood, or what was left of it. Shenkin danced forward then, interlacing his fingers to make one large fist he swung it across Biggins' jaw left to right then right to left. Biggins was a ruined man, a crumpled piece of battered bones. The ref went to hit Shenkin with his heavy stick. Shenkin's right fist moved no more than six inches but it caused havoc to the side of the referee's face. Shenkin caught him as he began to fall, he whispered in his ear, 'You need to lift my arm as the winner or they're going to have to carry you out of the ring. If you don't believe me take a long look at Biggins.' He needed no convincing.

'I declare,' he spluttered, 'Charlie Benson the winner by a knock down. Biggins is unable to come up to the scratch,' he said, lifting Shenkin's arm up high, then he sunk to the ground. Pandemonium broke out in the crowd: fights began, broken bottles were being thrown or used. The bookies were happy for most of the money was on Biggins

As a cordon of special constables was coming towards the barn, the fight lookouts shouted warnings. The crowd began to break up and run, scattering in every direction. Turner turned to leave. 'Surely you are not going without settling your debts first sir?' said Sir Edward, meaningfully.

'I am a magistrate sir. I cannot be found here, nor can these gentlemen around me.' They all nodded and again began to move towards the back door.

Sir Edward blocked their way. 'Then the sooner you all pay up the quicker you will be away.'

Shenkin, a towel hanging loose around his shoulders, came to Sir Edward's side. 'Is there a problem, Sir Edward?'

'These gentlemen are reluctant to hand over the money,' said Sir Edward. Turner and five others had their backs hard against the side of the ring. Sir Edward stood in front of them with Shenkin now to his right and Tinker to his left in a tight arc.

'I see,' said Shenkin. 'Gentlemen, I would expect better from such men of honour and standing, but if you would turn and take a look at Will and your ref, I am sure you would prefer to walk or run out of this barn's back door rather then straight to a hospital. However, the choice is yours sirs, so please take your time in your deliberations.'

The main door was being hammered on, the crowds had mostly dispersed through windows or under fencing. For heart beats only the hammering on the door made a sound, all else was still. Then with a deep sigh, one gentleman stepped forward, held up his betting slip and placed his money in Sir Edward's tall hat.

'Thank you, sir,' said Sir Edward.

Each in their turn did the same. Sir Edward ticked them off, then turned to Turner who grudgingly dropped the purse in the hat together with his betting slip and the money due it.

'Thank you gentlemen. Breeding will out.'

Turner turned to Major Harris. 'My apologies, Harris. I am sure your losses too are difficult to endure.'

Harris duly looked miserable. 'Indeed sir.' While his friend Captain Bellamy could hardly keep a straight face.

Turner shouted, 'Before they get to the back exit we must leave. I have coaches there at the ready.'

At last, the doors splintered and gave way. The constables rushed into an empty barn.

CHAPTER 29

Bellamy was still laughing when they got to the docks. 'Early in the morning gentlemen on the high tide, thank you again for a most entertaining afternoon and evening, also for my handsome winnings. As agreed, it secures you berths to Sydney.' Alighting from the rattler he again bid them goodnight as he and his laughter melted into the fast-approaching night.

Harris smiled. 'Well Benson you are a remarkable man sir.' It was the first time he had addressed him so. 'That bout was one of the best I've ever witnessed, indeed the best by far, and certainly the most profitable,' he said clinking the bag of silver coin in his pocket. At this even Shenkin, in spite of himself, laughed.

Then with a flourish, Harris tapped the roof of the coach. 'To the Inn, driver.'

Apart from Tinker who again had to bed down in the stables, they all sat with ale and wine in their hands and celebrated the win.

Sir Edward looked over at Shenkin, then taking him to one side he said. 'I know my friend, you can not reconcile this moment with Harris, given all that has passed, but you must Shenkin, if you wish to survive and honour the lives given up for this moment. We all have to compromise at times and your time will come believe me, when you can square your conscience,' he said, placing his hand on Shenkin's shoulder. Then in a louder voice, he said, 'Well Benson, what about the championship of New South Wales? I am sure the major will risk a bet.'

'Indeed I will,' said Harris, raising his glass.' So went the evening.

Come morning they assembled in the main room of the Inn. A morning sea mist and chill had settled over the Inn and docks. Harris, his military top coat wrapped around him, stepped outside. 'You to Sydney, I to Government House to report the successful outcome to the recovery of the escaped convicts, dead to be sure, but a good warning to others of like mind. But first

I'll see you to your ship sirs. Do not forget to let me know when Benson here fights again, Sir Edward.'

'Indeed I will not, Major,' said Sir Edward, holding Shenkin's arm back.

At the wharf their ship the HMS George, dipped and bobbed in the early morning light. She was a fifth-rate frigate armed with about thirty or so guns, fast and effective when necessary. She had been in Hobart to celebrate the town's first regatta and would now return to her home port in Port Jackson.

Bellamy, still in good humour welcomed them aboard. 'Good morning and welcome to the George, a fine ship, what? In a fight she'll out manoeuvre any first-class ship, allowing our guns to cause havoc from stem to stern of the enemy.' Then with great pride, he said, 'Given minimum coming about and a good blow, she'll have us in Sydney in eight to ten days. And damn it if she isn't mine and I love her like no woman I have ever known.' Bellamy said, with a gleeful laugh.

Sir Edward stepped aboard. 'Upon my life Bellamy you've not known the right women.' A chorus of laughter cut the chill air.

'Maybe not Sir Edward, maybe not, but with all my heart I do love this old wooden fortress. She was designed by William Rule in 1807. Why she's my only home, gentlemen and all I want in this fast-changing world. She's a sanctuary of steadfastness, a solid reliable piece of English oak,' said Bellamy, tapping the bulwark fondly.

Shenkin smiled. 'To find what you want in life is to know happiness, Captain I envy you sir.'

'Thank you Benson, by the by, you are sharing the midshipmen's quarters with Midshipman Mr John Rees, the young son of a wealthy Cardiff ship owner. He will take you below decks and introduce you around to our other young men.'

'Mr Rees,' called the captain.

'Sir.'

'Please show Mr Benson to your quarters and make him comfortable.'

'Aye aye, sir.'

Shenkin was confronted with a youth of no more than thirteen or fourteen: spotty faced, small of build and a little nervous. His uniform, which was well pressed, consisted of a dark blue frock coat with white collar tabs. While at his waist, attached to a black leather belt, hung a sword and his small feet were encased in silver-buckled shoes. However, none of it disguised his worried facial expression as he looked up at the powerful presence of Shenkin.

'I don't fight in my sleep midshipman, unless provoked, so do not be alarmed.'

'No, sir,' said Midshipman Rees with a forced smile, while around them laughter broke the morning air except for one of the crew. Standing slightly to the left of Bellamy was a tall thin officer whose bearing proclaimed him to be a man of the upper social rung.

'Sir Edward, may I introduce you to Acting Lieutenant James Garret-Jarvis with whom you will share a cabin. You are aware of his father I am sure, Rear Admiral Garret-Jarvis of Trafalgar and many other famous sea battles against the French. My acting lieutenant is hoping to follow in his father's footsteps, is that not so, Lieutenant?'

Garret-Jarvis bridled immediately, it was obvious the men did not get along. 'The Acting part of my title Sir Edward, is very temporary I assure you. My examination results will be announced soon and I am assured of my own command, channels within the channels of the sea, don't you know?'

Bellamy smiled a rather tight smile. 'It of course, requires my recommendation, so we shall see, but for now enough of naval politics, please make yourselves as comfortable as the limited space allows for I have much to do ship side to get us underway. I will see you all at dinner tonight.'

Bellamy stopped short. 'Before I forget, the boatswain will escort your aboriginal man to the hold where he has made a place for him.'

With that, and a wave of his hand to the boatswain, Bellamy strode towards the quarterdeck. The boatswain was a short powerfully built man, his face spoke of many weather-beaten years at sea. He was the most experienced of the deck seamen aboard. Boatswain Harry Wilson had served under more captains than he cared to remember and at fifty years of age, he regarded himself to be in his prime. His black short reefer jacket shone with brass buttons under which he wore a red waistcoat with a white shirt beneath. His white trousers were pressed razor sharp; they ended in black polished shoes. To top it off he wore a black hat complete with the same colour ribbon that flew in the morning wind. 'Right!' he said in a gruff voice. 'This way then my black-faced friend, mind the ropes, the rigging and, above all, the wet scrubbed deck and we'll have you bedded down in no time.' Then with a wink, he added, 'in fact, my dark-faced man, you'll have more room than the others and that's a fact.' His gruff voice laughing out loud causing the port seagulls to scatter across the sky.

As each followed their room mates to their respective quarters, Shenkin looked around him. The ship was a far cry from the convict ship, the Runnymede, that he came out from England in. This was a British Navy Frigate, all the brass fittings were shining and the wood polished down to the grain. Her ropes were coiled neatly in shape. The sailors were dressed in shipboard issued crew clothing, pressed and clean. She had a crew of one hundred and fifty and was armed with thirty-eight guns. She was neat and in Bristol fashion, that is to say, a place for everything and everything in its place, giving a feeling of ordered discipline and safety.

'I hope you have no misgivings about sharing the midshipmen's quarters sir, for we are a group of hopeful officers to be. But we know our place in this hard world of sea and ships.'

Shenkin smiled. 'Far from it I welcome your energetic company, young man one that is mostly unmarked by this hard world that is not restricted to the sea.'

'Indeed sir.'

By now they were, with much careful treading on Shenkin's part, below decks. Shenkin remembered how low he needed to bend so as not to hit his head on the timber beams also with an inward smile, how many times Regan did. How he missed that big Irishman. Even now he found himself turning around expecting to see him at his shoulder.

'Here we are sir, all well found,' said Midshipman Rees, bringing Shenkin back to the moment.

Shenkin was presented with an array of hammocks, swinging with the movement of the water, some had sleeping men who really were no more then children by the look of their fresh young faces.

Seeing Shenkin's look, he said, 'They were on duty during the night time watches sir.'

'Yes, of course,' said Shenkin

'This will be yours sir,' said Rees, adding, 'I do hope it's not too short for you, but it's comfortable enough. You can stow your belongings in the side locker there.'

'Thank you, Mr Rees. It will be fine, for I have slept in more cramped places, I assure you.'

The young man smiled. 'John please, no need for formalities in the mess and you are not Navy sir.'

'Indeed, then you must call me Charlie.'

'Right sir. I mean Charlie, do you know you are the first bare-knuckle fighter I've ever met? I do hope you will entertain us with stories of your many fights.'

'Indeed, starting tonight,' said Shenkin, shaking hands, their friendship formed.

'Here we are Sir Edward, not much to look at and certainly not a great deal of space, so I would ask you to be respectful of my part of the cabin and my belongings sir. Do not touch or move them, not used to sharing don't you know?'

Sir Edward gave an acid smile. 'I see nothing that would tempt me sir.' Then, looking around, he added, 'in fact nothing whatsoever.'

The lieutenant gave a shrug of his well-clothed shoulders, turned and walked out. *A fine beginning,* thought Sir Edward, *at least it's only for a few days, I hope.* It reminded him of his public school days.

Tinker settled into his berth in the hold, which was well ordered and clean. A makeshift hammock swung in time to the roll of the ship. The boatswain was right, there was indeed plenty of room. He'd be fine here.

They had been underway for a number hours or so: first down the Derwent River then, turning to port, they passed Port Arthur and were into the Tasman Sea. Sir Edward came down the companionway to talk to Shenkin. 'You seem at home already, and in better company I'll be bound, for our lieutenant is a man full of self-esteem and righteous indignation.'

'Well, it's just for a short period Sir Edward, but I must say rather you then me having to share the same air as that bloody pompous man.'

'Indeed, but the captain is a fine fellow so we're in good hands. We'll fare well and soon be back in Sydney, which is why I'm here,' said Sir Edward sitting carefully on one of the hammocks. 'I have been thinking you need to catch a rattler up to Charlie's farm as soon as possible, take a look around and meet his man up there, then lay low for a month or so.'

'But I am anxious to confront Feltsham and have it out with him, that's if I can keep my hands off his throat,' said Shenkin.

'We need to get a feel for how things are at the moment in Sydney. What is Lord Feltsham up to at this time, how is his standing in Sydney society and what is his story about Elizabeth and your child? Also we need to contact your Dr Tarn.'

'But you have your own place to run and business to see to. I can't expect you to give all your time to me when you have done so much already.'

'Shenkin, there are just three of us left to see this injustice through. I'll not forsake you now, nor, I'll wager, will Tinker.'

'Thank you Sir Edward, it means a great deal to me.'

'I'll not hear another word. We will soon be walking the rutted roads of Sydney again while planning the downfall of the man that has caused you all this pain,' said Sir Edward, with a smile. 'So we are agreed, Charlie's farm first, yes?'

'Agreed.'

Bellamy remained seated while he raised his glass. 'Gentlemen, I give you the Queen, may her reign be long.' All raised their glasses to a chorus of 'TO THE QUEEN, GOD BLESS HER.'

All had remained seated to give the Loyal Toast, which was the custom since King William IV, who had served as a naval officer and had experienced the discomfort of suddenly standing on board a vessel at sea, to give the Loyal Toast and had authorised that all in the Royal Navy should toast him while sitting down. So it had continued ever since, much to every officer's relief and comfort, for the beams were indeed low.

Sir Edward sipped his wine and sighed. 'Your man prepares a good meal, Captain: damn fine piece of meat cooked to perfection and that pudding tart why, we could almost be in Rules of London. Thomas Rule himself would not find fault with it, Captain Bellamy.'

'Good of you to say Sir Edward, very good indeed. I brought the cook with me, at my own expense I may add but he's worth it.' Bellamy closed his eyes for a moment then said, 'Last time I was in London I dined there, Rules that is with my wife sir, on game pie if I remember rightly, before going on to the opera, but don't ask me which opera for I fell asleep.'

Laughter filled the gun room which served as a dining room on a frigate. Its low bulkhead timbers creaked above. Around the table were the invited officers, midshipmen and their guests. Cigars, pipes and the port was brought to the table; soon the cabin was filled with clouds of smoke and red-flushed faces.

Shenkin leaned across the table. 'So you are to be an officer John. How soon will that be?'

'Another four years I fear, for I will be eighteen before I can sit my Lieutenant's examination.'

The captain caught the conversation. 'He shows great promise Benson, great promise indeed.'

'Thank you, sir,' said Midshipman Rees.

At this Lieutenant Garret-Jarvis broke in, 'His navigation had better improve or upon my life the little snot will have us in the South Pole instead of Sydney,' he said with a snigger, adding, 'the boy's a fool at navigation.'

The young midshipman blushed red. Shenkin turned to the lieutenant. 'And you sir, what do you favour navigating, the naval ladder or the social ladder?'

'I resent your assertion sir, particularly from someone who uses brawn rather than brains.'

'Resent it! Why, you represent it in all its worst forms. A man, who by accident of birth, connections and wealth, has gained a place in life that he has not earned nor, as far as I can see, in your case merits.'

Garret went to stand then remembered the stout timbers above him. However, the captain quickly intervened. 'Not at my table or on my ship, gentlemen. You will desist. Hold your glasses firmer and tempers longer. Do I make myself clear?'

'My apologies Captain Bellamy, for my outburst at your acting lieutenant's remarks,' said Shenkin, stressing the words Acting lieutenant.

This was too much for the lieutenant, who bent down while getting up from his chair and made to leave the cabin.

The captain placed his glass slowly on the table and said, 'You are not dismissed Lieutenant, sit down.' The atmosphere could be cut with one of the dining dinner knives. For heartbeats no one spoke. 'Now who has the port?' said the captain. The bottle travelled up the table on the left to Garret-Jarvis who passed it to the captain.

'Thank you, Lieutenant.' While he poured he turned to his Lieutenant. 'I am sure you must have duties to attend to so let me not detain you. You are dismissed sir, and goodnight.'

The junior Lieutenants went to move. 'No need gentlemen, please be seated and finish your drinks,' said the captain, without explanation.

Sir Edward Standish raised his glass and tipped it in acknowledgement to the captain and said, 'Now for me, the best restaurant in London is Whites of St James's, a private club I know and one is fortunate to be a member, but by all that's holy they lay the best table in London. Their Roast Mutton, or Stewed Rabbit followed by Plum Pudding and Mince Pies is a meal of wonder and joy, washed down with an excellent Bordeaux, say an 1818 Chateau Lafite a great vintage.'

'You know your fare, sir.'

'Indeed I do, Captain, but I have sadly had little opportunity to indulge it of late,' said Sir Edward, quickly adding, 'until tonight that is.'

'Good of you to say. My apologies we did not have a Lafite, but our Claret was the best we had to offer,' said Bellamy, turning to Shenkin. 'And you Benson, what favourite restaurant would you recommend?'

'I would say for me a basic meal of...' Shenkin hesitated. 'a wholesome meal for I am a simple man with basic needs.'

'Well, it has suited you well for a finer specimen of manhood I have yet to see sir,' said Bellamy, with a laugh.

'You are looking at the future champion of New South Wales, Captain Bellamy, can we count on your bet?'

'After Benson's recent performance, I have no doubt of it sir, you can indeed rely upon my support.'

The evening continued in a good-humoured spirit of friendship and companionship. Wine flowed voices became louder, even Midshipman Rees joined in the banter of high spirits, though his young eyes were brimful of tears from the cigar smoke. At that moment of time, in that sea-rolled dining room, all was well in the world Shenkin felt at ease for the first time in many years, ones that had been so full of loss and sorrow. He knew much more would need to be done to square the circle of his life, if indeed that was ever possible, but for now he just wanted to hold on to this precious moment when even justice seemed possible.

CHAPTER 30

The morning welcomed them with fresh winds and a ship sailing at full knots. 'Good morning, gentlemen. You slept well I trust, given the night before,' Captain Bellamy said, standing four square on the quarterdeck of his beloved ship, sea spray washing away the cobwebs of the night while Shenkin and Standish were holding onto anything that looked steadier then themselves.

'I had a chorus of young snoring and the comings and goings of wet clothes that brushed past me in the night. That apart I slept well enough,' said Shenkin.

'And you Sir Edward, what of your slumbers?'

'Well, your lieutenant snores as daintily as he walks. I could have sworn I was back in kindergarten.'

Their laughter was at that moment, drowned in a roar of wind, which was just as well for Garret-Jarvis was joining them.

'Good morning Lieutenant, the night went well I trust. Nothing to report, the ship behaved herself during your watch?'

'Yes, sir, all is well.'

'Good, splendid, take the ship, sir,' said the captain turning towards his cabin. Adding as he walked, 'Wake me if anything arises that you feel I need to be told of.'

'Aye aye sir.'

Shenkin touched the captain's arm. 'Would it be alright if I ran up and down the length of the ship for some exercise, Captain?'

'Well, don't bump into anyone or anything and above all don't fall off the ship for I'll not turn around and it's a hell of a swim to Sydney, understood?'

'Yes sir. Thank you sir. I'll try not to do either.'

The lieutenant grunted. 'You said something, Lieutenant?'

'No sir. Clearing my throat sir.'

'Well it's the morning for it,' said Bellamy, sarcastically.

After almost two hours, Shenkin, timed by Tinker on a fine Herringham Gold Trafalgar watch lent by Midshipman Rees, knew every gangway, companion ladder, pin-rail and neatly coiled rope, that he was told were called halyards, on both sides of the ship. Chill wind or not, he was soon building up a fine sweat while his lungs and muscles were beginning to burn with the effort of the exercise.

'Good bloody training big fellow, but according to this timepiece you were getting slower each time. Not good Shenkin, must do better tomorrow.'

'Right, better tomorrow. I'll get a wash down and fresh clothes. Meet you on the lower deck in a few minutes.'

Tinker held up a bunch of bananas that he had liberated from the hold. 'These plenty good for you, natural sugar followed by plenty water to wash away wine, yes?'

'Yes,' said Shenkin moving back along the forecastle deck. A sailor on the port side was pulling on a halyard which caught around Shenkin's legs. The boatswain's gruff voice bellowed across the deck. 'Watch that bloody halyard, you miserable landlubber.' But it was too late, Shenkin was whipped off his feet and came crashing down onto the deck with a loud thud. For a moment Shenkin was stunned Tinker, the boatswain and a number of the crew were around him.

Breaking through the circle of men Lieutenant Garret-Jarvis wanted to know what was going on. 'Well boatswain, speak up. What happened?'

'Its one of our passengers sir, he was...'

Shenkin cut him short. 'My own fault Lieutenant. I slipped on your well-scrubbed deck and your men came to my assistance. But I'm fine, no harm done. My apologies for interrupting the crew's work,' he said, turning to the crew members. 'Thank you all for your concerns.'

'If you're not familiar with the layout of a ship Benson, the last thing you should be doing is clambering about for hours on end.'

'Indeed, and you're quite right; it won't happen again.'

The lieutenant sneered. 'Indeed it will not. I'll have a word with the captain about it. Damn dangerous business for the crew and, more importantly the ship. I suggest you retire to your allocated quarters Benson, and get out of the bloody way,' said the Lieutenant, making his way back to the quarterdeck.

The boatswain lent Shenkin his arm and lifted him upright. 'I'll see you to below decks sir.'

Once they were together with Tinker and were out of sight and earshot the boatswain turned to Shenkin.

'Thank you sir, that man would have been put on punishment duties. He should have made sure no one was in the way before he began hauling away. I'll have a word with him sir, letting him know how lucky he was that you took the blame.'

'Its Harry isn't it?'

'It is sir,' said the boatswain.

'No damage done Harry, only to my pride in having to take a rebuke from the lieutenant.'

The boatswain smiled. 'I could see it took all your willpower to hold your temper. The lieutenant is not liked among the crew sir.'

'Or the passengers, Harry.'

Both men laughed as they made their way below but Tinker stopped them to take a closer look at Shenkin, running his hands over his arms and legs then his head. 'No broken bones thank goodness, but perhaps the lieutenant has a point. This is not the best place to train Sh…' Stopping himself, he went on, '…Charlie.'

If the boatswain spotted the mistake he said nothing. 'Right, I'll get him into to his hammock for a rest before the evening meal while you, my black-faced man, can go back to the hold.'

That evening they were again invited to join the captain for dinner. Sir Edward had come down to the midshipman's quarters to see Shenkin. 'Are you alright? I just heard about your fall. The lieutenant was reporting it to the captain. I left them to see for myself that you were not seriously hurt.'

'I am well Sir Edward, thank you. It was my own fault for suggesting it: not the place for running. I'll see you at the gun room for dinner.'

'Fine I'll see you then, but I fear the lieutenant will make the most of it and he appeared to have something more to add but wanted to leave it till tonight.'

The captain greeted Shenkin warmly with his hand upon Shenkin's shoulder. 'Nasty fall I understand Benson, but you seem well enough, is that so?'

'It is I'm fine, Captain Bellamy, and thank you for your concern. I'll not make the mistake again.'

The lieutenant, a glass of wine in hand, said, 'Indeed you will not sir. I'll not have it, a spell in irons would be the result.'

'You will not have it Lieutenant, you will not?' said Bellamy, adding, 'do not presume to issue threats on my ship, Acting Lieutenant.'

'I have the measure of this man sir, and am surprised Sir Edward associates with an ex-convict.' The serving of the meal, the clink of glasses and the general conversation became silent.

'Explain yourself Lieutenant, and choose your words very carefully.'

Garret-Jarvis permitted himself a slow sip of wine.

'Put the bloody wine down sir, and continue. For you are sorely stretching my temper.' The two men's different backgrounds and social standing became obvious. 'To question the characters of our passengers and guests at my invitation, to my table, on my ship, I regard as a breach of my standing and authority. I feel sure we have more than one set of chains on board sir. Do I make myself clear? You are not in your gilded home sir, you are in the British Navy and will defer to your superior officer before any high-handed accusations.'

The colour in the lieutenant's face said it all; he was being dressed down in front of everyone. 'I can prove the man's an ex-convict for as the boatswain was untangling Benson's legs, I clearly saw the unmistakable chain marks on his ankles. While a midshipman on HMS Franklin, we were commissioned as a convict ship bound for the penal colony in Sydney and I saw these same chain marks many times.'

Shenkin moved to stand then looking up at the timbers above, he sat back.

Addressing the captain he said, 'Captain, the lieutenant is...'

Bellamy raised his hand. 'You are an invited guest Mr Benson, aboard my ship. I judge a man by what he does, not what others say he is. I was on the quarterdeck when the incident happened and saw it all. You have nothing to explain sir, nothing.

You are at liberty to leave, Lieutenant, if you wish.'

The lieutenant moved his chair back with a scraping crash.

'Be assured sir, my father and the Admiralty will be acquainted with the facts.'

Captain Bellamy afforded himself a small smile. 'It's a long list that you have to report, Acting Lieutenant. Let them place it alongside my record.' Pausing for a moment, he added, 'that will be all. you are dismissed.'

'Steward,' Bellamy called out.

'Sir.'

'Stop listening at the door and serve dinner.'

'Sir.'

'Right!' said the captain. 'Who has the Claret?' He turned to Shenkin.

'Not another word Charlie. It's been a long time coming, before you even came aboard. Also I retire soon, so to hell with him and his nursery tell-tales.'

Sir Edward Standish stood between the beams. 'A toast gentlemen, the captain.'

'The Captain.'

'Indeed,' said the steward, spilling some gravy. Shame-faced, he said, 'Sorry, sir I got carried away like.'

For moment no one spoke; then they all laughed at once.

The rest of the voyage was uneventful with the lieutenant sour faced and excusing himself from the captain's table, which the captain did not question.

At last, to the sound of seagulls screaming around them, they were in sight of land on their portside and soon making their way along the coast. In no time, they were passing Sydney Cove and into Port Jackson. For Shenkin it seemed to take ages to get her into position but, with a loud splash as the crew moved efficiently around the decks, she was finally at anchor out in the bay.

Sir Edward standing at the captain's side, held out his hand. 'A fine voyage sir, our thanks to you and for your generosity during the crossing.'

'Its been my pleasure Sir Edward, to have you aboard, I assure you. I trust we will be able to meet up in Sydney when Benson fights again. In the meantime, with the evening fast approaching I'll have the boatswain make ready with the jolly boat to ferry you ashore.'

With farewells and handshakes all round, except for the lieutenant who just nodded, they were down the rope ladders and into the bobbing jolly boat, by which time it was getting dark. Lights were on the small but wide beam boat; under the command of the boatswain, the oars were soon dipping into the black water. The harbour lights looked welcoming but Harry Wilson leaned over to Shenkin. 'I'll land you down from the main harbour where it's darker if you follow my meaning he said, tapping the side of his noise.

Shenkin smiled. 'Thank you, Harry.'

'Obliged to you, Mr Wilson,' said Sir Edward.

'Right! Ship oars, douse lights.' The only light came from Tinker's bright white teeth.

With a bump they were at the harbour wall and about to stand on solid ground again.

Shenkin held his hand out to the boatswain. 'Thank you again, Harry.'

'Its been my pleasure sir. I wish you all the best for the future, and keep throwing punches at the face of your difficulties Shen... Mr Benson.' In a lower voice, he said, 'I saw that fight against Charlie Benson; a good man met a better one that night, good luck to you.'

'Thank you, Harry.'

Then with a dip of oars, they sailed into the night leaving their passengers looking for a coach. The rattle of iron-hoop-bound wheels on the uneven stony road prompted Sir Edward to step into the light of a wharfside pub and hail the coach down. Soon they were on their way back into Sydney where the reckoning would begin.

'Doctor Tarn's place first, Sir Edward,' said Shenkin settling back into his seat.

CHAPTER 31

'Who is it?'

'I remember once you called me a friend,' called Shenkin.

The door opened immediately. 'I'd know that voice anywhere,' said Patrick Tarn grabbing Shenkin by the shoulders. 'Come in, come in quickly. How and by what means are you back in Sydney? For I had given up hope of ever seeing you again Shenkin, and Regan. Where is that big lovable countryman of mine?'

'Dead, Doctor.'

'No, never, not Regan surely? I can't believe it,' said Tarn.

'It's a long story to be told over a glass of, well anything for we've been on the cold sea these past few hours.'

'Sit down, sit down, gentlemen. It's so good to see you again too, Sir Edward and Tinker, my dear friends. Let me open a bottle of rum to warm you all.'

Bottle at the ready, Tarn bid them sit while he filled their glasses.

Glasses in hand, of a reasonable shot of rum, with water for Tinker, Shenkin told their story.

Tarn sat still for a long time while Shenkin told him all that had happened while he slowly turned his glass, the fire light catching the deep colour of the rum. Finally, he said, 'It's an incredible escape Shenkin, and you do indeed look like Charlie Benson. I am so sorry about Elizabeth and your child, which I knew about of course here in Sydney. But Regan and Charlie Benson too? It's all so sad; it's been a very heavy price. While, here in Sydney, I regret to tell you that Lord Feltsham continues to scale the heights of power and influence I'm afraid.' He shrugged his shoulders. 'But tell me, what's your next move? Staying around Sydney would be very dangerous.'

Shenkin downed the last of his rum and said, 'Tomorrow, if you could put us up for the night, we'll go up to Blacktown to Charlie's farm where I'll lay low for a month or so.'

'Of course you must stay the night. I'll make the arrangements now.'

Shenkin nodded his head. 'I knew I could rely upon you Doctor, thank you. I continue to be in your debt.'

'Nonsense, I'll send my housekeeper out for some extra food in the morning for now we have enough for a light supper,' said Tarn. Opening the study door, he called out, 'Rachel, a moment please.'

After a moment or so, a young woman of about twenty came into the room. She had dark curly hair, which fell about her pretty heart-shaped face that one would have called innocent were it not for the hard knowing look in her eyes. The eyes told of hardship, awareness and an ill-treated abused life. However, she smiled at the doctor with a gaze that was full of trust and affection.

'Rachel, these gentlemen are staying the night. Can we arrange sleeping places for them?'

'Of course, Doctor. No beds I'm sorry to say, but I'll put something together that'll be comfy enough.'

Tarn smiled. 'Thank you Rachel. I know you'll do the best you can. However, you've never seen them here, do you understand?'

'Seen who, sir?'

'Exactly.'

When she had gone about her task, closing the door firmly behind her, Tarn turned to his guests.

'A lovely pretty child with an ugly past, I'm sorry to say. She came from England a year ago on a female convict ship, sentenced to eight years for disorderly conduct and stealing a yard of cloth and a petticoat. She had been on the streets since she was twelve. Her father threw her out for not letting him have sex with her. Her mother, a prostitute and drunkard, beat her for not sharing any money from stolen goods with her. I met her when I treated her for malnourishment and leg ulcers in the Female Prison in the Rocks only a few weeks after she had arrived. Too ill to take on any worthwhile work in the prison, I persuaded the court to let me employ her as a house maid and that I would stand warranty for her good behaviour. The upshot of it was that they were only too pleased to be rid of her. They were feeding her, but with nothing to show for it, so she has been here ever since. She just wanted kindness and care which had been denied her all her young life. But now I have a problem with the Mothers Guild here in Sydney.'

Shenkin raised his eyebrows. 'Mothers Guild, pray who are they, Doctor?'

'The guild is made up of the wives, widows and spinsters of the new so-called gentry here in Sydney, many of whom are of questionable backgrounds themselves, and converts are invariably the worst kind of hypocrites,' said Tarn.

Sir Edward nodded. 'Indeed they are, Doctor. I have met them by the hundreds in London society, busybodies with nothing better to do then tittle-tattle to each other.'

'So what are they saying, Doctor?' said Shenkin.

'That it is not morally acceptable that a young woman, convict or not, should be living in a house on her own with a bachelor man.'

Shenkin sighed. 'But a man, if you will forgive me for saying, who is old enough to be her father, a respected doctor and a man of high reputation, it's ridiculous.'

Tarn smiled a slow smile. 'Old enough to be her grandfather Shenkin, but such is the narrow-minded way of the guild members. I could ignore them of course, and continue to lose paying patients, already the wives are cancelling appointments which means the children will not be sent to me or, of course, the husbands. So I must find somewhere for her to go. But that is now not easy, given the malicious talk here in Sydney Town.'

Shenkin put his hand on Tarn's shoulder. 'She'll come with us to Blacktown, Doctor, where I understand there are females working in the houses and on the land. I'll undertake her safety and her protection if you'll let me.'

Sir Edward stood up, his glass in hand. 'Of course the perfect solution, Shenkin. Let's drink to it and to Rachel's future.'

Tarn looked from one to the other. 'My dear, dear friends, it would take such a worry from my mind. I cannot thank you enough.'

'Good, that's agreed then; tell her to pack tonight for tomorrow we leave early,' Shenkin said, raising his glass.

'Rachel,' called Tarn.

In a few moments Rachel came into the room, a blanket over her arm. 'You called, Doctor?'

'After you finish the sleeping arrangements, my dear, you must pack your belongings, for you are to leave in the morning with these friends of mine.'

Rachel stood very still, visually shocked, the blanket she was holding dropped to the floor. 'No please, Doctor, don't send me away from here. My work is satisfactory is it not?'

Tarn bade her sit down. 'It is indeed my dear, but it would be better if you were away from all that might harm you; did you not tell me people called you names and even threw stones at you while you were out shopping?'

Head held high, Rachel said, 'I do not care sir, for your kindness is worth all the hurt in the world.'

'Please my dear girl, do not make this even harder for me than it is, for this house will indeed seem empty and the poorer without you, but it is for the best I assure you. These men are trusted friends, also there will be other women where they are taking you who will make for good companionship. What is there here but an old man set in his ways, dreary and dull?'

Rachel, tears now filling her eyes, looked at Tarn. 'A dreary old man that I have come to love like no father I ever had,' she said, tears now in full flood.

'Then listen to your father's advice: go and be safe. I promise to come and visit you in your new home. Now away with you before this old Irishman shares your tears.'

Picking the blanket up she slowly left the room, closing the door quietly behind her, only her sobs sounded in the hallway.

'Take good care of her Shenkin, I beg you. My apologies, of course you will, you all will. I know that.'

'Of course we will,' said Sir Edward, an audible sniff coming from his aristocratic head.

'Another drink quick, before we are all affected by this unashamed show of emotion,' said Shenkin, his glass out in front of him.

Tinker, with clouded eyes, nodded. 'It's times like this that I too wish I had taken up this habit of fire drinking.'

The comment released the moment's sense of sadness and turned it into laughter.

'She'll be fine. Gentlemen, I give you Blacktown,' said Shenkin.

Glasses clinked as the call went up, 'Blacktown.'

Placing his glass down, Shenkin said, 'I'll need the money you've been holding for me, Doctor, for which I am most grateful.'

'It's ready whenever you wish it, Shenkin.'

'I'll take it with me then come morning, for I'll need it to put my plans in place; but first the sale of Charlie's stock, the money to go to his brother.

His man can acquaint me with all that is of the house and land, Tinker is going to find sheep for me, and Sir Edward promises to guide me through the running of a sheep farm.'

'You mean sheep station Shenkin, not farm,' said Sir Edward.

Shenkin gave a small sigh. 'I fear I have much to learn Doctor, but if I am to avenge myself of Lord Feltsham I must be ready.'

Sir Edward smiled, took a sip of his drink and turned to Shenkin. 'It will take time you know that, but I believe this will put you on the best path to achieve your plans, so let us drink finally to that aim.'

'To "Bare-Knuckle Sheep Station", Blacktown, gentlemen and all it stands for.'

'Of course, Bare-Knuckle farm, thank you, Sir Edward. Tinker, can you make a branding iron in the shape of a fist?'

'One or two fists, Shenkin?'

'One for the sheep and cattle and one for over the entrance to Charlie's farm; he'd like that.'

Excitement was in the air for the future as Rachel opened the door and announced. 'The beds are ready, Doctor.' Sobs still in her voice.

'Thank you, Rachel. You need to be ready to leave early tomorrow, so let us all say goodnight and get a good night's sleep.'

CHAPTER 32

Early the following morning after thanking Tarn for all his help, they set off for Blacktown. During the night the doctor had arranged for horses to be brought to the house and had given Shenkin a secure metal box containing the money that Goldspick had given for the diamond pendant.

Shenkin bought two of the horses, his first purchase in his new life. However, he was not looking forward to riding a horse again.

Blacktown was some twenty miles west of Sydney and Shenkin must have fallen off more times than that in the first ten miles, much to the laughter of Sir Edward, a fine horseman. Tinker, and even Rachel between her sobs, who rode behind Sir Edward clinging on to him for dear life, joined in the laughter. Tinker as always, ran by their side. A mere twenty miles was but a short stroll for him, his steady loping stride never faltering, except for picking Shenkin up off the ground with roars of laughter.

Soon, to Shenkin's great relief, they were at Parramatta where they stopped for water and food, and to clean their faces and clothes of dust. Tinker told them the name Parramatta meant 'the place where the eels lie' in the Darug language and that Government House there was more popular than Sydney's. Governor Arthur Phillip certainly preferred it when he established Parramatta as the second European settlement.

Blacktown was so named because of Governor Macquarie's land grants to aborigines, and the area of the settlements soon became known as Black's Town. Tinker told them two aborigines had helped soldiers travel overland in the early years of the colony and that they had been rewarded with a parcel of thirty acres. Tinker could not resist saying it was land that had been lived on for thousands of years by the Darug people, and vast in size; but these two were given just thirty acres for their trouble. Bitterness etched each word that Tinker spoke, for the sheer arrogance the act expressed.

Sir Edward gave a deep sigh. 'In such a way do stronger nations build Empires Tinker, and not just the British; but I understand your anger my friend.'

Shenkin placed his hand on Tinker's shoulder. 'We will soon be on Bare-Knuckle farm, or I should say station, Tinker where we will build our own empire, is that not so my friend?'

'If you say so, Shenkin, so it will be.'

How many times had Elizabeth and Regan said that? thought Shenkin. And as god was his judge, he would make it happen.

A few hours more and they were on the outskirts of Blacktown. Sir Edward opened the map Charlie Benson had given them. 'Over that hill and we should see the station,' he said, pointing to a raised ridge of ground not more then a half a mile ahead of them.

'It's good land Shenkin,' said Tinker, a handful of earth in his hand that he rubbed between his palms, then raised his cupped hands to his nose and smelt slowly, letting the reddish dust fall to the ground. 'Yes, good earth.'

Tommy Bright was at the entrance to the station. He was mounted on a white horse, a musket tucked under his right arm, his hand resting lightly over the hammer. A surprisingly small man, his stature made smaller by the powerful horse he sat astride, but his stare was rock steady.

'Welcome to our sheep station gentlemen. Sir Edward Standish, I have met before at various fights that Charlie fought. But the rest of you need to explain your visit before we go to the house,' he said, in a firm voice. His tone was flat, to the point, unapologetic.

Shenkin passed him Charlie's letter. He read it slowly, carefully, unhurriedly. Shenkin liked him immediately, a slow smile coming to his face. Turning to Sir Edward, he nodded. 'Charlie knew his man, Sir Edward.'

'Indeed'.

Lifting his head, Tommy Bright looked over at Shenkin. 'You certainly have the look of Charlie about you, even down to the scar. Had I been at that fight you would not have won Shenkin, but Charlie insisted you were the better fighter that night. I know better then anyone how hard that was for him to admit,' he said. Swallowing hard, he added, 'did he die well?'

'As he fought,' said Shenkin, leaving a pause. 'He was the best I ever met inside the ring and one of the very best I ever met outside of the ring.

'Thank you for that; we had been together for many years. He saved my life the day we met. I'll tell you about it one day if you earn it.'

Shenkin smiled. 'It's my aim to Tommy, if I may call you Tommy, for Charlie spoke of you many times.'

'You may so call me. I was his man in every corner of his life so, with this letter and the will, I am now yours.' For heartbeats no one spoke. Then Tommy, his head bent as if giving a private prayer, looked up. Finally, he said, 'Let's go home.'

Everyone relaxed as Tommy Bright turned his horse and led the way on to the sheep station land. 'We should be there in a day's ride. We'll camp here tonight, then at first light we ride to the home house.' He threw the words over his shoulder and rode over to a flat piece of ground upon which was erected a small timber building.

'A day's ride?' said Shenkin, in amazement. Sir Edward turned to him.

'Most sheep stations are large Shenkin. It seems you have been willed a sizeable amount of New South Wales,' he said. 'Why man, you can build one of the largest sheep stations on this continent; it's incredible and much larger than my place.'

'Tinker, what do you think?'

'Well Shenkin, it's a great deal to handle but land is land whatever the size. Together we'll tame it, and I think, by breeding not just sheep for their wool but also cattle for their meat.'

Tommy Bright turned in his saddle. 'I agree with your man, but it would take a lot of money to do that.'

Shenkin smiled, resting his hand on the metal box in his saddlebag containing the proceeds from the diamond pendant. 'I have some funds Tommy, and will also be fighting again. Incidentally, we're going to call the place Bare-Knuckle Sheep Station; I think Charlie would like that.'

'He would indeed, yes. "BKSS". I like it Shenkin. I like it.'

'Good, then so it will be,' said Shenkin.

'If you say so Shenkin, if you say so,' said Sir Edward, laughing.

Kangaroos jumped nervously at the sound of the laughter while many-coloured birds rose in the slowly darkening sky that spread out over Shenkin's land.

It was difficult for Shenkin to take it all in. The land before them went on and on it took his breath away. He had never owned anything before in his life now this, this overwhelming generosity from Charlie Benson, brought a lump to his throat. He'd not fail; he must not fail. It would be hard work with so much to learn but he would do it. By god's good grace he would build an empire and if not god's, then by his own sweat, determination and sheer bloody arrogance for this was the way to bring Feltsham down and get his daughter back, his Beth, his love. Shenkin looked up to the now dark sky.

'We are home, Elizabeth. From here, however long it may take, I will see that justice is done for you and our daughter. I swear it.'

It would be an incredible challenge: land to conquer, sheep to raise and cattle to breed; water to find and heat and diseases to fight, but each would be a step closer to Lord Percival Hugo Feltsham. The journey was set in place, the aim clear: this one man's downfall. The hate and need for revenge was burned as deep into Shenkin's soul as the iron marks around his ankles. He would prevail. He would succeed in the name of all those he had loved who had suffered because of this man. Looking up at the sky above BKSS land, Shenkin pledged his future life to it.

CHAPTER 33

Shenkin stood very still, his scarred face seemed made of stone as he looked out at the land from the wide veranda of the home house at Blacktown, west of Sydney. He was remembering all that had happened over these past years. He had been many things: a political dissident, a man transported to a penal colony for twenty years' hard labour, a coal miner, a bare-knuckle fighter, a wronged man. Now, at this moment on this day, he found himself the owner of a large sheep station that had been willed to him by his dying friend Charlie Benson. He was also still a convict on the run from the notorious Van Diemen's Land Port Arthur penal colony. Daniel Shenkin, aka Charlie Benson, a Welshman from old South Wales, now he found himself here in New South Wales, the owner of a sheep station. He had been sentenced to death, which was later commuted to transportation, for leading that uprising against the sovereign state of England. He had been sent to 'a place beyond the seas', the penal colony of Sydney. At Blacktown the nearest large town was Parramatta, it had been inhabited by the Darug aboriginals for over thirty thousand years. In their language it means, 'head of the waters, river of the eels'. The British had founded Parramatta in 1788, the year the First Fleet arrived when the land around Botany Bay and Sydney Cove had proved to poor to grow crops that were desperately needed to feed over a thousand con-victs, soldiers and administrators who had arrived from England. The then governor, Arthur Phillip, had reconnoitred several places before choosing Parramatta as the most promising place for a large farm. It was inland away from the sandy coast line, and at a point where the river became freshwater, which was necessary for good farming land.

He looked out at the fertile land in front of him, what he was trying to come to terms with was that it was now all his. The early evening light was casting shadows across the horizon for as far as the eye could see and it was all his, he kept repeating it to himself over and over again.

He shook his head at the incredibility of it all. Just under six feet tall, his burly powerful frame seemed to be carved from rock; he had come a long way from his black mining valley in South Wales.

Now all this. It was difficult to take in for he was no farmer, he was a coal miner, a bare-knuckle fighter, an escaped convict, a fugitive from justice, a hunted man. Since arriving in this place 'beyond the seas' he had lost the woman he loved and their child. He had survived the penal barracks in Sydney, and Port Arthur's brutal prison. Then the escape across Van Diemen's Land where he had lost two of his closest friends to the spears of unfriendly aboriginal tribes. One was Regan O'Hara, the wild Irishman, they had fought on the slag-heaped mountain above Merthyr Tydfil then become friends during the workers' fight for the right to vote. The other was Charlie Benson, his fellow bare-knuckle fighter who had helped him escape from the prison and had then insisted, while he lay dying, that he take over his identity and had willed him this property with his last breath. He had buried them both in that primeval forest, on Van Diemen's Land, cutting his own name on the cross of Charlie Benson. Much of what he had endured was down to one man, Lord Percival Hugo Feltsham, who Shenkin had sworn to get even with if he could go on surviving, for he was already on borrowed time. All of this past went around and around in Shenkin's mind, the spell finally broken by the arrival behind him of Sir Edward Standish, his benefactor who had also become a close friend ever since they had met at one of Shenkin's bare-knuckle fights. Their social class could not be further apart, but their bond of friendship was the closer because of it.

'Well Shenkin, how does it feel to be a landowner?' said Sir Edward, with a smile.

Shenkin turned to greet his friend. 'I just cannot believe it, Sir Edward. It's just too overwhelming,' said Shenkin, throwing his arms in the air. 'All this, why it's more then a man can accept as true.'

'Believe it Shenkin. Charlie acquired a truly superb piece of land; make the most of it.'

Shenkin nodded. 'Firstly, I need to know the number and value of the sheep already here so that I can pay Charlie's brother his inheritance.'

'Yes, of course. Tommy Bright has been acting as stockman so I'll discuss it with him in the morning. As to the labour force, well much of it is convict labour both the men and the women, so the costs are low and you'll need more if you intend to have cattle as well.'

Shenkin was not comfortable with this. 'I am here in this "place beyond the seas" because I fought for the rights of the working class Sir Edward. I organised a rising in old South Wales. People died on my encouragement as one of their leaders, do I now join the very profit-making company owners that I denounced?' Shenkin said, bitterness etched deep in every word he spoke.

'Yes,' said Sir Edward Standish, bluntly. 'If you want to make a success of this place.'

For a long drawn-out moment, silence hung in the air between them. Finally Sir Edward spoke.

'Listen to me Shenkin, you can change it from within, speak up for the convicts that work for you, give them their wages, their rights, but first make this place a solid financial success.' Sir Edward paused for a moment. 'It's called compromise, Shenkin. Can you do that for Elizabeth and your child, for Regan and Charlie Benson?'

Shenkin said nothing.

Silence strained the moment. Multi-coloured birds shrieked as they flew past to roost in the trees at the far end of the fenced field while opposite them Tommy Bright rode into view, running at his side were men carrying farming tools over to a row of low-built sheds.

'Well,' said Sir Edward, finally.

Shenkin stirred himself from his almost frozen state, the word betrayal spinning around in his mind. 'I…' he stuttered. 'It's too difficult I can't give up all I believe in, to betray all those beliefs.'

'It would certainly be a betrayal of those who died to make this moment happen, to bring you here to give you the chance to really make a difference, to help the working class man to a better future. Damn it Shenkin, wasn't that what your rising was about?' Not waiting for reply, Sir Edward went on. 'And not least of all, to enable you to take revenge on the man responsible for Elizabeth's death.'

'I value your advice and friendship Sir Edward, but would you please leave me? I need to come to terms with this in my own way.'

'Of course I understand,' he said, and left.

The evening wind caught the door behind him and slammed it shut, the sound vibrated through the enveloping darkness. The birds screamed again.

An owl, or some other bird or animal also startled by the noise, called into the night sky, a plaintive, melancholic sound. Whatever it was it echoed Shenkin's moment of soul searching. He knew he must keep faith with those who had believed in him, had given their lives to bring about this moment; but it was hard. What would his father have said? For he too had given his life during the rising in their Welsh valley for the rights of the working man, the right to be heard, the right to vote for their futures and that of their children. He knew Sir Edward was right, that this sheep station would give him the opportunity to change the lot of the working man, slowly at first, but if he was successful it would give him a voice to be listened to. Was that the compromise that Sir Edward spoke of? If not then he would remain a convict, a victim of an unjust world to be hunted like an animal. The vote would stay in the hands of the ruling classes who were there by an accident of birth, born into a world of privilege and money earned by others. Driving some to steal a loaf of bread or jug of milk to feed their families, turning them into criminals, to become convicts in a 'land beyond the seas', the hard brutal penal colonies of Australia.

Shenkin turned to the door into his study, yes his study, again finding it difficult to believe. He found Sir Edward smoking a long clay pipe at the side of the fireplace, for after the heat of the day there was now a chill in the air.

Sir Standish looked up. 'Well?' he said, through a cloud of smoke.

'Where and when do we begin?' Shenkin said.

'Excellent, you have made the right decision my friend. As to where, why, right here; and to the when, right now. We begin by valuing the stock. The numbers and the current market price, which I will help you with. You will pay Charlie's brother the price these would bring as his inheritance in Charlie's will.'

At supper that first night on his sheep station, they all sat around the long table in the main house, including the aboriginal Tinker who Shenkin insisted on having present.

The meal was mutton cooked outside by the convict women. The meal was enjoyed by all and washed down with the new John Tooth beer from their Sydney Kent Brewery, acquired by Tommy Bright, their stockman, on his last visit to Parramatta for provisions. For a long moment no one spoke, each aware that after all that they had gone though this was the decisive turning point.

CHAPTER 34

'Well, gentlemen, what do you think of the beer?' asked Tommy Bright in an effort to lighten the moment.

Sir Edward placed his tankard down. 'I am used to London Porter, sir, though I must say this is very agreeable, but let us turn our minds to the station.'

'Let us indeed, you want to know how large it is and how many sheep it supports, is that not so?'

Shenkin nodded.

'Well, it will support three to four times what we have at the moment. Charlie was slowly building it up when he had the money to do so. He was, as you know, no longer fighting, that income was being replaced by selling low quantities of wool to the larger stations both here in Parramatta and in Bathurst but it takes time and it's very labour intensive,' said Bright.

Again Shenkin nodded. 'Alright, I understand. Firstly, I want an evaluation on the present stock Tommy, money to this value will be put aside for Charlie's brother. Secondly, Tinker, can you give me a report, verbally, of the quality of the grazing and the level of water supply we can rely on.'

Tinker nodded.

'Thirdly, Sir Edward, can you act as my broker in handling the purchasing of more sheep, cattle and the machinery we need to support this increase?'

Sir Edward was relighting his pipe, satisfied that it was well packed down and burning well, he said, 'I need to ride over to my place first and speak to my stockman to assess the current well being of the station, after that I am at your disposal.'

'Thank you, Sir Edward. Gentlemen, let us drink to our plans,' said Shenkin.

After placing their glasses back on the table, Sir Edward said, 'There is another thing we have not discussed.'

'Which is?' said Shenkin, looking at Sir Edward through a cloud of smoke.

'Why, your next fight, Shenkin, under the name of Charlie Benson.'

'The purse money would be very useful but where? For I can't go to Sydney, where the money is.'

'Well that is not entirely true, sporting men will go where the main sporting events are, so why not Bathurst or Newcastle? I know a number of sporting gentlemen in those areas who would be interested to encourage, and indeed promote, bare-knuckle bouts. Also you would be more readily accepted as Charlie away from Sydney.'

Shenkin considered for a few moments then said, 'Very well, see what can be set up, Sir Edward.'

For the next month they were all busy putting their plans into action. The number and value of the sheep already on the station was established. Shenkin marked this money down for Captain Saxon, Charlie Benson's brother, who they learned was now on his way to England with a cargo of wool. Sir Edward had also spoken to some of his sporting gentlemen and a fight had been arranged with a local fighter at Bathurst, one John Billings a sheep shearer and a favourite fancy of William Tellman, a wealthy cattle owner in the area and a self styled gentleman. Tellman also owned a number of race horses, a sport that had quickly caught on since the importation of both Arab and English thoroughbred horses into the colony. Tellman was a keen gambler and had fancies in every weight of bare-knuckle fighter, but it was Billings who had made Tellman the most money.

Sir Edward said, 'He is good, Shenkin. Tellman has made a great deal of money on promoting him both at Bathurst and Parramatta and, given his wins, Tellman is finding it hard to match him. Ten fights to date, eight by knockouts and two by his opponent's corner having to call a halt to the fight to save their man from further punishment.'

Shenkin nodded. 'His age, height, build and reach?'

'Twenty-two or three, six foot three inches tall, powerful build, don't know his reach, he believes he is unbeatable, intends to fight in Sydney next. Since you left Sydney, the man to beat there is regarded by the colony as the New South Wales champion. He goes by the name of George Powell, an ex-convict now on a "ticket of leave" and working in the Fortune of War pub as a pot-man. He's the fancy of Major John Peterson-Palmer.'

Shenkin nodded. 'Right, Billings first. What's the purse, date and where?'

'Fifty pound purse, but a large crowd will attend making side bets worthwhile, and, as I said, the fight will be at Bathurst at a field just outside of the town at seven o'clock on the evening of the 21st, two weeks' time. All the arrangements are being made by Tellman, who believes after the beating Shenkin gave you, your best days are over and you're no longer the fighter you were,' said Sir Edward, with a smile.

'Then let's confirm the arrangement and thank you, Sir Edward.'

'I'll go to Bathurst tomorrow and place the purse.'

Turning to Tinker, Shenkin said, 'What of the grass and water, can it support what we have in mind?'

Sir Edward Standish noted that Shenkin was adapting fast to his new role of running a station and making the necessary decisions to bring their plans to fruition.

Tinker had grass in front of him and a pot of water from the station's river. 'Its more than we need and then some. Charlie chose his farm well, Shenkin; it will support a mix of stock too.'

'Thank you, Tinker.'

Turning to Tommy Bright, Shenkin said, 'You told me we need a number of rams, Tommy. What progress there?'

'There is an auction in Parramatta next Saturday and a friend tells me there will be a number of rams for sale. If we can successfully bid for them they would, together with the twenty-six we already have, more than meet our present needs.'

Shenkin sat back in his study chair with a sigh. 'We seem to be making good progress. What news of Lord Feltsham among the social circles of Sydney, Sir Edward?'

Lifting his arms in a display of resignation, he said, 'The bloody man goes from strength to strength, his sheep stations, of which he now has three, are all doing well with demands for wool in England at an all-time high.' Placing his hands in an open gesture of acceptance, he added, 'he is going to be difficult to match, Shenkin.'

'Then we have no time to lose Sir Edward, if we are to bring the bastard to account. So first, the fight, I'll train here on the station, of course. Tinker, can you pace me in running? And, Tommy will you act as my corner man, with Tinker as my cut man, since Charlie assured me you were one of the best?'

Tommy Bright pulled himself up to his full five foot three inch height. 'It'll be my pleasure Shenkin. I'll be interested to see what you have. It must be good, to have beaten Charlie.'

'If it isn't Tommy, then I'll be pleased to listen to your advice,' said Shenkin.

For the next two weeks they all worked hard from early morning to late at night, for apart from the fight preparations, the sheep had to be seen to, together with all the running needs of the station. Tommy Bright had engaged more convict labour and had also successfully bid for the rams that now had to be settled into their new surroundings.

Shenkin was running five miles every morning against Tinker's gruelling forced pace. The day before the fight, Tinker doubled up on the run and declared Shenkin fit.

The following evening, in a field outside of Bathurst, the noise of the crowd seemed, as it always did to Shenkin, a single roar that covered everything like a heavy blanket. Across from him, John Billings danced in his corner, full of the confidence of youth, eager to get on with the fight. The purses had been placed in the hands of one of the sporting gentleman present, of which there were a number. The side bets were plentiful and Sir Edward had placed a large bet on Charlie Benson to win; so far no one had doubted that it was Charlie Benson who was fighting. To Shenkin's regret, he did not see Feltsham at the ring side but it may have been just as well, he thought, given his true identity.

Tommy Bright leaned over to speak to Shenkin, or rather to shout above the noise of the crowd. 'He has a long reach, Shenkin. I'd say at least seventy-five inches; you'll need to fight inside his arms.'

Shenkin nodded. 'Yes, I'll lean back a little further than usual to ensure my head is out of reach, then force him to bend his arms by pulling him towards me. He has a powerful build but can he punch with all his weight? We'll see soon enough.'

Tinker and Shenkin had spent the last hour on a good vigorous work out, to bring up his sweat, and he felt relaxed but wished Regan was here too. Still, he heard him in his mind whispering encouragement laced with sarcastic remarks.

'Careful Shenkin, now don't go losing for we'll be needing money for a few jugs when it's all over. And I'm glad to see you haven't got that bloody pigtail any more, sure your father would be pleased too.'

It brought a smile to Shenkin's lips as they were called to up to the line. Each man held up his open hands to show there was nothing more than skin in their palms. The square had timber stakes in each corner with runs of rope joining the posts. The ground was uncovered, making the field's grass slippery under their feet, but Shenkin was used to this, for in his black valley up in the mountains of Wales it rarely stopped raining, so Shenkin knew how to use it to his advantage. Everyone moved back and they began to circle each other. The younger man, at six foot three inches, seemed to tower over Shenkin's five foot eleven, causing more bets to go on and many more ales to be slid down the dry throat of the animal called the crowd.

'Beat the bastard to a pulp, Johnny boy. Get that right hook going.'

'Hit the old man, Billings; he's no right to be in the same ring.'

'Put him away, Johnny boy.'

So the calls went on, but Shenkin heard none of it as he judged the other man. Then Billings threw his first blow, a left jab to Shenkin's head; he caught the blow on his upper arm. Strong yes, but Billings stood still as he gauged the distance; then he did it again. Shenkin smiled, the man was making it clear when he intended to use his right. *That's his first mistake*, thought Shenkin. Leaning back, Shenkin moved out of distance of Billings' reach; the blow hit thin air. Now, thought Shenkin, how good was he at taking a punch. Shenkin moved left, then neatly stepped right. That placed him inside Billings' swinging arms. Shenkin's right moved no more then a few inches, catching Billings across his head. Down he went onto his left knee.

The first round was over. Shenkin walked slowly back to his corner. 'Hell that was good, but don't put him away too early Shenkin, or you'll not fight again in this area,' said Tommy Bright.

Shenkin turned to Bright. 'He's overconfident Tommy, and sloppy in his movements. To make it look good, I'll have to carry him for a few rounds.'

Tommy Bright looked at Shenkin. 'I watched you Shenkin, and now I see what Charlie meant: you seem to float on your feet and that right had all your controlled power behind it, just enough to put him down but not out.' He gave a sigh. 'It's a rare gift,' he said, with unashamed admiration. After sixty seconds for the knock down, both men came up to the scratch again.

The fight went on for the next six rounds with Shenkin nursing Billings around the ring.

After almost two hours of both going to the ground, Shenkin had red marks around his arms and shoulders where he had blocked wild blows from Billings. Turning to his corner, Shenkin said, 'We need to finish this Tommy, it's becoming more difficult to make it look convincing. How do the bets look?'

'Sir Edward says he can't get any more on for you, the bookies are closing their books, so yes, it's time to go home,' he said, with a smile.

'Tinker, what do you think?'

Tinker's dazzling white teeth lit up the fading light. 'I agree, not a mark on your face and purse money to rattle in your pockets. Let's go home.'

Up to the scratch mark they came. John Billings smiled. 'I'm too good, Benson: you can't hurt me, you're too old and you'll be on the floor in this round. You'll not get up.'

Shenkin gave a small grin. Billings led with his left, then again he stood still to throw his right. Shenkin stepped inside the swinging windmill of arms, a short left hit Billings in the stomach then Shenkin's right moved up to Billings' chest, causing him to bend slightly at the impact of the now much stronger blows that caused Billings' mouth to fall open. He never saw Shenkin's right uppercut drive upwards to his now slack chin, a trap door opened and Billings went through it with a thud. It was all over.

Shocked silence stilled the crowd, followed by the usual roar of wonderment. Money changed hands, fights broke out, beer was spilled and half-eaten pies were trodden on. Billings was still unconscious in the now crowded ring.

'Give him air,' shouted Tellman, a look of disbelief on his face. He walked over to Shenkin. 'I've never seen a blow so well delivered, a lucky punch perhaps?'

'Not for your man sir, who may well have a broken jaw,' said Shenkin.

'No,' said Tellman, handing over the purse to Sir Edward, who then collected the side bets.

CHAPTER 35

By late evening they were all back at the sheep station counting the winnings.

'A good day's work, Shenkin,' said Sir Edward.

Tommy Bright stood up. 'Good? Why, it was the finest display of bare-knuckle fighting I have ever seen. Your father taught you well, Shenkin. You hit with every ounce of your body; that's a rare talent. I now see why you beat Charlie, who was the best I'd seen up to today. I wouldn't presume to teach you anything. It was a lesson in the craft of bare-knuckle fighting: a privilege to watch and an honour to be in your corner,' he said in a flurry of words.

'Thank you Tommy, good of you to say,' said Shenkin, a little embarrassed.

'Tellman took the defeat well, even saying it was the neatest knock down he had ever seen and would we be interested in him taking a percentage in you. I told him we'd get back to him but that I doubted it,' said Sir Edward.

'No, we keep this strictly between ourselves,' said Shenkin.

'Of course.'

For moments all was quiet, each man going over the events of the day. the spell was broken by Tinker.

'Can we talk about the running of the station.' Not waiting for a response, he continued, 'We have a number of predators on the land: dingoes, foxes, theft by aborigines, and some sheep just wander off into the bush. That means we need shepherds, who will also need to carry guns.'

'Right, where do we get them from?' said Shenkin.

'The shepherds from our convict labour. Given the guns, they will need to be carefully chosen.'

'Right, and the guns.'

'Tommy tells me there's a store in Parramatta where he can purchase a couple of muskets, together with at least two Baker rifles,' said Tinker, turning to Tommy Bright.

'That's right, the muskets will cost between three to four pounds each. The

Baker's much more costly, but the rifling inside the barrels causing the shot to spin means it's more accurate and has a longer range.'

'Get them Tommy; we may have more need of them than for dingos alone.'

Tommy nodded. 'Right.'

'We have the rams, which are no good without enough ewes. What progress do we have on that, Sir Edward?'

'Well Shenkin, you have a hundred and twenty thousand acres all told with, according to Tommy, around a thousand sheep already grazing with fifteen rams, plus the ones we've just purchased. It could support a great deal more than that, say, up to a flock of ten thousand in the long term. Now, with twenty more stud pedigree rams and more being added to our breeding programme as the station progresses, given one ram can service fifty ewes, we'll need two hundred rams if we build up to ten thousand sheep. A big enterprise Shenkin, it would take a great deal of money and effort but you have already begun.'

Shenkin nodded.

'And Feltsham, what does he have?'

'At the moment he has three sheep stations with a collective flock of around fifty thousand sheep, a wool mill, and the best machinery money can buy. So less labour intensive, higher outputs, resulting in a great deal more profit, it's a high mountain to climb Shenkin. His social standing has gone up now that he is married to an influential society lady with a small daughter from his previous beloved wife, whose memory he commemorates with a plaque in ex-convict architect Francis Greenway's St James' church on King Street. The plaque was placed with great ceremony and a bequest given to the church of an undisclosed amount, giving rise to rumour of a large donation, thus further establishing him as a great benefactor to Sydney.'

'The bastard, he'll not get away with it I swear it,' said Shenkin, his fist in a ball at his side.

'A heady peak to climb Shenkin, and all is on his side, even his wayward ways are ignored, given his power and social standing. To bring him down will be very difficult, particularly by a convict on the run.'

'Indeed Sir Edward, but not impossible. We are both gamblers are we not? So while we build the station up over the next months, will you put it about Sydney that Charlie Benson is looking for a chance to fight for the bare-knuckle championship with a purse of four thousand pounds?' A gasp went up from everyone around the table.

'What? Why that is a phenomenal figure Shenkin. It's never been that high for any sporting event here in the colony,' said Sir Edward, in amazement.

'How long will it take me to be as influential as Lord Feltsham?'

Sir Edward gave a slow, knowing smile. 'I take your meaning Shenkin, a short-cut, but if you lost, you'd be finished.'

'If I lost.'

'It's a huge gamble, Shenkin,' said Sir Edward, again.

The stillness in the room was palpable. Rachel came into the room with more wine but, sensing the mood, placed the wine down very quietly and left.

Eventually Shenkin looked around the table. 'Well, what do you all think?' Without waiting for a reply, Shenkin went on, 'Tinker, what do you think?'

'You are asking an aborigine, who places no value in material things, we own nothing and nothing owns us: the air, the water, the earth and fire are all free so I have nothing to lose.'

'Tommy, what do you think?'

'Charlie put his life savings into this place and he willed it to you to give you the chance of avenging yourself on Lord Feltsham, so it's your decision, which I would accept even if it left me without a job and home.'

Shenkin rested his hand upon Tommy's shoulder. 'Thank you.'

'Sir Edward, I know you feel it's a big gamble, but how else can I raise the money needed to fight Feltsham?'

Sir Edward reached for his clay pipe and began to fill it slowly. Then he lifted his head and looked at Shenkin. 'Do you have four thousand pounds in cash? No. Would they accept the deeds of this place as your side of the purse? Yes, they would. But it would include everything: the animals, the workers, the furniture, the outbuildings, the lot: the complete working sheep station. And if it was a profitable business too, which it is not at the moment, are you willing to risk it all? In fact there is a saying in the colony, "Is it a sheep station bet?" said Sir Edward, adding, 'it means the highest bet possible, the highest risk, an all-in gamble.'

Shenkin did not hesitate. 'Yes, all in Sir Edward, or nothing. How long will it take to build the station up to an attractive concern, one that would tempt a sporting man?'

'At least a year,' said Sir Edward.

'Right, we make a detailed list of everything we need. Can I raise a loan on the property from the bank?'

'When I put in your winnings from the fight, I think I can persuade them to give us a loan. I'll not mention the fight; banks don't like gambles. But I do know one bank director who is a gambling man. Bear in mind Shenkin, that you would then be in debt to the bank as well as committing it all on the purse money at the end of the year.'

'If I win, we'll be able to develop the station to take on Feltsham; if I lose, will it matter? I will have lost it all.'

Sir Edward nodded. 'Very well then. We now need to find someone who is prepared and able to put up a purse of four thousand pounds,' said Sir Edward, then in spite of the risk and because he too loved a gamble he smiled. 'Damn it, let's do it,' he said.

'Good, we are agreed we spend the next twelve months doing what is needed on the station: paddocks to be built, so we need to cut Mulga wood; more horses and guns to be bought; a larger shearing shed to be built and more blade shears to be bought together with an experienced shearer to lead a team; and washing-pool to be built. A lot to do, my friends but we can improvise to begin. Tommy, we'll need more convict labour.'

'Right! first thing in the morning.'

'While we busy ourselves, Sir Edward circulates among his sporting gentlemen friends in Sydney regarding the biggest sporting event the colony has ever seen and where it could be held.' A laugh went up and glasses were raised. 'The toast my friends, is the fight of the century,' said Shenkin.

Clink went the four glasses. 'The fight of the century,' went up the cry.

CHAPTER 36

For the next days, and then months, Shenkin and the others worked long hours as he watched his sheep station start to take shape. More sheep, merino, both ewes and rams, had been acquired by Tommy Bright which, he said, were expensive but produced the best wool. Another two horses had been purchased, together with four black Kelpie dogs for working the sheep. Three of the newly bought guns were in a cabinet in Shenkin's study under lock and key with the ammunition in a separate place. Four more, for guarding the sheep, were now with the shepherds, who had to have huts built for them out in the bush.

The practice in the mother country, to shepherd the sheep during the day, and yard them into folds at night, was strictly adhered to. In this way the shepherds were able to watch out for any injuries or disease. They lived in their huts for long periods; these were some distance from the home farm. Tommy Bright and Tinker had built huts which were provisioned with fresh food and drinking water at set intervals. Any ideas a convict might have of running away were discouraged by the vast wilderness around them. However, Shenkin made sure all their needs for well being were met. They were, in fact, taken care of far better than in any government penal prison. It soon became known that BKSS was the place to be indentured to.

By now, Shenkin was running low on money. The fight he hoped would bring in the money needed to complete the final stages of the sheep station was still many months ahead, that's if he still owned it after the fight.

Soon with Spring and the warmer weather coming, the shearing season was almost upon them. He intended to sell his amount of wool to one of the larger neighbouring sheep stations for cash. But firstly the sheep had to be dipped into a wash. Tommy Bright said the stream running through the station would be fine until they were able to build washing troughs; a trench in the middle of the shallow stream would do the job. Tinker agreed, since the larger station would most likely wash them all again with their own wool.

The extra convict labour, some twenty in all, were building accommodation huts: one for the men, the other for the females from Parramatta's female prison factory. Shenkin insisted they have a good diet with meat and fresh vegetables at least twice a week, also the bunks must have mattresses and the huts fresh water.

The following month they experienced a severe drought. Many of the convict labourers went down with heat stroke. Three died. One was a shepherd found dead in his hut. His flock of sheep, about three hundred in all, had wandered off; a number died. It took a few days to find them. Many were in a poor state and killed for their meat. The land was a cracked mosaic of dried powered earth, the hot wind blowing it up into spirals that choked man and beast. Most on the BKSS were Europeans, not used to heat and droughts. The women seemed to stand up to the climate better then the men. They simply did not fight the weather but continued on doing what was necessary. Shenkin was glad to have them, convicts or not. Late on yet another hot, throat-drying day there was a knock at Shenkin's study door.

'Come,' said Shenkin.

Rachel, still a little wary, stepped inside. 'Sorry to bother you but I'm concerned about one of the females.' Shenkin had put her in charge of the care of the females on the station.

'What is the problem, Rachel?'

'Well sir,' said Rachel.

'No need to call me sir, Rachel; please go on.'

'Well, it's like this: in the female factory in Parramatta there are about sixty children, all born to the female convicts who are punished for getting with child, most due to the attention of the guards. Well, when the babies are born they are taken away from the mothers. Terrible that is, I think. So, anyway, Rose is to come here as arranged by Mr Bright as part of the increased labour on the sheep station. She, Rose that is, was glad to be leaving the factory but her baby can't come and now she, Rose that is, won't eat. Not a morsel since she arrived two days ago,' said Rachel, tears beginning to well up in her eyes.

Shenkin moved a chair up closer to her, indicating for her to sit down. 'Now don't go upsetting yourself Rachel. I'll speak to Tommy Bright and we'll see what can be done. Are there any others with young children that are sill in the prison?'

'No, of the eight that arrived two days ago only Rose had a newborn babe.'

'Right, ask Mr Bright if he'd come in to see me.'

'Thank you, sir.' Stopping herself, she added, 'I mean thank you.'

Two days later, a bemused Tommy Bright rode into the sheep station by pony and trap. At his side in a wicker basket was the small bundle of a crying baby with a smiling mother sitting next to it, who was also crying.

Shenkin and a beaming Rachel helped mother and child into a small room that had been quickly built at the end of the females hut.

'What did they say, Tommy?'

'That they were pleased to get rid of another mouth to feed.'

'I thought so.' Turning to Tinker at his side, Shenkin said, 'Our future needs all the young it can get, and not just animals, for they are all our future.'

'If you say so Shenkin, so it will be.'

So the time went in the following months, full of dramas and long hard working hours under an increasingly hot sun. When at last the rains came, it was a moment to celebrate. Everyone stood outside, got drenched and cheered. It also brought sheep diseases: foot-rot scabs, ringworm and many more that sheep were prone to in that hard unforgiving land. It was a steep learning curve for all but Tommy Bright and Tinker, who fortunately seemed to have the answers to everything. Nevertheless those long months had taken them though a baptism of fire. The fight of the century had been forgotten; in its place was the need to survive. The fight was heat, dust, droughts and diseases. Strangely, it brought them even closer together. Finally, with Sir Edward's return, they were once again seated around the big table in the main house. All now had weather-beaten faces, hardened bodies and a grim determination.

Shenkin called for each to report their progress until late in the evening. They waited to hear what Sir Edward had to say.

Wine glass in hand and his pipe burning well, Sir Edward began, 'Well, my friends, it now seems you all know what running a sheep station is really about, for you wear it on your etched faces. There's nothing like practical knowledge for learning quickly.'

'It has been an interesting time, Sir Edward; we'll be better prepared next year, that's if I win the fight,' said Shenkin, adding, 'now tell us, what progress on the fight?'

Sir Edward smiled. 'Regarding the fight, I can report that all Sydney is thrilled at the prospect of the proposed bout and agape at the stake money involved which has proved to be a difficulty, because no one individual will match it, including the promoter of the champion, one Major John Peterson-Palmer, a former officer in the now long disbanded New South Wales Corps. As a very young lieutenant he vigorously enforced the law of illegal gambling on cock fighting and bare-knuckle prize fighting. He was also involved in the Rum Rebellion and was able to acquire a large stock of rum, which at that time was the main means of paying for land, goods and labour. He's now a rich man with large tracks of land in the Cowpastures area, together with landholdings in Parramatta, hence the ground for the fight. He's a game-keeper turned poacher who now actively promotes the so-called illegal sport of bare-knuckle fights. He's a wily old boy, but he feels a purse of this size is a little steep, as does every other sporting gentleman in the colony.'

Shenkin was silent for a moment then said. 'So how did you progress?'

Sir Edward Standish's aristocratic face beamed with self satisfaction. He paused for a moment then said, 'A good question Shenkin, one that I pondered over for a few days. Then I had an idea: I took out an announcement in the *Sydney Gazette* newspaper which said that the large stake for the proposed upcoming bare-knuckle bout between Charlie Benson and George Powell for the championship title of NSW could be met by a syndicate of four sporting men, each pledging one thousand pounds, and that I would wait to hear from the sporting fraternity for twenty-four hours. If there were no takers, I would withdraw the challenge. In less than the due time, four notable sports-men came forward,' said Sir Edward, a triumphant look upon his face.

'Excellent,' said Shenkin, adding, 'well done, my friend, well done.'

'You have yet to hear the best of it, Shenkin, one of the men is none other than Lord Percival Hugo Feltsham, who wanted to take two shares, but I refused the offer for I did not want to appear too eager,' said Sir Edward, with an even wider look of satisfaction upon his aristocratic face. 'So Shenkin, we have it arranged. Only the details remain to be agreed: the month, the time, and the place. Also, your friend Doctor Tarn will act as medical man for the bout.'

'Better and better this is excellent, now it only remains for me to win the fight,' said Shenkin, with a rather light smile. 'How good is this man, Sir Edward?'

'Well they are not bringing him to Sydney to lose. Of his last three fights he has won all by knockout with none going more than six rounds. He's formidable, Shenkin.'

'Right I'll need his height, weight, reach, age and the fight rules.'

All turned to Sir Edward, who was slowly lighting his clay pipe. Once fully underway, he said, 'Six foot, fifteen stone, reach seventy-three inches and at twenty-two he is in perfect condition. You'll fight under Broughton Rules not the new London Prize Rules.' Shenkin nodded. Without waiting for a reply, Sir Edward went on, 'I did see him fight once Shenkin. It was over a year ago, but he was very good; you'll need all your skill to beat him.' As he spoke a circle of smoke floated around him, filling the air with the rich dark flavour of his tobacco. For long heartbeats no one spoke; no one wanted to put words to their thinking.

Finally, Shenkin looked at each one in turn. 'I know my friends, if I lose, we lose everything that we have worked so hard for.' Then he added, 'If I lose, but if I win we could create an empire that will match anything in this "place beyond the seas", something we will be proud of. It will help build a great nation on the sweat, blood and determination of a people the old country threw out.'

Again there was a stillness in the air, mixed with the aroma of the strong tobacco. Tommy Bright broke the silence. 'Then there is no time to waste in preparing the station to be the best in New South Wales, and you Shenkin, with your training.'

'That is true Shenkin, you should be in bed, for early tomorrow you begin training in earnest. To begin with, put that glass down,' said Tinker, in a firm voice. They all gave way to laughter, if a little warily.

CHAPTER 37

Morning after morning, the day began at 6am with Tinker administering a daily dose of diuretic salts to purge Shenkin's body. At least he did not believe in blood letting to make way for healthy new blood, so Shenkin was saved that. Tinker said blood was blood, and that vigorous excise would put clean air into the blood, putting an end to any discussion about blood letting. For this vigorous exercise, Tinker set up a punishing schedule of running, bag work, lifting weights, which was mostly sheep (after all, as Tinker pointed out, Shenkin may as well do something that was useful while training), from paddock to paddock and, of course, pickling his knuckles in vinegar every evening to toughen the skin. Soon they were running twenty miles a day to get Shenkin down to his fighting weight. Nutrition was strict: no refined bread, but bread made from coarse fermented wheat. These were made by the women, in clay ovens they had built on the sheep station. It was to be eaten with meat but only from animals fed on grass. Drinking was reduced to a minimum and no sexual activity of any kind. This was due to the fact that Tinker had noticed Shenkin was becoming more aware of Rachel these days, which Shenkin strongly denied, then caught himself doing it. A month before the fight, Tinker announced they would continue his training out in the bush away from all distractions. Sir Edward and Tommy Bright would run the sheep station. In fact, they already were so that Shenkin could train, so the morning they left Shenkin discussed the forward plans for the station, yet again, with Sir Edward and said goodbye to everyone for a month, except, on Tinker's insistence, Rachel. Shenkin had to admit the station was beginning to take on the mantle of a well-run farm and, with more money in the coffers, they would have the frame work to make it very successful, if he won the fight!

Certainly the convict labourers could not believe their good fortune and, apart from a few malcontents, they returned the improved conditions with a decent day's work. The females, under Rachel's supervision, soon had the place fit to live in and were cooking fulsome meals. Two of their number were former cooks in grand houses in London before helping themselves to the silver, which had landed them a sentence of ten years' transportation. So, while the station was a mix of ill-fated men and women, some out of desperation, some out of the weakness of the moment, collectively they had all settled down to a better life on Bare-Knuckle Sheep Station than they had ever known before. Shenkin felt in this, he was still being true to his beliefs.

They rode into the bush for some hours until, under a rock outcrop, Tinker proclaimed that this was where they would make their training camp for the next month, because the species of birds, animals and plants he had seen in the area indicated that there was a water source nearby. So, they unloaded the pack horses and soon Tinker had a fire underway for their first evening meal under the fast-approaching night. Stars hung like crystal balls in the velvet black sky. It reminded Shenkin of his home on the mountain above the town of Merthyr Tydfil, except here it had no constant thumping of the iron works machinery, or a sky lit up with belching smoke and fire from the ovens. Here, it was loud with a silence that murmured in his ears like a lullaby. After the long ride, Shenkin was soon asleep in a dream full of footwork and punches with Regan, the friend he had lost to an aboriginal spear in the primeval forest of Van Diemen's Land, telling him to duck, weave and not hit empty air. 'Jesus, Shenkin, make the blows count or we'll never get back to the pub before they close.'

'Alright, you big bloody terrible man, last man standing pays the bar slip,' said Shenkin, waking up with a start for it was morning and Tinker was prodding his side.

'Time to run towards the rising sun Shenkin, and back again before breakfast.'

The sheer vastness of the outback was breathtaking. Shenkin had a sense that he was running into a never-ending landscape of brutal beauty. It was as if he was running back in time, to a time before man stained the land with his greed and contempt for everything except himself. A clean page presented itself to Shenkin, one which he must not harm or spoil by his arrogance and self will. Looking down at his running feet, Shenkin saw the dust of ages rise about him in a cascade of brown red flour. He pulled the scarf that Tinker had given him over his mouth and nose. For hours they ran on and on, until Shenkin's mind went into a trance of nothing but the hot dust around him.

At last Tinker called a halt. 'We have something to eat and drink here,' he said, dropping a bag onto the ground.

They were under the thin branches of a solitary tree that had markings on the trunk, which were obviously man made, but around them was a landscape of nothing but low brush and scrub.

'What does it mean, Tinker?'

'It means a water chain is near us. My people make these marks on trees or stones to let others on walkabout know that water is here,' said Tinker, adding, 'Our camp beneath the rock outcrop is also marked. You just didn't see it, my friend. Tomorrow I will dig a hole to the water course to top up our supply, for we will be here a number of weeks.'

'What about food, will we have enough?'

'I will find us food. Do not worry Shenkin; you will not go hungry.'

Shenkin settled down with his back resting on the trunk of the tree. It gave slightly under his weight. The welcome shade the tree gave was a relief from the now-burning sun. No cloud or bird travelled the sky, just the relentless heat. A lizard hurried across the burned earth in front of him, going where to what? For there was nothing.

The red ochre dust stuck to his clothes while sweat ran down his body like a river of warm water. The kangaroo skin that Tinker carried their water in, of which he had brought a number, seemed cool by comparison to the brown bread and cheese they ate, a banquet of culinary delight.

While they rested and ate, Tinker pointed to the shadow that one of the skeletal branches of the tree had cast on the ground. 'When it touches that small anthill,' he said, pointing to a busy group of tiny ants. 'We begin our run back and you can go into your dreamland again Shenkin.' The blackness of his skin was dotted with the brown earth, covering his nakedness like a mottled cape.

For the next two weeks this was their daily routine: they ran, they ate, then they slept under their stone shelter, which now had a small well of water and was home and a welcome sight to Shenkin at the end of each gruelling day. By the end of the second week, their food was being supplemented by tree and ground grubs that Tinker seemed to find from his wilderness larder. Shenkin was continually surprised how he found them. As to their taste, it was one that Shenkin began to get accustomed to. Tinker said they were a good source of energy so Shenkin ate them down, if not with relish, then as a mark of respect to Tinker that he knew best.

The day came when Tinker said it was time to return to the farm. Strangely, Shenkin was sad to leave this arid brutal land, for he had, for the first time in many years, found a certain peace in its sameness, its timeless quality of stillness and tranquillity. But he was down to his fighting weight, the training had been successful, so he must indeed return to reality. However, there was something else the bush had taught him; it was knowing the inner core of himself, and for this he was very grateful. He felt at peace. He knew this would not be complete until he had avenged himself on Lord Feltsham and hopefully regained his daughter. Nevertheless, he felt strangely calm.

The late evening of their return saw everyone out to welcome them back. Tommy Bright had good news of the station, Sir Edward was eager to tell of the fight preparations and Rachel had a lamb stew ready for their evening meal, to be washed down with cold beer that had been standing on the cool marble slabs in the kitchen.

'The station is coming along well,' said Tommy Bright. 'The convict labour are working well and have adapted to the new skills they need. You were right about the better food they now eat; it has lifted their spirits, and clean water to wash and drink has improved their health. They are, without doubt, fitter and wiser. We have new lambs, which the women convicts take care of as if they were babies.' Tommy said, laughing. 'And the real baby is beginning to crawl. Rose is in tears every time she sees him, which is often,' he said laughing again then, draining his tankard, he placed it on the table. 'But we need new sheds, more paddocks; and we will need more shears for removing the wool.'

Shenkin refilled his and Tommy's tankards. 'It seems we should go away more often, Tinker, for it looks as if the station has taken on a life of its own. As to what we need next, it's money, which we will have if I win this fight. If not, well, it won't matter. Is that not so, Sir Edward?'

'That is the top and bottom of it Shenkin, but if you win...'

Shenkin smiled. 'I will win or die trying.'

'If you say so Shenkin, so it will be,' said Tinker.

'Now what news of Sydney, are all the preparations underway?' said Shenkin, turning to Sir Edward.

'The bout will take place at Rosehill. Powell's promoter owns a large area of ground there where he has staged a number of sporting events. So it plays well into our plans, Shenkin for you will now not need to go into Sydney and risk the chance of being identified. Also, and this will be of much interest to you, Lord Feltsham is arranging a celebration party after the fight in honour of the winner.'

'Well,' said Shenkin, 'that will certainly urge me on. What an opportunity too, to make public who I really am.'

Sir Edward was for a moment alarmed, then realised Shenkin was joshing him.

'Do not be concerned Sir Edward, but I hope the time will come when I will have that pleasure,' said Shenkin, placing a hand on Sir Edward's arm.

'For a moment Shenkin, I thought you were becoming impatient for the truth.'

'No. Not yet my friend, but soon I hope, for my daughter Beth is getting older by the day and in the hands of the very man that was instrumental in killing her mother,' said Shenkin, biting off each word as he spoke.

'You have the deeds to the sheep station ready, also the undertaking that everything upon the farm goes into the stake?' said Sir Edward.

'Yes, all is ready.'

Tommy Bright said, 'I do not change my mind, but when you hear it like that, it's a frightening risk, Shenkin.'

'I know my friends, and I understand your concerns but I must risk it all if I am to achieve my aim. Nonetheless, your commitments weigh heavy on my mind. I give you my word, Powell will not have my determined spur to win,' said Shenkin, looking at each man around the table. 'So please join me in a toast.'

Tommy smiled. 'Well, what is the toast to be, Shenkin?'

'Why, to enjoy Lord Feltsham's celebration party of course.'

CHAPTER 38

Suddenly it was the day of the fight. It was to start at 7pm in the evening with the guarantee of record numbers attending. Blacktown was about ten to twelve miles away from Rosehill, so there was no chance of Shenkin stiffening up on a long journey. Tinker declared him as fit as he'd ever be, both physically and mentally. Tommy Bright had packed their wagon with all they were likely to need: body oil, grease for protecting the eyebrows, herbs to stop bleeding, fighting apparel, shoes and towels to wipe the blood and perspiration away. Shenkin insisted on resin for the soles of his shoes, to give him better grip on the grassy surfaces. Sir Edward had gone on ahead to ensure all was as agreed and to place the stake purse. By five o'clock in the evening they were all at the Rosehill field, which already had a crowed of some six to eight hundred, ready to watch and bet on the outcome of the prize fight. The streets were full of people and flags of, it seemed, every country, together with placards of who was going to win and what the odds were, mostly stacked against Charlie Benson. Some even predicted the round the fight would be over, with Powell shown with his arms in the air as the winner.

Sir Edward greeted them to the ring side. 'Everything is in hand Shenkin, but from now on,' he said, turning to them all, 'Shenkin must be referred to as Charlie Benson, understood?' They all nodded.

'Charlie, it's good to see you looking so well,' said Dr Tarn, with a warm handshake.

'You too, Doctor. I could not want a better man in my corner,' said Shenkin.

'But it's a hell of a risk,' said Tarn, nodding in the direction of the stake purse in a corner of the ring. Stakes of wood stood at each corner with a single line of rope joining them together. The stake opposite Shenkin was hung with the purse pouch, hence the term 'stake money'. It was in full view with two men each side of it, both held charged pistols in their hands.

At that moment the promoter, Major Peterson-Palmer, detached himself from a group of sporting gentlemen, which included Lord Feltsham. Shenkin flinched with anger at the sight of him.

'Sir Edward, is your man ready?' said the major, holding out his hand.

'We are indeed, Major Peterson-Palmer. May I introduce you to Charlie Benson, sir?'

The major cast his eyes over Shenkin. 'Well, you're certainly a fine looking man sir, but a little on the old side don't you think?' Not waiting for a reply, he continued. 'Didn't you lose very convincingly to a convict fighter a few years back? In fact, I'm told you then retired sir. Is that not so?' The major had a confident look upon his face as if he already had a quarter of BKSS sheep station in his back pocket. Still not waiting for a reply, the major turned and walked back to his group of fellow syndicate members. The laughter at whatever the major said to them was meant to unsettle Shenkin.

'Take no notice, Charlie it's just gamesmanship,' said Sir Edward.

'I have been the underdog many times before, Sir Edward, many times. In fact an overconfident other side is an advantage.'

Tarn began to examine him while Tommy and Tinker prepared him for the first round. The increasing roar of the crowd was deafening. Bets were being called and ale and pie sellers shouted their wares as did the local prostitutes.

'What about you, sweetheart, fancy a good time?' said one, close to the ring side.

'After the fight, Mary. I'll have the money then, for the old boy won't last long.'

'Well everyone seems confident in the other man Tinker,' said Shenkin.

'For now Charlie, for now.'

Lookouts were posted around the field to watch out for any blue-coated police, or 'bluebottles' as they were called. However, in the ringside seats were two judges and a senior member of the law enforcement agency of Sydney Town, who had placed good size bets on Powell to win. All three men were gathered around Lord Feltsham, who was offering them brandy in an expensive-looking silver flask, while still brushing off that invisible piece of lint from his top bespoke Savile Row coat.

An umpire walked into the ring, lifting his arms, he began to announce the bout but, given the noise of the crowd, only the front few rows were able to hear anything.

Not deterred, the umpire continued, 'In the right corner, wearing white breeches and red sash, is the challenger from Blacktown weighing in at 184lbs, Charlie Benson.' Shenkin danced into the centre of the roped-off ring. There was some clapping and shouting, but mostly booing, from the impatient crowd as shouts went up.

'Get on with it, or the pubs will be closing.'

'Give it to him, Muscles.'

'Light the bloody torches or we'll not see a thing.' It was indeed becoming darker, scheduled for 7pm, it was already well past the hour.

'In the left corner, wearing breeches with a black sash, the recognised champion of New South Wales, weighing in at 215lbs, Rosehill's very own George "the muscle" Powell.'

Into the ring danced the six foot Powell, robe already off, he looked every inch a champion. The light from the now-lit torches glistened across his well-muscled body. He was full of the confidence of youth: immortal.

The roar from the crowd was thunderous until in the end, the umpire had to call for quiet, which was not fully forthcoming, but better than it had been. A fight had broken out near the ring between two men and a woman. Three big men with heavy police sticks hit the brawlers over their heads. The woman jumped on one of the bouncers who turned fast, shaking her off his back. Finally, some order was restored. The two men were dragged away, both unconscious. Another umpire was now in the ring and called the fighters up to the scratch mark. Powell wore Blucher boots. His loose breeches came right down to the top of the heavily laced boots. Shenkin's breeches ended just below the knee and were tightened with a red ribbon. On his feet he wore light slipper-like shoes. Tinker had been soaking them in oil for the past three days; they fitted like a soft glove. Shenkin ground the soles of his shoes in resin and walked up to the mark.

Both umpires had each man open his palms upwards to ensure they did not conceal any iron bits. When satisfied, one of the umpires spoke to them.

'The fight will be fought under Broughton Rules. Are you both aware of these rules?'

Each man nodded.

'The sixty second rule will be strictly enforced, any man down on his knee after a blow, or who touches the ground or is knocked out and fails to get to the toe-line mark in the middle of the ring at the end of the count is considered the loser. Each round will only end when one man is down. No hitting the man who is down or grabbing beneath the waist. Any man slipping under the rope to avoid blows will be forcibly pushed back into the square. Any man not breaking when I say break will be pulled back by my assistants after thirty seconds, with blows around the head, if necessary.'

Shenkin gave the man a doubting look. 'That's not in Broughton Rules.'

'It is here,' said the umpire. Without waiting he continued, 'No limit for number of rounds. Last man standing is the winner, understood?'

Again each man nodded.

'Good, turn out your sashes for me to show they do not hide salt, mustard, grit or powder of any kind.'

Each man did, none was found.

'Good, return to your corners for final preparations. When I call you, come up to the middle of the ring and toe the line. Lift your arms when I call set-up. When I am satisfied that both of you are ready, I'll drop my arm for the bout to begin, understood?'

Again, the nod said it all. Then Powell looked straight at Shenkin. 'You should be at home in a rocking chair, an old man like you.'

Shenkin said nothing. Only a light smile spread across his bearded face. How he wished he still had his pigtail, he thought. By now the crowd were in an uproar of frustration that the fight was taking so long to begin. The flames from the torches cast shadows around the ring giving it an almost dream-like quality except for the noise. Major Peterson-Palmer and Lord Feltsham were smoking cigars, the embers glowed bright as they excitedly drew in the strong tobacco leaves. The umpires, one on each side of the ring, were ready. They both turned and acknowledged the sporting gentlemen at the ring side. Then the one who had gone over the rules with the fighters lifted his arm. It came down fast, accompanied by a screaming roar from the crowd. The fight was at last underway.

Tommy Bright tapped Shenkin on the shoulder. Tinker wiped off the last surplus oil from his arms, then they both went back to their corner. Shenkin felt the old surge of excitement as he waited for Powell to make the first move.

'Go get him, Charlie,' shouted Rachel, who had hidden in one of the wagons.

Sir Edward laughed. 'Now what are you doing here? It's no place for a lady.'

'Then that's just fine, for I'm no bleeding lady,' she said. 'The poor dear deserves all the help he can get.' At that moment Powell muscles glistening, moved over to their side of the ring. Rachel let out a gasp. 'He's big and strong he is. Jesus, that's a lot of man, that is.' She might have added more for Sir Edward saw it plain enough in her eyes.

'Now, Rachel none of your old ways here. Sit down and behave.'

'I'm just saying I am, that's all. He's good looking too, isn't he?'

'Rachel, watch the fight, or I'll send you home.'

'Alright, alright hope Shen… I mean Charlie, don't hurt him too much.'

'I think he can take care of himself,' said Sir Edward.

Both men moved around each other slowly, judging movements, the other man's reach and the stance of each other. Powell threw the first jab. Shenkin noted the long reach and laid the top of his body back slightly; the blow hit air. He also noticed Powell had a steady grip on the grassy ground, which with the coming of the evening was getting damp with the night dew falling. *The bastard's got spikes under the boots,* he thought, which was why they were so robust and laced so tight. *He thinks he'll not have to fight too long before winning so the extra weight does not matter. In any event, his legs are like tree trunks.* All this went around in Shenkin's mind as he assessed his opponent.

Another blow, this time a straight left, it caught Shenkin on the right upper arm, good strength, well-placed knuckles, thumbs well tucked in. Shenkin responded with a tentative left jab, it caught Powell high on the forehead. *He's big, but slow to weave he's also standing wide in his stance so he presents a large target,* thought Shenkin, the widest target area being his stomach. Shenkin's father would say kill the body and the head would fall. The crowd shouted and egged them on to make a fight of it, but Powell was smart enough to wait his moment to gauge this man in front of him who moved so fluidly for an older fighter.

'Cut the bastard down, George. Hit him with that right cross before I down this grog of mine.' Setting off laughter from the man's friends around him.

Powell dug his boots into the soft ground and threw a right to the body, followed by a left swing to the head that left a red mark on Shenkin's rib cage. The other missed by a good few inches as Shenkin ducked under it.

Powell's head swung in close, hitting Shenkin on the right of his face then back across the other side.

Rachel was on her feet. 'That's not nice that's not,' she shouted.

Turning to Tommy Bright, she said, 'Is that allowed, Mr Bright?'

'Yes, Rachel, it's allowed and much more.'

'I don't think that's fair. He's a miserable bastard. I take everything back, I does. I hope he gets a bloody good hammering.'

'So do we, Rachel, so do we.'

In the ring, the pace was moving up. Both fighters threw combination blows, both were beginning to show marks around the body, but both still looked strong.

Time to test him, thought Shenkin. Three body blows went in one after the other in rapid succession. Powell winced, then took a right to the top of his head. It sent him backwards. He shook his head in disbelief; the blows were brutal in their power. He backed away. Shenkin did not follow him; he waited for Powell to come back and, as he did, Shenkin hit him with a combination of blows to his midriff. A gasp came from Powell's mouth; the gasp was echoed by the crowd. Money started to change hands as the odds against Shenkin dropped. Powell led with a right. He again tried to punch his way into Shenkin's defence. A mistake, for Shenkin was well balanced. He trapped Powell's right arm under his own left side, swinging Powell to his right, exposing Powell's head. The right cross from Shenkin was heard loud and clear by the ringside seats. Powell went down on one knee, both surprise and doubt mixed in equal amounts on his young face. This had never happened before to him. To his credit, he got up quickly. Round one was over. It had taken thirty minuets.

Lord Feltsham's cigar fell to the ground. Anxiously he jumped to his feet in disbelief, as did all the sporting gentlemen around him. The crowd were for the first time subdued. Powell's corner were talking hurriedly to their man, who still had a look of deep concern on his young face.

Within the sixty seconds, both fighters were back to the scratch mark, toes again on the line. The umpire stepped back as they circled each other, this time at a more deliberate pace. Powell was no longer grinning, nor did he say anything, but realised for the first time in his young life he was in a bare-knuckle prize fight against a fighter who was experienced and dangerous. They ducked, weaved and punched with a combination of blows. A left jab to the head forced Shenkin to guard his chin closer. He countered with a right to Powell's stomach, causing him to flinch at the intensity of the power behind the blows.

Rachel grabbed Sir Edward's arm so tightly he called out to her, 'You're not in the ring, Rachel, let go of my arm.'

'Sorry, my lord, I was carried away like.' Then she shouted out, 'Be careful, Sh... I mean Charlie. Sorry, Sir Edward.'

'Keep calm, Rachel.' Turning back to the ring, Sir Edward Standish shouted, 'Watch his left Charlie. Now, hit him now.' Rachel began to laugh,

Tommy tutted and Tinker had towels and herbs in hand. Powell was down on one knee, the umpire began the count. He got up quickly and hit Shenkin with a left jab high on the head. Shenkin danced back, then moved right, then left around Powell. The now-wetter earth was causing them to slip; Powell's spikes were filling with earth and he slipped forward onto his knees. Shenkin moved back, giving the other man a chance to get back on his feet. As Powell did he rushed forward head down, into Shenkin's stomach. With a gasp, Shenkin went down on one knee, and stayed down for a breather. For the next three rounds both went down, taking advantage of Broughton's sixty second rule.

At the start of the tenth Powell rushed at Shenkin, chopping with an open right hand to the throat. The umpire called out, 'Closed fists at all times.' But the powerful chop had caught Shenkin, leaving a red welt across his throat. Gasping, he went down on one knee and waited for a few counts before getting up and going to his corner.

'Be careful, he's prepared to fight dirty. The calls from the umpire will be after the foul so the damage will be done. Remember, no one here wants you to win; you're only going to win this fight with a clear knockout,' said Tommy, while Tarn examined Shenkin's throat.

Shenkin nodded.

'No broken skin or real damage but it will be sore for some time; keep it protected,' shouted Tarn, above the steady roar of the crowd.

Tinker smeared it with a finger tip covered with some herb or other. He turned to the doctor. 'It brings the bruising out, Doctor Tarn,' said Tinker, by way of explanation.

At the scratch mark, Powell said, 'How's the throat Charlie, difficult to swallow?' The umpire laughed, then quickly stepped away.

Shenkin went into a clinch. He turned Powell around with his right arm pinned under Shenkin's left side. The right cross came in quick; it connected with Powell's jaw. Then Shenkin followed through with his elbow on the umpire's blind side. Powell went down in a heap, his corner ran into the ring. The umpire shouted as the crowd screamed. They brought Powell onto his feet while he was still doubled up. 'Sixty second count,' shouted the umpire, rushing to help Powell to his corner.

'Bloody hell, what did you hit him with?' said Tommy.

'Two can fight dirty. My father taught me all the tricks, Tommy,' said Shenkin between deep breaths.

'Time,' called the umpire, not that many could hear him.

Powell did not come up quickly. The umpire waited then shouted time again.

Then with help, Powell got to the mark. It was the fifteenth round. Pulling Powell into a clinch, Shenkin whispered into his ear, 'Foul me again and I'll return it double, got that?' Powell broke loose, as he did he hit Shenkin left, then right with his head. Shenkin felt something split in the area of one of his eyebrows. Shenkin dropped to his knee. Blood was in his eyes as Powell hit him again while he was down. Shenkin fell forward full length onto the wet grass. The umpire rushed forward to cover the view of the foul.

He got up slowly, Tommy at his side. 'Bastard has split the scar above the eyebrow,' said Tommy, back in their corner.

Tinker packed it with a mash of god knows what herbs. 'Stay away from him; it needs time to harden off,' he said.

Feltsham was cheering, the crowd were yelling, the umpire came to the corner. 'Does he want to retire,' he said cheerfully to Tommy Bright.

'No you bastard, but get in my way again and I'll cripple you for life,' Shenkin shouted. The umpire, even in the dim light on the corner, went a pale colour.

'Time,' he screamed.

Shenkin was at the scratch mark even before the umpire. Powell smiled. 'This fucking round your time is up,' he said. Then Shenkin hit him with a left cross followed by a right upper cut that completely span Powell around. As his front came back to face Shenkin, he hit him with a series of combination punches to the body: the chin, the head, the chin again. Powell went backwards under the barrage of blows then went down onto his back. It was the first full force knock down. Relative silence spread across every part of the crowd. Feltsham shouted, 'Get up, you useless bastard.'

Powell's corner handlers were in the ring. The umpire said nothing. Powell was bodily carried back to his corner. Sitting him up, they threw water over him. With a splutter and a shaking of his head, Powell came around.

Tommy and Sir Edward screamed, 'Count, count.' Nothing from the umpire who was looking over at the sporting gentlemen. One stood up; it was Major Peterson-Palmer. 'Yes! Damn it, count.'

Feltsham pulled him down. 'You stupid fool, we have too high a wager on this fight to lose.'

'I am many things sir, but not a cheat.' he said, disdainfully.

Feltsham sneered. 'Then you carry twice the loss of our purse,' he said in a rage of anger.

Another gentleman stood up. 'Sir, you are not a gentleman but a thoroughly poor sportsman. I assure you, whatever the outcome is we will share the loss or win equally. I give you my word, Major.'

The major thanked him and again called for the count. At least three minutes had passed. Both umpires said nothing while Powell began to recover. Finally, the count was called but slowly. Eventually, an aided Powell came up to the scratch mark. It was becoming a brutal punishing fight, blood streamed down both men's faces, but neither would give in. Powell's pride kept him going and for Shenkin, both his future and that of all those he cared about.

CHAPTER 39

For the next eight rounds they sent each other to the ground, but always came up in time to toe the line. Both carried welt marks about their bodies. Shenkin's scar had held up, but only just. Powell had swellings under both eyes, his whole body a mass of red welts, but he continued to have the stamina of youth to keep going. A chopping right from Shenkin followed by a left under the heart doubled Powell in two. Shenkin's right hook straightened Powell upright. Then a left to the head sent the younger man down, his right eye split open, the grass now turning red. Somehow Powell got to his feet; his team almost carried him back to his corner. But again they both toed the line. Powell charged in with his head down into Shenkin's stomach, then drove his head up under Shenkin's chin. In a heap, Shenkin lay gasping but he staggered to his feet. 'You've taken too much punishment. Your age is beginning to tell. Let me call it over. It's not worth this,' said Tommy Bright.

'He's right Shenkin, your one eye is nearly closed; the cut is wider,' said Tarn.

'The man that stops this fight will have me to answer to, do all of you understand?' said Shenkin, through a veil of blood.

The scratch mark was no more now than a pile of mud made of a mix of earth, sweat and blood. But both men stood on or near the spot. So the twenty-fifth round began. Feltsham shouted out, 'Get it finished. I've got plans for that sheep station.' The other gentlemen ushered him back to his seat.

In the ring, Shenkin was urged into a fury by the remark, hitting Powell with a swinging right that went over Powell's guard. It sent him down into the blood and mud but again he got up. However, he now had cuts over both eyes and a swelling on his lower jaw, causing his mouth to drop open. In the twenty-sixth they seemed to be holding each other up, then Powell dropped to his knee for the third time. Was it over? No, Powell's corner brought him to the line again, but slowly, and it took longer then sixty seconds.

After only a short few moments, Powell went down from a well-placed right cross. Back in their corners, each were summoning their last reserves of energy. Shenkin turned his bloody eyes over to Feltsham. Sir Edward whispered into Shenkin's ear, 'Yes Shenkin, that's your prize, not the money, not the championship, but his downfall: for Elizabeth, your daughter, Regan and Charlie Benson.'

Shenkin nodded his blood-drenched head. He turned to Tommy and Tinker. 'My father would say, when you're out of breath, then hold your breath and put all your strength into your fists.'

'I believe it. It takes energy to breathe,' said Tommy Bright.

'He's bloody strong, Tommy. I've hit him with good punches, but he's still standing while I'm beginning to feel the pace,' Shenkin said, between heavy breathing. 'I must finish this soon or all is lost.'

'Damn it, you've won the fight once; you have more ring-craft than him, so pin him to the rope and take him down. I know you can do it,' said Sir Edward, with an encouraging smile. Adding, 'think of Feltsham; he's in the other corner.'

'Thanks,' said Shenkin, between gritted teeth.

'Tinker, how is the scar?'

'Beginning to open; he's hitting it whenever he can. I'm not sure how long it will last. You must keep it protected at all costs.'

'Time,' shouted the umpire.

Round twenty-seven. *This should be over,* thought Shenkin, *his jaw must be made of oak.* He threw a straight left followed by a hard right into Powell's stomach. He went backwards but counter punched well. Blood began to trickle down Shenkin's cheek from the scar. He dropped to one knee.

'How bad is it, Doctor?' asked Sir Edward.

Tarn examined it carefully. 'Not good, I'm afraid. It's going to open fully with the next blow on it; the eye will close up.' The crowd were on their feet blaring and chanting, POWELL, POWELL.

'Damn it,' said Shenkin, gritting his teeth. adding, 'right, let's get this done.' As he took a deep breath

'Time.'

Lord Feltsham shouted, 'Down him, George; put him away.'

'Sir, do you mind? A little more decorum and less coarseness.' This from another of the sporting gentlemen. Feltsham ignored him.

Tinker had done the best he could with the eyebrow, since it was he who had given Shenkin the scar to replicate Charlie Benson's, he felt guilty. Still, what is done is done. Life goes on. Nothing stays the same.

They broke away from the line and began to move around each other, Powell now looking at him over swollen puffy eyes. A red swelling on his rib cage was slowly turning a bruised blue. He was wincing with each breath he took, but he continued to fight on. He hit out at Shenkin with a swinging overarm right that went nowhere, then countered with a left to the head. The crowd went wild with excitement. 'You got him, Muscles, finish him off,' came a shout near the ring side.

Rachel called out, 'Hold on, hold on, but don't get hurt, Charlie.'

'Now, now, Rachel, please control yourself,' said Doctor Tarn.

A short jab to Powell's head stopped his movement forward. Shenkin then hit him with a right cross, then a left cross, and another. Powell's head jerked in rhythm to the blows. They were across the ring and Shenkin had him trapped against the top rope. A left, then a right to the body, a tattoo of blows went up Powell's trunk leaving a series of marks up the length of his upper body. The skin on the swelling of Powell's rib cage split open.

The umpire pulled them apart, then stepped back quickly when Shenkin turned to look at him. Powell refused to go down. His right eye was cut both above and underneath. Blood streamed down his face. *The youngster's got courage, I'll give him that,* thought Shenkin. Then he hit Powell with a right upper cut that seemed to lift him off the ground. Down he went, his back against the stake in his own corner, blood flowing from under his left eye and nose. If Shenkin wasn't mistaken, the nose was broken.

They threw cold water over Powell, jammed a rag up his one nostril, smeared his slit eyebrow socket with grease, then dragged him up to the mark. Round twenty-eight began with Powell holding on at every opportunity, rubbing his forehead into Shenkin's now split-open scar.

Blood began running freely down Shenkin's face; he wiped it from his eyes to see. Powell broke loose and hit out with a right to the jaw. Shenkin lay his upper body back slightly and the blow grazed his face, leaving a trail of blood on Powell's fist.

Powell's corner shouted out, 'Now George, now, use everything!' He did, his elbows, forearms, head, then his heavy boots came down on Shenkin's inside shin, leaving the skin on his ankle torn wide. Powell squared himself for a two-handed barrage of blows; he was wide open. Shenkin took in a very deep breath, wiped blood from his eyes and hit Powell with what can only be described as the most brutal vicious right cross that anyone there had ever seen. Powell staggered backwards. Shenkin hit him with a swinging left, then a right to the abdomen. Powell's head dropped; the jaw fell open. He was fighting for breath. Shenkin stepped inside the sagging figure of Powell. Shenkin's right fist whipped across Powell's chin at a devastating speed. It travelled perhaps six inches, six violent brutal inches, with all of Shenkin's weight behind it. Powell's arms dropped. He stood for a few seconds, swaying on his boots, then it seemed to Shenkin that, in slow motion, Powell crashed to the ground.

'Count,' cried Sir Edward, Tommy and Tinker, together with the only female voice there.

'Foul,' shouted Feltsham in a somewhat vain attempt to reverse the irreversible, for Powell was spread eagled on the wet grass, his arms wide above him. Nothing would bring him back to the line; he was unconscious. Fights had broken out all over the field, wagers were paid and the bookmakers began to count the cost of the odds against Charlie Benson. Ale was being tipped, pies thrown and general bedlam ruled. The umpire raised Shenkin's arm, declaring him the winner and new Bare-Knuckle Champion of New South Wales, then quickly said, 'No hard feelings I hope, Mr Benson.'

Shenkin pulled his arm away and wiped blood from his eye. Turning to the crowd and the sporting gentlemen, Shenkin shouted, 'I have no wish to be champion. I thereby announce my retirement from the ring.'

There was an astonished response from the gentlemen while Sir Edward smiled and nodded. 'I thought that was what he would do.' Then, joining the sporting gentlemen, they all walked over to the stake purse post.

Major Peterson- Palmer turned to Sir Edward. 'Yours I believe, sir.'

'Thank you, Major. A tough fight, your man equipped himself well. Now, gentlemen, if you'll excuse me, for I have a number of side bets to collect.'

'Of course, Sir Edward, but be on your guard on your way home. That's a great deal of money to have on you. My congratulations again to Charlie Benson; that was without doubt the most devastating right I have, or I should think anyone else has, ever seen, he'll be a great loss to the sport, sir.'

'I will so convey it, Major, and thank you again,' said Sir Edward, rattling the purses above his head. Only Feltsham refused to acknowledge the win and had walked off in a display of bad manners.

The major looked after him. 'No gentleman sir, for it takes more than a title, it takes breeding,' he said.

'Indeed sir, but I feel Lord Feltsham's day of reckoning is not too far off,' said Sir Edward.

'Delighted to hear it, if I can be of any help in the matter please let me know.'

'I will indeed, sir, in the meantime, I bid you good night.'

Doctor Tarn, Tommy and Tinker were attending to Shenkin while Rachel, much to Shenkin's embarrassment, was kissing his arms. Sir Edward whispered into Shenkin's ear, 'By all that's holy, you've made a great deal of money. The side bets alone have yielded a large sum. Good god man, you're rich. We need an armed escort to get us back to the sheep station. If you agree, I'll hire the purse guards with cash on the nail.'

For the first time after any fight, Shenkin turned a bloody face to Sir Edward.

'Of course, my friend, whatever you feel is best.'

'Right, tomorrow we get it all into the bank. The guards will stay overnight at the station,' said Sir Edward, rattling the purses again. 'Incredible, Shenkin, this will build the best Sheep Station in New South Wales.'

Shenkin smiled a blood-splattered grin. 'Then it's the turn of that bastard over there, for his days are numbered,' he said, tipping his head towards Lord Feltsham, who had walked back to argue again with his fellow syndicate members. However, each gentleman left him standing on his own at the side of the ring, which, like Feltsham's superiority and self-esteem, was being dismantled.

'You'll need stitches in that eyebrow cut, at least six or eight. I'll come home with you; we can do it there. I'll need plenty of hot water, Rachel, and clean cloth. Tinker, can I leave the herb preparations to you?'

'They will be ready, Doctor Tarn,' said a now-smiling Tinker, adding, 'the packing will hold until then.'

'Tommy, how is Powell looking?' said Shenkin.

'He's still groggy; they're slapping his face but to no effect. I swear I've never seen a right cross with so much power, and with only a few inches of movement.'

With effort, Shenkin managed a full smile. 'My father beat the Swansea champion with that very cross,' he said with pride. 'But it was a close-run thing, Tommy, for he was good.'

'Not good enough, Shenkin, for if ever there was a true champion it was you tonight. Charlie would have been so proud.'

'I told him the New South Wales Championship would be in his name, for I owe him so very much, Tommy, and Regan too.'

Then, turning to Doctor Tarn, he said, 'I see there is no medical aid for Powell. Would you please see how he is and tell him I'll meet the cost of any care he may need?'

'Of course,' said Tarn, climbing into the ring and pushing his way over to Powell's corner.

Rachel had packed their belongings up and most were now in the wagons. 'We need to get him home, Sir Edward.'

'Indeed, Rachel, once Doctor Tarn is back we'll be on our way.'

Tarn bent under the rope. 'Well, he's coming around slowly. I gave him some smelling salts, but his jaw is broken in three places. I told them to get him to Sydney Hospital with a note from me to one of the surgeons there to reset the jaw. The surgeon, one Doctor Timms lives at the hospital so Powell should get immediate attention. I also said that you'll cover all payments for the treatment; Major Peterson-Palmer was very touched by your generosity.'

'Thank you, Doctor, let's go home.'

CHAPTER 40

While the excitement and celebrations at the sheep station went on. Shenkin had nine stitches put in by Tarn to close the scar. Finally, late in the evening, he was able to rest. The following day saw Sir Edward at the Bank of New South Wales on the Broadway known by all as 'The Wales'. Sir Edward demanded to see the president of the bank, John Thomas Campbell, who, together with his chief cashier, ushered him into his office. Ultimately they managed to stop talking about the fight. Sir Edward then lodged the money in the name of Charlie Benson. Against a signed note from Charlie Benson, Sir Edward drew out coin for immediate expenditures, this was in dump and holey dollar coins, made from Spanish silver dollars, amounting to five hundred pounds. So began the principal financial development of the Bare-Knuckle Sheep Station at Blacktown.

The first months of the second year proved only the beginning of the task to build BKSS into a successful sheep station, while a vindictive Feltsham undercut any wool price that Shenkin was able to bring to market. Indeed, he bragged he would ruin the BKSS and make Charlie Benson and his associates penniless.

'That is the word in Sydney Shenkin, and he has the resources to do it. He'll simply run one of his sheep stations at a loss to wipe you out,' said Sir Edward.

Shenkin nodded. 'Will this damn man never stop in his malicious, selfish behaviour? First me, now Charlie, one and the same but he just does not know it.' The words came out like a drawn knife, cold steel seeking a point of entry into this man who continued to be a danger to him.

But Feltsham was not the only problem, the year became one of the hottest New South Wales had endured since the 'First Fleet' arrived in 1788. The continent is one of the driest in the world, because of the land mass sitting under a subtropical high pressure belt which encourages the air to push down, preventing the lift required for rain, or so Sir Edward informed Shenkin. Even Lake George was drying up and the Darling River was hardly flowing. Whatever the cause, they were soon seeing the devastation to the land. The stream running through BKSS was dry; they had to bring water in from wherever they could get it and at a high price. Then the fires started. These were self-combustible fires, a wall of flames that ripped through the bush leaving nothing but scorched earth behind them. In front of them trees exploded, the sky turned dark and the burned debris flew hot in the air. Tommy Bright advised long trenches be dug, so everyone that could be spared was digging as if their lives depended upon it, which it did. The firebreaks would hold the flames back for a short time, enough to save some live stock or farming equipment. But the strong winds fanned flames across the wide trenches, forcing them to retreat in the face of the advancing furnace. Small animals were burned alive. The larger ones, opossums, kangaroos and dingoes, tried to out run it but the smell of burned roasted flesh was everywhere. Sir Edward's place was reduced to nothing but black ash. Shenkin helped to save what they could and brought it to BKSS, then he placed money to the value of the station into Sir Edward's bank account, much to his protestations but Shenkin insisted. They were now all committed to BKSS. The rain did finally come but it seemed they almost had to start again. So they did. Lord Feltsham, via the bank, offered to buy Charlie Benson out. Via the bank, Shenkin told him to 'go to hell'.

CHAPTER 41

It had taken two months for Shenkin to recover fully from the fight, and two years to build the sheep station into a prosperous enterprise. It had been a hard sharp leaning curve. Shenkin's daughter was ten years old when Sir Edward sat opposite Shenkin in the main house to discuss the next move in their plans. During the last two years a great deal had happened: Sir Edward had sold all his holdings to the BKSS group of which he was now the General Manager, Tommy Bright was Head Stockman, and Tinker a free man, as always, and a constant shadow wherever Shenkin went. Not long after the fight in Rosehill, a lone rider had come to the gates of the sheep station. One of the convict workers sent someone to the main house. By late day, Tommy Bright approached the visitor.

'What is it you want? This is private property.'

'My name is George Powell, sir and I would appreciate seeing Mr Benson if he would receive me.'

Tommy smiled and said, 'Glad to see you are on your feet, young man. That was a hell of a fight.'

'It was, and I've had two months in hospital to prove it. I've been back in Sydney these past three weeks trying to find work, but can't find anything so I leave for England in three days.'

'So what brings you here?'

Powell explained his reason for the visit, rather hesitant at first then in full flow.

'I see,' said Tommy, adding, 'I'm sure he'll see you. It's getting late so we'll put you up here overnight.'

The following morning, Tommy Bright took him up to the main house, where Powell met Shenkin in his study.

'Well, what's this, no fists up in front of you?' said Shenkin, with a laugh.

'No, sir, you rather curtailed my fighting career,' said Powell.

'Well, if not a rematch, then what brings you here? Tommy Bright said he'd prefer you to tell me. So what is it?'

'I wanted to thank you personally for all your help while I was in hospital; your Doctor Tarn ensured I had the best of care.'

Shenkin lifted his hands in a gesture of acceptance that it was nothing. 'Please, it was out of concern for a worthy opponent. You fought well; anyone would have done the same after such a monumental bout.'

'That is not so sir. I would not have if I had won,' he said, hanging his head low.

'Come, sit down. We'll share a glass together. Major Peterson-Palmer tells me you have recovered from the fight but no longer work at the Fortune of War pub, is that so?'

'It's the noise: it causes may head to hurt. Also the constant reminder from every man that drinks there of the fight and how much they lost. I can't blame them really; it was a heavy loss for everyone.'

'So what are you doing now, isn't the major able to find you work on his sheep farms out at the Cowpastures?' Not waiting for a reply, Shenkin went on, 'I understand you worked on a sheep station before going to Sydney to be the fancy for Major Peterson-Palmer.'

'That's correct. I grew up on a sheep station; been working with sheep since I was a six-year-old in paddocks, washing, and finally shearing. That's how I got the nickname 'Muscles'. I became really fast, went to shows all over New South Wales where I began bare-knuckle fighting too. But almost all of the major's labour are cheap convict workers, so he can't offer me anything. Also, thanks to you, he is finding it difficult to compete against the BKSS. No, I intend to work my passage to London where no one knows me and start all over again. Both my parents are dead so no one will miss me, but I couldn't go without thanking you for your help and paying the medical costs after the fight, Mr Benson.'

'You want to go to cold rainy London do you?'

'No, but it will mean no one can point a finger at me for losing them money,' said Powell, throwing his arms up in hopelessness.

Shenkin bid Powell sit then poured two liberal glasses of ale. When done, Shenkin went to the door. 'Rachel, could you ask Mr Bright if he'd be good enough to join us?'

'Yes, Sh… oh dear, yes, sir. I mean… oh dear.'

'Now, enjoy your ale while I light up this smelly old pipe of mine and I'll tell you all about myself, which will go no further then this room. I will deny it if you repeat it and put it down to a bad loser, understood?'

In some bewilderment, Powell nodded. So Shenkin told him everything.

'Come.' This in answer to the knock on the study door

'Tommy, you were saying yesterday that we need an extra good sheep shearer and extra help for you as a stockman, someone who knows all about sheep farming, someone strong enough to stand up to the long hard hours.'

'I did.'

'You, of course, remember our young friend here?'

'Indeed I do, last time I saw him he was flat on his back,' said Tommy Bright, with a grin.

Then he stepped forward. 'It's good to met you again. Bloody good fight. I meant to ask you, how's the jaw, you able to eat yet?'

'Well, I was on fluids for quite a few weeks; never knew anyone could hit that bloody hard.'

'Glad to see you've recovered. If it's any consolation, I'd never seen a right cross like that either and I've been around the fight game for a long time. Nothing to be ashamed of, youngster. Good news is, Charlie is retiring so you should be able to have another go at the championship, for you're certainly strong and good enough. You must be to go that many rounds with Charlie Benson.'

'No, I've just told Mr Benson, or rather Mr Shenkin, that I'm going to London.'

Tommy Bright turned to Shenkin in alarm. 'What?'

'It's alright, Tommy. I've told him everything.'

'But,' said Tommy, still taken aback.

'Tommy he has nothing, no job no family and very few friends. He'll not fight again, not with that fragile jaw. We gained much by the fight in terms of what it enabled us to do. Let's not add a life ruined because of it.' Shenkin paused for a moment. For heartbeats no one spoke, the strong tobacco smoke swirled up into the warm afternoon air. 'So I want you to take him on. He'll live here with us. He is strong, young and we need an experienced man, after all, we all need a little kindness from time to time.

'If you say so, Shenkin, so it will be,' he said.

Shenkin wasn't sure, but it looked as if there was a teardrop in the corner of the old man's eye. Sniffing, Tommy Bright wiped his gnarled hand across his eyes. 'Bloody hot dust gets everywhere. Right, follow me, George, you start earning your keep right away.'

'I don't now what to say, Shenkin. I...'

'Repay me with an honest day's work and welcome to the Bare-Knuckle Sheep Station.'

'You'll get the work done, I promise you that Shenkin, and thank you again.'

After they had left, Sir Edward came in from the veranda. 'No need to explain. I heard it all. Think you can trust him?'

'Yes, he had no need to come here. He simply wanted to thank me for the hospital bills and say goodbye. Let us give something back, always leave a little salt on the table.'

'You are a remarkable man, Daniel Shenkin. I'm glad I know you.'

'Now don't go sentimental on me, Sir Edward, for we have much revenge yet to do, is that not so?'

'If you say so, Shenkin, so it will be.'

They both laughed and relit their clay pipes until the room was dense with the fog of tobacco smoke.

After two successful years, Tommy Bright and Sir Edward were laying out their next set of plans. 'We need to build a wool mill Shenkin, two if possible. That way we have cost control over the preparation and treatment of the wool we produce.'

'If you think so Tommy, then make enquires regarding the costs and I agree, we'll build two if possible,' said Shenkin.

Sir Edward tapped out his pipe. 'I have spoken to Captain John Saxon, Shenkin. He thanks you for the money but says there was no need for interest on top. I told him you'd have it no other way. He sends this information about Feltsham and Moxey Shipping Line business, they're to put up their cargo prices to London. Apparently Feltsham is in need of money, because our superior wool at such competitive prices is leaving him with stock that he finds difficult to sell. Also his gambling debts increase daily and his wife spends money at an alarming rate. However, he understands your daughter is well but that Feltsham's wife continues to resent the girl.'

Shenkin smarted at the statement.

'This is the tittle-tattle from the wives of the other captains; he feels the sooner you can get her back the better.'

'I count the days till that can be done,' said Shenkin.

Sir Edward indicated his agreement. 'Of course, I told him as much. Regarding Feltsham's business activities, Saxon suggests, if possible, you own your own ships, which in your name he could secure on his next voyage to England.'

Shenkin smiled. 'John Saxon, like his brother, has been such a good friend over these years,' he said, his mind drifting back to the time when Charlie Benson was alive and how much he was indebted to both him and the good captain.

Shenkin lit a long clay pipe that he too now smoked and passed the tobacco pouch to Sir Edward. 'I have been thinking of that very thing for a month or so now. Also that the time is coming to do serious harm to Lord Feltham's fortunes. But first, how best to weaken Feltsham's financial base?' For some time, all was silence apart from the puffing of the pipes. 'What if Moxey could be persuaded to come over to us? We do need a large warehouse on the dock, do we not? What if we offered to buy the two Moxey has at a price he would find difficult to turn down, then put him on a ship back to London, a retired and wealthy man?' said Shenkin.

'Yes, he may be favourable to the idea,' agreed Sir Edward.

'We then privately buy out Moxey's interests in the ships he owns with Feltsham and commission them at an even lower carrying cargo price. Before Feltsham realises what is happening, since it is Moxey who deals with all the shipping side of the business, BKSS will sign a contact for the first shipments of wool to London at the reduced carrying costs.'

Sir Edward allowed himself a chuckle. 'You have learned the art of business fast, Shenkin. It would certainly isolate Feltsham and deal a damaging blow to his finances. May I also suggest you buy up his shares when possible: small amounts to start with, then in blocks as he becomes more desperate for money.'

Shenkin sat back further in his chair, puffed at his pipe and said, 'Set it in motion, Sir Edward, for I've waited a long time and many have sacrificed much to bring me to this point. I have a great deal to thank you for, my friend, indeed, each and every one of you.'

'It continues to be an interesting journey, Shenkin, and let's not forget we've all flourished by your single-minded drive,' said Sir Edward, standing up. 'I will leave for Sydney tomorrow.'

Over the weeks, and then months, BKSS wool became one of the leading exports in the colony. Vast sums of money were going into the bank until in the Autumn of that year, the president of the Bank of New South Wales asked if he could meet with Mr Charles Benson with a view to offering him a place on the board of directors.

'It would mean going into Sydney for the first time in three years; it's a risk is it not?' said Shenkin.

'Yes it is, but by now a small one. You've already been invited to a number of the Wool Industry's dinners, which I've attended on your behalf. A few of their senior members have been to the BKSS for meetings and it's very likely that you may well be offered next year's Chairmanship. Also, as you know, one of the Directors is Lord Feltsham. I understand, following the loss of Moxey and their ships, which we acquired privately at a very good price I might add, together with his continual losses on the wool market and at the gambling tables in Sydney, his shares continue to fall as does his line of credit.'

Shenkin did not speak for a while. 'He has reduced credit standing. Therefore his overdraft limit is under threat, is that not so?'

'It is,' said Sir Edward, affording himself a smile.

'Tell the bank I would be pleased to met with the president as soon as it can be arranged.'

Sir Edward slid a letter across the table carrying the name of the bank across the top. 'It's an official invitation for a meeting at your convenience. Just sign it with the time and date to meet.'

'Thank you my friend, ever ahead of the game. Let's have supper and discuss the details of the continued fall of his lordship Percival Hugo Feltsham.'

'I'll drink to that,' said Sir Edward, placing the whisky bottle on the table.

CHAPTER 42

'Good of you to come, for I understand you rarely travel far from Blacktown, sir.'

'No, there is little need. I find the world is slowly coming to me.'

The president laughed out loud. 'Indeed, indeed, BKSS wool is now exporting to so many places abroad, you do the colony well, sir. It will be our honour to have you on the board, don't you know?'

Shenkin sat at the president's invitation. 'Thank you,' he said, in response.

'However, before I accept your offer, I do have a stipulation.'

'Name it, sir, it will be done.'

Shenkin settled back into the Chesterfield chair to enjoy the moment. 'I want Lord Feltsham removed from the board,'

'What! Why? He has been with the bank for some time, sir, yes, indeed some time.'

Shenkin clasped his right hand upon his walking stick and began to get up.

The president stood up at the same time. 'Please, sir, will you not reconsider?'

Shenkin walked to the door then turned. 'Sir, I cannot join a bank who has upon their board a director who is in debt, a gambler with the bank's overdraft money, and a man of questionable morals. In fact, sir, I doubt that I should risk placing my own money in such a bank.'

'But, sir, I...'

'No buts, sir, you will hear from my General Manager, Sir Edward Standish, regarding the closing of the BKSS account. Good day, sir.'

'Wait, wait, let us not be hasty, sir, no indeed. We must look at this closely, yes indeed, closely, very closely.'

Feltsham's removal from the bank caused quite a stir in the colony. His wife found social invitations began to dry up. The husbands of the society ladies avoided him, even his circle of gambling friends became smaller. The bank had foreclosed on his account and his creditors began to hound him, leading to him having to put his sheep station at Bathurst up for sale. In a short time it became part of the BKSS group, but at much lower than the asking price. A month later, Feltsham was forced to sell his ships, one of which was the Runnymede which soon flew the BKSS flag. Among its first passengers was Josiah Moxey, not the captain this time. That was Captain John Saxon, who also held the position of Post Captain to the BKSS SHIPPING LINE.

No one would support or lend money to Feltsham, who became more and more desperate, even going to his old henchman, Ketch, who had gathered around him some very unsavoury individuals. Ketch's pub was now the centre for crime in the colony, no mean achievement given the reputation of the harbour side of Sydney Cove and the infamous Rocks. Ketch gloated over his lordship's plea for help. When he had finished begging, Ketch threw grog in his face, then had two of his bouncers throw him out onto the dirt of the dockside road.

Standing in the doorway, Ketch called out. 'Oh dear me, looks as if you've got lint on your sleeve, my lord. No, I'm wrong. It's stale ale and shit.'

A rattler passed the prone rumpled muck-covered figure on the ground; the driver lashed down with his whip. 'Get out of the way, you drunken bastard!' The horse's flying hoofs stamped across the body of Lord Percival Hugo Feltsham.

The following day, Sir Edward related the story to Shenkin. 'He is in an almshouse, alive, but battered and bruised. He is expected to be able to leave tomorrow. His main creditor, the bank, are holding the deeds to his property, a fine establishment I understand. Your daughter is still there, being taken care of by one of the servants ever since Feltsham's wife left him two weeks ago,' said Sir Edward.

Shenkin nodded. 'I see.'

'What do you want me to do?'

'We get a message to Feltsham that says we're interested in meeting him with a one time only offer for the balance of his assets here in the colony. The payment to be made in cash; but that there will be two terms attached,' said Shenkin.

'What if he declines?'

'We've made sure he can go nowhere else to raise money, have we not?'

'We have but he may decide to bluff it out.'

Shenkin agreed. 'We could bring more pressure to bear by insisting the bank place, in writing, their intention to sell his property to cover his outstanding overdraft within seven days. Failing to do so they would take legal action, rendering him bankrupt,' said Shenkin, his tone harsh.

'You are taking a very hard line, Shenkin. I do understand why, but if he is bankrupt we get nothing and he could face prison.'

'Indeed,' said Shenkin, unmoved. 'Either way we'll have ruined him.' Shenkin's tone remained hard.

Sir Edward stood up. 'I'll prepare the message ready for your signature. It will be delivered to him once the bank sends their letter.'

The following day, as a bank director, Shenkin countersigned the bank's letter, which was sent by rider that afternoon. Two days later, a meeting was arranged with Feltsham at the Woolpack Hotel in Parramatta.

Shenkin was shocked at the sight of Feltsham, who walked very unsteadily into the hotel, his clothes ill fitting due to loss of weight. The once haughty aristocrat who stood before him was a broken man.

In a weak trembling voice, he said, 'You had a proposal to put to me. What is it?' If the body was broken, the manner of speech was still superior in tone.

Shenkin indicated for him to sit. 'Simple, it is this. I will give you, in Spanish dollars, an agreed amount for all your assets here in the colony. You, in turn, will leave Sydney for a destination of your own choosing, never to return.'

'I see,' said Feltsham, removing yet again the absent lint from his frayed sleeve. 'And is that all? You mentioned two conditions in your message.'

'I did, the second is you leave my daughter behind and back in my care,' said Shenkin.

Feltsham got to his feet. 'What is this that you are saying? I don't understand.'

'Sit down, Lord Feltsham. You're in for a shock.'

Feltsham slumped back down into his chair. 'When you were directly responsible for Elizabeth's murder at the hands of Ketch and his gang of thugs, she was with child, my child Feltsham. Yes, my child, me, Daniel Shenkin, who you first met on the Runnymede all those years ago, the man you tried to kill at the Sydney convict barracks then had sent, together with Regan O'Hara, to Port Arthur penal colony. But I escaped, Feltsham. I took the name of Charlie Benson, who you saw me fight once not far from here.'

Lord Percival Hugo Feltsham had gone very pale. 'You! No, it cannot be. I do not believe it. Yet, sitting this close to you and listening to all you say that only Shenkin would know, I…' Feltsham's throat dried. He began to falter. 'It's just impossible.'

'Believe it, for did I not say on that night you had Elizabeth taken away in your carriage from the King's Wharf that I'd get even with you?'

Feltsham endeavoured to recover his equanimity. Finally, taking a deep breath, he said, 'You're an escaped convict. I'll have you returned to Port Arthur to complete your sentence.'

'Try it and I will put you in a debtors' jail for the rest of your life,' said Shenkin. The words cut the air like a knife.

For heartbeats in their private room, in their private world of the past, both sat very still. Noise drifted in from the bar while wheels rattled over the uneven road outside. Somewhere a dog barked, while dust floated around them in the beams of sunlight from the window. The silence became loud in their ears. It was the thump, thump of their own heartbeats.

Lord Feltsham was many things but he was not a fool. He knew money talked. He knew the BKSS now had a great deal of influence in the colony, that the ravings of a bankrupt would amount to nothing.

He finally spoke. 'How much?'

Shenkin placed his hands on the table. 'Ten thousand in coin.'

'Twelve thousand and I'll leave within the month. As for the brat, you can have her.'

Shenkin hit him full in the face, sending him backwards off his chair. Feltsham's nose was broken, blood flowed down his shabby coat. 'You mean Beth is free to come back to her father, do you not?'

A knock on the door was accompanied by the landlord's voice. 'Is everything alright in there, sirs?'

'Yes, we knocked a chair over, but could you bring me a glass of your best whisky, landlord? In fact, bring in a bottle.'

'Right away, sir, with two glasses.'

'No, just one glass,' said Shenkin, looking down at Feltsham who remained on the floor.

'Sir Edward Standish is outside in a carriage at the back of the hotel. The door in that corner opens onto it. He will take you back to your place, where you will sign papers transferring all your assets over to Charlie Benson. Sir Edward will then collect Beth and her governess and take them to my sheep station at Blacktown.

'Tomorrow, Sir Edward and two trusted friends will return to your place to help you pack. Sir Edward will have nine thousand in Spanish dollars for you. He will then escort you down to Sydney Cove, where a passage to New Zealand has been arranged for you. Once on board, the captain is instructed to ensure you stay on board any attempt to leave will, I assure you, be dealt with forcefully.'

Feltsham was now on his feet trying to stem the bleeding from his nose. 'You offered ten thousand.'

Shenkin lifted Feltsham's head. 'It's now seven thousand, my lord. Do you want to go for less?'

The door opened. The landlord placed the whisky on the table, a glass at the side of it. All the while he was staring at Feltsham's bloody face and the broken chair.

'Thank you, landlord. I note the charge for the private room. I will double the charge to cover any damage, and to ease your memory of what you have seen,' said Shenkin, placing silver coin in the landlord's hand.

The landlord smiled, putting the money quickly in his pocket. 'Seen what, sir?'

'Indeed,' said Shenkin. Adding, 'we will leave by the back door, if that is agreeable.'

'Of course, sir,' said the landlord, closing the door quietly behind him.

Shenkin filled his glass. 'To your departure, Lord Feltsham. If I see you again, I will kill you. Of that you can be sure, for the harm you've done to me and mine and others, indirectly. Do I make myself clear?'

For a moment there was silence. 'Well?' said Shenkin, raising his voice.

'Yes, damn you, yes.'

'Good, my next business is with Ketch, which I assure you will be swift and final,' said Shenkin, opening the back door, the other side of which stood Sir Edward.

'He is ready, Sir Edward. Would you go and fetch my daughter please?'

'My pleasure, Shenkin,' said Sir Edward, taking a firm hold of Feltsham's arm while directing him to the waiting carriage.

That evening they were all seated around the big table in the study. 'Well, my friends, first I would like you to met my daughter, Beth. Rachel, bring her in please,' called Shenkin at the door.

A young girl of ten years struggled to break free of Rachel's hand. The governess stood at her side in a bewildered state at everything that had happened in such a short few hours. The child stood defiant in the middle of the room. She fought to stop herself from crying, determined not to show weakness. Shenkin had seen that look before and smiled. Then, fighting his own tears back, Shenkin said, 'Gentlemen, my daughter, Beth.'

CHAPTER 43

Two nights later, down at Ketch's pub on the King's Wharf, Shenkin, together with George Powell, pushed the doors open. They were closely followed by three ex-convicts, who Shenkin knew from his time at Sydney convict barracks. Eyes turned to take in the sight of the two bare-knuckle fighters actually together.

Ketch looked up. 'If it's a rematch, Mr Benson, my money's on you.'

'No rematch, they tell me at the Fortune of War you're thinking of selling this place. Is that so?'

'Now why would I want to do that?' said Ketch, adjusting the patch over his eye.

'Been complaints about short changing customers and watering the ale, anybody here aware of that?'

'Yes, I never got me change at all when I was last in here,' said one of the men who had come in with Shenkin.

A man at the bar spat out his beer. 'Now that you says about watering down, this pint does taste more like piss than ale.'

'Smells like it too,' said another.

Ketch's henchmen stepped forward, the bigger of them broke a bottle over the bar edge; the jagged edge swung at the man still swilling his ale. Shenkin hit him once, spinning him along the bar rail. Another of Ketch's men went for Shenkin, only to be stopped short by a blow from George Powell's right fist.

Back to back, they moved down the length of the bar towards Ketch, who went for the shotgun under the bar. Shenkin kicked it out of his hand as the place erupted into a brawl. Bottles, grog and chairs went through the air. The big mirror behind the bar shattered as a table hit its centre, a thousand pieces span up into a cloud of glass snowflakes. Shenkin pushed Ketch into a small back room at the far end of the pub and closed the door. George Powell stood guard outside.

'At last, after all this time, Ketch, it's just you and me,' said Shenkin.

'Why me, Benson? What do you want with me?'

'Not Charlie Benson Ketch, although he certainly would detest you too. No, this moment is between Daniel Shenkin and Sergeant Thomas Ketch of the convict ship the Runnymede,' said Shenkin, taking off his coat and slowly rolling up his shirt sleeves.

'But… he was sent to Port Arthur to serve out his sentence, together with that big bastard Irishman. Why, they must both be dead by now, and good riddance says I.'

'Sadly, Regan O'Hara is dead, thanks indirectly to you and that lint-picking bastard Lord Feltsham, but not Daniel Shenkin. He stands before you to settle a few old scores and avenge the deaths of friends and loved ones that were better then you ever were.'

A look of terror spread slowly across Ketch's face then, after a moment, he spoke, 'Now wait Shenkin, it was Feltsham that put me to it I swear it.'

Shenkin's face was hard, merciless. 'Even your brutal behaviour to convicts in the hold of the Runnymede, chained men unable to defend themselves. Beaten, starved, to be treated like animals. Above all there's Elizabeth Moxey and the night you visited her with a gang of thugs and raped her.'

'No, no, it was Feltsham, he arranged that. He gave me money to do it but I never intended them to rape her, I swear. We went there to teach you and O'Hara a lesson but it all got out of hand, I swear.'

'Just watched did you, Ketch? And did nothing? Like everything else that Feltsham employed you for, his vicious dog on a chain that he could unleash when he wanted you to do his dirty work. You took very little persuading, Ketch, because the money was good and your nature enjoyed it. But I have met with Feltsham and he was just as surprised as you are to see me still alive. You will not be doing his bidding again Ketch, for he is a broken man, just as you will soon be. Listen to the damage being done to your pub. So much noise no one will hear you scream Ketch, no one.' Ketch turned away. 'Look at me Ketch. I am an "avenging angel" for all those you've murdered or hurt in your far too long miserable life. Say a prayer Ketch, if you know any, for tomorrow will start without you. The first blow will be for Elizabeth and my daughter, Beth,' Shenkin said, stepping forward.

Spinning around, Ketch suddenly had a knife in his hand. 'Should have come in here armed, you Welsh bastard. I'll cut you up so bad they'll carry you out of here in a bucket,' he said, the old sadistic grimace back on his face.

He thrust the knife towards Shenkin, who backed away and moved to his left.

'Well, well, what have we here? Another Kettlewell? Another Teal? Now you know what happened to them, Ketch, don't you? But I'll say this, it's what they did and they were good at it too. You're big in size Ketch, I'll give you that, but you're out of condition with all this soft living, holding up a bar. Whereas I've been a bare-knuckle fighter all my life, just like them; it's what I do for a living.'

Ketch circled around Shenkin. 'I'll let the knife even things up. Sharp as hell it is, which is where you're going, Shenkin.' At this he dashed forward, driving the knife upwards towards Shenkin's stomach. Shenkin caught Ketch's knife wrist, forcing it upwards. When it was level with Ketch's throat, he turned the knife inwards and gazed into Ketch's one eye. A bottle or chair smashed against the door.

Shenkin heard George Powell shout, 'Can't go in there; it's a private room, mate, best fight it out here.'

The red veins in the eye were turning to a deeper red as Ketch strained to hold back the knife, but slowly it got closer and closer. The tip cut into the outer skin.

'Let god be my judge,' cried Shenkin, as he drove the knife into Ketch's throat. Ketch gave a small gurgling sound and Shenkin knew he had hit the jugular vein. Ketch went limp as the blood gushed towards Shenkin. Letting Ketch slide to the floor, Shenkin kept the knife in Ketch's hand. Standing, Shenkin turned quickly to the door and knocked. George Powell opened it. Shenkin ducked as a bottle came through the air. 'We can get out from the back door. Signal to our men to follow you,' said Shenkin. Blood covered his shirt front. Hurriedly, he put on his top coat.

Out on the road a carriage pulled up. Tommy Bright swung the doors open and the carriage rocked as they all got in. Tommy pressed his feet hard onto the front board as he flicked his whip forward with a loud crack. The end stung the lead horse on his rump and they were off at a gallop. Dust flew up into the air as the carriage swayed around the corner of the street. They passed a number of police wagons heading for the front of the pub, almost hitting the side of one of them. A constable called out but they were already around the corner in a cloud of dust. By the early hours of the morning they were back in Blacktown, sitting in another pub's private room where Sir Edward and Doctor Tarn sat with drinks at the ready. Entering the room from the back door of the building that Sir Edward had unlocked, Shenkin crossed the room and thumped on the door to the main bar. The landlord, in his nightwear, entered with an oil lamp in his hand.

'It's bloody late, gents and I needs my sleep I do.'

'Just one final bottle of your best brandy landlord, then we'll be off,' said Shenkin, making himself unsteady on his feet. Adding, 'I'll top the bill up with a generous pile of extra coin for the inconvenience we've caused, and the lateness.'

'Well that's good of you sir, thank you. I'm just saying you've been here for bleeding hours and the wife and me, we needs our sleep, like.'

'We have indeed, landlord. We thank you for your hospitality and we'll soon be on our way,' said Shenkin, closing the door.

Sir Edward, relieved to be able to stop trying to make the noise of a full room, one complete with smoke from the sixth full pipe of the night, he turned to Shenkin.

'Need I ask?'

'No,' said Shenkin, adding, 'all is now accounted for the slate is clean.' Only my soul carries the burden of what I've done this, night, which I can live with. So let's go home my friends, and thank you.'

Doctor Tarn leaned towards Shenkin. 'We all share a little of that rightful burden Shenkin. May Elizabeth, Regan and Charlie rest in peace now,' he said, making the sign of the cross.

'Amen to that,' said Sir Edward.

'Indeed,' said Shenkin. 'So many years, so much sadness, from this day on we concentrate on building the BKSS into a company that will benefit this "place beyond the seas", this prison with a wall twelve thousand miles thick. We will show what disadvantaged people and convicts can do. We will build a great nation.'

'If you say so, Shenkin, so it will be,' said Sir Edward.

Doctor Patrick Tarn laughed, then raised his glass. 'Gentlemen, a toast to the future of BKSS and to the next generation, to Beth Shenkin.'

In the years that followed they reared their sheep. They crossbred them for better quality wool. Shenkin expanded by purchasing sheep stations in other parts of the continent: Queensland, Perth and even Tasmania, where he began to breed cattle. He opened factories to process both sheep and cattle meat. Until late in the century they were one of the largest exporters of wool and meat in Australia. Over these long years they had had successes and sadness. All had been explained to Beth, who over the years had grown into the very image of her mother. Tommy Bright died in an accident in the bush, and then Doctor Tarn in the same year from typhoid while treating the sick during an outbreak. Then there were the droughts, bushfires, sheep and cattle diseases, and volatile market prices that forced Shenkin to diversify. He sent Sir Edward to London to discuss with the government of the day. He opened a London office, and his shipping line, under John Saxon, were the fastest ships to London's Canary Wharf. George Powell married Rachel and Shenkin walked the bride down the aisle at a wedding where many tears were shed. Tinker read an aboriginal wedding poem that had a lot to do with many children and dreamland, his hair now a cloud of cotton white.

Shenkin was invited to receptions and presentations of the wool industry. He became Chairman of the Bank, where he instigated low interest loans for the poor. He gave money to the reintroduction of ex-convicts into society and a large donation to the hospital where Tarn died to build a new wing, to be called the Patrick Tarn Wing. The governor invited him to Government House but time and again he regretted he was unable to attend due to the pressures of business. He explained to Sir Edward that he could not compromise the governor by allowing him to entertain an escaped convict. While in London, Sir Edward had married the daughter of an Earl. His family had welcomed their black sheep back into the family and he lived again in the family 16th-century stone pile outside of London in Surrey, his old nursery now filled with the crying and laughter of his son and daughter. While Sir Edward advanced the continuing success of the BKSS on the London stock exchange, Shenkin did the same in Australia. It seemed to Shenkin that the time passed quickly now, as his hair too turned a snowy white. The day came when, at his own request, Sir Edward asked to return to Sydney to retire. Shenkin made over the deeds of Sir Edward's old sheep station back into his friend's name and Sir Edward settled down there to a quiet contented life. John Saxon returned from a voyage to New Zealand with a shipment of farming equipment and news of Lord Feltsham.

'Sit yourself down John. You had a good sailing, I hope,' said Shenkin, offering the captain a glass of ale.

'I did, and have just unloaded the cargo of sheep you ordered, all safe in the pens. They take them up to your Bathurst station tomorrow.'

'Good, now what's this about Feltsham?'

The captain went quiet for a while then, in a small voice, he said, 'He's dead, Shenkin.'

'What? How and when?' said Shenkin, sitting up straight in his chair.

John Saxon settled back into his own chair and took a deep draught of ale. 'He'd been involved in cheating Maoris out of their land rights. The sales were to newly arrived farmers from England on the South Island. It was, of course, a swindle from top to bottom that resulted in the loss of a great deal of land belonging to the Maori people. The upshot of it was that when Feltsham was found out, he committed suicide. They found him in his lodgings, hanging from one of the beams, or so it was accepted by the authorities who had no wish to get involved in a land dispute between the Maoris and the farmers. All monies where returned and a fair price was agreed. Feltsham's burial was in a pauper's grave outside of Dunedin which, given our interest in his lordship, I decided to attend. Only one other person attended: he was a Maori elder who stood high on a grass rise above the burial ground. The two Maori grave diggers lifted the body of Feltsham from a cart and turned to look upwards to the elder, who gave a signal. They then dropped Feltsham face down into the grave. When I again looked up to the elder, he had already turned and was walking away.'

For heartbeats neither spoke. Finally, Shenkin said, 'It is a just ending for a man who caused so much harm during his life.'

'Indeed,' said Saxon.

After a drawn-out silence, Shenkin lifted his head.

'So, it's over, at long last. A stain on my life and many others is finally removed; rest in peace Elizabeth, Regan and Charlie.'

John Saxon rested his arm on Shenkin's shoulder, stood up and left Shenkin to his memories. The past and present went through Shenkin's mind, as they did more and more these days. Late in the evening a knock at the study door was followed by the entrance of a young beautiful woman. Every day now she grew to look more like her mother. It always took Shenkin's breath away. It was good to have her back from that expensive finishing school in England, but he could still hear that Australian accent, he was pleased to say. Behind her stood Sir Edward's two children, Winifred and Justin, visiting their father for the next month and full of all they wanted to do and see. *Ah! Youth,* thought Shenkin. *It's all too tiring.*

'Well, are we going riding in the morning, Father? I did say we were going over to Uncle Edward's for tea later, remember? Justin is teaching me how to play croquet. Are you not, Justin?'

'Indeed, if I can stop you from swearing at the ball.'

'I remember, but be careful of those mallets. They look heavy to me,' said Shenkin.

'Don't fuss so, Father. Justin is very careful for me.'

'Is he?' said Shenkin, lifting his scarred eyebrow.

Shenkin had to admit, Justin Standish was a handsome young man. He had been seeing a great deal of Beth since Sir Edward had returned to New South Wales.

That evening, while Sir Edward and Shenkin were playing chess, as was their wont on a Sunday these past few years, Sir Edward slowly filled his second pipe with his favourite tobacco, of which he had brought back a tidy stock from London's Grand Cigar Divan on the Strand. When he finished filling his pipe he handed the finely decorated tobacco jar to Shenkin.

Shenkin busied himself filling his own clay pipe, that by now had dark stained marks on the bowl and stem. He regarded it as a good companion.

Dual plumes of smoke rose in the air around them, floating up to the ceiling where they settled in the equally dark brown stain of their pipes. They were content and returned to their chess. Shenkin was white with an opening move of Queen pawn to four.

Sir Edward made his move and looked up at Shenkin through a cloud of smoke.

Shenkin smiled. 'What has happened to the gambler I knew? For it looks like you are planning a Sicilian defence, my friend.'

Sir Edward drew deeply upon his pipe. 'We'll see, but be careful of your next move. Talking of which, I have a meeting tomorrow with the governor at Government House in Sydney.'

'Is this something to do with the increases we're facing on exports? For I have made a few notes upon the subject,' said Shenkin, his hand hovering over a pawn.

'Not entirely; I believe he will be requesting to met you again after that donation you made to the building of a new water plant. He feels after everything else you have done in the colony, he must this time acknowledge your generosity.'

Shenkin raised his hands in dismay. But Sir Edward stilled him. 'Let me at least speak with him to explain please Shenkin, after all this time and all you have achieved, including being one of the leaders of the first congress of trade unions'

'And send me back to Port Arthur into the bargain. Is that it, Sir Edward?'

'You are so stubborn. It's like my name; you still call me Sir Edward after all this time when I have been asking you to call me Edward for years now.'

'I still see you as that: down to his last few hundred pounds, a sporting gentleman placing it all on a bare-knuckle fighter you had only just met. Incidentally, your mind is not on the game, my friend.'

Silence rained for some time as each studied the board that was slowly disappearing in a fog of smoke. Shenkin gave a sigh of satisfaction. 'So much for the Sicilian my friend. Checkmate, I believe.'

'Well I'm damned, so it is, my mind is on the meeting with the governor and what excuse I can make this time regarding your refusal to meet him. Anyway, one last glass and a puff and I must be going. It'll be an early start tomorrow if I'm to get to Sydney in time for the meeting. I will take your observations on this tax increase with me.'

'We have not spoken about Beth and Justin. Do you think it's serious?' said Shenkin, rather nervously.

Sir Edward smiled. 'I've never known you to be lost for words Shenkin, but yes. I think it is, do you object?'

'Is it not you who should be questioning it, Edward. There, I have, after all these years, called you Edward.'

'And about time too.' They both laughed with companionable good humour.

'But the daughter of a convict Edward, an escaped convict at that.'

'No, not a convict but my oldest and dearest friend: a true nobleman. One who has paid back his debt, if there ever was one, to society many times over,' said Sir Edward Standish, sincerity and affection clothed each word.

'It will not matter here in New South Wales but London, your family and fellow nobility. Is that not something to consider?'

'You are forgetting I walked away from it once before. Friendship is far more important, is it not?'

'Indeed, and thank you. Now off you go before we both start getting emotional in our old age.'

Three days later, Beth came into the study and announced she was getting engaged. 'To whom, my dear?' Not waiting for a reply, Shenkin added, 'is it anyone I know?'

'What?' said Beth, ready for a row written all over her face.

'Just wondering, for if it was Justin Standish, for instance, then I would be delighted, but someone else? Then I am not so sure… ' Shenkin was unable to finish the sentence because Beth had her arms around his neck crying.

'Father, Father, how did you know?'

'Well, your mother could never hide anything from me either and she too, I know, would be pleased. Besides, we all have eyes, do we not? Even Tinker asked only yesterday when could he cast the stones of how many grandchildren I would have, and he would teach them real life.'

That same afternoon, Sir Edward walked in from the balcony. In his hand was a roll of parchment paper. Shenkin noted the red ribbon and seal holding it together. 'What's this, a rescinding of the tax bill?'

'Something far better, and for you to read my dear friend, but I suggest you sit down first,' said Sir Edward, pulling their tobacco jar towards him.

Shenkin sat down and carefully broke the seal. 'It's my bloody arrest, I'll wager.'

When he had finished Shenkin, with a shaking hand, poured himself a whisky. He handed one glass to Sir Edward.

'I can't believe it Edward. I just cannot believe it. A Royal Pardon, but how, when, and who?'

'It's called the Royal Prerogative of Mercy, Shenkin, and the governor has been petitioning for it for some time. In fact, ever since I told him the whole story six months ago. I felt if it all went wrong, well, I could help you escape from Port Arthur all over again.'

The eyes of Shenkin were brimful of tears as he embraced his lifelong friend. 'Thank you, Edward, thank you.'

Sitting in Government House a week later, Shenkin shook the hand of the governor, Sir Augustus Loftus. 'Thank you, Governor, for all your efforts in achieving the pardon,' said Shenkin.

Sir Augustus smiled. 'It seemed it was the only way to get you to come here, and I understand your daughter is to marry. Is that so?'

'It is, Governor.'

'Good, for the telling of your story to my wife prompted her to say she would be delighted to help with the wedding arrangements. It would also give her the opportunity to thank you for your financial assistance in setting up the building of a new wing for the orphan children's hospital.'

'That is most kind of her. Please express my thanks to her ladyship.'

'I will indeed, but tell me, for it is something I have given thought to, what will be the first thing you will do, now that you are free of any stain of the past?'

'After the wedding, Governor, I am going home,' said Shenkin.

'To Blacktown?'

'No, home to my black valley in the mountains of Wales, for I have been weary and slow these past months. I arrived here in chains, Governor, in 1832. It is now time to go home before, according to my doctors, it is too late.'

'Let my doctor examine you, Mr Shenkin. We must take care of the man who has done so much for the colony.' It was the first time he had heard his name spoken by anyone outside of his small group.

'That is most kind, Governor, but I am aware of my condition and it comes as no surprise to me that, at the age of sixty-five years, it's been a very full life.'

'I understand, sir,' said Governor Loftus, holding out his hand. Adding, 'On behalf of the government, thank you for everything you have done for New South Wales and Australia.'

The following day, Beth came rushing into the study. 'Did you hear that the governor is to give a reception to mark my wedding? Isn't it wonderful? Now tell me, what did the doctor say?'

'That I'll outlive you all. But a long rest may be a good thing, say at least a year to eighteen months away from the sheep station work and its worries.'

Beth became alarmed. Shenkin held out his arms. 'Now there's no need to be concerned. You get married to Justin, then off to London to meet the Standish family. I just need this break, and the doctor says it's all that I need and then I'll be fine.

'There, did I not say you were just tired? And this hot weather drains us all.'

'You did indeed,' said Shenkin.

After Beth had left he sat down very slowly. *Maybe a two to three years but it could be less the Chief Colonial Medical Surgeon for Sydney had said. It was due to recurring aortic aneurysms of the heart. He could operate but could give no guarantee of success. Indeed, it may cause him to be confined to his bed for the remainder of his life. So I must keep going for the wedding. I don't want to miss that, and then the voyage across the sea and home. If the doctor is right, I'll just about have the time.*

The wedding and all the festivities surrounding it were very tiring for Shenkin but he got through it, and the compensation was to see how happy Beth was. The couple honeymooned in London.

CHAPTER 44

It was to be over two years before Shenkin felt ready to face the long hard journey back to his South Wales valley.

They sailed to London in one of the BKSS new 'Windjammer' ships. Shenkin had the main cabin which he reflected, was a long way from the hold of the Runnymede. Tinker accompanied him and was always at his side, whether he knew or not. Shenkin never asked, but he had a strong feeling that he did because Tinker did not pack Shenkin's tobacco pipe or whisky flask and always made sure a chair was close to hand. The invigorating sea air improved the way Shenkin felt, for which he was grateful. Captain John Saxon entertained and dined them well every night, unless his duties took him onto the bridge. However, all in all, it was a good fast passage which soon saw them at anchor in London. Shenkin and John Saxon, once the unloading of their cargo of wool had been attended to, spent the night at the George Hotel. Beth and Justin were still living at the Standish's country seat. Beth had given birth to a son, and another child was on the way. Beth had charmed the Standish family and they loved her. She was busy, not only as a mother, but in charitable works for under-privileged women in the East End of London, while Justin was now the member of parliament for the constituency of Surrey.

John Saxon turned to Shenkin. 'What are your instructions for your return to Sydney, a month or two months?'

Shenkin, catching his breath after the walk from the dockside to the George, finally spoke. 'I shall not be returning my dear friend. You will receive all further orders for the shipping line from Sir Edward.'

Saxon nodded. 'I thought as much' he said, sadness engraved in every word.

'So you guessed too John. Do you think Beth knows?'

'No, they are both, thankfully, lost in their own world of happiness, love and Beth's charitable work.'

'Yes, and so they should be,' said Shenkin.

'When will you leave for Wales? Do not tell me this is our last night together old friend.'

'I must recover from the voyage, say a day or two? I think Tinker will insist, for I am sure he knows. I may just have a small whisky before Tinker arrives to tuck me in for the night.'

'I'll join you,' said Saxon, grim faced.

The glasses charged, John Saxon lifted his. 'To you Shenkin. It has been my great privilege to know you.'

'And I you John. Keep an eye on that daughter of mine.'

Shenkin's agents had made enquiries about the Shenkin family and had sent him a full report, attached to which was a short list of properties and businesses for sale. There were two houses for sale: one in Merthyr Tydfil and one towards Brecon. He knew the description of the Merthyr property immediately, for his mother had scrubbed its floors many times. He instructed them to purchase it without delay, the place to be put in order ready for his and Beth's arrival.

The day he finally arrived back home in his black valley it was raining and cold. Tinker had a blueish look about him while everyone they passed stood and looked in wonder at this strange black man with snowy white hair.

Carrying wreaths, they walked slowly up to the cemetery were Shenkin knelt for a long time while Tinker stood on the stone path that separated the graves. The headstones of the three marked graves read: Idris Shenkin, Megan Shenkin and Rachel Shenkin. Shenkin's agents had failed to find the whereabouts of Owen Shenkin, only that after the death of Rachel he had left the valley and never returned.

In the weeks that followed, the big house was being made ready for a reunion celebration of Beth and Justin. An army of local cleaners, decorators and fitters of furnishings from Cardiff and London whirled around Shenkin and Tinker like a bushfire. They kept out of the way in the west wing of the house, which Shenkin intended to close off. Shenkin could hear his mother's voice. '*Clean house and clean air I'll have, or I'll want to know why.*'

'*Take those boots off before you go in the house Daniel, or there'll be hell to pay,*' his da *would say with a laugh. So long ago, so very very long ago.*

Tinker put another cushion behind his back. 'Don't fuss Tinker, please I'm fine. What's the time?'

'Ten minutes since you asked me last. They'll soon be here so don't get all distressed,' said Tinker adding, 'take your medicine, that I don't hold with, if we were on walkabout, I'd make a large bowl of good herbal tea.'

'What do you think of the house now?'

'I prefer the stars and bright moon light,' said Tinker, in a huff.

'You should have gone back with John Saxon, as I said.'

'My place is here. Now open your mouth for me to pour this devil's liquid into it.'

Shenkin swallowed it down as he reached out to Tinker. Black and white hands clasped tight together in friendship and love.

'I'll soon be out of your white hair Tinker, then you can go home to Bare-Knuckle Sheep Station.'

They sat in silence, this black man and this white man, and waited for their Beth.

That evening they dined on Welsh lamb, roast potatoes, thick gravy and mint sauce, while Beth and Justin told them of their adventures in London and his grandson. Beth had reassured Shenkin time and again that her pregnancy was going well, that he had nothing to worry about, but he still did.

The next day Shenkin showed them his town: the pit where he nearly died under a roof fall and the old miner's cottage on Quarry Row. Until Tinker said quietly, 'We should go back to the house for you to rest. All this walking and talking is tiring you Shenkin, and me.'

It was in the early hours of the morning that Tinker called one of the servants to fetch a doctor. Then he woke Beth. 'But why did he not say he was this ill?' said Beth, after Tinker had told her everything.

'Because he is a stubborn sixty-eight-year-old man and he did not want to spoil your time in his Welsh valley,' said Tinker.

'You should go in now my dear, for he is fading fast,' said the doctor, holding the door open.

Tinker sat down outside, held his head in his hands and wept.

Shenkin's fight-scarred face lay still on the pillow. His eyes flickered at the sound of the door opening.

In a breathy voice Shenkin said, 'Is that you, Elizabeth?'

'It's B...' she said, then stopped. 'Yes, it's me, my darling. You've been a long time,' she said, holding his gnarled hand.

Shenkin's scarred face broke into a smile. 'I promise I'll never leave you again, cariad.' Then his big bare-knuckled hand went limp in Beth's. His head rolled over to one side. His last breath left his body like a long contented sigh; they were together again.

Beth leaned close to him, kissed his cheek and whispered into his ear. 'If you say so Shenkin, so it will be.'

HISTORICAL NOTE

Between 1788 and 1868 some 160,000 convicts were transported from Britain and Ireland to penal colonies in Australia. The British Government had been transporting convicts overseas to their American colonies in the early 18th century right up to the American Revolution, when an alternative site needed to be found to relieve the overcrowding of British prisons and hulks. In 1770, James Cook charted and claimed possession of the east coast of Australia for Britain. This proved to be the perfect site for a penal colony and on the 20th of January 1788 the First Fleet of eleven convict ships arrived at Botany Bay to found Sydney, New South Wales. Later, other penal colonies were established. Among them was the notorious penal prison of Port Arthur on Van Diemen's Land, now Tasmania. Located 97km (61mi) from Hobart it was named after George Arthur, the lieutenant governor of Van Diemen's Land. From 1833 until 1853, Port Arthur was the destination for the most hardened of convicted British criminals. These were secondary offenders who had committed crimes after arriving in Australia. The prison at Port Arthur had some of the harshest punishments and strictest security measures of the British penal system. It was no surprise that many of the inmates developed mental problems, due to what was called the 'Silent System', and an asylum was built on the site. Not many actually lasted the term of their sentences. The penal site is on a peninsula and forms a natural secure area by being surrounded by water, which was reputed to be shark infested. The 30m wide isthmus of Eaglehawk Neck is the only connection to the mainland. It was fenced and guarded by soldiers, man traps and half-starved dogs. In many ways it was much like Alcatraz Island in the United States, made totally secure by its very geographic placement.

It was regarded as an inescapable prison, but even so it did not discourage some from trying. A convict named Martin Cash did successfully escape along with two others. One of the most bizarre was the escape attempt made by George 'Billy' Hunt. Hunt disguised himself using a kangaroo hide and tried to cross Eaglehawk Neck. The guards, thinking the kangaroo meat would supplement their meagre food supply, tried to shoot him. Seeing them all sighting him up, Hunt immediately threw off the disguise and surrendered, receiving 150 lashes for the attempted escape.

Port Arthur was a harsh brutal penal settlement, easy to get into if you were a hardened criminal in the 19th century, but, once there, impossible to get out. Some tales suggest that prisoners committed murder, an offence punishable by death, just to escape the brutal life of the penal camp. Those who did die there were buried on the Isle of the Dead. Some 1,646 graves were actually recorded, but only 180, of prison staff and military personnel, are marked.

Against this backdrop, Daniel Shenkin and Regan O'Hara had to plot their escape. Their good fortune was that they had both inside and outside help. Without that collaboration it would have been almost impossible. And to then march across Van Diemen's Land to get to Hobart, and, when there, find a ship prepared to take them to Sydney for Shenkin to have his revenge. Simply put, his driving force was his hate for Feltsham and the wrongs that the harsh world of the 19th century had done him. It had marked his soul and steeled his determination, he would survive.

I hope I have been truthful to the inmates of Port Arthur penal settlement. Whatever their crimes, many were victims of the times they lived in when severe sentences were imposed for what we would now consider to be minor offences. Finally, any errors are, of course, entirely the fault of the author.

Davey Davies
January 2023

Ingram Content Group UK Ltd.
Milton Keynes UK
UKHW010925310523
422635UK00004B/141